Praise for

The Way of Women

"Two dozen years ago we watched in horror as Mount St. Helens erupted on our television screens, fearing for the safety of those who lived beneath her shadow. In *The Way of Women,* Lauraine Snelling takes us there in graphic, moving detail as she explores the lives of three women deeply affected by the natural disaster. Her careful research and vivid descriptions make the mountain come alive, and the unique challenges each woman faces draw us day by ash-covered day toward a satisfying end."

—LIZ CURTIS HIGGS, best-selling author of *Thorn in My Heart*

"In *The Way of Women,* Lauraine Snelling goes beyond her usual grand storytelling in giving us insights into landscapes, history, and life. This time, through her memorable characters, Lauraine explores the explosiveness of loss, taking us to the depths of our need for relationships in turbulent times. Grief and disaster can be transforming if we allow God to work in our lives. That's one way of women I'll take with me from a story that sings with the beauty of the northwest landscape and Lauraine's own lovely language. 'The creek gossiped with the rocks' and 'Wait—a four letter word worse than cursing' are phrases worthy of remembering, as is this fine story of God's power to use each of us to help heal each other and restore ourselves in the process."

—JANE KIRKPATRICK, award-winning author of *A Name of Her Own*

"Reminding us that love can spring forth from ashes, that life can emerge from death, Lauraine Snelling writes a gripping and powerful novel that will inspire and uplift you."

—LYNNE HINTON, author of *The Last Odd Day*

THE WAY OF WOMEN

OTHER NOVELS
BY LAURAINE SNELLING

The Healing Quilt
Dakota
The Gift

Dakotah Treasures Series
Ruby
Pearl

Red River of the North Series
An Untamed Land
A New Day Rising
A Land to Call Home
The Reaper's Song
Tender Mercies
Blessing in Disguise

A Dream to Follow
Believing the Dream
More Than a Dream

Secret Refuge Series
Daughter of Twin Oaks
Sisters of the Confederacy
The Long Way Home

THE WAY OF WOMEN

A NOVEL

LAURAINE SNELLING

WATERBROOK
PRESS

The Way of Women
Published by WaterBrook Press
2375 Telstar Drive, Suite 160
Colorado Springs, Colorado 80920
A division of Random House, Inc.

Though Mount St. Helens and its environs are real, the characters and events in this book are fictional, and any resemblance to actual persons or events is coincidental.

ISBN 1-57856-787-4

Library of Congress Cataloging-in-Publication Data
Snelling, Lauraine.
The way of women / Lauraine Snelling.— 1st ed.
p. cm.
ISBN 1-57856-787-4
1. Saint Helens, Mount (Wash.)—Eruption, 1980—Fiction. 2. Saint Helens, Mount, Region (Wash.)—Fiction. 3. Women—Washington (State)—Fiction. 4. Washington (State)—Fiction. 5. Female friendship—Fiction. I. Title.
PS3569.N39W39 2004
813'.54—dc22

2004002175

Printed in Canada
2004—First Edition

10 9 8 7 6 5 4 3 2 1

To all my women friends
without whom I would be lost.

And to my mother, my hero,
who is now at home in heaven.

Acknowledgments

Since this book started in 1983, my public thanks to Linda Waltmire is long overdue for all her hours of copying the newspaper articles of the eruption and making sure I got all available information. Thanks, friend. Marcia Mitchell provided airplane and flight information, and Susan Edmonds at the Frank Hutchinson Cancer Research Center in Seattle let me go through archives and provided information on early bone-marrow transplants. Thanks to Kathleen, Kitty, Mona, and Eileen for reading and critiquing. Our writer's retreats are high points for me both production-wise and spirit-wise. You are all great brainstormers and wonderful friends.

Cheers for my editor, Dudley Delffs, at Waterbrook Press, who encouraged me to push the envelope—a scary thing. Thanks to all the people at Waterbrook for your encouragement and the pleasure of working with you. My agent, Deidre Knight, rates five stars. Thanks my friend.

Cecile, you had no idea what you signed up for when you agreed to be my assistant. Diamond you are, and what a ride we are having. Thank you, God, for all my friends and family who put up with so much and help keep this storyteller on track.

Much has been published about the eruption of Mount St. Helens, and I think I've read and watched most of it. But I'll never forget the happy hours we spent on her flanks, the awe we felt watching what looked like a concrete pillar rising miles in the sky in the early days, and the tears I shed at the sight of the devastation and again when I saw new green sprouting from the ashes. To God be the glory as life is reborn from ashes and we go forward.

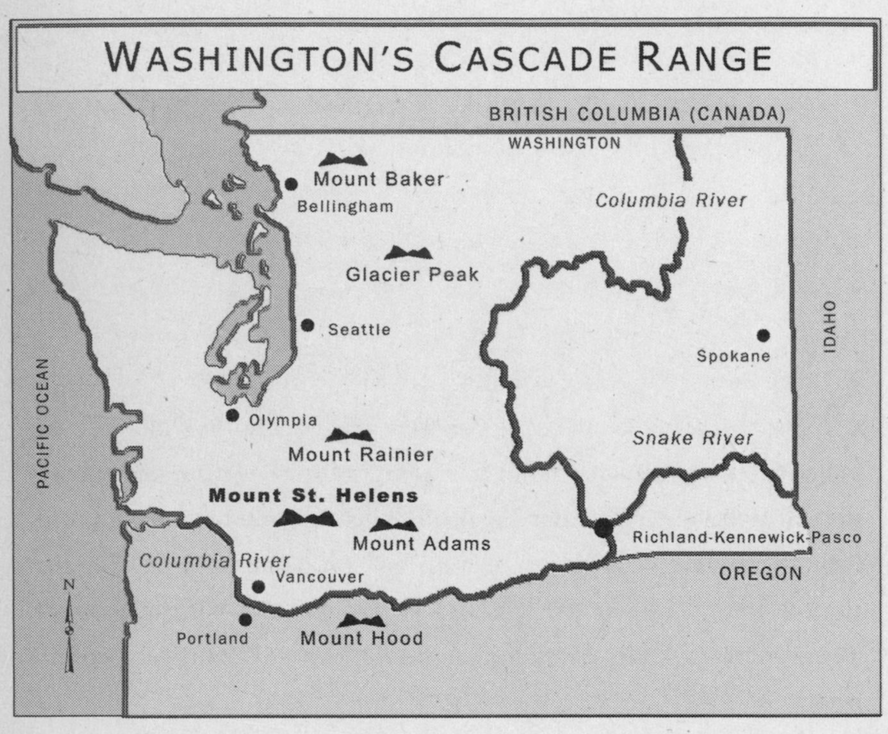
WASHINGTON'S CASCADE RANGE
BRITISH COLUMBIA (CANADA)
WASHINGTON
Mount Baker
Bellingham
Columbia River
Glacier Peak
Seattle
Spokane
IDAHO
PACIFIC OCEAN
Olympia
Mount Rainier
Snake River
Mount St. Helens
Mount Adams
Richland-Kennewick-Pasco
Columbia River
Vancouver
OREGON
N
Portland
Mount Hood

PROLOGUE

MAY 18, 2000

Some days are for remembering.

The visitor stared out across the silver-gray river bottom of the Toutle Valley. Twenty years ago, Mount St. Helens had spewed her insides all over the valleys, laying timber out like wind-flattened stalks of grain and turning the river into a cauldron of rock and ash, snow, and ice. She had turned death loose on the hills and valleys in one cataclysmic stroke. Twenty years ago, life changed in an instant, and no one had any control over it.

Least of all The Lady.

What direction would life have taken had this not happened?

The anniversary commemoration had attracted international attention around the now-quiet mountainside. Media events and photo ops could be had at various points as the world today remembered Reid Blackburn, Harry Truman, David Johnston, and the others who perished. A bronze plaque listing the names was comforted by a recently planted grove of trees. The visitor read the names and remembered many of the individual lives they represented. It was difficult to be present at the base of such an altar of loss, but far more difficult not to have come, not to have remembered.

It had been called a holocaust, a natural disaster of mega proportions, an act of God. But looking down at the river twisting its way between banks of ash, like café au lait in a silver frame, one could see alder and willow now taller than saplings, their green leaves sparkling in the sun.

Life does return and it can be good again, can't it?

The visitor lingered and tried to recall how much had changed over the span of twenty years, what had grown out of the soil of grief. The visitor sensed a hint of green just now beginning to show within. But there was so much to overcome. So much to remember.

1

Frank

May 18, 1980

The scream ripped through him again.

He jerked upright in bed as the cold damp sheets slid away from his sweat-drenched body. Fumbling for the half-empty bourbon bottle on the bedside stand, he ignored the glass and raised the bottle to his lips. Warmth flowed around his internal core as the liquid glugged down his throat.

Cowlitz County Sheriff Frank McKenzie was not by nature a screaming man.

He had not screamed that night twenty-two months ago when he had returned from a fruitless search for a reported lost child and found his wife and ten-year-old son murdered. He had not screamed at the note stuffed in his son's hand lying on the table: *Now we're even.* He had not screamed when the killer was remanded to a psychiatric hospital.

Maybe all the screams just echoed in the empty caverns of his mind. He was never sure.

Empty mind. Empty heart. Empty life.

Frank hoisted the bottle again. Empty. He flung it across the room in a slivered crash against the far wall.

Sig, a mammoth-shouldered German shepherd, whined low in his throat and shoved a cold nose into Frank's shoulder. Sig had the best tracking nose in all of Washington State. He was also the most loyal friend and guard a man could have. But Sig had been up on the mountain that night with Frank, not in his usual place guarding Barbara and Jacob.

Frank flopped back on the pillow, a rip in its case. The stench of his own unwashed body and bed made even him wrinkle his nose. Sig inched his muzzle under his master's flaccid hand lying on the sheets. After a moment, the dog lifted gently, a persistent hint. Frank mechanically massaged the dog's ears and the back of his skull until they both dozed off.

When Frank awoke again, the shard of silver dawn had succumbed to the onslaught of morning. Sunlight stabbed his eyes. The clamor of the phone crashed in his ears.

Muttering profanities, he reached for the missing bottle.

Sig barked. A short, sharp demand.

"Sig, shut up!" Frank fumbled for the insistent phone. "Yeah!"

"I'm sorry to bother you this lovely morning…" The female dispatcher's voice clearly belied her words.

"Then don't!" Frank started to drop the phone back in its cradle. His glance slid over the dirty laundry hiding floor and chair. A framed 8 x 10 photograph of Jacob hugging Sig hung lopsided on the wall above the pile of glass.

"Frank McKenzie! Don't you dare hang up that phone!" Her tone penetrated his fog.

He brought the receiver back to his ear.

"And don't you swear at me either!" She took a deep breath. "Now.

Let's start this conversation again." At the sound of his muttering, her voice sharpened. "I don't care how big a hangover you have, you agreed to take those homeowners through the roadblocks up to Spirit Lake this morning at eight. You're late!"

Frank blinked at his watch. She was right. 8:05.

"Tell 'em I'll be there in half an hour." He slammed the receiver down, cutting off her reply.

2

Katheryn

March 23, 1980

A family that loved one another and showed it, that's all she wanted. Katheryn Sommers glanced around the room, being careful not to catch anyone's eye. Brian, so much younger than the others, melted into himself, watching his brother and sister carry on what they called a "discussion" but which left others feeling ready to jump in to break up a brawl.

"But you haven't looked at all the facts." Kevin sent his sister a look of disgust.

"Sometimes facts aren't the only important criteria." Susan's green eyes, so like her mother's, flashed as she tapped her younger brother on an arm, still tanned from attending college in Arizona. "You, my dear brother, forget all about intuition, gut reaction. Remember that time I—"

"You don't need to bring that up again. You're just like an elephant. You never forget when someone else makes an error in judgment." His eyebrows flattened, his tone needled.

"Kids, let's..." Katheryn stopped, knowing the futility of interfering.

"Why? I don't forget when I make a mistake either. But then, that's not so bad because I make them so rarely." Her teasing smile made him grate his teeth. "My intuition, you know..." She tossed her head enough to send auburn hair, usually worn in a braid, over her shoulder.

"Yeah, right, Miss Perfect. What a pile of—"

"Okay, time out." Katheryn formed the universal sports T with her hands. "Kevin, you and your dad take Brian out to shoot some hoops. And no, it's not raining. Blow off some steam."

Kevin rolled his eyes, started a rebuttal, but instead unfolded his six-foot-four athlete's body. "Come on, Chip, I'll take you two on."

Since Brian's first birthday, ten years earlier, Kevin had called him Chip, as in "chip off the old block." Katheryn was sure Kevin often referred to his father as the old block, albeit never aloud or at least not in her hearing.

"I'll go." Susan stretched as she stood, her pregnancy just beginning to show. "I can still take you on the court."

"No, this is a guy thing. You can help me in the kitchen."

Katheryn turned to go but stopped short. "Honey?" She kept the sharp reproach from her voice with studied calm.

David Sommers blinked and brought his attention back from wherever he'd been. She'd known he'd not been seeing anything out the window, but staring, his mind off somewhere else, inside himself, shoulders slumped as if the load were caving them in.

"Go with the boys, okay? Run off some of their energy at the hoop." She repeated the information without succumbing to sarcasm. She knew he hadn't heard her the first time. And often he didn't the second time either.

He nodded as he stood. "You coming, Suz?"

"Nope, Mom says she needs help in the kitchen." Susan watched her father walk one beat faster than a shuffle, snag his Windbreaker off the hall tree, and go outside.

She watched her mother as the closing of the door echoed behind him. "How long has he been like this?"

Katheryn massaged her lower lip with the tip of her tongue. "Been coming on for some time."

"Has he had a physical lately?" Capable Susan, who'd begun by specializing in pediatrics but switched to psychiatry instead, had just finished her residency and was starting her own practice.

"Yes, I insisted." Katheryn led the way to the kitchen. "The roast will be ready in about half an hour. I thought you could peel the potatoes."

"Of course." Susan opened the drawer to get the peeler while her mother fetched the potatoes from the pantry. "So, have you any ideas what triggered the depression this time?"

"The usual. Midlife crisis. Male menopause. He didn't get promoted to dean of the English Department. All of the above and then some."

"Why was he passed over?"

"I wish I knew." *I wish he would talk, tell me.* She trapped another sigh. One only bred another, and she was afraid a chain reaction would lead to her sobbing. The only control was not to start.

"Mom, you know Kevin and I don't mean anything by our discussions. It might sound worse than it is." Susan touched her mother's arm and smiled when they looked into each other's eyes. "I know about returning-home behaviors. We both do."

"I know, I guess." Katheryn twisted her mouth, wishing she could believe anything of late. Other than God is in His heaven and all is right with the world; the first half believable, the second in serious question. At least in her world.

"There are some studies, you know, on male menopause. I could look them up for you, see if they fit."

Katheryn turned on a burner and set the pot with water for the potatoes on to heat. Keeping her hands busy gave her mind free rein.

"If it's ordinary depression, one of the antidepressants might help."

"I'd thought of that. But you know how your father is about taking pills."

Susan rinsed off the peeled potatoes and took them to the stove to cut into the steaming water. "How small you want the pieces?"

"We'll mash them." *Like I feel, cut up small and mashed to mush.* This time the sigh ambushed her.

"Need more than this?"

Katheryn checked and nodded. "I'll use the leftovers for potato cakes tomorrow. Your dad loves those." Although sometimes she wondered why she bothered, making special things to tempt his appetite, going out of her way to provoke a smile or sometimes even an argument. All to no avail. Her husband existed in some gray parallel universe. Often she speculated that he lived there by choice, making no effort to change.

"You ever thought of screaming at him?"

"Gave it up for Lent last year and never bothered to pick it up again."

Susan snorted in the back of her throat. "Bet you feel that way more often than you want to admit."

Katheryn knew her daughter was using some of her counseling tools on her mother, but she felt more relief than resentment. The latter reared its ugly head most often in the middle of the night when David slept in the recliner in the family room rather than in the bed beside her. He said he slept better there, that the television acted more like white noise. She'd even considered moving a television into their bedroom, but the thought of sleeping through a war movie or another western made her shudder.

"You want me to try to talk with him?"

Katheryn realized she'd been staring out the window, not even seeing the shadows of the guys at the hoop. Good heavens, was this a contagious disease?

"Better you than me, but don't take it as an affront to your expertise if you draw a blank."

Susan started to say something but stopped midword.

Katheryn glanced at her daughter. "Are you all right?"

"Yes, at least I think so." Awe painted Susan's face. She laid a hand on her rounded belly. "Mom, I think I just felt the baby move. Like tiny wings fluttering?" She stared at her mother.

Katheryn rolled her lips together, fighting the burning behind her eyes and nose. "The first time?"

"Uh-huh." Susan stared down at her middle, holding her breath. Her face lit from within, incandescent and luminous, transforming her features.

"He's real, Mom."

"He?" They both whispered as if loud talk might frighten away the flutters.

"Jonathon David, for both our fathers."

"Could be a girl, you know."

Susan shook her head. "No, your first grandchild is a boy."

"Dinner ready yet?" Kevin stuck his head around the door.

"Fifteen minutes. Time for two more games of HORSE." Katheryn stabbed the potatoes. Holding the fork in the air, she shook her head ever so gently. "Think I'll hold off on knitting a blue sweater yet."

"Bet you money."

How often had she heard that challenge. But Susan used it only when she was double-dog certain she was right.

"Maybe I'll use variegated yarn."

"Did you sic Susan on me?" David asked that night, sitting on the edge of their bed, aligning his shoes so only the toes peeked out from under the dust ruffle.

Katheryn turned from hanging up her green woolen jumper. Hunter green, one of her favorite colors, one that used to elicit welcome comments like "that color makes your hair glow like fire" from the man on the other side of the room. He'd once said green made her skin look like cream. She'd stored up his compliments, all the richer for being few and far between.

"What made you think that?" Always better to answer a question with a question if you might not like the answer you'd have to give.

"Oh, the questions she asked."

"Funny, she practiced her counseling techniques on her mother today too." She fingered a silk negligee but chose a warm flannel gown instead, sliding it over her head before turning around.

David sat facing the other wall, elbows on knees, his shoulder blades peaking the cotton of his T-shirt.

When had he gotten so thin?

Never meaty, David wore ropy muscles, the norm for distance runners and rock climbers, sinewy cords for rappelling off cliffs and traversing granite faces.

Angel wings, Katherine had called shoulder blades like those of her men when son Kevin had been young, all bones and firecracker energy.

Katheryn knelt on the bed and stroked his back. Counting his vertebrae and ribs would take no effort. "Susan felt the baby move, the first time."

"Oh, good." David folded back the covers and slid beneath them, immediately rolling on his side—away from her.

Katheryn trapped the sigh between lips clenched together.

Maybe she'd dissolve Valium in his coffee.

3

The Mountain

She could feel it deep within her core, like the first faint flutter of a tiny fetus. She raised herself from the long years of hibernation, curious about the new stirrings. Concentrating now, she waited for it to flutter again. Weeks passed. Her stone-and-earth body betrayed no new movement, so she decided it was merely a surface shift and drifted back to sleep.

But then, like a fevered dream, the sensation disturbed her again. The pulsations birthed deep within her moved inexorably closer to the surface as the days continued. As they peaked and receded like waves on a sandy shore, she fought the nausea that was building within her. She could not rest.

4

Mellie

March 25, 1980

Melissa Sedor lay silently and watched dawn silver the morning. The thin curtains almost disappeared with the light showing through a weave so weak it looked as weary as she felt.

I should have put tinfoil over the window, she thought, *or even cardboard. But if I can't have light, how can I exist?*

And yet if darkness helped her daughter Lissa sleep for even a few extra minutes, she must do it. The Bible said there was healing in sleep; or was that Shakespeare? But she knew if she moved now, Lissa would wake instantly, and in that same moment the pain would strike and another tightrope day begin.

God, surely you can do something. Her cry atrophied from lack of response. If God were indeed listening, wouldn't Harvey have a job by now, wouldn't Lissa's pain lessen, wouldn't the sun break through the clouds long enough to remind them that spring hadn't forgotten to stop by the Pacific Northwest?

Lissa, a bundle of bones collapsed in sleep, moaned. At five, all color had been leached from her face by the relentless disease, all strength drained from one born running and dancing through each moment of life. Mellie wished she dare withdraw her arm that had fallen asleep some hours earlier, but the touch of her mother's hand made sleep possible for Lissa, even though most touch hurt. Mellie, as Harvey called his childhood bride of seven years, had learned to sleep in any position and without moving. But oh, she rarely slept in bed where her husband was as restless with worry as Lissa lay immobile with weakness.

Today the doctors were to give their decisions on a protocol to fight the invader. Mellie thought it more a battle plan.

"Mommy?"

"Yes, darling."

"I'm cold."

"I'll get your blanket." Mellie reached to the foot of the bed, where the beloved quilt made by Lissa's godmother had been kicked off in the last bout with a temperature that took great delight in spiking and ebbing at will.

"Don't go."

"I won't." She and Harvey took turns each night. She'd slept the early shift, if you could call her collapse on the mattress rest. Fear jarred her awake more often than not.

"You go take a shower and see if you can sleep some again." Harvey, hair askew like he'd been tearing at it in his sleep, stopped in the doorway to yawn.

"Daddy?"

"I'm here, baby. Mommy's going to rest."

"Can you tell me a story?" Her pale lashes fluttered open, revealing eyes darkened by the pain killers.

"As soon as I can talk." The two adults changed places with a brief hug in the process.

"I'll put the coffee on."

"Get some rest."

"I will." They spoke softly, for loud noises jerked their baby's nerve endings like an angry puppeteer.

"Once upon a time…"

Mellie left the voice behind. If only "once upon a time" worked for them. Once upon a time there was a mommy and a daddy, and they had a little girl named Lissa who could run and play from sunup to sundown and never get tired.

That "once upon a time" had been reality less than six months earlier. *Please, God, let her be well again.* Mellie filled the teakettle from the tap and set it on the burner to heat while she measured grounds into the receptacle for the water to drip through. Harvey liked dripped coffee rather than perked. She poured herself a glass of water and, while sipping, leaned against the counter and rubbed one bare foot on top of the other. Why couldn't she remember to put on her slippers? She'd slept with one blanket around her and an extra one around her feet.

In bed it was Harvey's job to warm her feet. She'd not had warm feet since this misery began. The kettle whistled, and she poured the sputtering water into the top half of the stainless-steel pot. On her way to the bathroom, she could hear Harvey's voice murmuring one of his made-up-on-the-spot tales of a thumb-size little girl named Issa.

A few minutes later, Mellie delivered the coffee to the sickroom, earning a smile from her grateful husband. Back in their bedroom, she crawled under the covers, seeking any warmth left by Harvey's body. He should have slept longer. He needed his strength to find a job, one with medical insurance. One close to home so he could continue to help with Lissa's care. But so often truck-driving jobs were for the long haul, cross-country like the three of them had done before Lissa started walking.

Harvey loved trucks as much as she loved being at home, but so far no one had agreed to hire a man who lived a love affair with eighteen-wheelers.

Harvey woke her in time to dress for their appointment. "Lissa and I are all ready to go."

"Thanks. Make sure you bring her mittens and hat."

"You get dressed."

Lissa sat between them on the front seat of their blue Ford pickup that Harvey kept running by sheer loving care and attention. "Will the doctor hurt me again?"

"No, I don't think so. We just have to talk with him." Mellie dropped a kiss on wispy hair that stood straight up as soon as Lissa pulled off her knit cap. The little girl hated being bound by clothes—hats, shoes, mittens, all came off as soon she was inside. They only went on by repeated cajoling or a stern frown from her father. When she was cold, her cuddly quilt was the garment of choice. It lay folded in her mother's lap.

Lissa dozed through the drive from Tacoma to Seattle and woke when they left the freeway.

"Will she stick me?"

"Who?"

"That lady in white."

"Oh, the nurse?" Mellie and Harvey exchanged half-smiles across the seat. Lissa, usually stoic, had already come to the point of screaming at the sight of a needle and syringe. At first she had recognized the different health workers, but now "the lady in white" could mean any female.

Harvey left them at the front door of the Fred Hutchinson Cancer Research Center and went to park the car.

"Daddy coming?" Lissa looked up at her mother.

"Yes." Mellie checked her watch. If Harvey didn't hurry, they'd be late. "We'll go on to the elevator."

"Daddy." Lissa turned to watch the door.

"He'll catch up with us." Mellie knew how Lissa felt. Alone. Afraid. Feelings that were bleached of their sharp colors whenever Harvey appeared.

"Daddy's coming." Lissa's radiant smile caught in Mellie's throat.

Their daughter lifted her arms for her daddy to pick her up.

"It might hurt you." He leaned over to look in her eyes.

"Don't care. Carry me, please."

He swooped her into his arms, stepped into the elevator, and let her punch the button for their floor.

"If I was little Issa, you could put me in your pocket to carry." Arms locked around his neck, she leaned back to watch his face.

"But how would you breathe in my pocket?"

"I would look out the top."

"And what would you see if you looked out the top?"

She shook her head as if amazed at his question. "Why, I'd see elevator walls and the door opening, just like now."

"Of course, how could I be so silly?" They turned right and made their way down the hall, her clutch around his neck tightening as they neared the office.

Mellie glanced up to check on her daughter. Lissa had closed her eyes. The mother understood. If only closing her eyes could postpone the next step. She turned the doorknob and let Harvey go through first, fighting the urge to run back the way they'd come. Fighting to get enough air, as if by stepping into the office she'd stepped through a portal and, inside like some tangible thing, the air refused to be pulled into her lungs.

Harvey spoke to the woman behind the counter.

"He's ready for you." She picked up a thick folder and nodded to the entry door. "Follow me."

Lord, other times we've had to wait. Waiting isn't such a bad thing. Mellie opened the door and again let Harvey and Lissa precede her.

The receptionist motioned them into the office. "Please be seated, and Dr. Thomas will be right with you." She laid the four-inch folder on the dark wood desk.

Mellie could no more sit back in the chair and relax than she could fly out the window. Her fingers knit themselves around the strap of her purse, and her teeth clamped together to keep the fear locked within. *But it could be good news.* She sucked in a breath of air that failed to contain enough oxygen, so she had to breathe quick again.

Harvey finished helping Lissa gain some kind of comfort leaning against him and laid a hand on his wife's arm.

The simple touch made her eyes burn.

"Good morning." Dr. Thomas, mandatory stethoscope in the pocket of his white lab coat, stopped beside Harvey to shake his hand. "And how's Miss Lissa today?" His smile coaxed one from her. She looked from his gentle face down to his tie.

"You gots a Smurf tie."

"I do?" He glanced down and looked back at her. "Why, I really do." He held the tie out with one hand. "Do you like it?"

"Uh-huh."

"So does another little girl, so she gave me this for my birthday." He perched on the edge of the desk and picked up the folder.

His face first assumed a doctor's blankness, then he smiled instead.

Mellie watched him, hoping to read more from his face and body than she would from his words.

"Lissa, how would you like to go pick out a lollipop and a toy with Nurse Campbell?"

Lissa stared at him for a moment, as if gauging how far she could trust him. "No shots?"

"No shots."

"Gots purple?"

"I sure do hope so."

The nurse poked her head around the door. "You coming, Lissa?"

Lissa checked her father's face for permission and, at his nod, slid to the floor. "Can I get one for my daddy and my mommy?"

"I'm sure we can arrange that."

Lissa took the nurse's hand, and together they walked out the door.

"She's a sharpie, that one." Dr. Thomas smiled, but the smile faded again when he returned to the folder. "I wish I had better news for you."

Mellie swallowed the invisible gravel that cluttered her throat.

"We can give Lissa more chemo, but that is nothing more than a palliative. We have had some success with a new procedure, but it is long and hard and still considered experimental."

"And without it?" Harvey took Mellie's hand in his.

"We're buying time."

"Do you do it here?"

"Yes, but there is a waiting list."

"How does it work?"

"We have seven days of continuous radiation, followed by heavy doses of chemotherapy. We remove bone marrow from the patient and then reintroduce it later into the body in the hope that it will overcome the damaged tissue and heal the body. Lissa would be in a sterile room for a month. You would be on the other side of the plastic sheets. You would be fully gowned and masked, even having to wear gloves and booties."

"You mean I couldn't touch her, hold her?" Mellie stared at the doctor as if he'd lost his mind.

He nodded. "Anything could start an infection, and her body would have no immunity to fight with."

The silence in the room shrieked against Mellie's ears. She fought the desire to clamp her hands over her ears, to run out of the room.

"And you would promise that this would work?"

"It has in other cases like this."

"But not in all cases." Harvey's voice wore sorrow like a shroud.

"That's right. I hate to ask this, but what kind of insurance do you have?"

"Teamsters."

Mellie glanced at him. *But you said the insurance ran out.*

He must have sensed her scrutiny, but without looking at her, he took back her hand. And squeezed.

"We can check to see how their policy works on experimental procedures."

"But what if..."

"We'll cross that bridge if we come to it." Dr. Thomas glanced from one parent to the other. "I just wish I had better news to give you."

"When would this start?" Harvey cleared his throat.

"I want you to know that I've run this case by the best doctors in the field. They are pretty much recommending the same treatment."

"And if this doesn't work?"

"We'll just pray that it does." Dr. Thomas stood. "I'll be in touch as soon as I know more."

"Fine." Harvey stood and reached to shake the doctor's hand.

It's not fine. Nothing may ever be fine again! Mellie kept her scream inside and stood also. She could hear Lissa's voice at the doorway. *Fine: a four-letter synonym for hell.*

5

MITCH

MARCH 27, 1980

Army Corps of Engineer Captain Mitchell Ross hated going home. It wasn't that he didn't enjoy his family. He loved his two sons and was a fairly good father. He was a decent husband too, when he wasn't cheating, which was much less often of late. His charming, very talented wife, Karen, had an exceptional sense of humor and an enormous capacity for forgiveness. His home, while unremarkable on the outside, was decorated with treasures from all over the world, collected from his various posts of duty.

The current problem lay with his latest love affair, the most insidious of his life. Her name was Helen, Mount St. Helens to be exact.

Ross had been posted to the Corps of Engineers Portland office when he'd made captain a year earlier. His chief responsibilities were the dams on the Columbia River, specifically the expansion of Bonneville Dam, thirty miles upriver from Portland, Oregon.

Hooked on danger, he climbed mountains. It made him feel in control, sure of his own strength, and if he slipped sometimes, the surge of adrenaline beat any drug high available to man. With him life was always the thrill of the chase.

He'd been to the top of St. Helens before he even moved his family to their new post. The climb was strenuous but not dangerous. She was called the cream cone by climbers; a long walk with little rock work. On later climbs he had explored her more challenging faces.

Wednesday, March 27, had begun like any other, except he wasn't running the hour ahead he had planned. And so with, "Sorry, no time for breakfast," he kissed Karen goodbye as he flew out the door. The kiss he blew toward his eighteen-month-old son, perched on her hip, missed.

"Remember dinner with the Fromsbys," Karen called after him.

"Right."

"Not now!" Cars had already begun to line up as he approached the I-5 freeway. The bridge between Portland and Vancouver was up. Mitch, waiting for the tug to push two connected barges under the span, drummed his fingers on the steering wheel. He adjusted his tie in the rearview mirror and caught sight of the frown lines between his eyebrows.

"Cool it, buster." His self command had the desired effect. He slumped back in the seat, turned off the engine, and opened his briefcase. *Might as well make the best of the time.* The paperwork he was always behind on didn't give a fig where he did it.

Half an hour later he handed his secretary the forms he had reviewed. "Sorry, I'm late, Carol. The bridge was up. My one day in the office this week, and that had to happen."

"Don't worry, it's only eight o'clock. But the phone's been going crazy."

She handed him a sheaf of messages. "Most of those came in yesterday, and I couldn't reach you. I numbered them by priority." She checked her calendar. "You have a staff meeting at noon. I've ordered sandwiches." She glanced up. "Anything else?"

"No." He shook his head while grinning at her. "You've covered everything, as capably as usual. Thanks."

The hours evaporated. At eleven thirty he called for another cup of coffee, relieved to be able to see his desk in between the dwindling stacks of triplicate forms. He rolled his head and neck around, trying to touch his ears to his shoulders. Desk work always tightened him up more than being on site.

The meeting touched on the possibilities of an eruption on St. Helens due to all the earthquake activity the last few days. Mitch felt himself come alive at the discussion, especially when the presenter said the seismograph reports were almost a continuous line because the tremors were so close together.

"But none of them are very strong?" Mitch knew only what he'd read in the newspaper the nights before.

"No, but they are coming closer to the surface. Something is happening under that peak, and if it goes like the ones in Japan, it could be disastrous."

"But it could be nothing, too," Mitch said.

"True. At this point we don't know what will happen." The older man rubbed a hand across his balding dome. "But I feel we should be prepared for the worst."

Mitch tossed the reports on his desk when he returned to his cubicle. A morning shot he'd taken of The Lady graced one of the sand-colored partition walls. Pink tinged, she greeted the sunrise with majestic nonchalance. He stared at the picture, trying to visualize what was going on beneath her. *God, I've got to get up there and soon.*

With a groan he settled back at his desk and picked up another report. The army would someday suffocate in paperwork. The intercom buzzed. "Phone call from Seattle. He says it is urgent."

"Thanks." Mitch pushed the button as he lifted the receiver. He leaned back in his chair, glad of the reprieve. "Ross, here."

"She did what?" He slammed his heels back on the floor, his chair at immediate attention. "I know there's been earthquake activity there the last few days." He listened intently, all the while shaking his head. "Well, I'll be... We have a real live, active volcano right here in our own backyard." He dropped the handset in the cradle and called to his crew. "Get the radio. We've got ourselves a hot one."

Radio reports throughout the afternoon reiterated what he'd heard. David Johnston, a geologist monitoring the situation from the base of St. Helens, said, "A vertical explosion could spew ash five to ten miles into the air. It's not as precise as predicting the birth of a baby," he continued. "It might not erupt in this episode, but it's heating up. It could be minutes or months."

The news announcer continued after signing Johnston off. "A mudflow estimated at up to two thousand feet in length is pouring down the northeast face of the 9,677-foot mountain, and gray-brown ash covers the snow all the way to the tree line."

Mitch tried to picture the scene in his mind. But he had no frame of reference. He checked back to the commentator.

"Two crescent-shaped crevices have opened up from the new crater, extending through the wall of the ancient crater."

Mitch knew of that crater. He had explored it several times, wondering at the power that could create both mountain and hole.

"Rapid snowmelt and mudflows appear to be the greatest threat," the commentator continued. "Mudflows have been known to travel at sixty miles per hour on cushions of hot gas. They can cover tens of miles once unleashed. As a precaution, Pacific Power and Light will be lowering the levels in the reservoirs..."

Mitch knew all about that. Draining the water system was standard operating procedure. He shook his head. SOP. Standard Operating Procedure. What was SOP in this case when no one knew what was going to happen? So far there had been no reports of damage. The last eruption in 1857 had blown debris as far as Montana. Other team members from the office floated in and out, eager to discuss various possibilities.

He'd finally left the office at six, after forcing himself to clean up his entire backlog.

"And who knows," concluded a different announcer, "how long this one might last? Are we at the beginning or the end?"

Good question, Mitch thought. Hoping to pick up more coverage, he switched to another station on his car radio. He looked longingly at the planes parked at Pearson Airpark. But they'd said the airspace within ten miles and twenty thousand feet of the mountain was restricted. Besides, it would be too dark soon. *I'll go up tomorrow.*

Blast. He'd promised the boys a trip to the zoo if the weather was nice. But wasn't a mountain erupting forty miles away more important than seeing the monkeys?

He shook his head. Not to kids it wasn't. *Karen would kill me if I reneged now.*

6

Jenn

April 15, 1980

She woke with a start.

Her mind searched the haze of the party the night before. Whose hand was this that groped her breast, even in sleep? The miasma of stale sheets and spilled booze stung her nose as she lifted the covers. With the stealth of an attacking savage, she slipped from the bed, picked up her clothing, and, through glazed eyes, found the bathroom.

With wisdom learned from similar mornings-after, she left the light off, both to keep from alerting the supine man in the bed and to keep from catching a glimpse of herself in the mirror. She knew only too well what she looked like at the moment. And that sight would remind her how far she'd fallen.

She dressed, made it out the door, and down the hall without detection.

Stiletto heels stabbed the concrete of a New York sidewalk. In rhythm with her steps, she lacerated herself for her actions.

Why?

Why the coke?

Why the men?

And the most important question of all: *Why live?*

As the dawn chill penetrated her fog, she brushed drooping strands of hair from her eyes and the corner of her mouth. Early morning commuters trickled up from the subway. The smell of fresh coffee both enticed and repulsed her nauseous stomach. The celebrated face of the '70s was coming alive again. But no one would recognize her; most never did, even when she looked her best. The face only showed itself to the eye of the camera.

The face she lived with every day had moved behind the camera. Now her name carried the distinction, Jennifer Elizabeth Stockton; better known in the current mags as J. E. Stockton, ex-model, current fashion photographer *extraordinaire.*

She pulled her mink coat closer. She'd always maintained a model's leanness, but lately *gaunt* better described the body she ignored in the mirror. Along with a few other choice and not so gentle names. She thought of herself as permafrost in the tundra. Even when the surface melts, the frozen core reigns.

Two blocks later her right heel snapped off in a steel grate. Cursing under her breath, she hobbled to the corner and whistled at the first taxi she'd seen that blustery morning.

She leaned back on the seat, eyes closed against the cabby's questioning glance in the rearview mirror. Her address was all she could force past lips now clenched against the tremors rocking her body. She breathed deeply, forcing herself to swallow the bile bouncing in her throat.

When the driver stopped in front of her apartment building, she thrust several bills into his hand and threw herself from the vehicle just in time to heave her guts into a planter. She vomited again and yet again. Sanity ebbed away, and a black cloud was taking over when the familiar voice of the doorman penetrated her stupor.

"Now, miss." A strong arm that half led, half carried her inside accompanied the voice. His Irish brogue deepened in his concern. "And you'll be all right in a moment, here." He locked the front door with his free hand and then helped her across the marble foyer and into the elevator. When her knees buckled, he caught her up in brawny arms and punched the button for the penthouse.

Her second waking of the day felt little better than the first, but at least she was alone—in her own apartment—in her own bed. Flat on her back, willing the world to stand still. She stared at the twenty-by-twenty-eight, triple-matted, and framed photo on the wall. Rosy-topped Mount St. Helens in all her evening glory. Jenn had taken the shot from the north end of Spirit Lake to catch the full reflection. The Lady and the lake. With a sky so blue it hurt her eyes, she had felt the fir needles under her feet and heard spring singing in the moving bows above her. It had been her last weekend living at home, before she left, seeking fame and fortune, for the Big Apple.

The ache to see her mountain again pierced her numbed senses. But since the eruption, she couldn't bear to see the changes in her mountain. While she'd watched every newscast, read every word written about it, and commiserated with her parents when they called, she'd refused to go home. Made all kinds of excuses. Sure, she'd been busy, had deadlines, had premieres to attend…

Today she knew she had made a putrid hash of her life and couldn't live without seeing The Lady one more day. Maybe it was time to do something that truly mattered to her. Two hours later she boarded a flight to Portland Oregon. J. E. Stockton was going home.

As soon as she snapped her seat belt, she closed her eyes and slipped into a no man's land of shifting shapes and feelings. Her head hurt.

Captain Mitchell Ross folded his army-green dress jacket and carefully placed it in the overhead compartment. He started to loosen his tie but stopped when he looked at the woman in the window seat. *Interesting face,* he thought and wondered about the body hidden in the expensive mink coat. She never stirred when he sat down and buckled his seat belt. Either she was ill, the smudges under her eyes testified to that, or she was exhausted, or...

Jenn resurfaced as she sensed someone invading her space. She'd felt him sit down. Her seat mate was obviously a man, his aftershave expensive and sexy. She allowed her lashes to raise a fraction of an inch and found herself looking into the dark blue eyes of the officer staring at her.

"You're awake."

"I haven't been asleep."

"Are you all right?" His elbow pressed into her from the armrest shared between their seats. "You look like—"

"Hell?"

He grinned, showing perfect teeth. "Well, I certainly wouldn't go that far. I thought more along the lines of ill."

"You could say that." She turned her face to the window, hoping to discourage him. She'd seen that light of interest too often, in too many men. She refused to play the game—not now, not ever again.

Slightly disgruntled at such on obvious, even rude, turnoff, Mitch settled back in his seat. Rarely was he forced to play the part of pursuer. He loosened his tie and dug in his breast pocket for a pack of chewing gum. Ordinarily he would offer a stick to his seat mate. He glanced again at the woman in mink. If she stayed bundled up like that, she'd have heatstroke. He shrugged. Not his problem, but she looked bad.

Mitch smiled to himself as the plane gathered power, thundering down the runway. He heard the fine-tuned roar deepen and the frame shudder just before the wheels left the concrete and the aircraft thrust itself into the ascent. *His* fingers itched to be on the stick, *his* feet on the pedals and *his* eyes scanning both the horizon and the instrument panels. *Pilots always have more fun than passengers,* he thought. Or at least, most of the time. Other flights as a passenger had been most profitable, in terms of pleasure, that is.

While Jenn slept through the drinks and meal, Mitch settled in for a boring flight. He'd flirted mildly with the flight attendant, strictly out of habit, and tried to ignore his seat mate. When he leaned his seat back and closed his eyes to catch a few winks himself, even his years of military conditioning failed him. He'd slept standing against a German wall and curled in a Korean foxhole, but the aura of the woman in the mink precluded any rest for him in the plane seat next to her.

Disgusted at his reaction, he turned and let himself study her. God, she was thin. What was she, one of those anorexics? He checked her emaciated left hand. No wedding ring and no evidence of a recent removal. Long fingers and recently manicured nails with soft pink polish. No artificial nails. He liked that. Her body was effectively hidden in the coat.

But her face, he permitted his stare. High cheekbones, strong chin, straight nose—cataloged they sounded ordinary, but there was strength there and a hidden seductiveness. His fingers itched again, this time for a camera. He'd bet three months' pay that face would come alive through the all-seeing lens.

"Finished?" Her voice slashed through his reverie. She didn't bother to open her eyes.

Mitch smiled, a disarming smile that covered a multitude of pranks when growing up. That same grin usually devastated his female companions. Not in this case.

He tried another tack. "Do you hate everybody, or is there something about me you particularly dislike?"

Jenn snorted. She flicked her fingers like one would to shoo away a bothersome insect. "Look, soldier boy, I tried to give you a polite hint. I don't want anything you have to offer. I'm not interested. Now, is that cut and dried enough for you, or do you need a memo from your commanding officer?" She hadn't even the energy to glare at him, but that lack pounded exclamation points behind her statement.

Mitch stared at her a fraction longer. Nothing in her face betrayed the vitriol with which she'd just doused him.

"No wonder you're so comfortable in that coat—must be mighty cold in there." He shook his head. "Pardon me, ma'am, for bothering you." He faced front. "Maybe next time we meet, you'll be in a more humane mood."

Jenn didn't bother to answer. *Whatever makes you think there will be a next time?*

Turbulence over the Rockies reminded her that she had a stomach. She felt it flutter back in place after a vertical drop. Another quick dip, and the morning's nausea forced her to think of the bag in the magazine pouch in front of her. *Don't be stupid,* her inner voice prodded. *You have nothing left to heave. What do you want to do, make a complete jackass of yourself again? Let this army jock think you need his strong arm? Come on, J. E., where's this control you're so proud of?*

Jenn breathed deeply once, then again, and let her spine slump against the seat. She dropped her chin into the cushion of the mink collar and allowed the relaxation to permeate her body. She swallowed past the bile crowding her throat and, with a super convulsive effort, choked down the bitter phlegm. Her eyes remained closed until the flight captain's voice broke into her consciousness.

"Ladies and gentlemen, we'll be on the ground in Portland in about ten minutes. You can see Mount St. Helens steaming off to the right. As I'm sure you all know, she's been puffing off and on for several weeks now. Our flights between here and Seattle have had some spectacular views. Those of you on the left can see Mount Hood. There's some speculation that he could blow too, if St. Helens really lets go. I hope you've had a pleasant flight. The crew and I thank you for flying the friendly skies."

Jenn leaned her forehead against the window, her heart aching at the gray tears staining The Lady's once pristine slopes. Spring coming to the Pacific Northwest meant peaks still glistening from a late snowfall or cloud cover on the many dismal days. Today the clouds had parted to show the steam rising from the crest of the peak like vertical puffs from a locomotive champing to leave the station. The tear that sneaked past her iron will and rolled down her cheek gave mute testimony to her pain. J. E. Stockton had come home.

7

FRANK

MARCH 28, 1980

Rockin' and arollin', eh?" Frank clamped the phone between ear and shoulder.

Harry Truman's string of cuss words blasted his ear.

"Okay, old man. I hear you. So things are falling off the shelves up there on the mountainside, and your cats are ricocheting off the wall in fear." Frank nodded to the young officer who beckoned from the doorway. "I gotta go, Harry. I'll try to get up there tomorrow."

"There's a woman outside who says her son ran off, hasn't been home for three days."

"Why'd she take so long to get on in here?" Frank paused as his desk shuddered. Another one. The quakes were coming closer together. *Swarms,* the government guys called them.

"She says she tried to call us but could never get through. I'm kind of wondering if—you know—she's all there."

"Now, that's a police term if I ever heard one." *Dumb young punks were supposed to get some kind of training at the academy, just not sure what kind. Two o'clock and it feels more like five.*

They'd had a meeting just this morning with some of the government hotshots, some saying the mountain could blow any second, others saying it could be years. No one knew what was going on, and he was gettin' on to not caring. Just let him run his office and get out of his way.

"Maybelle, honey, could you check your records? See if we got any calls from…" He glanced to the deputy.

"A Mrs. Betty Jones."

"How old you say her boy was?"

"Fourteen?"

"And did she check with his friends?"

"Said so."

"And he's not been to school?"

"I don't know, sir."

"Bring her…"

"No calls listed to that name, Frank." Maybelle glanced to check on the waiting room. "Is that her?" Her whisper made the deputy draw closer.

"Yes ma'am."

"I see." She turned back to Frank. "Let's go back to your office."

Frank reviewed his study of the woman wearing baggy gray sweats, her mousy hair pulled back in a club. Her swollen face showed the ravages of tears, or something.

He followed Maybelle down the hall. "What is it?"

"Poor woman." Maybelle sighed before looking up at the sheriff. "Her only son died three years ago. She's been hospitalized at Stillacom off and on."

Frank felt himself shut down, like a door slamming in his head. He kept from uttering the words he was thinking, only because he knew Maybelle would be offended.

"How about if I take her home with me?"

"Right. Maybelle Hartman, keeper of lost waifs."

"You have any other suggestions?"

The floor trembled beneath their feet.

"Guess we'll have to get used to them, right?" Frank motioned toward the floor.

"Makes my heart near to stop, but guess so. What do you say?"

"Sure, take her home for the night until we can get ahold of her doctor."

"They might just put her back there."

"Would that be so bad? At least she'd be safe."

"She's not a danger to anyone. Just lookin' for her boy."

Frank watched his dispatcher leave the room. *All heart, that woman, but don't cross her once she gets her mind made up.* He turned back to his paper-shrouded desk. *If only a big wind would blow through and take all the forms and reports away.*

I could be just like that woman. The thought made his stomach clench. *I need a drink.* He glanced at the clock. With no emergencies he could leave at five. Leastways that's when he was supposed to leave. He should stay and clean up this mess.

When five rolled round he was out the door and on his way home. He passed the bar without a qualm. No one was going to drive him home tonight. He had plenty on hand, and besides, he didn't feel like talking with anyone.

Sometimes laughing and BS-ing fit his mood, but tonight—tonight he wanted to be alone. Tomorrow was the day.

Some anniversaries were better forgotten. If only he could.

Three years since the worst day of his life.

8 The Mountain

In spite of her expectant tremors, the first blast caught her by surprise. She had hoped to seep the pressure off bit by bit, but the heat within crescendoed until she could feel her snowy mantle begin to melt and slip away, a lady's shawl discarded in haste. Ash dirtied her spring gown of white. Tears formed a gray brown-stream pouring from a wound in her crater. While the initial discharge relieved some of her turmoil, she realized that the pressure remained. The worst was yet to come.

9

JENN

APRIL 18, 1980

Sorry, miss. You can't go any farther."

Jenn frowned at the young trooper. She knew he was only doing his job, but that fact did nothing for her spirits. She donned her "charming" smile. "Look, I grew up here. I know this area like the proverbial back of my hand." She peered at his nametag. "I also know, Officer Tanner, that you can make exceptions to any rule. Can't I sign a release that says I'm going up at my own risk?"

"I'm sorry." He shook his head. "Governor Ray said no exceptions. I'm just obeying orders."

Jenn thrummed her fingers on the steering wheel of her rented four-wheel-drive pickup. Getting up to Spirit Lake gnawed like a rabid badger at her insides. "Look…"

"What's the problem, Tanner?"

Jenn turned her head at the commanding voice. It sounded vaguely familiar.

"This lady insists on going up to Spirit Lake, Sheriff." Officer Tanner stepped back from the truck window at Frank's gesture.

"Now, ma'am, I'm sure Officer Tanner here has explained the situation." McKenzie tipped his hat brim back with one finger.

"Hello, Frank." Jenn removed her oversize dark glasses and turned in the seat to face him. Would her childhood idol even recognize her?

"Well, I'll be blowed over." Frank's smile made it all the way to his hazel eyes for the first time in months. "Jennie's come home." He turned and grinned at the young officer as if he should be excited too.

Jenn flinched at the diminutive. Jenn was okay, J.E. better, but Frank wouldn't know that.

"Yes sir." Officer Tanner glanced back at the cars lining up behind the pickup. "Uh, maybe since you know this person, you could, um..."

"You're right. You go deal with those others, and I'll take over here." Frank waved in dismissal. "Thanks, Tanner."

Jenn studied Frank briefly during his exchange with Tanner. The man had aged! He looked like he could barely crawl out of bed. Had his family's tragedy made him physically ill? When he turned back and leaned closer, she caught a whiff of whiskey. Did it take a drink to get him out of bed every morning? Her musings failed to alter her smile. What were they? Two of a kind?

"Sorry for all that." He extended his hand. "Welcome home."

"I won't be home until I get up to the lake. Can't you do something about that?" Her eyes darkened with intensity. "I *have* to get up there."

"I know you do, squirt. You and The Lady always had a special affinity." The ancient nickname slipped out without his awareness. "Park your truck over there and come with me. I have to go up and try to talk old

Harry Truman out again. Won't do any good, but it's a great way to spend the morning."

"Thanks." She felt like bouncing in the seat, just like she used to. Strange, so many memories she hadn't thought of for years. *What is happening to J. E. Stockton?* Man calls her squirt, and she immediately regresses to that tomboy who tagged along behind Frank even after he joined the county force, even after he brought home his bride.

She parked her truck at the back of the parking lot and swung her camera and daypack out in one fluid motion when she stepped from the cab. The camera was an extension of her soul, her graceful body a product of years of grueling dance and ramp work. She started to lock the door but brought herself up short with a small grin. She was home. No one locked houses here, let alone cars. Cowlitz County was a far cry from the crime-ridden city where she made her living.

She opened the door of the forest-green Blazer and froze. The massive German shepherd facing her from the seat lifted one lip slightly. The growl remained in his throat, audible only to Jenn. An expletive escaped before she clamped her mouth shut.

Sig watched her, waiting for her next move.

"Frank. Call off your dog!" Jenn matched the monster, stare for stare. He was magnificent. Frank laughed, a carefree sound that Jenn failed to appreciate.

"Backseat, Sig." He rumpled the dog's alert ears and thumped him on the shoulder. With a thrust of his powerful hindquarters, the animal pushed himself over the seat. He assumed his sitting position on the rear seat, tongue lolling, eyes still on the woman.

"She's a friend, Sig. A friend." Like a soldier ordered "at ease," the dog immediately relaxed and, with a quick swipe of his tongue, cleaned the sheriff's right ear. Frank wiped his ear dry and extended a hand to pull Jenn's backpack into the center of the seat. "You're not afraid of him, are you?"

"No. Just respectful." She followed her gear in. "Eye to eye, no one with any brains would argue with him." Jenn looked over her shoulder to accentuate her point, then slammed the door. "I'm ready when you are."

When Frank failed to move, Jenn glanced up. At the intensity of his gaze, she locked herself into an assumed nonchalance, one of the poses for which the camera made her famous. Her head tilted slightly as if resisting his gaze.

Frank studied her, his piercing stare wandering from the top of her head, lifeless hair easily tamed with a bone clasp, to her eyes, the purple shadows under them huge in her face. He noted the hollows under the cheekbones, the once strong chin, now all bone, her neck no longer graceful but gaunt. "You look like something out of a death camp. What has that city done to you? Or what've you done to yourself?" He grabbed her chin in brutal fingers and turned her face to the light. "You fall or someone work you over?" The bruise on her temple tried to tell its own story.

"None of your business, Frank McKenzie." The ice in her voice belied the fire in her eyes. "Besides, look who's talking." She jerked her chin free, conscious but uncaring that there'd be another bruise. "You're only forty-four. Yet you look sixty—and a sick sixty at that."

"Yeah. Well, I guess I earned my scars the hard way." The cynical bite in his tone contradicted the desolation in his eyes.

"And you think I didn't?" Blue eyes locked with hazel, as if the two were sworn enemies rather than friends who'd been separated for years. Jenn gave up the contest, hating the emptiness she saw in his soul. "Frank." She laid her hand on his sleeve. "I'm sorry. I thought you'd have gotten over that by now."

"I know. What's a wife and kid in the grand scheme of things?"

"I didn't mean that the way it sounded."

"Yeah. I know." Frank worked his hands loose from the steering wheel. He shifted the Blazer into first, checked his side mirror, and pulled out onto the road. "Let's go rout out old Harry, squirt." He reached over and patted her knee. "Maybe he'll pour us some of his special stock as a welcome home for 'the face of the seventies.' He has one of your magazine covers up on his wall, you know. Along with all the other celebrities who've visited the lodge. Says he knew you before when…"

It was obvious that they were to return to banalities, so Jenn buried her ravaged feelings and dug her camera out to mask any pain in her eyes. Why could this man crack her armor with a few choice words when no one else had even nicked it in the last years? And heaven knows, they'd tried.

The gray clouds scudding overhead matched the turbulent, gray river. Both mirrored Jenn's feelings. The brief flareup with McKenzie only served to deepen the depths of her grayness. She was counting on the mountain to bring her back to life, but each milepost they passed intensified her fear rather than heightening her anticipation. What if the mountain were dying too? *Don't be stupid!* She cut her thoughts off. Mountains don't die. Only people and living things die. And dreams. And hopes. She glanced at the hard profile of the concentrating driver. And those you love. Dying is hard, but murder? She tried to comprehend how he must have felt. The horror eluded her, but empathy and its cousin sympathy found a home. She shifted, staring out the window, to hide the drops seeping from her eyes. When that failed, she rolled her eyes upward, clenched her jaw, and commanded her emotions back into their burrow. Who was she crying for anyway? Frank? Herself? The Lady?

The weathered cedar siding of Mount St. Helens' Lodge melded into the lowering mist as Frank parked in the empty parking lot. Spirit Lake needed a clear day to mirror the proud peak. Today tips of white on the rolling waves were the only color in the murky lake. Mount St. Helens hid herself in the gunmetal clouds. The brisk wind off the lake gave Jenn an excuse for the moisture in her eyes as she stepped from the cab. She fished in her pocket for a tissue while pulling her gear out with her left hand. With her pack slung over her shoulder and her camera around her neck, she finally had both hands free to blow her nose and wipe her eyes.

Frank beat her to it. His hard fingers gripped her chin, gently this time, as he tilted her face upward. He wiped each eye, the tear path over her jaw, then handed her the handkerchief. "Blow."

She mutely obeyed and handed the red square back. He nodded. "That's better." He stared into the eyes still brightened by the tears he'd been aware of but refused to comment on. He unclenched his jaw by conscious effort. "So I'm a sick sixty." He shook his head. "Let's see what Harry's serving this morning." He transferred his grip to her elbow and aimed her toward the lodge. At Sig's short, sharp bark, Frank shook his head. "Sorry, fella. Stay. You drive those cats of Harry's crazy." Frank slammed the door. The sound was lost in the moaning of the wind in the giant Douglas fir trees that sheltered the aged building from storms off the lake.

They ducked their heads and clattered up the worn stairs to the lodge as the first squall whipped through the windbreak and spattered giant tears across the landscape.

"Anybody home?" The wind wrenched the door from Frank's grasp and slammed it against the wall. He shoved Jenn inside, then stepped out to pull the door securely shut behind him.

Jenn shook the drops from her hair while allowing her eyes to adjust to the gloom. The main lighting came from a roaring fire in the rough rock fireplace, since the storm had darkened the windows. "Harry," she called, raising her voice against the wind. "You here?"

Frank took her elbow again and led her across the cavernous room. "Harry!" He thumped the scarred wooden counter. A ragged-eared tomcat, jarred from his nap on the counter, leaped to the floor and disappeared around the corner.

"I'm comin'. I'm comin'. What's your hurry?" Harry shuffled through the door still muttering, gray hair standing on end, bulbous nose and cheeks stained a permanent blush from his favorite beverage. He stopped, peered at the couple through sleepy eyes, then a grin split his face from ear to ear. "Well, I'll be…" Harry finished his sentence with his trademark run of profanities. He nodded as if confirming what his eyes told him. "Ya growed up, kid." He wiped his hand on his pant leg and reached for Jenn's hand. "What'n blazes are you doing up here? Thought you'd forgotten all about us, you'n all that big city glamour." He glanced back at the picture on the wall. Even in the dimness, the striking beauty of the face on the cover of *Time* magazine arrested one's attention. He peered at the woman in front of him, then back at the cover. He stared at her a lifetime, his woodsman's eyes trained to note minute detail. He nodded, a barely perceptible motion. "Had to come home, did ya? Back to The Lady?" He squeezed the hand he still held and grasped her elbow with the other. "You poor child, why'd ya wait so long?"

While Jenn usually hated pity, she felt the moisture rising again at the depths of his scrutiny. It stabbed like needles, piercing her soul as she held his gaze.

"I don't know, Harry"—she swallowed—"but I'm here now." The needles lanced the pustules deep within where she'd buried her bitterness and disappointment and left them to fester. She clenched her teeth and squeezed his hand, fighting against the incipient tears. "So, Truman, what's happened to your famous hospitality? Frank promised me you'd kept a good supply up here and..."

"And, darlin', you need a drink. Cocoa, Frank?" He grinned up at the sheriff leaning on the counter. "Or...?"

"Always the comedian, aren't you?" Frank thumped the old man on the shoulder. "Let's have some 'or,' and make it a stiff one. By the way, I brought you a couple of cases of Coke. 'Fraid you might run out."

"If you ain't a real friend." Harry led them toward the bar. "Got plenty of Schenley. Stuff goes pretty far now, since those busybodies in Olympia won't let nobody come up here." Never able to say three words without cussing, some of which he ran together and used as one adjective, he busied himself behind the counter as Jenn and Frank perched on the stools in front of the bar. He set up three glasses, ice, whiskey, and topped them off with Coke from a can, but not much of the latter. After sliding two drinks across the bar, he raised his own. "To comin' home, darlin'. To comin' home."

Jenn swallowed against the rising tide and raised her glass in salute. The barely diluted whiskey burned a path through the gathering tears and warmed a puddle in her middle. *What's happening to me?* she thought. *I don't cry and mush about like this. Get your act together, girl. Tears don't belong in your life. You're tough. Remember?* She coughed and slid her empty glass back across the counter.

"Last time you was here, you was too young for my special brew." Harry refilled the glass, the Coke barely staining the amber Schenley. "Now, you want a second? Quicklike—what's gone on with you, girl?"

"Just fill it up, Harry. The story's much too long and boring."

Frank watched the by-play, already on his third drink. He'd poured his own after the first splashed down and begged for a chaser. By now he could feel the glow creeping around his gut and out to his extremities. He sipped, finally taking time to allow his tongue some appreciation of the smooth, warm whiskey flavor. His eyes and mind searched for clues to Jenn's comment. Whatever had happened to her, it certainly wouldn't be boring. She bristled like a baby porcupine before it had any sense, ready to throw its quills at any distraction. Frank glanced down at the tabby cat twining around his ankles. Sig would have a field day with cat scent all over him. At the same moment, the ratchety *chir-r-r-r* of a raccoon preceded a sleepy bandit face from the dark end of the bar. Cat and coon shared the premises on an equal basis, but for the top heavy number of felines.

"Well, look at you." The smile in Jenn's voice broke across her face as she spied the newcomer. The raccoon tried to slip a hand into Harry's glass but dodged when the man pushed him away. Harry reached in his breast pocket before the raccoon could and handed Jenn a peanut.

"Here. Give the old fool this, and he'll be your friend for all time."

Jenn held the peanut out on the flat of her palm. The raccoon snatched it with one black paw. Black eyes sparkled in the light as he held it daintily with both front paws, chewed the shell open, and picked the nut meat out. Jenn dug in her pack for her strobe, attached it to her camera, and snapped off the lens cap. "Give him another peanut," she ordered and focused.

The raccoon ambled toward her, sniffing cautiously at the strange contraption. When a peanut materialized in front of his nose, he sat back on his haunches and proceeded to dine. The first flash sent him scurrying for cover, but another peanut turned him back around. The best shot was of the tubby bandit dunking a peanut in one of the glasses.

Watching the photographer in action, Frank searched for traces of the little girl he once knew in the professional before him. She was quick, her motions smooth and yet unhurried. She muttered to her subject more in the way of encouragement, as if the animal could understand every suggestion she made.

"More peanuts!" The snap in her soft tone was a definite command. "Now, back away." The two men did as ordered. The raccoon lapped it all up—the liquor, the peanuts, and the attention.

Jenn swiped an errant strand of aged honey hair back from her cheek as she dropped the camera back around her neck and dug the lens cover out of her shirt pocket. She laughed, pointing to her waddling subject. "He beats most of the models I've worked with lately. Can't say much for the lighting, but, Harry, you're a great assistant. Bet he'll sleep for a week after all that." She scratched the animal behind its ears and stroked down the silky back. "No wonder they used to make coats out of your cousins." She continued stroking. The raccoon rolled over for her to scratch his tummy. His soft purring encouraged her to keep it up.

"What a sweetheart." She laughed, suddenly conscious that she'd gone off into her own world. She started to pick up her drink but remembered whose hands had been in it last. Besides, it was empty. She paused. Her ear tuned to an inner voice as her eyes sought Frank's. A miniature freshet of joy trickled from around her icy interior, like snowmelt in the first rays of spring sun.

Frank's hard stare was like looking into reflective sunglasses. He raised his drink, as in a toast, and tossed it back with one swallow.

Frozen again, Jenn turned. "Make it a stiff one, Harry." When she failed to rub his belly anymore, the raccoon sniffed at the other glasses and then ambled off into the darkness.

"He'll sleep good now," Harry broke the painful silence. "At least till I feed the cats."

Frank turned back to the bar, his elbows resting on the worn surface. He poured a straight shot and swallowed appreciatively, nodding at Harry. "That was a great show, old man. Now, when are you coming out?"

Muttering his usual, Harry bristled like one of the old cats in a squall. "You know better'n that, Frank. I said I was staying here, and I meant every word of it. If I leave here and that mountain takes my home, I'll just die anyway, so I'm staying." He hoisted a bottle. "Me'n my special stock here. We'll wait it out in a secret shaft I know of." His ruddy face sobered. "And if it's my time to go, I can't think of any other place on this whole earth that I'd rather be. This is my home. Why, you know I even own the top of The Lady. Went toe-to-toe, me and Burlington Northern." He stared into the glass in his hand. "You can't make me go, Frank." His voice softened. "Don't try to make me go."

Frank took a deep breath. "Just doing my job, old man. They tell me to go up and reason with old Harry, so now I can say I've done so. Again. I didn't expect you to change your mind and besides, Jenn and I"—he brushed her arm—"we were really hoping The Lady'd be out. The sky was clearing in Toutle."

Jenn flinched at his touch. He was as changeable as spring weather. Who—where was the real Frank McKenzie?

The sheriff continued. "This city gal here needed to get out and get her boots dirty. Sight her camera on our mountain, 'stead of some idiot walking bundle of bones." He slurred his words only slightly.

"Sight all you want. I'm not leavin', but you come on back any day. We'll all still be here, me'n the cats and coon. And of course, St. Helens. She sure is making it hard to sleep at night. Those earthquakes giving me a crick in my neck."

"Earthquakes?" Jenn joined back in the conversation.

"Yeah. All that rockin' and rollin' even knocked some stuff off my shelves. Lost a brand-new bottle the other night. Smashed all over the floor. What a waste." He ran his fingers through his thinning hair, making it stand even higher. "Shame."

"Have the quakes done any more damage that you know of?" Frank asked.

"Not down here, but I know that's what opened those two craters at the summit. Keeps all the geologists hyped up too. They got tracking equipment scattered all over the place. Talked to a couple up by Dog's Head. They say that there bulge to the subpeak happened in the last eruption, 'bout a hundred years ago. Now it's swelling again. Been avalanches, too. 'Course, everyone you talk to has a different theory." Harry shook his head. "Near as I can tell, they're all guessing what'll happen next, just like the rest of us." He picked up a half-grown black cat and cuddled the animal under his chin, all the while stroking the soft fur. "The only thing I know for sure is that I sure ain't leaving."

"I get the point, Harry." Frank pulled himself upright. He hadn't felt so relaxed in a long time, a mighty long time. "But we'd better get ourselves back down that road. I've done my duty, the most pleasurable part of my duty. Next time I come, you need anything?"

"Na. When you coming?"

Frank switched his gaze to meet the questioning look in Jenn's eyes. "The next time the mountain decides to show herself. She's what this photographer friend of ours came to see. You don't suppose she made the trek clear across the continent to have a drink or two with a couple of old has-beens like us, do you?"

"Speak for yourself, you young pup. I gotta lot of living yet in this old hide of mine. You just get yourselves up here, and I'll walk your legs right into the ground. You'll get some real pictures, gal, you stick with old Harry."

Jenn laughed as she shook her head. "I'll look forward to it."

"I'll bring in those cases of Coke." Frank slipped his down vest back on.

"You think I can't carry in my own drinks?" Harry puffed up like a bantamweight prizefighter.

"Stow it, Harry. Sig would chew you in pieces if you opened that door. You know that."

Water beaded and ran in rivulets down his vest by the time Frank set the two cases of Coke on the counter. He shook the drops off his felt hat. "Pouring harder than ever. Keeps up very long, and we'll have more flooding. The Toutle's a mess already. Come on, lady, let's hit the road before it washes away."

"Thanks, Harry. These have been the best hours I've spent in a long time."

"Don't wait so long, girl." Harry walked them to the door. "See you, sheriff. You keep all those gawkers away now, you hear. Don't let old Harry make a penny up here. My boats are gonna rot out with no one to rent them. And what's a lodge without guests? That's right. You and old Dixie Lee. Keep an honest man from earning an honest living."

"Maybe it'll all calm down by the time fishing season opens. Then you'll really be in the bucks."

"Yeah, and overrun by all them sightseers."

Frank snorted as he swung open the door. "Can't have it both ways, old man."

"Nope, just wish we was back the way it was. I've had a good life here. The best." Harry stared at his boot toes a moment. "See you soon?"

"Soon." Jenn gripped his hand. "Very soon."

Frank and Jenn dove for the Blazer, both of them laughing as they ducked their heads against the squall that tried to wrest the car door from Frank's grasp. Jenn threw herself up to the seat just as Sig leaped into the back, his tail brushing across her face. She sputtered, wiping both dog hair and raindrops off her chin, then honked the horn at Harry when she realized the fogged windshield prevented him from seeing her wave.

Frank honked again as he backed the truck and turned to head down the loopy road. Beautiful it was any time of year, but treacherous would be more likely today. Good thing he had four-wheel drive. They might need it.

His concern proved unfounded when they pulled into the Toutle parking lot, an hour and a half later. The river had nearly crested the road in a couple of places, but Highway 504 was holding its own. Both Frank and Jenn had retreated to their inner dungeons as they returned to civilization, neither of them speaking for the final twenty-five miles.

"Thanks for the ride." Jenn picked up her pack, prepared to step out. Her teeth clenched on some of the choice words she'd been rehearsing to deliver. Instead she went with her heart. "If you ever want, I mean, need to talk about what happened, I've been told I'm a good listener." *Besides, I'm your friend from those eons ago.*

"You get some rest," he ordered, eyes straight ahead. "And for heaven's sake, eat."

"Who do you think you are?" She bit off each word precisely. "My keeper?"

"By the looks of you, somebody'd better be."

She let the slam of the door answer for her. *And see if I offer again. Ha!* her inner voice added. Sometimes only the wounded recognized each other.

10

Harvey

April 30, 1980

But, Daddy. I don't want you to go."

"I'm sorry, baby." Harvey Sedor swallowed past the lump in his throat. "I have no choice." He hugged five-year-old Lissa to his chest. With callused fingers, the tip on the index finger lost to a saw blade on a past job, he brushed the limp strands of blond hair from her pale face. Her skin had become thin and transparent, like cellophane covering blue veins. The treatments had done that to her. But the poisons the doctors had dripped and injected into her innocent body weren't doing their job. The cancer seemed to feed on them instead. And now they were down to experimental procedures, a bone marrow transplant followed by months of isolation. They also had no money and no more insurance.

When Harvey allowed himself to think of the mounting medical bills, despair settled on him like oily smoke from burning tires. That kind of smoke seeped into every pore, coated throat linings, and reddened eyes. The smell of it clung to one's hands for days. Despair was like that.

He rocked her gently, knowing how easily she bruised. Her thin arms clung to his neck as if she knew something he was unwilling, no, unable to tell her. He thought she had fallen asleep until she lifted her gaze to his.

The purple bruises under her eyes tore at him. "Daddy?"

"Yes."

"Am I going to die?"

"No!" The denial was an explosion tearing out his heart. *Not if I have anything to say about it!* A taunt. A scream. A prayer. He flung his challenge at the heavens. "No," he whispered against her hair.

"'Cause Suzie said dying's not a bad thing except..."

"Except what?"

"I don't want to leave you and Mommy." She took his face in her soft hands and looked deep into his eyes. "That's why I don't want you to go away now."

"But I've gone away on jobs before. Daddies have to work."

"I know." She settled back under his chin. She was quiet, absorbed in her thoughts.

He could feel her thinking, as if her mind reached into his and ferreted out the secret plans. He was being fanciful. No matter how close they had become in the hours of transport and treatment, mind reading was impossible. Wasn't it?

"Suzie said that when you're dead, you don't hurt no more."

God! Let her live! Take me! Let her live! He'd pleaded those prayers before, for whatever good it did. God must be sitting on His hands, for He certainly wasn't healing this precious child.

"Guess I'll go to sleep now." She hugged him again.

He wanted to crush her to him, hold her safe from the invisible marauder, but instead he laid her gently in her bed and kissed her frail cheek. "Goodnight, baby. Sweet dreams. God loves you, and so do I." He choked on the nightly ritual and shut out the light.

Harvey leaned against the archway into the living room, reliving each syllable of their talk. If he'd had any doubts as to his actions, they'd evaporated in the heat of his despair. The doctor had said "no treatment, no life." This was their last chance.

He strode into the bedroom, hoisted his suitcase, and entered the kitchen to pick up his red-and-white cooler, packed and ready. Mellie tightened the Thermos lid as he put both arms around her from behind and kissed her on the neck.

"Harv, I don't want you to go." Her shoulder-length hair, slightly darker than her daughter's, swung forward and hid the quiver in her determined chin.

"You sound like your daughter."

"We need you here. I know you said you'd be back for the preops but…"

"It's the only job I could find. And you know how good the Teamsters insurance plan is. We'll get the help we need." He tightened his arms, so she leaned back against him. "Mellie, I don't know anything else to do." The fridge hummed loud in the silence. He could feel her heart thumping against her narrow rib cage. *Wiry* was a description she hated, but it suited her. She'd manage. "Now, you know where all the papers are if anything should happen to me?"

She nodded.

"And I'll call you with a phone number as soon as I've got a place to stay." Her silence made him want to blurt out his carefully contrived plans. They'd never kept secrets from each other. He took a deep breath.

"I'll only be about two hours away. Chehalis isn't the end of the world, you know." His attempt at being lighthearted failed for both of them.

"Those logging trucks go right up on the mountain, and Dixie Lee ordered everyone out of there. I don't care about the insurance. We'll find another way to—"

"No. We won't." His voice fell flat. A period. Final.

Mellie scrubbed the tears from her eyes, bit her lip until she could taste blood, and drew a ragged breath. "I'll talk to you later then."

Harvey nodded.

He waved to her as he climbed into the cab of their well-used pickup. *Goodbye, my love. I know this is our only way, so please forgive me once you understand.* He backed out of the driveway of their east Tacoma home, blinked his headlights at the slim figure standing in the door, and fought down the urge to cancel his plans. The freeway beckoned.

Once through the Tacoma interchanges, he allowed thoughts to surface of the insurance policy that he'd tucked away among the papers in his file box: $500,000 and double indemnity for an accidental death times two. There had always been accidents for logging trucks. One more wouldn't even make a ripple in the lake of life. And his family would be taken care of. The house, the car, the credit cards, all paid for because of those small premiums. But the biggie. Lissa's chance for life. His throat clenched with a sober awareness of his intention. A life for a life. A fair exchange.

He turned the radio up loud and forced himself to listen to the blaring rock-and-roll. "No turning back, no turning back." He pulled off the freeway at State Highway 504 and, a mile later, turned into the truck yard. Harvey Sedor reported to the office. God had given him this job, but would He sanction the plan that Harv had built around such provision?

11
Jenn

April 30, 1980

Never one to wait for help, J. E. Stockton took matters into her own capable hands when the weather cleared. According to the *Columbian,* southwest Washington's largest daily newspaper, Pearson Airpark off Highway 14 had become the nerve center for small aircraft.

Monday morning she turned her pickup off Highway 14 at Industrial Way, followed the signs to the airfield, and parked behind the corrugated metal hangers. By the number of vehicles in the parking lot, she wasn't the only one with flying in mind.

She grabbed her daypack by the shoulder straps, stuffed her down vest in the front pocket, and set off to locate a pilot. *I should have called for a reservation,* she thought as she strode around the corner.

Five planes were lined up at the west end of the concrete runway, ready for takeoff. Several others were warming up, prior to trundling down to join the line.

As Jenn approached the building marked OFFICE, she could see another line; this one of men waiting in front of the counter.

It seemed like a hundred conversations going on at the same time, all in cocktail party decibels as she opened the door. The cacophony and the cigarette smoke hit her simultaneously. Wrinkling her nose at the smell, Jenn stepped into line behind two gesticulating men.

"I don't care what your studies indicate," said the bearded one. "This mountain is going to blow. The only question is when? The quakes have progressed to harmonic tremors. That means magma is moving around under that peak." He threw up his hands. "It'll only get worse."

"Sam, there's been earthquake activity under these peaks before. Why, Baker's been puffing for years. Even Rainier steams at times." Dennis, the younger of the two, shoved his hands into his back pockets. "You can't just shut the area down. People have a right to get into their property around Spirit Lake, and I sure wouldn't want to be the one to tell those loggers to take a vacation. They've been known to turn a hair nasty when they can't work."

Jenn almost commented. *Could be my dad they're discussing. And yes, he can get testy when someone else tries to tell him what to do. Likely where I got my own stubborn streak.*

Sam stuck his brushy jaw out farther. "You mark my words, if those loggers, the gawkers, and those homeowners don't stay away, it's gonna cost them more'n a few days' wages. Those other mountains don't have a crater in their summit bigger'n two football fields, now do they?"

The other man shook his head.

"And, Dennis, those mountains aren't spitting ash and steam a couple of miles up in the air, are they?" He hammered his point home with a stiff forefinger on Dennis's chest.

The clean-shaven, wiry young man shook his head. "But still…"

"No buts…"

"Excuse me, you two." The harried-looking man behind the counter interrupted them. "Finish your argument in the air. Hank is ready for you in the twin-engine Beechcraft. He said to hustle. His schedule's going nuts in short order."

The two men waved their thanks as they left the room.

"Next!"

"I'd like to hire a pilot and aircraft." Jenn took her place at the counter.

"Where to, ma'am? And what type?" He studied the paperwork on the counter.

"I want to get as close to that crater as I can, and some time around the rest of the peak. I'm a photographer and…"

"You and everyone else," the agent muttered as he shook his head. He raised his eyes to hers. "It'll be a couple of hours, if you get up today at all."

Oh, please. Jenn turned on her megawatt smile, the one that transformed her face into stunning. "Is there any chance of something sooner? I've been waiting for days for the…"

"As he said, you and everyone else," responded a masculine voice from behind her. "But I'm going up, and who am I to turn down a fellow photographer?"

"Thank you so much." Jenn turned as she spoke, her smile radiating even more voltage. "I'll pay whatever…" She raked her gaze up and down the smiling man in front of her. Shutters closed off the candlepower of her eyes. "Oh. It's you."

"And hello to you, too. Thought for a minute the spring thaw had come." Mitchell Ross extended his hand. He waited. "Guess I was wrong."

Jenn stared at his hand, none of her warring emotions visible on her sober face. It was him, the intrusive hustler of the flight from New York.

But what are my choices? Him or a long wait. And the weather can change any minute. She gripped his hand and shook it.

"I'm J. E. Stockton, and"—the words stuck in her throat—"and thanks, Sergeant."

"The name is Mitch," he said. "Captain Mitchell Ross."

"And you're for hire?" Jenn kept her tone noncommittal. It was a shame the barb hadn't hit home. She'd remembered his rank all right. No matter how abhorrently rotten she'd felt that afternoon, her mind still cataloged facts and pictures like the bars on his tunic and remembered them.

"No."

"But you said..." She watched cockiness settle on his shoulders like a cloak.

"No. You said you'd pay anything. I said I'd not let a fellow photographer down. I'm going up around the mountain, and you're welcome to fly with me. But I am *not* for hire." He pushed the bill of his khaki baseball hat up with one finger so his dark blue eyes were clear of the shade. "Well?" He glanced at his watch, his tone snapped into military cadence. "Flight time is 0915 hours. That's my plane over there." He pointed at a four-seater, red-and-white Cessna, anchored to blocks about a hundred yards to their left.

I despise feeling like a penitent. She always paid her own way. On the flight to Portland, she'd put him in his place and left him there. She'd pegged him immediately. One of those men so used to women chasing him that he just turned on the charm and waited. She'd trimmed his charm down a notch or two. But today she broke into a trot to catch up with the rapidly striding officer. He'd released both chocks before she caught up.

"Welcome aboard, ma'am." The gleam in his eyes matched the glint off the plane's window. He unlatched the door on the passenger side and offered Jenn a hand up on to the slanted wing.

Jenn's sense of humor finally pushed past her scowl. *So I've been outmaneuvered. So what? I'm going up over the mountain, and that's what matters.* Wasn't that what she needed, almost more than breath itself? She allowed her weight to lean into the hand cupped under her elbow. She nodded, little demons dancing in her eyes and at the edge of her lips. "Thank you, Sergeant."

Mitch threw back his head, his belt of laughter audible above the roar of a taxiing aircraft. He was still chuckling as he lowered himself into the pilot's seat, slammed the flimsy door, and hooked his seat harness.

"Well, Ms. Stockton." His glance checked her already-fastened belt and looked behind to see where she'd stowed her gear. He nodded approval. "I see you know your way around small planes, too."

"Yes. I do. But for the record, my name is Jenn. I hate 'Ms.' anything. I go by J. E. professionally, but out here I'm Jenn." She finished screwing her wide-angle lens in place and zipped the camera pack. "And I have a bargain to make." She turned the full intensity of her gaze on him.

He watched her silently, waiting.

"You don't hit on me and I won't dig at you." She held out her hand. "Agreed?"

"Agreed." They shook on it, two business people closing on terms. "But may I say one other thing?"

She looked at him, with one honey eyebrow raised.

"You're in a whale of a lot better shape today than when I first saw you. I'm glad."

Jenn nodded. "So am I."

By the time Mitch had completed his preflight checks, the line of planes at the end of the runway had taken off. They taxied, turned, and, with an increasing roar of the engines, lifted into the air. He glanced at his passenger.

Pleasure lightened her face, a half-smile flirted with perfect, nibbling her full lower lip. While her cheekbones were still much too prominent, a faint blush softened the stark angles. Dark glasses hid her eyes, but her entire body radiated excitement. She leaned against the belt, intent not only on the landscape flashing below, but on the ash-dusted mountain that loomed ahead of them.

Mitch routinely checked his gauges, but his gaze homed back to her, drawn by her joyous concentration. It was hard to equate this vibrant woman with the frozen creature of the earlier plane ride.

He tapped her shoulder. "Lake Merwin." He pointed to the azure lake below and to their left.

She nodded and pointed to the long lake to their right. "Swift Reservoir?"

"Yes. Yale Lake is right below us. We've been letting water out of all three just in case the eruption blows this way. Trying to keep the flooding down. Lewis River carries a lot of spring melt as it is."

He pointed to an open field with a scattered herd of animals. "Elk. They haven't headed up to summer pasture yet."

Jenn focused her camera as he banked the plane to give her a good shot.

She grinned as she turned back to him. "They're grazing among those houses down there, just like a herd of cattle."

"Yeah, but no fences."

Mitch took them up to ten thousand feet as they came around the southwest flank of the mountain. From the south, the only indication of the mountain's travail was the dusting of gray ash over the dazzling snowpack and plumes of steam that periodically penetrated the stratosphere and mimicked clouds hovering over the peak.

Jenn sucked in her breath at the size of the crater visible from the west and north. The men at the airpark hadn't exaggerated. Football fields or aircraft carriers were the only way to compare the size.

"We'll go around once at this altitude and the next run several thousand feet above her." Mitch nodded toward the mountain.

Jenn felt a pain in her gut at the desecration of such a magnificent mountain. The crater had fallen in, creating a hole hundreds of feet deep, the sides of it a gray-and-black mosaic of rock and ash. Deep gashes radiated away from the crater and appeared at other stress spots. The mountain was cracking from the pressure within. Although Jenn had read that the north face was bulging, she couldn't discern it yet with the naked eye.

Jenn grabbed for her case behind the seat.

"Out of film?"

"Uh-huh." She completed the loading with automatic fingers, sneaking glances at the mountain as if it might do something while she wasn't looking. *Come on, come on.*

Spirit Lake lay below them now, bounded on the south by the two lodges. "You ever been to the lodge?" He pointed to the smoke rising from the lodge chimney.

"Yes." She snapped pictures as she spoke. "Frank McKenzie and I were up there last week. He hasn't changed a bit."

"So you're from around here, then."

"Born and reared in Longview. That mountain was my playground growing up. I've been to the top three times and hiked more of her trails than most people in the forest service."

"But you left."

"Yeah." *Because you wanted more,* her inner voice chided. *Well, you sure got what you wanted. More headaches, more sex, more money, more...* The tone dripped acid. She shrugged. Well, the fame and money part weren't so bad. Just the garbage that went along with it.

Her monosyllabic reply effectively cut him off. Jenn knew he could feel the distance she threw between them with that one word. He turned his full attention back to his flying and the mountain.

The view from above and to the north gave them direct access to the crater. As Jenn refocused her camera, the upper side crumbled in on itself. An ice-and-rock avalanche sent steam and ash billowing upward. The plane bucked in the pressure change. She sucked in her breath at the sheer magnificence of the glistening gash and the boiling turbulence. Her automatic fingers kept the camera clicking throughout.

"That'll be some footage." Mitch had the plane under control again, his hands and feet as automatic on the controls as hers had been on the camera.

Jenn leaned back against the seat, a sense of awe robbing her of speech. Her fingers dug again in the pack for film. For a moment she had glimpsed a minute portion of the power smoldering below her.

The flight back to Vancouver passed without comment until Mitch banked for his approach.

"She's really going to blow, isn't she?" Jenn hardly recognized her voice. It was as if the power captured beneath ice and rock had stolen any energy she had left.

"What?" Mitch hollered above the whine of the engine.

Jenn shook her head. Maybe by the time they left the plane, she'd be in control again. Right now she wasn't sure if she wanted to weep or rage. Or maybe both. *What in heaven's name is going to happen to my mountain?*

12

THE MOUNTAIN

The waves were so continuous she could no longer distinguish one from another. She shuddered from the onslaught, remembered the sensations from centuries before only too well. Her sense of control shifted with the cavernous roiling inside. Perhaps if she remained calm she could circumvent the natural sequence. She knew about change, and its inevitability, but like the flurry of activity by those around her, she tried to maintain control. No, she had done all she could do to withhold the fiery force within her, the liquid magma rising like bile. It was her time.

13
Harvey

May 11, 1980

Harvey felt the load shift.

How easy it would be, he thought as his body automatically compensated with both foot and hand motions to keep the rig under control. He shifted down, the growl of the gears filling the eighteen-wheeler cab. He'd been watching for just the perfect place. He couldn't afford an injury, so the drop-off had to be steep, a sharp curve to miss so the weight of the load would carry him over.

Lissa would have her surgery.

But he'd needed several paychecks first, money to tide his family over until the insurance came through. He knew there would be inquiries; the insurance companies would fight those claims every step of the way. That's why there could be no doubt that it had been an accident.

He thought of the horror stories he'd heard down at the Castle Rock Café. Tales of disaster when logs took trucks out, drivers who'd maybe had one too many. Well, no chance of that. He'd not had a drink since he got here. No matter how the guys teased him, he always ordered a plain Coke, no ice. He'd forced himself to hang around the bar a couple of times, just so no one would accuse him of being a loner. Oh yes, he'd thought of all the angles. Now just to locate the perfect place.

He checked both directions as he pulled out on Highway 504. It was a habit because no one but loggers and the scientific research teams were allowed in the red zone. In fact, the loggers had just been given permits to haul again, since the mountain had been quiet for the last couple of weeks. He slipped through the gears easily and sped down the road. Asphalt was a treat after the switchbacks on the rutted logging tracks. He thought back to the conversation with his two women the night before. Lissa, holding her own for a change, bragged about the two pounds she'd gained. "And I have a new stuffed rabbit, Daddy," she giggled. "Guess what I named him."

"What, baby?" Harv thrilled to hear the joy in her voice.

"Harvey." She waited for his response.

"Harvey? Whatever happened to Peter or Bugs Bunny?"

"Daddy." He could hear the exasperation in her voice. "He's all white with pink ears. Those others are gray. And besides…" She paused.

"Besides?" Harv waited for her punch line.

"Harvey's a magic rabbit and…"

"And?" Harv loved the way she explained things to him, always so definite and particular.

"Harvey's your name," she crowed. "You're a magic rabbit." Her giggle brought tears to his eyes and lodged emotion in his throat.

Oh, God. If only I were magic, what I would do for you. "Well, you hug that Harvey hard tonight, and I'll be home to see you soon. Put Mommy back on the phone, okay?"

"Okay, Daddy. I love you." She giggled again. "Harvey."

"Goodnight, baby." He scrubbed the back of his hand over his eyes. *God above, how precious she is.*

"Harv?" Mellie's soft voice filled his ear. He leaned against the phone booth wall. A drizzle had begun, and the chill wind sneaking in under the door caused him to shiver. He wasn't used to standing still this long.

"Yes? Mel, she sounds wonderful."

"When are you coming home?"

"Soon. I promise you. I just can't turn down any extra time they offer me. We've been driving right through the weekends since the rollback. Scuttlebutt says we'll be off the weekend of the twenty-fifth. That's less than two weeks away."

"Oh, Harv, I miss you so. The final precheckup is the twenty-sixth. Do you think you can stay through for that? Then maybe we'll know the actual beginning date."

"I don't know. I'll ask. But I hate like anything to miss a day. You need every penny."

"We need you more."

He couldn't argue with her. By that time it would all be over. He closed his eyes against the pain. *If only I could see them one more time.* "I know. I know. I'll see what I can do. Goodnight, Mellie. Hug each other from me." He hung the receiver back in its cradle.

Harv snapped himself back to the present. The rain on the windshield and the tears that soaked his eyes and soul blurred the curving road. He tapped the brakes; the corner ahead was coming up much too fast. He slammed the gears downward, double clutching and pumping the brake at the same time. The cab skidded. Eighteen tires screamed out their fury. "No!" His mind echoed the screaming tires. "Not yet!" He hit the gas at the last moment. His back and shoulder muscles corded with strain against the buck of the wheel.

He manhandled the rig around the curve, the trailer fishtailing behind him. *Thank you, God, that no one was coming.* He'd been all over the road, including both shoulders. He eased the vehicle down until he could stop by the side.

Fear's acrid stench filled the cab. Harvey wiped his sweaty palms on the front of his flannel shirt. His heart pounded. The blood pulsating around his skull and the rasp of his breathing drowned out the engine at rest. He slumped with his forehead resting on his hands at the top of the steering wheel. Would he be able to overcome his body's instinct to survive?

Blast if he knew.

He shook his head as though the weight was more than he could bear. *I have no choice.*

14

David and Katheryn

May 16, 1980

"But, David, you know going up on Mount St. Helens is against the law."

"I know."

The weariness in his voice and the slump of his shoulders drew her to him. Katheryn Sommers knew from long years of experience that her man was near the end of his tether. She pulled out a kitchen chair and gently pushed him into it. Her strong fingers massaged his rigid muscles. She tried again. "I know you've been through…"

"Hell?"

"Uh-huh." Her fingers prodded and pinched. "But I just don't feel right about this camping trip. That mountain is too unstable. Pictures show the Toutle River flooding already."

"No one knows for sure when, or even if, she's going to erupt. She's been blowing smoke for weeks now. Besides, if I don't get back up there, maybe I'll be the one who blows."

"I know but..."

"No more buts. You know I don't spend enough time with Brian." David Sommers leaned back against her healing fingers. "He's growing up without me, like the others did. How many times have you told me that yourself?" Katheryn winced at the accusation.

"I know." Katheryn caught herself before she added another "but." They had been over and over this argument the last two nights. *Lord, help me change his mind.* "Look." She brushed a lock of shoulder-length auburn hair back behind her ear as she struggled for some kind of compromise. "You know how glad I am that you've taken this time for Brian. And for yourself. But what if you went to Mount Rainier instead?" She could tell by the set of his shoulders that her arguments were useless.

"Katheryn, my love." He turned and grasped one of her hands in his. "I can't explain this connection I have with Mount St. Helens, but you know it's been that way all my life. How many times have I gone to her and always come back renewed? Right now, for sanity's sake, I *need* to go back there. Call it reverting back to childhood or whatever, but somehow any peace and the restoration of my life are bound up on that mountain. I have to go back. Now." His voice cracked on the final word.

She knew any further argument was useless. While he couldn't define his need for the mountain, how could she explain the tiny, inner rodents that gnawed with shrieks and chitterings every time she thought of him leaving? Sane and rational reasons she gave for his behavior did nothing to disperse them. Besides, Governor Dixie Lee Ray herself had ordered the mountain closed. She had established a red zone that made it illegal for anyone to penetrate the boundaries without special permission. David knew all this; they'd dogged it to death more than once.

"How are you going to get in? There are roadblocks all over."

Her husband shook his head. "You think with all the time I've spent on that mountain I can't get past roadblocks? She's so crisscrossed with logging roads it would take every trooper in the state of Washington and the National Guard combined to close it all off." He rose and wearily stuffed the last of the supplies in his backpack.

"You about ready, Dad?' Eleven-year-old Brian bounded into the kitchen. "I'm all packed. I put another coat of mink oil on our hiking boots."

"Sure, Son. We'll leave just as soon as your mother fixes us some breakfast."

"You said we could stop at McDonald's."

"You're right." David turned and gently kissed his wife. His smile belied the bleakness in his eyes. "I love you," he whispered. He hauled the pack up by one strap and clasped his other hand on the boy's shoulder. "Grab your gear, Son. Let's hit the road."

Katheryn hugged them both before they went out the door. She swallowed useless warnings, her desire to give them a happy send-off paramount in her mind. She would not be the one to cancel their plans, even if she could.

"See you Sunday night," she called just before they closed the doors on the old blue VW bug. She continued waving until she could no longer see the taillights in the predawn darkness.

She crawled back into bed, grateful for the warmth of the electric blanket. No matter how nice the weather had been, May mornings could be brisk in Seattle. She huddled into herself, not sure whether the shivers were from the weather, the worry, or the petitioning heaven for their safe keeping. While the warmth eventually relaxed her muscles, sleep failed to reclaim her mind. It leaped ahead of the blue bug to the smoldering mountain.

Brian chattered nonstop for the first hour, filling his father in on all his recent activities. "Mostly"—he leaned back with a sigh—"I'm glad to be out of school today."

"I'll bet." David forced himself to respond. "Hooky for a day always cheers a kid up. You having any more trouble with that big, rough kid? Ah, what's his name?"

"You mean Kenny?" Brian drew the name out, derision evident in the tone. "Na-a-a. He got suspended for a while. Now he plays it cool."

"Meaning?"

"Huh?"

"Cool. What do you mean by that?"

"Aw, Dad."

David chuckled at the pained expression on his son's face. He'd automatically switched from a father's questions to an English professor's questions. *Be specific. Say what you mean. Write what you mean.* How many thousands of times had he said those words or written them on theme papers? Good thing he didn't keep count. His mind careened off like a rabbit in a maze. What was causing this despair? He'd tried to shrug it off as spring fever, but spring fever had never before brought recurrent thoughts of ramming his car against some concrete abutment. He had so much to be grateful for. *Then why can't I be grateful?*

As they approached the town of Chehalis, David watched the dawn paint Mount Rainier in glowing pinks, drink dry the fog lakes in the valleys, and strew diamonds in the grass along the concrete roadside. With a nudge of regret he turned his attention instead to the exit signs. They pulled off the freeway at the familiar golden arches.

"Hey, at least wait till we quit moving." David's words faded into the door slam as Brian leaped out.

"Sorry." Brian watched and matched his steps to his father's as they crossed the parking lot. "I'm sure hungry, aren't you?"

After half an hour, a stack of pancakes, and Brian's flock of incessant questions and comments, they were back on the road.

"Dad?"

"Uh-huh?"

"Are you okay?" Brian's voice squeaked on the last syllable.

David took a deep breath. "Sure. Why?"

"Well, you hardly ate, and..." He screwed up his face, searching for words to convey his concern.

David cursed himself in the recesses of his mind. He'd forgotten how sensitive his youngest child could be. He decided to be honest.

"Brian, you're correct. Something's wrong. No, not wrong. Just not right." *Right, be specific,* the little voice from his shoulder mimicked his words. "I mean." He took a deep breath and started again. "It has nothing to do with you. Maybe if I knew what was wrong, I could fix it. But sometimes in life there are no immediate answers. You just keep muddling along until the thing either goes away or at least makes itself known." He paused again. "And sometimes feelings have nothing to do with things. Stuff just piles up and..." Another pause.

"And then you head for the mountain?"

"How did you know?"

"Mom said..." Brian shrugged. "And I watched you, you know, get quieter. You run more."

Yeah, running it off didn't work this time either. David reached over and tousled the boy's strawberry-blond hair, so much like his own used to be, before the gray silvered it. "You take after your mother. She's one smart woman. Make sure you listen to her." *Like I should do more often and don't or can't.* He swung the car off I-5 at the 504 exit. "Keep your eyes peeled for troopers now. We've got to sneak around the roadblocks, or we might as well be camping in Kelso."

Several miles passed before they caught a glimpse of the Toutle River. David had tried to prepare himself for gray water rather than the milky runoff from snowpack or the crystalline blue of the summer river. Even so, the river shocked him. Roiling masses of concrete-colored water ate away the banks and hurtled stumps and brush ahead to drown in the turbulence around the next bend.

"Dad, look!" Brian turned to his father.

"My God!" David tried to breathe around the rage restricting his chest. *What in God's name has happened to my river, my mountain?* All the newscasts had not prepared him for the actuality. He had loved Mount St. Helens from the time his father took his firstborn to meet The Lady. Awe and reverence inspired awe and reverence, even in a toddler.

David stopped the car when they reached a high point that gave them a full view of the mountain. His anger turned to agony. He stared at the desecration caused by the ash and steam eruptions over the last two months. Once pristine glaciers now trailed tears of black. Her snow-cone symmetry sank with craters, and her subpeak, Dog's Head, bulged above the shale slide. Steam vents shot smoke signals into the stratosphere in a language he could only define as pain.

Neither said another word until David parked the car in a small campground near the river. The trail they planned to take started at the back of the camp.

"You put rocks in here or something?" David asked as he held the blue pack for Brian to slip his arms into.

Glad to have some return to their usual banter, Brian shook his head and grinned. "Nope, I've got the good stuff. You got the rocks."

"You're right." David shrugged his shoulders to get the straps in the right places. The weight of the pack settled as he buckled the hip strap. "What'd you do, pack enough for a week?" He worked the pads into place on the shoulder straps. "Friday through Sunday is only three days as I count them. I'm sure we'll find a restaurant somewhere on the way home."

"You've said, 'always be prepared for any emergency.' " Brian tried to look serious as he quoted. "Besides, I put your camera and stuff on top. I figured you'd want it."

David lightly slapped the boy on the rear as they turned toward the trail. "Thanks."

Twilight found them miles up the trail, sweaty, and hungry. David could feel himself easing out of the shroud of despair that had enveloped him the last weeks, maybe even months. His resurgence had started with the first pain in his side as he tried to keep up on the switchbacks. Brian was definitely in better shape than his father. Not one to ask for quarter, David suffered, got his second wind, and felt the internal heaviness leach out with each drop of perspiration.

They pitched the blue nylon pup tent, pounding the stakes through the fir needles into the dirt crust. The small clearing was a hiker's dream: a fire pit already stone ringed, aged logs for table and chairs, Douglas fir trees to whisper secrets in the wind above them, and a tumbling creek to sing them to sleep.

David inhaled a breath of hope. "Let's find some firewood."

Brian's gentle snores didn't keep David awake. The rat race in his mind did. That plus the rocks and sticks that lurked under the blanket of fir needles and poked every bone that touched the ground. *On top of everything else, I'm getting old.* That thought was one burden too many. *The ground never used to bother me.* Neither had lazy, uneducated students, grouchy coworkers, class overloads, legislatures that refused raises to university staff, traffic, a house that needed repairs and painting, and insufficient time and energy to do things the right way. Maybe it was time to leave teaching. *To do what?* He rolled a few inches to the left to dodge the boulder grinding into his hipbone.

An owl screeched in flight. Some small animal skittered across the ground by the head of the tent. David drew in a deep breath and, with its release, let the worries float out into the night air to meld with the perfume of a mountain spring night. Fir branches rubbed and scraped in the breeze above. The creek gossiped with the rocks. He slept.

By Saturday noon, they reached timberline. Every viewpoint revealed The Lady in distress. The newly created crater at the north summit belched steam fumaroles into the fleeing clouds. The snowpack cried muddy creeks. Cinder-gray ash weighted fir bows like dirty snow. To the north, Spirit Lake shimmered beneath the intermittent sun, its deep blue a reflection bowl for the struggling peak.

David and Brian shrugged out of their packs and grabbed a bag of trail mix. They climbed to the top of a granite point. Far below them a miniature Mount St. Helens Lodge bounded the edge of the lake.

David opened his camera case and focused on the scene below. *Harry Truman's Lodge,* he thought, remembering back to a time when Coke glasses were filled with Harry's special brew and imbibed in front of a roaring fire. Harry thought he owned the mountain. "Wonder how Harry's doing?" He adjusted the f-stops on the camera body.

"That song about him sure hit the top fast."

"The old reprobate."

"Dad! I thought you liked him."

"Sure I do. He's a genuine character. But if the mountain really does blow like they're predicting, he'll get himself killed, and someone else will die looking for him."

For a second Brian forgot to chew. "How?"

"Well, if the mountain really does erupt..." David turned the wide-angle lens toward the peak. After a long pause, without pressing the shutter, he put his gear away.

"Dad?"

"Uh-huh?" David slumped, eyes closed. "I don't want to remember her this way. Next time we come, she'll be herself again."

After shouldering their packs, Brian asked. "You want to go higher?"

"No. I had thought about looking in the crater, but let's leave well enough alone. You want to head on down to the Lodge?" The thought of a shot of Harry's special stock bit a desire into his throat.

"Na. The lake's too cold for swimming yet." Brian glanced at the man beside him. "You want to?"

David thought a moment. "No. Let's head back for camp. See if there are any trout in that stream. I know you packed plenty of food, but creek-fresh trout tonight or in the morning sure sounds good to me."

After supper at the campfire, as Brian roasted marshmallows on a willow stick, David thought of home. *I wish Katheryn were here. She'd help me sort through this muddle. Why can I talk about great writers and thinkers, even grammar, for hours, but can never explain or describe this heaviness that settles near me?*

"Dad, you want one?" Brian held out a marshmallow, light brown on all sides and mushy in the middle, just the way his father liked them.

"Perfect, thank you."

"Another?"

"No thanks." The marshmallow being turned burst into flame. "At least not that one."

Brian blew it out. "I know, that's for me." He pulled off the crispy coat, ate it, and held the gooey center over the coals. "I love you, Dad." His whisper danced with the sparks against the black of the night.

Sleep that night came quickly. David's last thought as he shifted his aching legs away from a root stabbing him was one of gratitude. Tomorrow would be a new day. And maybe a granddaddy trout lurked in the shaded hole just beyond the knobby knees of that giant cedar.

15

Katheryn

May 17, 1980

Cleaning failed to keep her mind occupied.

Katheryn threw her cloth in the sink, wrenched the rubber gloves from her hands, and tossed the slippery things into the sink after the cloth. *I've had it—give it up, dope,* she dumped her thoughts after them.

No matter how hard she worked, she couldn't keep her mind away from the mountain—and her two men. David had been so down lately, and there seemed no way to get him to open up and talk about it.

Maybe he didn't want to figure out what was bothering him. Why was this time any different than the other years, other than deeper depression, or so it seemed?

And you let Brian go up with him, in spite of your doubts and fears. That was the part that rubbed raw right now. If David needed to go, so be it, but to put Brian in harm's way...

And you let him. The voice refused to shut up.

"How could I do that?"

How could you not? The calmer, more rational side of her brain kicked in. All these years she'd lived by the creed that David was the head of the household, and therefore he had the final say on things. If they disagreed and were not able to come to an agreement, she believed he should lead. That's what Scripture said. That's what she'd heard preached.

But now!

I'm worrying needlessly. And I know that worry is a sin, an elevator going down and taking me with it. She drew in a deep breath. "Father, forgive my worrying. Please free me now so I can…can what? Thank you for knowing me better than I know myself, and please keep those men of mine safe up there. Let them have a wonderful weekend and come home refreshed with wild stories of their adventures. Thanks for listening. And loving us all."

She wandered around the now sparkling house. All the windows were divested of their spotted winter look, and the rich cherry wood dining room set sent burnished reflections back to the cheery sun now able to penetrate the windows. She stopped at the French doors from the family room to the deck. Two tubs of Red Emperor tulips nodded in the slight breeze. The daffodils needed to be replaced, she saw. Their yellow trumpets had gone to seed heads. The air tasted like spring with freshly turned earth, hyacinths, sprouting grass, and budding leaves all blended into one heady fragrance as she bent to snap off the seed pods. *Perhaps snapdragons would be a showy change,* she thought, pulling out a couple of weeds at the same time.

Back in the kitchen, she turned on the teapot. She hadn't felt much like eating, but the clock on the stove reminded her that lunchtime had come and gone. When the cranberry herb tea and peanut butter toast were ready, she took them into her office.

You have absolutely no more excuses, she scolded herself. The house was immaculate, the errands run, the ingredients on hand for the chocolate-chip cookies she would bake for her returning campers, and her weekly letter sealed and stamped for her mother. She finished her lunch, brushed auburn strands of hair back from her face, and drew the disk for her third young adult novel from its protective sleeve. She slipped it into the computer, brought up chapter four, and immersed herself in the peccadilloes of thirteen-year-old Brandy Evans. Three hours later she was still tapping away at the keyboard.

Dusk shrouded the yard when she stretched her arms above her head. She massaged the muscles in the back of her neck and looked around the room, amazed that tortoise-time had escalated to hare. On her way to the kitchen for a refill on the tea, she thought of her campers, most likely cooking dinner at their campfire. *I can't believe it.* Eight already. She switched on the burner. David and Brian were most likely already in the sack. The thought of her husband's sore muscles made her conscious of her own.

A gentle "woof" at the door reminded her that Lucky wanted in. In fact, the German short-hair Lab had probably been begging for admittance for who knew how long. "I'm sorry, Lucky. I lost track of time." *And everything else.* She gave the liver-red dog an extra pat to make up for the lack of attention. Lucky sat and offered one paw, as if she were the one who had been remiss. Katheryn knelt down, shook the proffered paw, and rubbed the dog's broad head. Her strong fingers found Lucky's favorite place behind her soft ears and stroked. The dog's eyes closed in ecstasy.

Katheryn smiled. "Ah, if only it were this easy to keep everyone as happy." She rose from her kneeling position, her right knee cracking in the process. "Age. Don't ever get old, you hear."

She poured the hot water over the tea bag in her ceramic mug and, while it steeped, explored the contents of the fridge, the freezer, and finally the cupboard. "Those two guys of ours probably had fresh trout for dinner," she carried on her conversation with the dog. "Want some cheese?" Lucky answered with a bark. "Dumb question. You always want some of anything."

After slicing the farmer cheese and arranging it with crackers on a small plate, she took mug and plate into the family room and set them on the coffee table. Lucky wiggled in between the sofa and the table, both eyes fixed on the food. Katheryn tucked her long, denim-clad legs under her as she curled in the corner of the sofa after turning on the television. Lucky glanced from food to face and back.

"I get the hint." Katheryn laughed as she tossed a bit of cheese in the air. Lucky caught it with only a slight clicking of her jaws. The ritual continued until the meal had disappeared. Katheryn smiled when the dog leaned into her knees. "You're good company, you know that?" Lucky sighed and closed her eyes.

The ringing phone made her heart leap. Perhaps they were on their way home and calling to tell her to get some dinner ready.

"Hello."

"Hi, Katheryn, this is Ann Wholly."

They chatted for a couple of minutes, all the while Katheryn wondering at the purpose. While they could be called acquaintances, since both of their husbands had tenure at the university, she'd not label the woman a friend. However, Ann always knew the inside scoop on faculty business.

"I'm sure you are wondering why I'm calling..."

Actually, a lot. Most likely you have some pet project you are hoping to get me to volunteer to help on. "It's nice to hear from you."

"Yes, well, I think I've heard something really interesting, something you and David might really like."

Spare me the suspense. "Yes?"

"Rumor has it that Williamson turned down the position."

"You're kidding." Williamson was the one who got the appointment over David. Katheryn's heart skipped a beat.

"Not in the least. Same rumor said they will now offer it to David, who should have had it in the first place. You'd better not say anything—ah, that's silly of me. I'd tell my husband in a heartbeat. I'm betting David will get the call on Monday."

Katheryn couldn't stop smiling, not that she wanted to. *David, if only I could reach you. This should blow that gray cloud away for certain.* "Thanks, Ann. I cannot tell you how pleased I am. Thank you for calling."

"You are most welcome. Let's get together for lunch when this is all over."

"Yes, of course. Have a great evening." Katheryn hung up the phone and leaned her forehead against the coolness of the wall. "Thank you, Lord. What a homecoming this will be."

Katheryn sank down in David's recliner, but rather than paying attention to the sitcom on the television, she pictured David's joy when she'd tell him. She patted Lucky, who leaned against her knee, and when she'd calmed down, her mind wandered back to the plot of the book she'd been working on. Brandy, a spunky young girl, trying to adjust to junior high, was in trouble again. This time with her mother. Katheryn was loosely patterning the girl on Susan, the Sommers' oldest daughter. Except Brandy's stunts were funnier, and Katheryn wasn't *her* mother.

When nothing about Mount St. Helens appeared on the late news, Katheryn breathed a sigh of relief and snapped off the set. She stretched, hands clasped way above her head, and gently turned from side to side. She thought again of how sore David must be. "Sure wish they'd come home tonight." She let Lucky out for a last run, put the dishes in the dishwasher, readmitted the dog, and headed for bed. Maybe she'd get another twenty pages in tomorrow. May 18. Maybe she should invite their older children for dinner tomorrow night. It would be a nice homecoming and a great way to celebrate the good news. *I'll call them in the morning,* she promised herself just before dropping off to sleep.

16

The Mountain

She sighed in relief as the tremors slackened. Like sunburned skin grown cool, her mantle seemed to relax into the rocky fortress of her ascending slope. Perhaps her friends would be allowed back to float on her lake and climb on her flanks. Such hurrying and scurrying, like ants when someone invaded their hill. Could this possibly be the reprieve she'd been seeking? Had the Creator of all earth heard her cries and taken pity on her travail? Although the pains of the destruction she birthed had subsided, she feared that the internal calm was fleeting, the worst yet to come.

17

Jenn

May 17, 1980

Were any of them usable?

Jenn studied the slides one at a time as she clicked through her viewer. The mountain, from so many angles, rivers, reservoirs, grazing elk, Spirit Lake Lodge with the raccoon, cats, and Harry Truman. The ones she didn't like landed in the wastebasket. Was there a story in all these? Were any worth even sending out?

When had the thought first seeped in, the dream to change from fashion photography to photojournalist? *Could I make a living at this?*

She brought up one of the mountain with what looked like a concrete pillar stuck in her top, a gray ash that the sunset had tinged with rose.

Clicking off the viewer, she set to numbering the slides, adding contact information, and sorting them into the plastic sheets according to categories. In a notebook, she kept a record of the numbers and topic.

She'd rather be outside on this glorious spring day, but after a couple hours shooting in the early morning, she'd brought back the darkroom supplies she'd picked up in Longview and set to looking at boxes of slides.

One more hour of this, and she'd set up again the darkroom her folks had built for her while she was still in high school.

All these years they'd left it, as if knowing that someday she'd return. She still marveled at that, not that they'd needed the large closet-size space that had brought her such joy—and some recognition.

"Jenn?" Her mother's voice interrupted her musings.

"Yes, in here. Come on in."

Her mother, Clare, entered the room and glanced around, a smile showing the dimple in her right cheek. "I cannot believe you are actually here." She motioned around the room with a hand gentle enough to dry a child's tears and strong enough to pull dandelions. "I've threatened more than once to turn this into a sewing room but just never got around to it."

"Right." Jenn clicked on the viewer. "Want to see a couple of these?"

"Dinner's in the oven." Clare sat down at the table. "You've taken all these since you've been home?"

"These and about six other rolls that are being developed. I'm going to do the black-and-whites myself this evening."

"Mmm, this is lovely." Clare Stockton nodded while smiling at the slide of a drift of narcissus glowing under a newly leafed alder in their backyard.

"You always say that."

"No, I don't. Some aren't lovely, but powerful. Hard to believe that little camera we gave you one Christmas would lead to this."

"I was twelve." Jenn put another slide in the viewer. "And every dime I could earn went for film or developing. Some kids called me old one eye."

Her mother let out a bark of laughter. "Now, that's really an attractive pose."

"You don't get a view like that often." The slide was of her mother bending over digging in her flower bed, from the rear.

"Thank God for small miracles."

"I think that one could be a good cover shot. See the space in the upper half for titles and such?"

"I'll burn it first."

"Why, your face isn't showing. Who would know it was you? The flowers are lovely, some gardening magazine I think."

"Jennifer Elizabeth Stockton…"

"Uh-oh, now I know I'm in trouble." Jenn laughed as she put her slides away.

"Oh, I forgot to tell you. Frank called."

"Did he leave a message?" In spite of herself, her heart fluttered. Or at least something skipped in her midsection.

"Said he'd call you again tomorrow. I invited him to drop by for dinner, but he said he had to catch up on all the paperwork at the office."

Good excuse as any.

"I remember when you thought Frank was—"

"Don't dig up old stuff." Jenn interrupted her mother's reminiscence.

"I thought—"

"Mother, he's not the man he used to be. He's a—"

"Any one been through what he's been through would most certainly change."

"He's a drunk."

"No, I hear he drinks pretty heavy, but he's not a drunk."

And besides, who are you to criticize? What kind of excuse do you have for your past behavior? Nobody slaughtered your wife and son.

"Jenn, I think he needs you."

"Yeah, well, he can turn off a friend faster than anyone I know."

Clare stood. "Don't give up on him."

Jenn snorted. "You know me, the original Good Samaritan. Speak my mind and keep coming back for more. Persistence, sheer bullheadedness, all my middle names." *And right now, I could use a drink too.*

"You want a cup of tea?"

"Sure, Mom. I'll be out in a minute." *Tea, my mother's panacea for whatever ails one.*

Jenn clicked the viewer off, then back on to slip in one last slide. Frank McKenzie stood looking off into the distance, his Stetson tipped back enough for the light to reveal the lines that gouged forehead and cheek, the pouches under eyes that could light with warmth but rarely did—anymore.

"Ah, Frank, don't be too far gone. Surely my old friend is still in there somewhere."

18

MELLIE

MAY 17, 1980

When's Daddy coming home?" Lissa looked up from the picture she was coloring. Light from the hanging lamp above the kitchen table turned her wispy blond locks to platinum.

"Soon." Mellie stirred the hamburger browning in a cast-iron skillet.

"That's what you always say." A whisper of a whine crept into the little girl's voice. She rubbed her head fretfully. "I want my daddy now."

Mellie took a deep breath. "You know I can't say when, Lissa. Daddy will come home as soon as he can." In spite of the good news from the cancer center, today was not one of their better days. The spring storm that seemed to blow right through the windows had kept them both inside.

Lissa couldn't get warm enough, even though they'd spent the better part of the afternoon cuddled together under the comforter on the sofa.

Mellie left the meat sizzling gently on the burner and lifted her daughter up into her arms. Lissa straddled her mother's legs so she could lean against Mellie's chest as they shared the kitchen chair.

"I want Daddy to come home too, you know that." *God, how desperately I want Harv home,* she thought. But she was the adult here. She was the one left home to comfort their sick little daughter. Sometimes she raged at the injustice of being the chief caregiver. Harvey at least had new scenes, new faces, a job that challenged him. His whole life didn't center around treatments and comfort and illness. Here she was, stuck in a drafty house with a child so sick that—she gave herself a mental shake. Self-pity only created more self-pity. But, oh, God, how she needed someone to put his arms around her and rock her in his lap. And let her cry until the tears finally dried. Why was crying in someone's arms so much more comforting than crying alone in her bed at night?

She hugged Lissa closer and kissed the downy hair. "Maybe Daddy will call tonight." She kissed the same spot again. "Want to help me make the s'ghetti sauce?"

Lissa nodded. "I get to stir?"

"Yup. While I chop the onions. But you have to be real careful."

Lissa raised her eyes to her mother's. "You could tell me a story while I stir, if you wanted to."

Mellie laughed as she pulled out a chair and placed it in front of the stove for her daughter to stand on. "How about you tell me a story instead?" She finished turning the browning meat and handed Lissa the spatula. "Now, wait till I tell you to stir." She began chopping the onion. "Well, are you telling the story?"

"I'm thinking."

The swift stroke of the knife on the board joined the sizzle of meat in kitchen music. Mellie dumped the onion bits into the pan. "Now stir carefully."

Lissa concentrated, pushing the ingredients back and forth. "Mommy?"

"Uh-huh?" Mellie had her head in the lower cupboard as she searched for the tomato sauce.

"You start."

"Okay. Once upon a time…" She pushed a can of green beans off to the side and reached in the back corner for the last of the tomatoes. She straightened up triumphantly, three cans of sauce in her hands. "Once upon a time…" she prompted as she opened each and poured them in the pan. She covered the little hand holding the turner. When she looked into her daughter's face, she saw a tear slip from the lowered lashes and slide down Lissa's cheek. With one arm around the thin little body, Mellie continued helping her daughter stir the sauce, the storytelling forgotten.

Please, God, she pleaded in the recesses of her mind. *Please make Harv call tonight. I have some good news to tell him for a change.*

Mellie felt a bone-melting weariness invade her body when she sat down at the dinner table. Some days it was almost beyond human strength to keep from dissolving into a puddle of tears. Right now she felt as if the tears were draining out of her heart, flowing off to the Puget Sound and thus out to sea. If she closed her eyes, she could sense the rocking wave action, the floating of no more cares. No more pain. No more heartbreak. Cradled on the deep she melded with the eternity that rolled the breakers onto the shore and bared the beaches at the tide.

"Mommy?"

Mellie's eyes flew open at the hesitant query. No pain would mean no Lissa. She nearly cried out at the sacrilege of it all. Automatically, she took a bite of the cooling spaghetti. And gagged.

"Mommy, are you all right?" Terror made her voice squeak.

Mellie could only nod as she coughed into the sink. Her abrupt leap from the chair toppled it to the floor.

"Whew." She wiped her face on a paper towel and turned back to the table. "Went down the wrong spout, that's all."

A cruel hand squeezed her heart when she saw the fear on Lissa's face. A tiny drop of blood beaded on her baby's pale lower lip where her teeth had bitten through the skin.

They clutched each other, the fear a real presence that snaked tightly around them. "It's all right." Mellie wasn't sure if her words were for herself or Lissa. "We're going to be fine." They headed for their corner of the sofa and wrapped the bright blue afghan around them. Safe in the circle of lamplight with warmth creeping back into her bones, Mellie wiped a drop of moisture from the corner of her eye. She could feel returning courage staring down the monster that had attacked them, staring as it slithered back into some shadowy, nocturnal corner. A recalcitrant sob turned into a hiccup as she drew in a deep breath.

Lissa breathed softly, her breath so faint that Mellie found herself listening for each exhalation. *Oh, if I could only fall asleep so easily.*

Mother and daughter had both dozed off when the phone summoned them back to reality.

"Daddy?" Lissa's eyes flew open.

"I hope so." Mellie carried Lissa on her hip across the room as she rose to answer. She sat Lissa on the counter and, in the same motion, picked up the receiver. "Hello." Her voice sounded breathy, even to herself.

"Mellie?" Harvey's rich baritone seemed to fill the kitchen. The fear monster dissipated, like wispy fog in the sunshine.

"Daddy! Daddy!" Lissa grabbed for the phone with both hands.

Mellie let her take it, her joy matching her daughter's. Thank God for telephones.

Light came back into the pale little face as Lissa laughed at something

Harvey said. A cloud passed over. "Mommy coughed and coughed. Daddy, when are you coming home? I want my daddy, here. Now." A hint of the imperious princess dispensing orders emerged. She giggled, a little girl again, then clutched the phone to her shoulder. "He's coming home. Tomorrow night."

Mellie glanced up at the calendar. Sunday evening he'd be home. May eighteenth. Hallelujah! In time for the… "Say goodbye, Lissa." She ordered. "Now."

"Bye, Daddy. Mommy's getting mad." She giggled again as she held the phone out. Light and life had come back into her body.

"Oh, Harv, I'm so glad you're coming home. I have wonderful news too. Dr. Thomas called yesterday and gave me another number to call. Between the Cancer Society, a research grant, and several private donors, funds are available to help pay for Lissa's treatment." She ignored his questions. "I'm not sure. They said they'd talk more with us when we came in for the preop. But, Harv, you can come home. To stay. We don't need for you to work on the mountain. You can come home."

Harvey laughed along with her. All his plans. He could toss them into the turgid Toutle. He breathed in a deep breath of life, understanding what prisoners on death row felt like at an eleventh-hour stay of execution. He could kiss Baker Camp, the logging trucks, and mutinous Mount St. Helens goodbye. He'd be home for as long as Mellie and Lissa needed him. Surely there were other jobs available by now. The thoughts made him giddy with relief.

"I'll be home by eight in the evening," he promised. "I have to drive all day, but keep the coffee hot for me."

19

David and Brian

May 18, 1980

Dawn rimmed the top of The Lady in gold and took David's breath away. While getting up before dawn was not his passion, this view was. He sat on the rocky outcropping, coffee cup in hand, and watched the world come alive. Joy in the morning, he could feel it again. Was it the sticks and rocks that poked him all night that brought feeling back or the majesty before him? Down below in a small clearing two deer grazed by a mirror pond.

He inhaled, breathing in clear crisp air with the nip of evergreen laced with fresh coffee. When the gold rim succumbed to stronger light, he tossed the dregs of his coffee at a struggling pine seedling and headed back to camp. If they were going to have fish for breakfast, Brian had to get out of the sack.

"Come on, Son, the trout are calling our names."

Brian rubbed sleepy eyes and pushed out of his sleeping bag. "You already started the fire. Didn't you sleep?"

"Like a king. I'm hungry for trout, how about you?"

"Bet I get the first one." Brian pulled his clothes out of the sleeping bag, where they'd kept dry, and shivered into pants and sweatshirt. He sat on a log to pull on his boots.

They picked up their gear and headed for the creek, not ten yards away.

David felt his shoulders relax as he worked his line free and cast into a dark pool just up creek. The fly hardly lighted before a trout struck.

"I got one," Brian sang out.

David looked over his shoulder to see his son reeling in a brownie that leaped and fought all the way. "Way to go, Son." He kept his own line taunt, letting the fish have enough line to fight but not loose enough to spit free.

"We gonna take some home?"

"Your mom would love trout for dinner, if we can catch that many." David slipped his catch into the bag at his waist and prepared to cast again. If life could get any better than this, he didn't know how. The mountain had accomplished her healing again. He laughed to himself. *God, it's not the mountain that heals me but you. I just seem to listen better here. I don't know why the cares wash away when I get out in the woods like this, but they do. Why do I wait so long, make myself and others so miserable?*

He worked the long tip until he had enough line free, and then he cast, the fly settling in a patch of silver. The fly floated slowly toward the ripples. Nothing.

"Got me another one." Brian's laugh brought a smile to his father's face.

David drew his line in and cast again, back to where he'd caught the first one. With a zing that gave him the same rush, a trout hit it and tore for deeper water.

Ah, Katheryn, how can you forgive me for the way I've acted? You keep loving me no matter what. Somehow I'll make it up to you.

They stopped with six trout, four of which came from Brian's bag, and while David cleaned the fish in the creek, Brian built up the fire, hauled out the frying pan, and set the bacon grease from the morning before and the cornmeal on the wooden table.

"Ready?" David laid the cleaned fish on the table. Brian handed him the plastic bag of cornmeal-flour mix and set the frying pan on the crackling fire.

There is no fragrance like sizzling trout cooked right after catching it in a camp like this. David inhaled again, watching as Brian carefully turned the browning trout over in the pan.

"You're doing a great job, Son."

Brian grinned over his shoulder. "Thanks. You and Mom taught me."

David rubbed the top of Brian's head. "You're a good kid, you know that?"

"Get your plate."

David pushed the coffeepot over a hotter spot and took his plate back to the table. One bite and he shut his eyes to better savor the rush of flavor. "Perfecto."

Brian sat across the table. The trout disappeared as if by magic, leaving both of them with satisfied grins. When Brian belched, they both laughed.

"Let's get packed up. Get those trout on ice as soon as we can."

"Dad, look!" Brian pointed toward the mountain.

David turned. A puff of ash rose from the new crater, as if the mountain burped. While they watched, another cloud, darker and more dense, grew. David grabbed for his camera. He pointed it at the mountain, clicking as the clouds roiled and reared, when it looked like the entire north face was slipping downward.

"Brian, we gotta get outta here. Run!"

"I'll get the—"

"No! Run!"

They tore off down the trail, making about fifty yards when the blast hit them.

20

Frank

May 18, 1980

"Oh my God, look!"

Frank spun around, following the pointing finger. "The mountain." A whisper only, as if his vocal cords strangled at the magnitude of the sight.

Ash, steam, and roiling clouds climbed higher by the moment, billowing, filling the eastern sky. The mountain itself was not visible from where they stood in the parking lot in Toutle, the parking lot where over a hundred cars waited to follow Frank up Highway 504 to Spirit Lake.

The police-band radio squawked from his dashboard. "Mayday, Mayday. Mount St. Helens has erupted. Alert, everyone, Mount St. Helens has erupted. Oh my God, the north face is going!"

Frank leaned inside and grabbed his mic. He held it against his chest as he watched the ash cloud grow. How could a mountain be blowing up and life here, so close to it, go on as if nothing were amiss?

"Sheriff! What do you hear?" The property owners who'd been ready to have his head served barbeque style for being late only a few minutes ago now congregated together, some crying, others still open-mouthed in awe at the terrible beauty filling the eastern sky, climbing higher and wider into the stratosphere.

"What's going to happen?" One of his deputies kept his voice low so as to not panic the gathered crowd.

"I have no idea." Frank shook his head. His mind finally kicked into gear, and he realized only seconds had passed since the first shout, seconds that felt like minutes stretching into a time warp. He dropped his mic back in the cradle, ordered Sig to stay, and walked to the rear of the Blazer. Popping the rear door, he reached inside for a bullhorn. The squawk as he turned it on served to galvanize him into action.

"Okay, folks, we obviously won't be traveling 504 this morning, so I suggest you all head on home immediately. We need to clear this area for emergency vehicles."

"Thank God we weren't up there."

"Or on our way. If we think the Toutle is flooded now, just wait a while."

One woman came up to Frank. "Sorry for being so angry with you. God sure took care of all of us today."

"Thank you, ma'am." Frank touched the brim of his hat. Amazing how his head had cleared its alcohol-induced fog after the dispatcher's phone call. Shock did that to one.

21

Katheryn

May 18, 1980

"Maybe they'll come home early." Katheryn stretched her arms over her head, pushing against the headboard. She flexed her toes and rotated her ankles. *You'd better get going, or you'll be late for church. You could stay home and write, finish another chapter before they get home. After all, how often do you get this kind of quiet? And besides, you're on a roll.*

She tried to ignore the inner argument while slipping her arms into the sleeves of her chenille robe. "Hurry home, David. I have such magnificent news."

Lucky whined at the door. Out of habit Katheryn had closed the bedroom door the night before. Lucky slept on a folded blanket at the foot of the bed. While she'd been known to sneak up on the bed when Katheryn slept alone, last night she'd stayed on the floor.

Katheryn closed the window that she kept open a crack even in the coldest months, slid her feet into sheepskin slippers, and led the way down the stairs, Lucky's toenails clicking beside her on the dark oak risers.

"There you go, girl. Looks to be a lovely day." She inhaled a breath of spring as she watched the dog pause at the edge of the deck and sniff the air. She couldn't help but do the same. Someone had started a fireplace or wood stove, the narcissus blooming in one wine-barrel tub sweetened the mix, and, sure enough, the skunk had visited again during the night. How such a wild creature could manage in a suburban development like theirs was beyond her. She watched as Lucky did her business in the designated area, then followed an invisible trail over to the six-foot cedar fence. Tail wagging, Lucky checked out the immediate area, returned to the depression, and gave it a thorough sniff test.

"Come on, girl, that critter is long gone." Which was good if the skunk was the trespasser Lucky had followed. Their meeting would have been bad news. "You don't want a tomato juice bath again, do you?" It had taken three tall cans to get the odor out of the dog's hide, three baths for the dog, two for the handlers, and one for the entire bathroom. Amazing how one dog giving a vigorous shaking could paint an entire bathroom in red dots of tomato juice.

Katheryn poured dry dog food in the ceramic dog dish Kevin had made one year in an art class. She added a dessert topping of canned food and set the dish on the floor to the appreciative thwacking of the dog's tail against the side of her robe.

Church or no, the discussion still waged.

She inhaled the coffee fragrance when she opened the can to measure grounds into the percolator. Today could be deemed a good day for smells. *Have I included any in Brandy's story? Or am I missing out on that one of the senses? What about the other senses? What about taste and hearing?*

Once showered, dressed, and with industrial strength coffee in hand, she headed back to her office. The clock on her desk read ten the next time she came up for air, thanks to a rumbling stomach and a ringing telephone.

"Oh, go away." She swept her now dry but not styled hair back from her forehead. Picking up the phone and clamping it between shoulder and ear, she kept her fingers on the keys.

"Hello… Oh, good morning, Mother."

Typing while listening wasn't terribly hard for someone who routinely juggled three balls at the same time. "I know. I'm glad you are having a good time. Florida must be heating up by now."

She got Brandy in trouble once more and pulled the page out of the roller.

"Oh, our good news… Susan felt the baby move for the first time. I forgot to tell you that last time we talked." She held the ten typed pages by the side and tapped them on the desk, creating the order of another chapter.

"You did what?" Her smile widened as she punched the three holes and inserted the pages in the growing notebook. "Is he nice? What does he do for a living? You sound positively giddy." Katheryn leaned back in her chair and gave her mother her full concentration. "Bernie what?" Doodling with one hand, she shook her head at the design of linking hearts that appeared from under her pencil. She'd not heard such joy in her mother's voice since before her father's death two years earlier. And while Jessica Woods had said no one could ever replace her Ronald, the tone said differently now.

Katheryn fought a pang of resentment, banishing it with the sword of grace. Her mother certainly deserved some happiness at this stage in a life that had never been easy.

"Can I tell the family?"

Lucky wandered over from her spot in the sun on the carpet and placed one paw on Katheryn's knee. Switching from doodling to petting the dog took no concentration, and it soothed her as much as it did Lucky.

Her stomach rumbled again. "So, when will you be home?" Jessica had flown to Florida to visit her sister back in February, sure that she'd stay only a few weeks, which turned into three months.

"He asked you to what?" She sat upright, dislodging the dog in the jerking of the chair. "Ah, I don't know. Do you have to be in such a rush? I mean, come on, Mom, we haven't even met the man. Surely you should come home first and let him come visit you…us and…" She pushed her hair back again, electricity standing strands on end while the rest swept back to hang limply. Why hadn't she done her hair? Set the hot rollers? Put on her makeup. She could always deal better with a crisis when she had her armor in place.

"Mom, please, no, I'm not saying you are making a mistake…" Even though he could be some gold digger after her money. While Jessica was not wealthy, she had a home all paid for and enough in the bank and investments to live comfortably for the rest of her life. Her husband had provided well for her.

"Mother, please don't cry. I'm not judging Ben or Bernie or whatever his name is. I'm sure I will love him to pieces, but please, come home and let's all talk this over without any pressure. David will—I mean, all of us want to meet him first, and if you do decide to marry again, I really want to be there." She stared out the window, noticing the geranium needed both watering and pruning.

Sensing her unease, Lucky laid her head on Katheryn's knee and whined for attention.

"Good, I'll talk to you again this evening, and yes, of course, if Bernie is there, I'd love to chat with him." *What kind of a man would be in such a hurry? What's his agenda?* "Bye, Mother, and give Aunt Estelle a hug for me." *I'll just bet she approves, if it would get you moved down there. Of course she's a great judge of men. She's only had four husbands, tried all kinds.*

Katheryn hung up the phone, reminding herself that she was being unchristian and judgmental without knowing all the facts. But what a shock! Why had her mother not mentioned this man before? Why did she have such an unpleasant taste regarding this whole thing? Boy, will David have something to say about this.

"Come on, girl, time for some brunch, since I missed breakfast a long time ago." Strange how the house seemed lonely today when most of the days her men were gone off to work or school anyway. Was it because David hadn't called like he usually did during the day, just to touch base? Although he hadn't been doing that so often these last months either. One thing she'd learned about depression, the person suffering from it had a hard time thinking of anyone—but himself. "Should call it the 'me disease.'"

Lucky wagged her tail, glanced toward the cupboard where the doggy treats were stored and then back to Katheryn.

"All right, I get the picture." She dug out a treat, and the crunch of teeth on the rock-hard food filled the quiet kitchen.

Katheryn opened the cupboard doors and stared at the boxes and cans therein. Too late for cereal, too early for tuna. She moved to the fridge. Too early for salad, the leftover lasagna probably wore a gray-green dress by now, too lazy for bacon and eggs. She reminded herself she had planned to bake an apple pie for David—his favorite.

In a few minutes, she took mug and filled plate back to her office and the waiting manuscript. Brandy, here I come. *If I can keep going for a couple more hours, I'll have the rough draft finished—a major accomplishment. More good news to share. David, hurry home.*

"Nuts." The ringing phone jerked her back from Brandy's world. She glanced at the clock as she reached for the receiver, wishing she could ignore the persistent whine as other authors she knew did. She had a perfectly good answering machine, which was rarely used other than when no one was home.

"Hello."

"Mom."

At the tone of Susan's voice, Katheryn bit back her request to talk later. "What's wrong?"

"H-has Dad come home yet?"

"Nope, he said late afternoon. What's wrong?"

"Nothing, I hope. Have you had the television or radio on?"

"When I'm home alone? Get serious."

"Ah…"

"Just spit it out, honey, you're making me nervous." Katheryn stared at the calendar on her desk. David Larson's cartoon of an ant heap usually made her smile. She picked up a pencil to doodle with.

"Mom, Mount St. Helens erupted this morning at about eight thirty. Do you have any idea what—where Dad was camping?"

Katheryn's pencil dropped to the floor. Frozen in place. Nothing moved; not breath, not heartbeat, not corpuscle.

"Mom!"

Katheryn blinked and wet her lips with her tongue. "I… I'm here."

22

Mellie

May 18, 1980

"Daddy's coming home, Daddy's coming home." Lissa spun in a circle in the middle of the kitchen floor.

Mellie watched her daughter, resisting the urge to reach out and grab her to keep her from falling and possibly bruising. These brief bursts of energy, reminding her of the way life used to be, when Lissa danced and sang her way through each moment, were treasures to be hoarded, stored in the secret places of her heart. She forced herself to sing along.

Lissa wound down into a heap on the floor, still smiling, her arms wrapped around her middle. "Do you think he's already left?"

"No, he said he'd leave around four, or as soon as he delivered his last load."

"And he's going to stay home?"

"We'll see." So much depends on… Mellie tucked a strand of hair behind her ear. As soon as she had dinner in the oven, she and Lissa would take a long bubble bath together. They'd play with the bubbles and make fancy hairstyles with the shampoo froth. She glanced at the clock. Ten. If she cooked the roast on two hundred, it would be melting tender by five or six.

"Mr. Johnson would like to come for dinner."

"I thought of that too. Do you want to call him?" Mr. Johnson lived next door and over the last two years had taken the place of the grandfathers who lived too far away to be a regular part of their lives. Not that they particularly wanted to.

Lissa held the receiver to her ear. "What is his number?"

Mellie repeated the number slowly so Lissa could dial. "Tell him around five." She kept one ear on the conversation as she chopped onions to season the roast. Lissa's giggle said Charles Johnson was teasing her in the gentle way he had that always brought a sparkle to her daughter's eyes.

"He said he would love to come, and can he bring something?" Lissa held the receiver against her chest.

"Ask him if he has any of his frozen corn left."

Lissa relayed the message and giggled again. "Do you want five pounds or ten?" She deepened her voice in imitation of their neighbor.

Mellie laughed too. "Tell him enough for four people for dinner."

"He wants to know if you want sweet pickles, too?"

Mellie nodded. Mr. Johnson not only had the best garden in the country, but he made his own pickles and jams and froze all the vegetables he could. Knowing him, he'd bring some surprise for Lissa also. When one time she'd accused him of spoiling the little girl, he'd looked hurt. "But she's my only grandchild," he'd said, and Mellie never mentioned such a thing again.

Lissa said goodbye and hung up the phone. She picked up her rabbit and, clutching the stuffed animal in one arm, wrapped the other around her mother's slender hips.

"You need a snuggle?"

"Uh-huh."

Mellie fitted the top on the roaster pan and, after sliding the pan in the oven, turned off the burner. Ignoring the breakfast dishes and the preparation mess, she scooped up her daughter and deposited the two of them in the rocker in front of the window, where the sun could warm her shoulders.

Laying her cheek on Lissa's soft hair, she let her mind relax along with her body. For the first time in a while, things seemed to be turning around for them. She pushed with her toe and set the rocker to creaking in gentle harmony with the soothing motion. Within moments, Lissa slumped against her breast, sound asleep, Mellie's eyelids grew heavy, and slowly the chair ceased its song.

A knock on the door sometime later roused Mellie from her nap. Gently, carefully, she lifted Lissa as she stood and laid her on the couch. Mr. Johnson always knocked three, pause, and one, softly so that if Lissa were sleeping, she might not hear. Mellie opened the door, her welcome smile wide. "Come in." She kept her voice low so that Lissa could sleep on.

"Are you listening to the radio or television?" He, too, whispered, bending slightly from his former basketball star height.

She shook her head. "Come into the kitchen and I'll put the coffee on." They both glanced over at the sleeping child and, like coconspirators, tiptoed into the other room.

"Oh, it smells heavenly in here." Charles Johnson inhaled once and then again. He set his basket full of goodies on the table, paused, then turned to Mellie, who was filling the coffeepot at the sink.

"Mellie, where did you say Harvey was driving truck?"

"Above the Toutle River, down by Castle Rock, why?"

"That's on Mount St. Helens?"

"Yes." At the slight quaver in his voice she turned to look up at him. "Mr. Johnson, what is it?"

"Mount St. Helens erupted this morning. I didn't turn the TV on until I'd read the paper after church."

Mellie fumbled for the burner with the coffeepot. "H-how bad?" *Oh, God, not now. Where Harvey is, keep him safe, oh, God, please.*

23

JENN

MAY 18, 1980

Jenn, come here! Now!"

Jenn bailed out of bed at the sound of her father yelling. Norman Stockton never yelled. He hardly spoke ten words in a row and usually in a near monotone unless he was really riled about something. Had the world come to an end or what?

She grabbed her short terry robe off the oak bedpost and shoved her arms in the sleeves as she clambered down the stairs. "Where are you?"

"Out on the deck." Her mother answered as she most usually did to any question not directed to Norm personally and even then if one needed an answer in a timely fashion.

Jenn finger-combed her hair back, wishing she had a rubber band. She pulled open the sliding glass door that still stuck after all these years. Another of those things on her mother's honey-do list that her father never looked at until the item ceased to function.

"Oh my God." Tears burned as she spoke the words. "When did it start?"

"About eight thirty. Didn't you feel the earthquake?" Clare glanced over her shoulder. "You didn't put any slippers on. You'll freeze your feet."

"I guess not." Jenn came to join her mother and father at the aged cedar railing. She sniffed back the tears, but one leaked out and meandered down her cheek.

"Instead of going up, she blew out the north face. Wish I'd had a telescope." Norm never took his eyes from the spectacle mushrooming before them.

Moment by moment, the clouds of ash, rock, and steam billowed out, covering the mountain, filling the sky. Silver, black, gray, and every tone in between, heart-wrenching violence of an indescribable beauty.

"Where are you going?" Clare turned as Jenn left her side.

"To get my camera. I need to be recording all this. If I'd only known..." The slamming of the door cut off her answer.

Jenn ran back up the stairs, snagged her backpack and tripod out of the corner, started back down, and ran back to dig more film out of her suitcase. Praying five rolls were enough, she castigated herself for not stopping for more as she thundered down the stairs and out to the deck. With sure hands she pulled out the telescoping legs of the tripod, set it up, and screwed the camera body in place. All the while she kept an eye on the ever-expanding mountain. So much she was missing out on because she'd not been prepared. Lightning forked in the midst of the black and gray miasma.

Her father left the deck and returned in a few moments with a portable radio.

"Vancouver, Vancouver, this is it!"

She glanced at her father only to have him shrug.

"That's the voice of volcanologist David Johnston," said the radio announcer. "Mount St. Helens erupted at 8:31 this morning, sending a blast northeast that leveled trees and is sending an ash-and-debris cloud eastward. We have no idea of the damage so far, nor the death toll or what will happen next. The Toutle Valley is being evacuated, and everyone is ordered to stay away from the red zone. Rescue personnel are arriving, and sightseers will only hamper rescue attempts. We at KEX Vancouver will keep you informed as we receive more information here in the station."

Jenn was putting in the third roll when she realized her legs and feet were indeed freezing as her mother had warned. While the sun was out, the temperature was still too cold for shorts.

"Here." Her mother set a cup of coffee on the railing and handed another to her husband. "You want some breakfast now?" She dropped Jenn's slippers at her feet.

Jenn took a sip of the coffee and shook her head. "Later maybe."

Norm grunted, never taking his gaze from the cataclysm to the east.

"How come we never heard anything?"

"Beats me."

Jenn glanced over at her father, who'd been cutting timber on the foothills of the Cascade Mountain range most of his life. Was that a tear she saw on his sunburned cheek?

"You could have been up there." The thought dried her throat.

He nodded. "Happened on a weekday and I woulda been. A lot of us would."

"You think Harry..." She stopped at her father's shaking head.

"Unless he knew something earlier than anyone else—na, bet him and his lodge are blown off the face of the earth."

"Or buried by debris."

"He always talked about his secret tunnels and a stash of booze. If he got back there, perhaps he made it."

Jenn knew her father didn't have a great deal of respect for the foul-mouthed Harry Truman; the man was so cantankerous he'd offended nearly everyone at one time or another. Still, he'd always been good to her. Thinking back to the visit when she and Frank tried to talk him off the mountain, she had to blink before sighting a different lens. She resumed clicking the bulb every three to five seconds. Nine o'clock and the clouds had only grown bigger. What was happening up there? Agony ripped at her heart like the curved beak of an eagle tearing its prey. Talons nailed her to earth when she ached to fly free, fly closer to The Lady writhing in travail.

"Here, you might as well eat while you watch." Clare set a plate of scrambled eggs and bacon on the deck railing. "Eat before it gets cold." She handed Norm a plate also. "Don't suppose we're going to church." She glanced at her husband. "Didn't think so."

"Better we stay off the roads."

"Hadn't thought of that." She settled in the aluminum folding chair and began eating, like the others, keeping her gaze on the furious clouds that obscured the mountain.

By eleven if Jenn had heard the "this is it" call once, she'd heard it fifteen times. She removed her camera from the tripod and set it back in the foam slot in her camera pack.

"Where you goin'?" Her father kept his gaze on the east.

"Got to get more film, see if I can get any closer."

"You can see more from right here than anywhere else," her mother said.

"I might just come right back. You want anything from the store? It'll be a few minutes till I get dressed."

"Let me think on it."

After cleaning off the rack of Kodak film at the grocery store, where the mountain was the only item of discussion, Jenn debated whether to return home or try somewhere else. The debate, if there really had been one, died when she found herself on the freeway heading south to Vancouver.

I have to get up there, see what is really going on.

An hour later, a curt voice informed her, "They've closed the air space, miss. No one is going up."

Jenn slammed her hand down on the counter. *Military. Surely they're letting someone fly.* Pearson Airpark wasn't the only field within driving distance. She threw a "thanks" over her shoulder and headed for the door. *Thanks for nothing.*

"No matter where you try, they'll say the same thing."

Jenn waved over her shoulder and reached for the door handle, only to have it pulled open at the same moment.

"Well, if it isn't my favorite photographer." Mitch Ross stepped back to let her pass.

"They won't let you fly. Air space is closed." Jenn stared toward the mountain, where the cloud rose fifteen miles into the stratosphere. How could the sun be shining, birds singing here, when forty miles north, her mountain was dying?

"I'm sorry we didn't get to go back up there."

"Yeah, me too." Where was Frank? Had he taken that group up like he planned?

How many lives had already been lost?

"Do you get any special privileges as military?" Perhaps he'd take her with him as he had that other time. Although she hated being beholden to the guy, she'd do anything to get closer to the mountain, to see what was really happening. Radio reports were still so ambiguous.

"Not today. I was just going to reserve a plane for the first chance I can get. But from what I'm hearing, the red zone didn't begin to cover the areas of destruction."

"Did the sheriff go up, do you know?"

Mitch shook his head. "Darnedest story. Frank McKenzie overslept. Had some real hot customers when he didn't show up on time, but I'll tell you, bet they're singing his praises now. And grateful to be alive."

"I was up there. No one is allowed in except for emergency vehicles and rescue personnel."

"On 504?"

"Right. No farther than Castle Rock on I-5." Jenn wrapped her arms around her front. While the sun was glorious, here in the shade a breeze made her shiver. Or was it sympathy pangs for her mountain?

"Bet there's enough turbulence around that poor mountain to wipe out any small plane that went up anyway. They're routing the commercial flights clear out over the ocean." Mitch dug a pack of chewing gum out of his shirt pocket and held it out.

"Thanks." Jenn took a stick and peeled off the green wrapper, then the tinfoil. When the taste of mint hit her tongue, she realized she hadn't eaten more than a couple bites in spite of her mother's insistence, and here it was after noon. Her stomach reminded her of the fact at the same moment.

"I'd take you out to lunch, but I need to get back to the office." Silk smoothed his tone, and one eyebrow arched above his sunglasses.

"I can take myself, thank you." *Why did he have to do the come-on bit? Was he even aware that his tone changed? Or was it some inherent gene that kicked in without his knowledge?*

"I can let you know what I hear."

"Thanks, so can the radio and television."

"You have police band?"

She ignored him as she strode back to her pickup. How she wished she had police band, but if she gave that guy an inch, he'd take two football fields. Guess that agreement the other day in the plane only held true for that trip. He'd promised not to hit on her, but the promise sure hadn't lasted long. *You, fool, he might take you up when he goes.*

He just invited you out to lunch.

Yeah, but he wanted more than that. His eyes said so.

She shifted into reverse and scoped the parking lot. There he was, just backing out. Honking her horn, she pulled up beside him, rolling her window down in the same motion. When he leaned across the cab and did the same, she sucked up all her pride and stuck her head out the window. "May I go with you when you go up?"

"Sure, how do I get hold of you?"

She gave him her parents' phone number. "Thanks."

He touched the brim of his hat. "See you."

If it took sleeping with him to get up, then—so be it. Anything for her mountain. After one more look at The Lady, she headed back to her parents' house, the house that had once been home and now felt as if she didn't deserve to stay there. No matter how many times her mother commented on how good it felt to have her home, her dad hadn't said much.

She took 205 northward. Might just as well have stayed on the deck with her parents. The cloud of ash and steam had drifted east and, according to the radio, was blanketing eastern Washington in ash heavy enough to obliterate the sun.

Since every time she looked toward the mountain she had to fight the tears, she fought to keep her focus on the road. Gawkers lined the shoulders at every spot where the mountain itself was usually visible. Still, all they could see was roiling gray to black clouds, shot periodically with lightning flashes.

East of Portland, up the Columbia River, Mount Hood glistened white in the sun as if nothing was remiss with his sister. Would Mount St. Helens ever be the same?

In order to keep her sanity, Jenn thought back to one of her thousands of visits to Spirit Lake, the mirror for The Lady on a clear day. Years ago, she and Baldy, the family black Lab, and her constant companion, had left the others at a multifamily picnic and walked on around the shore.

"Go get 'em, fella." She tossed another pumice stone in the clear water. Baldy swam out to it and brought it back, since the pumice floated. When she tossed out a waterlogged one, he dove for it too, the lake so clear a pebble was visible twenty feet down.

Sitting on a log, she clasped her hands around one knee and watched a flock of mallards brake for landing. Baldy shook, showering her with half the lake, then sat by her side, most likely watching the ducks also. In the winter, he retrieved the ducks her father shot.

"I'm not going to stay here all my life, you know." She wasn't sure whom she was trying to convince, herself or the dog. "Soon as I get that diploma, I'm out of here. New York, here I come."

Baldy leaned closer, making sure his ears were within reach of her hands. When she didn't get the hint, he sighed, then whined low in his throat.

"I won that competition, you know."

Baldy turned his head to gaze up at her, resting all his seventy pounds against her leg. Her jeans were soaked from his wet fur.

She could almost feel the dog's presence as she brushed moisture from her eyes again. Like so many of her dreams, Baldy had died in the intervening years. Would she ever dare to dream again?

24

Mellie

May 18, 1980

"Mommy, you're squeezing me."

Mellie reined in her more than adequate imagination and loosened the lock she had on her daughter. "Sorry, pumpkin, I..." *I what? I cannot hear, I cannot see, I cannot touch? For my sight is blinded, but for fear; my ears hear nothing but his voice. "I'll be home Sunday night." He had promised. Here I am holding my daughter and I nearly squeeze her to pieces, all without knowing. God, you cannot take Harvey. You cannot leave Lissa fatherless. After all we've been through, you finally send a light in the tunnel, and now you snuff it out?*

Don't be silly, you're borrowing trouble. Harv could be on his way home now, for all you know. The more rational side of her brain spoke softly, as if gentleness could pacify the panicked side.

"I didn't want to be the bearer of bad tidings." Mr. Johnson looked as if she'd been lashing out at him, screaming like the woman down the street who cussed worse than a drunken logger.

Come on, Mellie, get control here. She sat on a chair, still holding Lissa but more loosely now. Fighting to get air, to stop the battle waging in her head, she finally sucked in a deep breath. Why did she feel like there wasn't enough oxygen in the air? She rotated her shoulders and shuffled her feet, all the while concentrating on each muscle movement, willing life into her icy body.

"Mommy, you're scaring me." Lissa put her hands on either side of her mother's face and held her straight. Even so, her gaze wandered from right to left, tracking nothing.

"We don't know anything for sure." Mr. Johnson nodded, but while his words veered off, his head kept moving.

"True."

"You got to keep the faith."

"I know." For Lissa's sake if nothing else.

"You want me to turn on the TV?"

"I can do that." Lissa slid from her mother's lap. She took three steps and looked over her shoulder. "You want to watch cartoons?"

"Turn it to five."

Lissa made a face but headed on into the living room without an argument. Within moments a news announcer could be heard but not understood.

"Mommy, look!"

The two adults exchanged sighs and made their way into the other room.

"…late breaking news of the eruption of Mount St. Helens." A used car salesman waved toward a battalion of cars for sale, balloons bobbing above in the breeze.

"Try channel four." In spite of the commercial, all she could see in her mind was the swift glimpse of virulent clouds of ash and steam and whatever else the mountain was sending up. Gray, black, all the colors of sorrow.

All the other stations had gone to commercial breaks also.

After they'd watched the same film clips enough times to send Lissa hunting for her rabbit, Mellie forced herself to her feet, then clutched the sofa arm. Her right foot refused to function, nearly pitching her to her knees.

"Ouch."

"You all right?" Mr. Johnson half rose.

"Just my foot's asleep. Oh, ahh." She wiggled her toes and flinched some more.

"Nothing to do but wait it out."

"You mean my foot? Or…?"

"Either."

She took a tentative step. And stopped until the needles quit dancing.

"Can I get you anything—coffee, tea?"

"No, thank you. I should be getting on home, but…" He stared at his hands clasped between his knees. His bony face made his eyes look even deeper. "If there's any way I can help, well, you'd ask wouldn't you?" Now those eyes pleaded for an answer.

Mellie nodded. "But what can anyone do right now but wait?"

"True, for right now."

When Lissa left her place in front of the television and cuddled next to her mother on the sofa, Mr. Johnson heaved himself to his feet.

"Think I'll head on home."

"But you'll come back for dinner. It should be ready about five."

"You sure it won't be a bother?"

Mellie shook her head. He always asked that question. "Never."

"I'll see myself out. You just take care of that little sweetheart there."

"Bye, Mr. J." Lissa waved, a small flicker of her hand.

"I'll bring you back a surprise."

"Really?" The word *surprise* always perked her up. "What is it?"

"Then it wouldn't be a surprise, now, would it?"

Mellie smiled at their ritual, knowing he got as much pleasure out of it as she did.

"You rest a bit, and the surprise will be here before you know it."

He gently closed the door behind him, leaving Mellie to wish for the only surprise that had any meaning right now. A call from her husband saying he was all right, Harv walking through the door right then. She stroked Lissa's fine hair, grateful at the ease her daughter slipped into sleep. If only she could do the same. If only they'd been able to go to church, but with Lissa being so vulnerable to any kind of infection, that pleasure, too, had been taken from her. Usually, she watched one of the television preachers, but they'd slept in due to a restless night. As if any night were not restless.

Sometimes she listened to the Lutheran Hour, but if she moved now, Lissa would wake. Mellie chewed on the inside of her cheek, far too tense to sleep now, her usual habit when Lissa dozed. Otherwise, she would not have been able to keep going.

She leaned her head against the cushion and closed her eyes. Traveling back in time, her well-used antidote for overcoming the pain of the moment, she blotted out the visual of the mountain in agony. Had it only been a year ago when she and Harv took Lissa to Point Defiance for her fourth birthday? Not even a year.

"Harv, don't let her touch them." She'd shuddered at the thought of octopus tentacles touching her skin.

Harv whispered over his shoulder. "You want her to grow up to be a scaredy-cat like you?" The love in his eyes sucked the sting from his words.

She shook her head and brushed the fine tendrils of ash-blond hair from her face, locking the straight strands behind her ears. "Just don't ask me to do that." She watched as Harv leaned over the concrete lip of the petting pool and, reaching down in the shallow water, stroked the tentacle of the octopus, who had suctioned himself to the side.

"Me, Daddy. Me too." Lissa nearly climbed up his leg so she could see better. When he hoisted her up to sit on the ledge, she leaned over with absolute trust that he would hold on to her.

"Ooh, Mommy, look." One hand in the water, Lissa glanced over her shoulder.

Mellie took two steps forward and forced herself to do as her daughter pleaded. The tip of a suction-laden tentacle wrapped like a string about Lissa's tiny finger.

"Easy," Harv whispered, his face painted with pride in his gutsy little daughter.

Mellie swallowed a shriek and, clutching Harv's shirt sleeve, buried her face in his upper arm. "That's good, sweetie." *No, that's bad, get her out of there.*

"What does it feel like?" Harv asked.

"Like...like he likes me."

"Lissa and her friend, the octopus?"

"Uh-huh. His eyes are open."

"Hold still."

"I am."

I'm not. Mellie tried to stop the tremors that lightninged up and down her entire body. *What if the creature...?*

"Don't worry."

How many times had Harv given her that advice through the years? *Don't worry. I'm not worried, I'm terrified. And he doesn't get it.*

"What does he eat, Daddy?"

"Oh, crabs and fish, sea creatures."

"He's gone. Bye." Lissa straightened up and wrapped her arm around her father's neck. She stared at her straight finger, decorated with tiny pink suction marks, then into her daddy's eyes. "Can we do it again?"

Harv hugged her to him. "Someday, let's go look for a book about octopuses."

"Octopi." Mellie turned from the concrete pool wall and stuck her arm through her husband's. "'Octopi' is the plural."

Her mind switched from happier days to the burgeoning clouds she'd seen on the television. *Harv, where are you? Please call. I need you to call.*

A knock on the door brought her back from nightmare-ridden sleep, her neck cramped from lying sideways on the couch. Lissa still lay with her head in her mother's lap, sound asleep, her breath puffing out lips that had once been rosy. Mellie held her daughter's head while she slipped out and laid her back on a pillow, for a change without a cry of protest.

Mr. Johnson gave her an apologetic smile. "I woke you, didn't I? I'm sorry. You need your rest whenever you can get it."

"That's all right." They both were whispering.

"I'll come back later."

"No." She laid a hand on his arm. "She'll be awake by the time I make the gravy." They tiptoed into the kitchen, and Mellie gently closed the door behind them.

"Have you heard anything new?"

Mr. Johnson shook his head as he set a box wrapped in pink paper on the table.

Mellie pulled the roaster pan from the oven and set it on a cold burner. With each motion of dipping potatoes and carrots from pan to bowl, she reminded God that Harv should be walking in the door any minute now. She set the crockery bowl in the cooling oven to keep warm, and with the meat on a platter ready to slice, she turned on the burner to start the gravy.

"Can I help you?"

She nodded. "There's a salad in the fridge, covered with plastic wrap, that you could slice some tomatoes into." She pointed to the two tomatoes she'd been saving for this special occasion. Harv loved tomatoes, even the winter ones. But these were special, grown in Mr. Johnson's greenhouse, so they were vine ripened and had real flavor.

Lord, please, let him be here to enjoy the tomatoes, please, please.

She dumped flour in a cereal bowl, added water, and stirred it into a paste to add to the now bubbling juices in the pan. With each flick of the whisk, she repeated her plea. *Harv loves my gravy, Lord. Let him come home to enjoy it. Please, please bring him home.*

"Mommy." The plaintive cry from the living room announced the end of Lissa's sleeping time. The tone said it was time for more pain pills. With the new prescription, they no longer waited until the pain grew severe but tried to keep a maintenance dose in her increasingly frail body. Even so, sometimes the pain got away from them.

"Here, let me." Mr. Johnson took the whisk from her hand and nodded toward the waif now standing in the doorway. "She needs you."

Mellie took the bottle and dropper from the shelf and the juice from the fridge. Pouring them together, she knelt in front of Lissa and handed her the small glass. "Drink it all."

Lissa nodded, downed the drink, and handed the glass back, swiping the back of her hand across her mouth. Purple streaked her cheek. "Hi, Mr. J."

"Hi yourself. That box on the table might be for you." He gave the gravy another whisking and shut off the burner.

"My s'prise?"

"Could be. You'd better check."

Lissa glanced at her mother, caught the nod, and, dragging her blanket by one corner, took the box and sank to the floor. "I like pink."

"Now, how do you s'pose I knew that?"

"I told you." She glanced down at her pink overalls and shirt. "And my clothes are pink." She dug into the wrapping paper folded at the sides.

Mellie watched, keeping her hands in her lap when they longed to make things easier for the little one.

With the tip of her tongue peeking out from between taut lips, Lissa finally got the paper loose without tearing it like so many other children would have. She loved pretty things and would often draw on the back of wrapping paper, tracing around the designs and coloring them in herself, then folding the paper into hats and boats and even butterflies. Harv had taught her such folding when she was too ill to play but well enough to want something to do. Harv had taught his daughter many things.

"Mommy, look." Lissa held a foot-long stick with a heavy string attached to a bit of brown-gray fur.

"For Kitty and me."

"You'd better look deeper."

" 'Kay." Lissa pulled more pink tissue paper out of the box before raising another wrapped package. Her eyes sparkled as she set to unwrapping it.

"You are so good to her. Thank you."

"Most welcome. Seeing her excited gives me great joy."

"Ooh." Lissa held up a card with a pink bead bracelet and a ring with a pink stone attached to it. "Thank you." Lissa stood and leaned against him. "Please, help me put it on."

Mr. Johnson, I love you. Mellie wanted to hug the man herself.

While the other two admired the new jewelry, Mellie glanced at the clock: 5:00 p.m. He should have been home by now. Or called.

God, what will I do if he never comes home?

25

Katheryn

May 18, 1980

Surely he'll call as soon as they get out.

At the ringing of the telephone, Katheryn turned from her pacing and flung herself across the room. *Please, God, let it be them!*

"Katheryn?"

"Yes." She slumped against the wall, needing the solidity to hold her up.

"Have you heard?"

"Yes, Mother, if you are referring to the eruption."

"Did they go up there after all?"

"Yes. And no, I have not heard from them." She closed her eyes and expelled the breath she didn't realize she'd been holding. "Please, I have to get off the line so David can get through. I'll call you as soon as I know anything."

"Are you going down there?"

"I don't know. Goodbye, Mother." Katheryn hung up the phone, knowing she'd cut her mother off, but right now the incessant questions were more than she could bear.

Back to the pacing lit by flashes of anger. Why had he insisted on going to the mountain when experts proclaimed it unstable? *David, I swear when you get home, I'll kill you myself. Oh, God, Brian, my son. Please, I want to see my son again. Surely you wouldn't take my son.*

She switched on the television, turned it off when nothing new was reported, then turned on the radio only to hear "Vancouver, Vancouver, this is it." If she heard that one more time, she'd rip the cord from the wall and heave the thing across the room. No sense listening. He'd call. Or someone would call. But what if they were injured so badly they couldn't call?

The front doorbell rang, but before she could get to it, Susan used her key to enter. "Mom! I came as soon as I could." The two women met in the middle of the room, arms locking them together.

Tearless, Katheryn held her daughter as Susan cried on her shoulder. Fury burned hotter than a cutting torch, drying her tears before they reached her eyes. She stroked her daughter's back with one hand, choked out the comforting phrases her mother heart could do without thought, and fought to keep the rage not only under control, but undetected.

Susan had always been her father's favorite, his princess back in the days before the depression had fogged his world. His pride in her academic accomplishments knew no bounds.

Katheryn used every micron of her will to keep thinking about the past, to pay attention to her daughter, even to pet the dog, who whined plaintively at their feet—anything to keep thought away from the mountain and the events exploding there.

The phone rang again. She tore from her daughter's embrace and leaped again for the receiver.

"Mom, where's..."

"On the mountain. That's all I know. I have to keep the line open so they can call me as soon as they reach civilization." She knew her tone was abrupt and rude, but anything further was impossible at the moment.

"Wait!"

She could hear the tears in his voice.

"Their camp was right in the blast zone." His voice choked. "Unless they camped somewhere else."

"Kevin, I don't know. All we can do is hope and pray. Truly, we need this line clear."

"I'm on my way over."

"Susan is already here." Katheryn stared at the receiver after it clicked in her ear. He hung up. Never had one of her children hung up on her, but then never had she told them to get off the line either.

Except during their teen years when the two fought over the phone and David finally put in a second line so he could call home when he wanted to. Back in the days when he called home.

Not like now. With that she jerked back to the present to find herself standing in front of the coffeepot. David would need fresh coffee when he got home.

She needed coffee. And besides, her hands needed action. Concrete, useful action before they tore her hair out.

"I can do that."

"Thanks, honey, but I will."

"Kevin's coming home?"

"On his way. Let the dog out, will you?"

Lucky refused to leave her side, ignoring Susan's cajoling.

"Your tulips are glorious." Susan cupped her elbows with her hands, remaining in the open door.

Such inconsequential things. Tulips, coffee, a dog needing a run. The things of life that go on even when death is stalking unknown numbers not a hundred miles south.

If only there were something I could do. She set the full teakettle on the largest burner and took the pot over to the sink to rinse out. Measure the coffee, make sure the lid is secure on the green can. Wait for the kettle to whistle. *Wait*—a four-letter word worse than any cursing. Wait for the water to boil. Wait for the phone to ring. Wait to hear if her son and husband still lived.

"We could call the hospital in Longview."

"There isn't one in Castle Rock?" Susan turned from her contemplations, tear tracks glistening on her cheeks.

"I doubt it." Wait.

"The news said not to call. All the lines are tied up or needed for emergency calls."

Katheryn cocked an eyebrow. Easy for them to say. Did not her fear qualify as an emergency? "I'm going down there."

"When? They said to stay away." Susan took the now screaming kettle and poured the hot water in the upper level of the dripolator.

"Now." Katheryn froze for an instant when the phone rang. Her stomach strangled her windpipe. "Hello."

"Katheryn, you hung up on me."

"Mother, please, I have to keep the line clear."

"You haven't heard anything, then?"

"No."

"Whatever possessed David to—"

Katheryn clicked the phone back in the cradle, whispering, "Goodbye, Mother," as she did so. She shook her head, then leaned against the cool wall, her forehead absorbing the comfort where her heart was unable.

"Grandma?"

A faint nod.

"You want me to call her back?"

"Please." Katheryn hesitated when the phone rang right beside her ear. She stared for an eternal moment, then forced her hand to obey the signals from her brain that said pick it up.

Why did "hello" seem like such a monumental stumbling block?

"Katheryn, have you heard anything?" David's father this time.

"No."

"They did go camping, right?"

"Yes." She knew David had spoken with his parents last Thursday and presumably told them he was going back up on the mountain.

"I tried to talk him out of it."

"Me too." Katheryn sank down on the chair where she usually sat to pay bills or plan menus. Her gaze caught the picture David had taken on one of their camping trips. He and Brian with a string of trout. Had they caught trout the last two mornings? Or in the evening? Was their last meal fresh trout dusted in corn meal and fried in bacon grease? *Stop that! You can't give up yet!* The stern voice brought her back to the conversation on the phone. "Sorry, Dad, but I have to keep this line clear for them to call. Right, I'll have him call you the second he walks in the door." She hung up again and stretched her head first to one shoulder and then to the other.

Susan tapped her on the arm and handed her a cup of coffee laced with cream and a spoon of sugar, just the way she liked it best. Most of the time, she eschewed the cream and sugar in the effort to maintain some kind of decent hip line.

She cupped her hands around the warmth, sipped half while staring out the kitchen window, and plunked the remainder down on the tile counter. "You stay here for the phone. I'll call you from pay phones along the way."

"I'll come with you."

"No."

"What good will it do to go down there. You can't get anywhere near Toutle or 504."

"I have to do something."

"Dad always said to stay where you are until someone finds you."

"I'm not the one who is lost." *And someone'd better be looking for them.* No one in authority knows they were—she corrected herself—are on Mount St. Helens.

26

The Mountain

She cried out in her agony, writhing and squirming in convulsive spasms that would not cease. "Creator of all things, I ache," she screamed. Struggling against the life blood streaming from her heart, she finally realized the futility of her efforts and resigned herself to waiting. It had passed before and would pass again. If she could only endure the pain in the meantime.

27

Mellie

May 18, 1980

I'd take you down there if you want me to."

Mellie paused in the act of removing the dishes from the table. She left the unused place setting in place.

"I mean, I know you don't drive and…"

"Would you really?"

Mr. Johnson nodded.

Mellie kept herself from throwing her arms around the man only by her certainty that he'd be terribly embarrassed. While he patted Lissa on the shoulder and enjoyed her spontaneous hugs, he'd never touched her more than to shake her hand.

"Thank you, but I think we'd better stay here for when Harv calls. Perhaps he had to help someone, and maybe the phones are out." How she wished she had a phone number for Harv, but he always called from a pay phone. *Why, oh why didn't I insist on an emergency number?*

Because you never insisted on anything. The thought caught her by surprise. Harv had always been so good to her, hardly even making fun of her fears, the fears that plagued her through the nights, so bad sometimes she woke up screaming. So bad that some days she felt frozen, unable to move, as if she'd turned to salt like that woman in the Bible.

She thought for a moment, trying to remember the woman's name, but only Harv's came to mind. He'd know the answer. *I'll ask him when he gets here,* she promised herself.

"Can I go watch TV?" Lissa left off toying with her meat, giving her mother a pleading smile.

"One more bite of each."

"Do I hafta?"

"Yes. You hardly eat enough to keep a mouse alive, let alone a little girl."

"Kitty could eat it. She likes meat."

"Pretend you're Kitty and you eat it."

Lissa propped her head on her hand and lined the remaining three out of five bites of meat across the top of her plate.

If your daddy were here, you'd eat without question. He'd be making you giggle, and the food would be gone before you know it. Why can't I make you giggle and eat and... Mellie cut off the thoughts and turned on the faucet to fill the sink and soak the dishes.

"I'll bet Kitty would like to play with her toy, you know, the one I brought today." Mr. Johnson winked at the little girl.

Lissa nodded and scooted from her chair.

"After you finish eating," said Mellie.

She sighed and climbed back up. "Will you play too, Mommy?"

"After dessert. I promised Mr. Johnson a piece of pie."

"Daddy likes cherry pie. That's his fav'rit."

"What's your favorite?" asked Mr. Johnson.

"Ice cream."

"Ice cream pie?"

"Ice cream doesn't come in a pie." She gave him one of her "silly grownup" looks.

"Sorry." He leaned forward. "But my aunt Bertha used to make the best strawberry-and-ice-cream pie. She'd drizzle chocolate on top."

Lissa got down from the table and stood next to their guest. "My mommy could make you a pie like that. She can make anything." She leaned her head against his shoulder.

For a change Mr. Johnson didn't bolt for the door. Instead, he rested his cheek on Lissa's head. Mellie ignored the sheen of tears in his eyes and picked up Lissa's still unfinished plate to scrape and wash.

An hour later, the dessert served and eaten, the dishes finished, Kitty entertaining the two in front of the television, and still an empty place setting at the table. Mellie leaned on the counter, propped on stiff elbows that compensated for shaking knees. *Lord, I know something has happened to Harv, or he would have called by now. What can I do? If only I had listened to him all these years and learned how to drive. Why did I let my fear get in the way?* She closed her eyes at the wrench in her midsection at the thought of getting behind the wheel of a car.

"Mommy, the mountain is 'rupting again."

Mellie rushed into the living room and sank to the edge of the sofa.

"Nothing new." Mr. Johnson nodded toward the screen. "Same as we heard before. Same pictures, too."

"Nothing about the Toutle?"

"Flooding," he said. "Six o'clock news might carry more."

Mellie wrapped her arms around her knees. Surely Harv would be walking in the door any minute. She would reheat his dinner, and she and Lissa would sit together at the table and listen to all his news, told around bites and chewing and nodding his approval at her cooking his favorite meal. She dug her thumbnails into the bed of her index fingers, anything to quiet the voices who'd only grown more insistent in her head.

"A cloud of ash has spread clear to Spokane and points east," the announcer said, showing clips of ash-shrouded streetlights in Yakima. "Everyone is advised to stay home and inside. Breathing the ash could cause severe respiratory problems."

Mellie watched until the end of the segment without any more real news. When Mr. Johnson stood up, she followed suit.

"My offer still holds."

"Thank you, but I'm sure Harv will be calling any minute. Besides, I know you don't drive after dark anymore, and..."

"I will if you want."

Fighting the tears his kindness generated, Mellie sighed and nodded. What if Harv weren't home by morning? They had that appointment with the doctor at eleven.

She bid Mr. Johnson goodnight and closed the door behind him, only to lean against it when her knees threatened to give way. Desolation crept around her, seeping into her pores, smothering, sucking the air from her lungs. The smell of fear drove her to the bathroom, where she turned the shower on, and, stripping, stepped under the hot needles. She pulled the band from her hair and tossed it in the direction of the counter.

"Mommy."

"Yes."

"You all right?"

"Yes, why?"

"'Cause you're taking a shower."

Better than crawling in bed and pulling the covers over my head. "I know. I'll be out in a minute."

28

Katheryn

May 18, 1980

How could this be such a perfect May day? Azaleas blooming, welcome sunshine, the Space Needle white against a cerulean sky, traffic moving freely. To the south, gray clouds like mounds of furious thunderheads were striving upward to be caught by the high western winds and feathered east, the sun lighting the gauzy gray.

She glanced at the clock. Twelve thirty. It had taken her half an hour to throw some things in a suitcase. Susan would take Lucky home with her, after staying at the house for the day or until David called.

She'd even remembered to bring her portable typewriter with her, as if tending to small details would keep the horror at bay. Surely she'd arrive at Castle Rock to give their names to whoever would be in charge, and someone would find them, or they would already be in a local hospital, or... The "ors" were beyond contemplation. She swung into a drive-in for sustaining coffee and a phone call home.

Susan picked up on the first ring. "No, Mom, no word, but the pictures coming over the television are horrendous. If..." She gulped and blew her nose. "If Dad camped in his usual spot…" Her voice broke again. "Mom, it was right in the blast zone."

Katheryn leaned her forehead against the black phone case on the wall. "He"—her voice broke before she continued—"had several favorite places." *David, if you get out of this alive, I swear I'm going to kill you for endangering Brian like this.* Rage, far beyond red and into blue-white hot, made her clench the receiver so hard, it might have liquefied.

"Mom, are you there?"

"Yes. We'd better get off the phone in case they call. Can Bruce come and be with you?"

"He's at the firehouse. Kevin should be here pretty soon."

"Okay. I'm south of Tacoma. I'll call you when I get to Castle Rock." She hung up and took a sip of her coffee, walked back into the drive-in, and added cream and sugar. Right now she needed something sweet.

Back on the road, she forced her mind to think about her characters. What would happen next in the tale of Brandy versus junior-high-school life? But no matter how hard she tried to control her thoughts, they kept veering off like billiard balls and heading directly for the mountain.

"God, if you are the God of love I've always known, you couldn't take both my husband and son like this. You wouldn't—would you? I promise, I'll do whatever you want if you keep them safe. Is this like Abraham, where you asked him to sacrifice his son? I'll give up writing, go work in a shelter, whatever you want. Tell me, what can I do?"

Why is it, when you need God the most, He always goes utterly silent? Not that He'd spoken directly to her, but often she'd sensed His presence with such a feeling of peace and joy, she'd been unable to contain it. Why not now?

Cars lined both sides of the road with people pointing and staring off to the east. Slowing down along with the traffic, she looked toward the southeast to see a swelling cloud of gray and black, leaping high into the atmosphere and flowing east. The mountain again? They couldn't usually see Mount St. Helens from here, only Mount Rainier, standing sentinel in all its magnificent white beauty. The cloud dominated the entire southern horizon. Tears, hot and scalding, burned her eyes and nose. She drank some more coffee and used the napkin to wipe her eyes.

Turning the radio on, she flicked from one station to another until she located the classical music and set the dial there. One of Grieg's symphonies filled the car. She'd come to love the Norwegian composer's grandeur and energy. The music flowed around and through her, carrying her along like the rushing mountain streams of the land of her forebears as it skipped over rocks and rotting trees to catapult over cliffs, falling in a continuous, tumultuous cascade to the waiting fjord waters below.

She turned off at the exit for Highway 504. The flashing lights of patrol cars announced the barricades before she could see the signs.

"I'm sorry, ma'am, this road is closed due to the eruption."

"I see. Surely you have some area set up for families of those who were on the mountain?"

"No one was supposed to be on the mountain." The weariness along with impatience in his voice made her aware he'd already said this more times than he wanted.

"Yes, well, some men don't listen to reason." *Why not air all the family's dirty laundry up front? Get it out in the open and let someone in authority deal with it.* For sure she'd not had any control over the situation. Not that she ever had. Were all men as hardheaded and self-absorbed as hers? She checked that train of thought and added, *He hadn't been until the depres-*

sion started. Sure, they'd had arguments, but they were both reasonable people and knew enough to compromise and kiss and make up.

"I have to tell someone in charge where to look for them."

"Them?"

"My husband took our youngest son along." The words burned like acid on her tongue. *Why, oh why did I let him take Brian along?*

Guilt, that's why. But why do I feel guilty for his father's actions? She jerked her runaway thoughts back to the matter at hand.

"Surely someone is coordinating search and rescue?"

Careful, Katheryn, don't go tromping on any male egos. Gentle and sweet and keep it that way.

"You could go into Longview to the Cascade Middle School. They've designated that a relief center." He looked toward the car behind her, an obvious hint to move on.

"Thanks." She knew he didn't hear her, but she was grateful for at least somewhere to go.

Hours later and with the only glimmer of success being that she'd found someone who took down contact information, she phoned home again.

Kevin answered this time. "Nope, no word." His voice cracked, and he cleared his throat. "You want me to come down there?"

"No, they are overrun with people like me. Keep telling us to all go home and wait there." She rubbed her forehead, where a headache alternately pounded or simmered. "They are setting up shelters, but I think I'll go look for a motel before they are all full, leave the shelters for those displaced from their homes."

"Are you all right, Mom?"

"Why?"

"You sound distant, sort of..."

"Kevin, don't worry about me. See if you can figure out any way to get information. Call the TV stations, radio, state patrol, anything. I'll call back later. At least if I get a hotel room, you'll have a place to call. Where's Susan?"

"She took Lucky and went home. I'll call her and tell her you called. Or you want to call her?"

"No, they are asking us to restrict phone calls. The lines are all tied up so emergency calls can't get through."

She finally found a motel in Klammath, not the kind she'd usually have stayed in, but beggars could not be choosers. After she'd struck out in Kelso, then Longview, they'd started saying they were full. A compassionate desk clerk had suggested Klammath. The farther south she had to go, the more she wished she'd located one before doing anything else. Maybe she should have stayed home or returned north after registering David and Brian Sommers as missing. MIA, missing in action, like her brother in Vietnam. The brother who'd been so cocky about wiping out the commies, about American firepower and superior forces. MIA. Rage snapped and steamed again. The government tried to sweep all the MIAs under the proverbial rug. But this wasn't national government here. This was the home of regional government, mixed-up services, and to her it all looked like the left hand had no idea what the right hand was doing, or if there was even a right hand. You'd have thought there would have been some sort of disaster plan in action. After all, they'd had months of warning.

But like David, too many thought it would all blow over, that the mountain would settle back down. And now they paid for it.

"No, you cannot think that way. They are alive." She knew they weren't at any of the hospitals; she'd checked every one. But people were still being rescued.

She flipped on the television, hoping against hope for some good news.

The ash cloud brought everything to a halt in Eastern Washington, blanketed Idaho, and was causing troubles in Montana. The last flurry of earthquakes of any magnitude had occurred around five, and the wall of mud and water from the North Fork of the Toutle River was taking out bridges and anything in its way. The earlier flow from the South Fork had abated and left the I-5 bridges still standing, and the feared flooding at Castle Rock hadn't happen. Ash and mudflows had now reached the Columbia River.

Katheryn called Kevin one more time, then Susan, trying to reassure them both, took two sleeping pills, and crawled into bed. *If I don't sleep, I'll not be any good when we do find them.* Even so, she'd rehashed the last time she saw them, wondered again what else she could have done, and cried her pillow wet before falling into a dark cavern where monsters hulked and earthquakes rumbled, raining loose rocks down around her.

29

MELLIE

MAY 19, 1980

The night tortured her with one minute after another. Why hadn't she agreed to let Mr. Johnson take them to Castle Rock? Where was Harv? Lurid pictures of him lying injured warred with scenes of raging waters pulling him under, crushed between rocks and logs. The phone remained silent. Several times she checked for a dial tone, in between pacing from Lissa's room to the kitchen to the living room and back to throw herself on the bed she and Harv shared so seldom lately.

Will I ever sleep in his strong arms again?

Dawn brought no joy, in spite of the verse she'd once memorized. Darkness endures for the night, but "joy comes with the morning." Somewhere during the night, she'd remembered that verse and clung to it.

When the clock struck seven, she picked up the phone and dialed Mr. Johnson's number. "I can't stand this any longer."

"How soon can you be ready to leave?"

"Half an hour."

"I'll be there."

She gathered Lissa's medications, a change of clothing for her, a quilt, and some snacks. All the while her heart beat faster, and sweat alternated with shivers at the thought of leaving the house and going to look for Harv. When she heard the car, she scooped the sleeping Lissa up, grabbed the bag she'd packed, and headed outside.

"Where we going?"

"To find Daddy."

"Oh."

Her fingernails dug permanent scars into the palms of her hands on the drive south.

"Did you eat breakfast?" Mr. Johnson asked when they hit Olympia.

Mellie shook her head. "I couldn't."

"We could stop at McDonald's. My treat."

"We couldn't impose like…"

Mr. Johnson sighed. "Look, somtimes you need to accept help when it is offered. I know you two don't ever ask for help, and I admire your gumption, but when I needed help you were right there. Those last months you made life easier for both Helen and me, and now it's my turn to do for you. That's what neighbors are for."

"But—"

"No buts. Now, I need some coffee, and I know Lissa likes Egg McMuffins."

"Yeah."

"I could pay…" She stopped when he shook his head. His jaw tightened. She trapped a sigh of her own. "Thank you."

Back on the road, as the car ate up the miles, silence gnawed at Mellie's nerve ends. Lissa lay asleep on the backseat, her tummy full and her rabbit clutched in one arm. Lack of sleep made Mellie's eyes itch and burn, but every time she closed them, pictures from the television news flared anew on the backs of her eyelids.

Flashing lights on the freeway announced that I-5 was closed to all traffic. Mr. Johnson switched on the radio to the station whose call letters were posted on the sign.

"The I-5 bridge across the Toutle is closed until further notice," the station announced. "Authorities are assessing the damage to the concrete structure."

"What are we going to do?" Mellie stared straight ahead. So close and yet… *Harv, where are you?*

"I'm going to go on up to the closure and ask the patrolmen there what to do. They'll be turning traffic away, so someone has to know where we can get help."

"You're in luck," the trooper said when he leaned in the rolled-down window. "We just got word that we can open the freeway again. Otherwise, you'd have had to go out to the coast and around."

"You have any idea where we might find information on this young woman's husband? He's a trucker out of Baker Camp."

"And you've heard nothing from him?"

"No." Mellie answered before Mr. Johnson. "He was supposed to be home late yesterday afternoon."

"They're still finding survivors, bringing them out by helicopter. You go on down to Longview. There's what passes for a command post down there. See if they can help you."

"Thank you." Mr. Johnson nodded as he spoke and sent a smile Mellie's way. "We'll do that."

Oh, please, God, some word, please some word.

"Well, will you look at that."

Used to the green hills all along the highway, Mellie stared at the gray mud, debris-filled, and still steaming river, roiling under the bridge nearly up to the span. The sight shocked her awake. Mud rings high on the remaining trees showed how deep the flow had been.

"Mommy, I hurt."

Mellie turned to look over the seat.

Lissa rubbed her forehead and then her stomach. "Can I sit in the front with you?"

Mellie nodded and helped Lissa clamber up beside her.

"When is her next appointment?"

"It was today. I called and left a message telling them we couldn't come. The appointment desk wasn't open, so I have to call back later."

"Ah…"

She glanced his way to see consternation written all over his face.

"Wasn't this the big one for…?"

"Yes." Silence but for the hum of the motor. She left off staring at her hands, knuckles white from the clench, and sighed. "But…but I couldn't go without Harv. He promised he'd be there, and…" Her right forefinger dug a hole in her left. "I have to find him."

Despair not only looked gray but smelled like the color of ash as well.

He nodded gently. "I hear you. We'll see what we can see."

The green-and-white highway sign for Longview reared up in front of them.

"Where will we look?" Mellie stared at the evergreens that lined the freeway. To look at the world here, nothing had happened. No gray ash, no raging waters, no destruction of any kind. As long as they couldn't see the Cowlitz River.

"I figure we'll go to the police station. They'll know where the shelters and emergency centers are."

"And the hospital."

Lissa stirred beside her. "I don't want to go to the hospital."

"Not for you, pumpkin." Mellie dropped a reassuring kiss on her daughter's hair.

Mr. Johnson stretched his neck from side to side when they halted at a stop sign, then rubbed his chest.

"You all right?" Fear and concern together tightened her vocal cords.

"Yeah, must be heartburn. I should know better than to have two extra cups of coffee in the morning."

When they parked in the visitor's space in front of the police station, Mellie unsnapped her seat belt. "You stay here with Mr. Johnson, sweetie. I'll be right back."

"I want to go with you."

"Not a place for little girls. You stay…"

"How about we all go in? I want to hear what they have to say too."

Mellie nodded. "All right, Lissa, put your jacket on, then." As she spoke, Mellie fished the jacket out of the backseat and held it so Lissa could put her arms in. At the sound of a grunt, she glanced over at their driver, who was now rubbing his left arm and stretching his neck again.

"Worse?"

"I think so." He dug in his pocket and, taking out a small vial, put a pill under his tongue.

"What was that?"

"A tablet the doctor gave me. Give me just a minute and I'll be fine. You go on ahead."

Mellie started to open the car door, then shut it. "I'll wait."

He leaned back against the headrest.

"Mommy, is Mr. Johnson sick?"

Oh, God, I hope not.

"I'll be fine in just a minute."

Mellie studied his face. Did he look gray around the mouth? *God, what do I do?*

Lissa whimpered beside her and burrowed into her mother's side.

"I'll be right back." Mellie opened the door and, shaking her head at her daughter, dashed into the building. Warm air, disinfectant, and misery combined in a hard-to-breathe miasma. Two other people stood in line at the information desk. *Be polite. No, what if…?* She waited only a second before announcing. "My friend—in the car—he might be having a heart attack."

30

Katheryn

May 19, 1980

In the morning Katheryn woke, rubbing her head. If this was what a hangover felt like, no wonder she'd never wanted to drink, at least not to the drunken stage. After downing a glass of water, she flopped back down on the pillows, wishing for the oblivion of sleep, knowing she had to begin her search again. Her heart leaped when the phone rang.

"Sorry to wake you, Mom, but they found Dad's car."

"Where? Any sign of Brian?"

"No, the blue bug is roosting in the top of an alder tree that stayed upright after the final surge of the North Fork."

"How'd it get there?"

"The river carried it down. Fully loaded logging trucks floated down on top of the sludge. Huge rocks, chunks of ice, trees, houses, you name it."

Katheryn closed her eyes against the pictures he created in her mind. *The car. Who cared about the stupid car? Where were David and Brian? Lord, you know where they are. Are you keeping them safe like you promised?*

"Mom?"

"I'm here."

"You want me to come down there? Susan can come here."

"Susan has a practice to attend to, and that will help keep her mind occupied. What about your job?"

"I told them about the situation, and they gave me some time off."

"We'd better get off the phone in case someone calls."

"Oh, Grandma called. She said you hung up on her."

"Twice."

"I see." A hint of chuckle colored his voice. "Grandpa called too. He wondered if you wanted him to come help look."

All I need is one more person to take care of. "No, they won't let anyone up there." *And I'm not stupid enough to want to try. Unless I could hire a helicopter.* But she knew all the choppers were already searching the area, and the area where David and Brian would have been was totally obliterated.

"I have to go. I'll call you if I hear anything."

"Me too. And Mom..."

"Yes?"

"I love you."

Katheryn choked back the onslaught of tears. "Me too." Kevin had such a hard time saying those three little words that when they came they were more precious than diamonds. She hung up and wiped her eyes. How could they burn so when her tears watered them so frequently? *Get your rear in gear, woman. If they are out there, it is your job to find them.*

And if they're not? The inner voice was nearly her undoing.

Back to the shelter in Longview, only to stand in line and hear the same rhetoric as the day before. "We have no word as yet, but as soon as we know anything, we will inform you via the numbers you have given us."

Katheryn sucked in a deep breath. "You needn't call me. I shall be right here, sitting over in that corner, like I did late yesterday afternoon. I'm the one with the portable typewriter." While she made some effort to keep the bite from her voice, at the fleeting look on the woman's face, she knew she'd not managed well. *"I'm sorry" is in order,* she told herself. But the clearing of a throat behind her reminded her she'd taken up her prescribed bit of time.

Katheryn went back to her space and stared at the blank page. Who gave a rip if Brandy and her friend got to take part in a play? Was there another scene she could write? How about a letter to David?

Her fingers hit the keys at twice their usual speed. Anger, rage, fear, poured out as line after line ran across the paper. Tears dripped from her chin as she yelled at him in caps, pleaded in underline, and called him names she'd never before said or written, selfish becoming an adjective for many.

Feeling like someone was watching her, she glanced up, hoping it was the woman behind the counter, but instead another woman, this one two seats away, was shaking her head. When their gazes met, the woman half smiled.

"You've sure been beating those keys. I expect that machine to break in two any minute now."

"Oh, I guess I have. Was I bothering you?"

"No, not at all." She raised an *Enquirer* magazine. "Was trying to read, is all. Can't seem to keep my mind on anything."

Oh, please Lord, the last thing I want is aimless chitchat. Or someone else's sob story. I have enough troubles of my own at this minute.

"You a reporter?"

"No." Perhaps brevity would give her the right idea. *Katheryn Ann*

Sommers, you are rude—and cruel. The voice sounded amazingly like that of her mother. On whom she'd hung up the day before—twice. And not called yet today.

What kind of monster was she becoming?

She stared at what she'd written. Did she even want to save this? Hardly. She ripped out the sheet, crumpled it into her pocket, and turned to the woman.

"I'm an author. I write children's books." She glanced down at her hands, then back to the open-mouthed woman. "But I was writing a letter to my husband..."

"He lost up on the mountain?"

"Seems so at the moment." She forced herself to continue. "What about you?"

"Same. He was called to go up and fix a friend's truck so they could take some valuables out of their house along the Toutle, just in case, you know?"

"Were they in the red zone?"

"Red, green, what difference did it make? That mountain didn't pay no attention to no red zone."

"True." Katheryn glanced over to the television set that had been set up in the corner. Several children sat in front of it watching cartoons, although she had a feeling that hadn't been the original purpose of bringing it in.

They chatted a bit more before the woman got up. "I gotta visit the ladies' room. Will you watch my things?"

"Sure." Katheryn glanced back at her machine, then on around the room. Other than the children playing and an infant sleeping in a car carrier, most of the people in the chairs sat staring at nothing. One man, head tipped back, snored in spurts and stops. Phones rang and machines clattered behind a three-quarter partition, as if life went on behind the partitions but had stopped in front, waiting, holding its breath.

The woman returned, smiled her thanks, and went back to her magazine.

Katheryn flipped through the pages until she came to the current one and rolled it into the typewriter. She reread what she'd written last, typed two sentences, didn't like them, then reread the last paragraph and felt like dumping the whole thing on the floor and jumping up and down on it. Or drop-kicking the machine across the room. Sitting still was impossible. *I've got to do something! Something active!* She stuffed her typewriter in its case and headed out the door.

You should tell them you'll be right back, common sense reminded her. *What if they hear something?*

If I don't get out of here, I'm afraid of what I'll do. She shoved a hand through her hair and straight-armed the outside door open. She dumped her things in the trunk of the car, pocketed her keys, and strode down the street, her heels tattooing the concrete.

Sometime later, breath fighting to keep up with stride, she paused and bent over, one hand cradling the stitch in her side. How far had she gone, and where was she? More important, where was the center?

After stopping in at a convenience store for a cup of coffee and instructions, she headed back. Surely there was something she could do there while she waited. You can write, her self suggested. *You've gotten yourself calmed down enough now, and when you get lost in your story, the time will fly by.*

The baby was awake and crying, two children squabbling and the two young mothers talking to each other, ignoring the fracas. Another woman sat in the corner, tears leaking down her face.

Katheryn ignored the chaos, pulled out a pad of paper, and wrote three paragraphs. Decent or not, she'd gotten herself back in control, and she could always go back on the rewrite to fix it.

The baby's higher-pitched wail, like fingernails on a blackboard, shivered her spine. She glanced over at the two young mothers. One was crying, the other comforting her. *Someone comfort that baby,* she thought.

Finally, she closed the top on her typewriter, set it under her seat, and crossed the room. Bending over the baby, she glanced to see if the mother, whichever one was the mother, would take the hint. When not, she rocked the carrier, crooning comforting mother sounds while she checked for moisture. Sure enough, soaked. "No wonder you're upset, little one. Let's see if we can help you out." She dug a paper diaper out of the bag, along with changing pad and powder. The woman had at least come prepared.

"What are you doing?"

"Changing your baby. She's been screaming for who knows how long." Katheryn plastered a reassuring smile on lips that wanted to accuse baby abuse. "Do you mind if I take care of her for a bit. I need to get practiced up for my coming grandchild."

"I guess."

"Thank you." But she couldn't stay mad at a grieving woman with a helpless baby, and within minutes Katheryn had her changed, redressed in a dry outfit, and cuddled against her shoulder. If there was anything more comforting than a sweet smelling baby against one's shoulder, she had yet to think of it. Other than seeing her son dash through the door and call her name.

When the young woman finally reached for her baby, Katheryn handed her back and returned to her place. She opened her typewriter and forced herself to return to her story. Glancing up, she caught a nod and smile from the woman behind the desk, and Katheryn smiled back. When she glanced up from rewriting a paragraph for the third time, the woman beckoned her over.

"First, I want to say thank you for my sanity," the woman said, nodding toward the now fed and sleeping baby. "I don't understand young mothers nowadays."

Katheryn made an agreeing sound, all the while wondering what was coming next.

"Let me get to the point. You have such a capable presence about you that I wondered if you would help us a bit. Things are so terribly confusing, all slapdash together, and the people coming here are in desperate need of a comforting presence. If you could just greet them, perhaps, and get a bit of information about them. Many of them could go right to a shelter, and unless they are indeed looking for someone lost or injured, they could be better served elsewhere and not have to stand in this line for no reason. I mean, you don't have to do this, and you could leave when you want but..."

Katheryn momentarily compared her work that was going nowhere with the good feeling of helping with the baby and nodded. She spent the next hours greeting people, offering condolences, pointing out the rest rooms, and in general making herself useful and easing the burden on the harried staff of one.

At three she left to get another cup of coffee, a necessity after tasting the sludge in the back room. How could the sun be shining when a heavy fog hungover her?

31

THE MOUNTAIN

She writhed in the agony of her rocks and ash hurling into the air, miles into the stratosphere, dusting the world with her insides. Gases, melted rock, bits of her soul poured forth, in gray and black destruction. Would it never end? Other times had lasted for suns and moons; would this one too? Her slopes were barren and scarred, drenched in mud and ash, leaking water like tears from buried glacier ice. *I'm sorry, I'm so sorry, I could not help this.* Her cries rose heavenward, along with the prayers of His people. *God, save us.*

32

Mellie

May 19, 1980

Please, where are you taking him?"

"Stand back, miss." The paramedic spoke kindly but firmly as they slid the gurney into the back of the ambulance.

His face now white, Mr. Johnson gave a feeble wave. He'd already said he was sorry more times than she wanted to count. The EMT finally asked him to concentrate on breathing, assured him that someone else would take care of his daughter.

Mellie had not set them straight on that account. If being his daughter made it easier for him and for her to get information later, so be it. Having a dad like Mr. Johnson was one of her dreams anyway, an easy replacement for the man who'd given her life and then tried to beat it out of her more than once.

She held Lissa close in her arms, the little girl wide-eyed at all the commotion.

What will we do now? The thought plagued like an infected splinter.

"If you want to follow us, miss, we're going to the St. John's Medical Center in Longview."

"I…I can't." Her look must have communicated the terror she felt, for he paused.

"You can't?"

"I can't drive. That's why he…ah…brought us down here." One wouldn't call one's father "Mr." That would be a sure giveaway.

"I see."

"Come on, Enders, we're ready to roll."

He waved in response but remained next to Mellie.

"Will he be all right?"

"I think so. Tests will tell." He held up a hand. "Stay right here." In less than thirty seconds, he was back with a female officer in tow. "Officer Stedman will help you. Take care now."

Ah, if you only knew.

By the time she gave a brief answer to Officer Stedman's questions, the ambulance had outdistanced its wail. Or was the wail going on in her head?

"Let me get this straight. You don't drive, that car or any car, your father…"

Mellie winced. Was not saying anything a real lie, or…?

"Mr. Johnson is our neighbor." Lissa lifted her head far enough from her mother's shoulder to speak clearly.

Officer Stedman looked to Mellie. "That true?"

Mellie nodded. "I never said I was… They assumed that, and I just never…" A sigh came from the soles of her feet.

"So, where is it you really want to go?"

"To the hospital for now. We came down from Tacoma to find my husband. He was working up on the mountain when it erupted. He was supposed to be home yesterday afternoon, and it's not like Harv—I mean—he always calls."

"I see."

"We were on our way to the center to…" Her throat clogged at the kindness on the young woman's face.

"Let me check with the desk. I'll be right back. You might want to go sit in the car there. We're going to have to move it, or it'll get towed."

If only I could drive. Mellie opened the car door and set Lissa on the front seat. The keys were still in the ignition, so someone could move it. To where? What if something happened to Mr. Johnson's car? He took such good care of it, just like he took good care of everything.

The tears made her eyes burn, and her nose start to run. Her chest felt tight, like a band that some evil fiend was tightening moment by moment. She sank onto the car seat. No way could she take a deep breath as her vision narrowed and her head threatened to rise off and float away.

"Mommy. Mommy." Lissa's voice sounded far away and going further.

"Put your head down between your knees." A firm hand on the back of her neck accompanied the order. "Easy now, breathe easy. Would a paper bag help?"

Mellie shook her head but did as the officer ordered. She kept her eyes closed and finally was able to swallow the bile that threatened to erupt. *Throw up, pass out, stupid, stupid. Can't you do anything right? Harv, help me. That's the trouble, you always expect someone else to…but I can't.* She felt like shrieking, tearing her hair out, anything to stop the war raging in her head.

"Better now?"

Mellie nodded and slowly raised her head. At least she could breathe, and the scenery around her slid back into place.

"Mommy, you scared me." Lissa glared at her, fear fighting with fury.

"Me too, baby." She hugged Lissa tight to her side.

"Okay, I'm going to move this car around the corner to the public parking lot—no one should bother it there. Then I'll give you a ride over to the hospital or the shelter, whichever you prefer."

"Are they near each other?"

"Five blocks or so, I guess."

"Okay." Which one, make a decision. The blackness hovered on the edge of her vision, waiting to pounce again with the least provocation. She bit her bottom lip, grateful for the pain. Pain she could deal with.

"The hospital. Do you suppose they'll let me see him?"

"Since you're next of kin, I'm sure they will."

Mellie stared up at the woman and caught a small wink with a slight tip of her head. "Thank you."

"You're welcome. Now, you wait inside the door until I get back. Your little girl doesn't look too good. We don't need anyone else getting sick."

"Thank you." *If you only knew.*

A few minutes later Officer Stedman drove them by the center and then on to the hospital. "Now, you can find your way back there, right?" The officer looked back over the seat to her passengers in the rear.

"Yes." Mellie looked up from writing down the address. "I can't begin to thank you enough."

"Yeah, well, we cops aren't all bad, you know."

"I never knew one who was."

"You take care, now. And, Lissa, honey, when you see your daddy, you can tell him you rode in a police car."

Lissa nodded, her eyes round as she studied all the gadgets.

Mellie waved when she and Lissa stood on the sidewalk in front of

St. John's Medical Center. Taking Lissa's hand, along with a deep breath, she walked up to the front door. How to tell Lissa not to say that Mr. Johnson was only their neighbor again ranked high on her list of priorities.

"You might have to stay in the waiting room by yourself for a few minutes."

Lissa sighed. "Don't want to." Her voice sounded weaker again, more tired.

"I know, but they don't let little children into sick rooms. Are you hungry?"

"No. Just yucky."

Mellie laid the back of her hand against Lissa's forehead. Sure enough, warmer than she should be. *You came to find Harv. Oh, God, I forgot to call.* She searched for a clock, finally finding one on a wall. "Come on, we need to find a phone."

"Carry me."

"Oh, baby..." Mellie scooped her daughter into her arms again, their bag over her other arm, Lissa clutching her blanket. She dug her address book out to remember her PIN. Harv had insisted she write it down so that if she were somewhere without money and needed to make a phone call, she could charge it to their home phone.

She'd not done this before. *What do I do? What did he tell me?* She closed her eyes, the better to remember. Her fingers started to shake, her heart to pound. When in doubt, dial 0 for operator. When a voice came on the line, she stammered and started again. Lissa's head against her chest somehow gave her courage. "I need to make a call to Seattle and charge it to my home phone." Reading the numbers requested, she heaved a sigh of relief when the office in Seattle answered. "I... I'm Mellie Sedor, and I had an appointment with Dr. Thomas this morning. I... We won't be able to make it."

"We worked you in because the report said it was critical."

"I know but...but my husband was on the mountain when it erupted. He..." She choked on the words. "He didn't call. I... I'm in Longview trying to find something out about him."

"I'm sorry to hear that." The woman's voice gentled. "When do you think you might be able to come?"

If only I knew. "I'm not sure. Mr. Johnson, who might drive me, is in the hospital here with a heart attack."

"I see."

No you don't. How can you?

"Let me put you down for Friday at eleven—that's the next opening I have. You call me as soon as you know if you can make it or not. All right?"

Mellie nodded as she answered, Lissa's hair tickling her chin. "Yes, of course." After hanging up, she slumped against the wall of the phone booth. *Harv, where are you? I need you. Lissa needs you! All I want to do is go home, and we can't even do that without Mr. Johnson. What are we going to do?*

Someone tapped on the door, so she rose and left the safety of the phone booth. Stopping at the information desk, she propped Lissa on the counter, keeping one arm securely around her. When she told the man in a pink office smock her situation, he picked up the phone, talked with someone, and said, "They admitted him to the CCU." At her blank look, he added, "The coronary care unit. You take the elevator to the third floor and follow the signs. When you get to the closed door, ring the bell, and a nurse will tell you what to do next."

"Thank you." *At least he didn't ask me if I am a relative.* When they arrived at the NO ADMITTANCE door, she lifted the phone and waited, as the instruction sign said to do.

After she identified herself, the nurse told her that they were still settling him in, and while he was asking for her, someone would come for her when he was ready.

"He's doing all right, then?"

"As well as can be expected. You'll only be able to see him for a few minutes. He needs to rest."

"Thank you." Mellie hung up the phone, carried Lissa into the waiting room, and set them both down on the couch.

"Mommy, I have to go."

"Can you wait awhile?"

"No."

Sometime later, settled again, this time with Lissa drowsing off, Mellie closed her eyes, wishing only for her own bed and the covers to pull up over her head. Safe in bed with Lissa well again and Harv driving in the driveway.

She jerked upright. What if he'd gotten home and was trying to find her? Sliding out carefully and laying Lissa's head on her purse, she looked around for a phone.

Hoping against hope, she dialed the phone in the hallway outside the waiting room, only to listen to the phone ring, five, seven, ten times before she hung up. Back in the waiting room, she sat in a chair near the burgundy couch and flipped through a *People* magazine. She'd finished two more before a nurse entered the room.

"Ms. Sedor." She kept her voice low after glancing at the sleeping child. "You can come in now."

"All right." Mellie rose, debating whether she should pick up Lissa or leave her sleeping.

"You'll only be a couple of minutes. I can show you the way and come back out here and watch her."

"Would you really?"

"Come."

Mellie followed the nurse past several beds separated by hanging curtains, being careful to not look at the patients, and trying to block out the beeps and hums of all the machines. Mr. Johnson's eyes lit up when he saw her, and he gave a feeble wave with the hand not attached to lines and monitors.

"I'm sorry." His voice sounded faint, as if he didn't have enough air to breathe, let alone use for talking.

"No, I'm the one. I should never have asked you to do this." She took his hand and leaned her cheek on the back of it. "But don't you worry. You just get well."

"Nice to…have…a daughter." He spoke slowly, stopping often.

"Ah…"

"I told 'em you are, so you play along."

Mellie nodded. "Was it your heart?"

"But not a bad one. I'll be out of here in a day or so."

"Home?"

He shook his head. "Other floor. Can you drive my car?"

"No." Panic flared like gas on a charcoal fire. "I… It's in a parking lot. Officer Stedman moved it and brought us here. The center is only a few blocks."

"How's Lissa?"

"Sleeping in the waiting room."

"You go on over there. I had the nurse bag up my wallet and watch. You take 'em. There's money there if you need it."

"Oh, I couldn't..."

He raised his head, causing the machine to beep, so she nodded. Anything to keep him calm.

"I have to go. The nurse is staying with Lissa in case she wakes and finds me gone." She leaned over and kissed his cheek. "I'll be back by evening. You just rest, and don't worry about us."

"Right." His left eyebrow arched. He squeezed her hand. "Later."

She left the room, fighting the tears and the terror that tore at her throat. What else could she do? Harv missing, Mr. Johnson in the hospital, and Lissa so sick. Who would help her?

33

Frank and Jenn

May 19, 1980

"Frank McKenzie, I've known you too long to take any bull, so just put a smile on your face and ask, please." Maybelle Hartman exchanged glare for glare with the man standing in front of her desk. He finally shook his head.

"Please." The other words he usually used and she refused to tolerate hung in the air anyway.

"Good." She handed him an envelope that she retrieved from the drawer that always banged into her comfortable middle. "And you be nice to her. I remember when she followed you around like you were her hero and caused the moon and the stars to remain in their required courses."

"You're laying it on a bit thick."

"You always were blind to her, still are, far as I can see."

Frank slit the envelope open with his pocketknife and folded the blade back to put the knife away. While his hands focused on the job at hand, his gaze narrowed at the arrival of more civilian cars in front of the station.

Maybelle followed his line of vision. "I thought they'd set up a roadblock to send all of them to the shelter."

"I thought so too." Frank folded the envelope and stuck it in his breast pocket before striding toward the door, his left hand reaching for his walkie-talkie.

He'd rather be out in the field than behind a desk any day. He paused at the top of the three concrete steps. "Can I help you?"

"We're looking for information about our son."

"Was he up on the mountain?" *Where he wasn't supposed to be. If people had obeyed the restrictions…no sense going there,* it dug at him, like a tick burrowing under his skin. Both created an itch that scratching only made worse.

"Yes."

He gave them the instructions to find the center and headed for his Blazer, where Sig waited. With the windows rolled down, the big dog sat in the front seat, watching the woman who leaned against the right front fender.

"Good morning, Sheriff."

Frank thought to the message in his pocket. He should have read it. He nodded. "No, you cannot go up with one of the rescue birds. They need every available space for lifting out the wounded."

"If you think you can read my mind, you just blew it."

"Oh." He stopped about three feet away from her. "You're looking better."

"Why, thank you. Heaven above, a compliment."

Was she laughing at him? Frank assessed her again. The bruises around her eyes had faded, some color returned to her cheeks, and she'd lost the war-orphan look. But her eyes, that was the real difference. No longer dead, but alive, and if laughing at him was part of the parcel, so be it.

"So, if you don't want to go up..."

"I didn't say that. Of course I'd like to be up in a plane or helicopter and see what's going on up there, but..."

She paused and he waited, settling back on his heels, his shoulders dropping a notch or two.

"But...?"

One eyebrow rose, as did her chin. "But no one would take me, and I don't have a national television network at my beck and call."

"They aren't going up either."

"So, I thought maybe you'd let me ride along with you, just in case, you know..."

"In case?" Ah, there came the sparks, that old pugnacious chin. She never could hide that for long. Her veneer was slipping.

"You get to go behind the barriers or up to the staging area. I promise to stay out of the way of the rescue efforts."

"Right, one look at you and those flyboys will be falling all over themselves to do your bidding."

"Why, Sheriff, I do believe you just gave me another compliment. And you're still standing."

He stopped his retort. "Standing?"

"Why, you haven't keeled over with a heart attack."

His snort widened her smile.

"You promise not to pester?"

"Pester! Frank McKenzie, I haven't pestered anyone since I was twelve. Of all the pigheaded..."

"Get in. We're wasting time. Over, Sig." Frank strode around the rear of the truck, his heart lighter than any time in the last twenty-four hours.

Getting her riled did that for him, always had. *Pigheaded* had been one of her favorite names for him, and he'd be willing to lay dollar to doughnuts, she'd not said it since she left home. Indeed, her New York veneer was not only slipping, it had developed serious cracking.

"Why do you want to tag along with me?"

"You get to go where no one will let me otherwise."

"And here I thought you admired my friendly personality."

Her turn to snort, which she did in an entirely unsophisticated manner. "I'm thinking of a photo essay about the heroes behind the scenes, like the mechanics on the choppers, ambulance drivers, shelter personnel, that kind of thing."

"You might talk to Maybelle. She keeps us all on track."

"I tried to take her picture, and she about threw me out."

"I'll talk with her."

"Oh, that ought to help a lot."

"I *am* her boss."

Another snort. "They're letting traffic through on 5 again?"

"As of 8:00 a.m. after the engineers finished checking for damage from the flood. That wall of mud and debris from the North Fork nearly took it out."

"Along with the flood plain of Castle Rock. Sure glad my folks' place is high up in the hills." She patted her camera. "I wanted to stay out all night shooting, but that doesn't work so well. I got some good shots at daybreak." She studied his profile for a moment. "You been even near a bed lately? I left a message at your house, but you never returned my call."

"Haven't been there. Slept a bit at the office. You think it's bad now. If that jam at Spirit Lake goes..." He shook his head. "It'll make the flooding so far seem like child's play."

Jenn melted back in the seat. "I heard some hydrologists and engineers talking about ways to minimize the damage."

"They can talk all they want. There's nothing they can do but pray—and talk some more."

"You know Mitchell Ross?"

"Army Corps of Engineers?"

She nodded.

"How'd you meet him?"

"On my flight from New York."

He saw her jaw tighten. "What happened. Did he hit on you?"

"Tried to. How'd you know?"

"He has a reputation as a skirt chaser." The CB crackling caught his attention. He picked up the mic and responded, then hung it up. "The governor wants a report. Why can't she watch television like the rest of them? Those reporters seem to know more than we do."

"Or at least think they do."

He turned the vehicle into Toledo Airfield, where the rescue choppers were deployed. "You get in anyone's way and you're back in the truck."

"Give it a rest, Frank. I'm a big girl now."

While she muttered into her camera case, he still heard her just before he slammed the door and strode across to the hangar. He caught himself whistling under his breath as he watched another Huey from the National Guard lift off.

Jenn watched him go, finished changing the lens on her camera, checked that she had enough film, and slammed the door behind her. An incoming chopper hovered and landed, an ambulance already in motion. With the blades still rotating but visible now, two men in fatigues, gas masks dangling, hauled out a stretcher with an elderly woman strapped in it. Jenn made it just in time to snap one of the airmen handing the woman a muddy and wriggling dog. She wished she were close enough to get a shot of the woman's face, but the EMTs blocked her view, and within moments the ambulance siren clicked on and headed out.

Jenn hovered on the outskirts, trying to hear what the flyboys had to say. Something about a flooded house was all she could pick up.

But they took time to bring in the dog, too. She wanted to hug them.

The next landing produced two body bags and a horror story about finding the two in their car. The heat and gases that stripped the paint off the car had most likely killed the occupants instantly. From the airfield she could see the tall pillar that still rose from the decimated mountain. Such awesome beauty, such terrible destruction.

When Frank waved for her, she capped her lens and returned to the Blazer. "Any suggestions where else I might go?"

"Not where you want, I'm sure."

"I was out along the Cowlitz this morning. I'd go up the Toutle if I could..."

"You can't."

"There's Swift Reservoir and Lake Merwin. Some real characters live out that way, but somehow..." She massaged her bottom lip with her teeth. "I hate to leave here in case something happens and I miss it."

"Have you had lunch yet?"

"Not sure I had breakfast. My poor mother is positive I am going to starve to death. Her goal since I came home is to fatten me up."

"She'd have to go some." At the look she gave him, he said. "I'm not blind, you know."

Ignoring his comment on her appearance, she continued. "Is there a list of those missing?"

"We're compiling one as people report in."

"What if someone wanted to disappear, start a new life? I mean, like finding all the bodies might never happen. Like Harry. If the sediment is over a hundred feet deep like they say…"

"I know, that's one of the difficulties. When do you stop looking?"

"Have they brought in dogs yet?"

"The surface is too hot, the mud too unstable."

"What about the farmers? Are they letting them go back up to see if they can save any of their livestock?"

"Not yet. If that sediment dam goes at the lake, that wall of water could travel a hundred miles an hour."

Jenn shuddered. "I listened to the interview of that couple that made it out. What a miracle."

"They could so easily have been ground to pieces between all those logs." He slammed the heel of his hand on the steering wheel. "But if they'd stayed out of there like they were supposed to… Idiots, total idiots. Then someone else gets killed going in to locate the blasted fools who weren't supposed to be there in the first place. If someone's got a death wish, they don't need to take innocents out with them."

Jenn understood the rage. He had to deal with death and injuries all the time. When did it get to be too much? Especially after it happened to those he loved.

"I need a drink."

"I'll buy you a cup of coffee."

"You're on."

She knew he wanted something stronger, and not long ago she would have too, but somehow… She thought back to the wasted woman who flew west and left the drugs and booze behind. She who'd needed uppers to get rolling in the morning hadn't thought of one in three weeks.

Ever since she came home.

"Penny for your thoughts."

"Not worth even that." But they were; to her they were. Seemed like the life in New York had happened to another person, in another lifetime, or at least an alternate universe. As if in crossing the Rockies, she'd gone back in time, or like a snake, had shed her old skin and was now growing a new one.

"Sheriff"—Maybelle's voice crackled into the silence—"you'd better get your rear back in here. The big shots have arrived."

He muttered several swear words and pulled a U-turn at the next intersection. "I'll take you up on the coffee another time, or would you like to have dinner with me tonight?"

"You could come out to my folks' house." Now, why had she said that? *Stockton, how appallingly down home can you get? What was she thinking?*

He smiled at her over his shoulder. "I'd like that. Tell your mom I'll call if I can't make it. I haven't seen your folks in too long a time."

Jenn caught back a smart retort. "Mom tried to get ahold of you. See you." She gathered up her backpack and headed for her truck. Perhaps a round of the shelters would be a good idea. She checked her pockets for her miniature tape recorder. All together; now get some lunch, call home, no, may be better to go tell her mom in person. After all, how long had it been since she'd had someone to fuss over?

34

Mellie and Katheryn

May 19, 1980

The five-block walk seemed like five miles.

"Mommy?"

"Um. Keep going." Mellie pulled open the door to Cascade Middle School.

A woman with auburn hair and a warm smile to match greeted her. "Hi, I'm Katheryn, and I'm just helping out here."

Mellie introduced herself and Lissa. "I'm looking for my husband, Harv. He drives a logging truck and was supposed to come home yesterday afternoon."

"I see. Then you are in the right place. You'll have some forms to fill out, so if you take a chair, I'll get them for you." *You both look too tired to stand.*

No one had Harv's name listed, either as a rescued survivor or a missing person. After filling out the forms Katheryn brought her, Mellie only wanted to sink into a hole and forget the world existed. *Right now, I'd settle for a folding chair or a blanket on the floor,* she thought.

"We don't have lists from all the shelters," the woman in charge told her. "We'll call you." But if Harv was well enough to be in a shelter, he would have called home. If she were at home to answer.

Mellie and Lissa took one of the chairs against the wall.

"Don't give up, honey," one of the others waiting said. "They are finding survivors all the time and bringing them out by helicopter. Best thing you can do is keep watching the news like the rest of us are doing. You hear it on the news faster than through officials. 'Course, they always wait to announce names until next of kin is located."

"I should have stayed home."

"Yeah, like me. I had to come search, just in case my hubby was injured too bad to be able to talk." The round woman in jeans and a Seattle Mariners sweatshirt nodded toward Lissa. "Your little girl don't look too good."

"She's been ill." Mellie rocked Lissa, sitting in the chair, softly kissing her head.

"She going to be okay?"

"I pray so."

"You mind me asking what's wrong?"

Yes, but… "She has a rare form of leukemia." There she'd said the words to a perfect stranger.

"Ah, no, not that little angel. I'm so sorry."

"Mrs. Wilhelm." The announcement broke into their discussion.

"That's me." The woman took a deep breath and stood. "Here."

"Would you come with me, please."

Mellie watched her go. Good or bad, at least the woman might know something.

Never had minutes stretched so long. When Lissa woke up, she rubbed her head fretfully. "I want to go home. Where's Daddy?"

"I don't know." Three simple words to carry such a load of despair.

"When's he coming?"

Mellie tried swallowing, but her throat refused, too dry for her vocal cords to work right. How could a dry throat burn along with the backs of her eyes and her nose? She leaned her head against Lissa's. "He'll come as soon as he can."

If only she could believe that. With every passing hour the horror drew closer.

"We'll be closing in half an hour. If any of you have no place to go to, there is room here at the shelter." The office worker who'd been answering questions all day crossed the room to talk to one of the others who waited.

Mellie watched her nod and smile. Could they stay in the waiting room at the hospital? Or should she stay here? If only she could drive. She opened her purse to look at the car keys and the wallet he'd insisted she take. The three dollars remaining in her billfold would barely buy them dinner at a fast-food place. And they'd about finished off the snacks she'd brought along. All that remained was one piece of cheese, and that was something Lissa would eat.

"Ma'am?"

"Yes." The woman stopped in front of them.

"You say there's room here at the shelter?"

"Yes."

"I see. But I need to check on my father at the hospital before we check in here."

"Was he injured on the mountain?"

"No, he had a heart attack when we got down here. We drove from Tacoma. It's my husband we are searching for."

"Boy, never rains but it pours." She shook her head. "Do you know the way?"

"Yes, we walked from the hospital to here."

"Don't you have a car?"

"I…I don't drive."

"Can your little girl walk that far?"

"No, I'll carry her."

"Perhaps you'd better see a doctor for her. How about I drop you off at the hospital, or if you would like, you could call over there and see how your father is doing, then you could stay here."

Mellie ducked her head, trying to think, to make a decision, but all she saw was confusion.

"I could give her a ride." Katheryn, who'd been four seats over, put away her notebook. "There are no more rooms to be had around here."

"That would be very kind of you." The woman in charge laid a hand on Mellie's shoulder. "Did you bring clothes or anything along?"

"Only for Lissa. We didn't plan on spending the night." Mellie shifted the sleeping Lissa in order to stand. *We didn't plan any of this. Who would have ever thought…?*

"My name is Katheryn Sommers. My husband and son are missing in the eruption."

"Mellie Sedor. My husband, Harv, was driving a logging truck up there."

"Mommy, I gotta go potty."

"Don't worry, I'll wait for you." Katheryn dug her keys out.

"Thank you." When she returned most of the others had left, but Katheryn waited, as she'd promised.

"Were you really planning to walk all the way?"

"A policewoman took us to the hospital, then I walked here."

"I see. You'll have to give me instructions to get to the hospital." She slung her bag over her shoulder. "I should have started looking for a place to stay when I first got here. As it is, I'm staying in Klammath." She held the door for Mellie. "You wait here. I'm parked around the side. I'll bring up the car."

"That's okay. I can walk it."

Once they were settled in the car, Mellie kept her arms wrapped around Lissa. They'd driven a couple of blocks before Katheryn asked, "What's your little girl's name?"

"Lissa. She's five."

"I heard you mention leukemia."

"Yes. I shouldn't have brought her out like this, but…"

"I know. You had to try to find your husband."

"I mean, how do they know who to even look for? Or where?"

"At least he was working there, so someone has a record. No one else but me knew my son and his father were even up there."

"Why'd they—?" Mellie clamped her lips shut. How rude. After all, this was none of her business.

"Why did they go up camping like that?" Katheryn stared straight ahead. "It's a long story. I'll tell you later." She stopped the car at the front of the hospital. "I'll go park and be waiting for you inside near the door."

"Thank you." By the time she got to the CCU, Mellie could have dropped down on a couch and fallen instantly asleep. If sleep would come. She was so exhausted that she might not be able to even if she stumbled into a bed. Her eyes burned, and the urge to rub them itched. However, her hands and arms were full. No fingers free to even rub her nose.

She set Lissa on a chair in the hall. "I'm going over to ring that buzzer, okay? You stay right here."

Lissa nodded, without even opening her eyes. The transparent skin around her eyes showed purple like the bruises that happened so easily now.

Mellie leaned against the wall while she picked up the phone. In response to the nurse's question, she said she was here to see Mr. Johnson.

"Are you a member of his family?"

Mellie nodded, grateful she couldn't be seen. "His daughter."

"He's sleeping, but you can come in. Open the door when you hear it buzz."

"Thank you." Mellie hung up the phone, picked up Lissa, settled her on her hip, and waited for the door.

"I'm sorry, but you can't bring a child in here."

"But—"

"She'll have to stay in the waiting room."

"Please, just let me see him. We'll only stay a moment."

"All right, but no farther than the foot of the bed." The nurse walked with them. "He is sleeping comfortably. There have been no more episodes. The doctor said we'll move him to a regular floor in the morning if he continues as he has."

Mellie stared at the sleeping man, his bed half raised. Color had returned to his face, and in spite of the nose prongs and beeping machines, he looked to be sleeping peacefully.

"I love you, Mr. Johnson," Lissa whispered.

Mellie hugged her daughter close. Too many times it had been Lissa lying in a hospital bed.

"You can call for information in the morning."

"When he wakes, tell him we were here, would you, please? And that we are staying at a shelter."

"I'll do that." The nurse ushered them out, and the door clicked behind them.

The sight of Katheryn waiting, someone that she at least knew by name, drew Mellie across the room. At Katheryn's question, Mellie nodded and almost smiled. "He's doing good—sleeping now."

"I'm glad."

A few minutes later they drove into the parking lot of the Cascade Middle School.

"Are you sure you don't want a doctor to see Lissa?"

"I'll give her some medicine and she'll perk up."

And what was going to sustain her through the night? *Please, God, let Lissa sleep through the night so she feels better in the morning. Let them find Harv and bring him to us. Please.*

35

THE MOUNTAIN

She wore a gaping wound, her blood flowing out in rivers of gray. Her breath rose in streams of smoke. Down in her bowels, the tremors continued, and she could not rest. She had buried many friends and drowned her own kindred. Who would forgive her for such cataclysm? Who would blame her Creator?

36

Mellie and Katheryn

May 19, 1980, evening

"Mommy, I want to go home."

"I know. Me too. But we need to stay here tonight."

"Will Mr. Johnson be better tomorrow?"

Mellie exchanged a look of commiseration with Katheryn. "Yes, but not enough to drive."

"But what if Daddy is looking for us?" Lissa laid her head on her mother's shoulder. "I want my daddy."

"Me too, baby, me too." Mellie stared around the gymnasium of the Cascade Middle School. She saw people of every age, kids playing, some people looking into nowhere, the weight of sorrow or fear pressing them into their chairs. Off in the corner two men were setting up more cots, in line with the others, where blankets and pillows were stacked in the middle. One family had taken over a corner group, the mother instructing her children in making up the beds.

Fragrances of cooking food floated from the cafeteria, overlaying that of floor wax, sour gym clothes, and pine-scented cleaning products.

A baby wailed in one corner, and Katheryn's attention followed the sound. Sure enough, the same young woman she'd seen at the center.

"For Pete's sake." Her mutter carried to Mellie.

"What?"

"That baby that's crying—I hope you'll all be able to get some rest." She hoisted her purse strap farther up on her shoulder. "If there's nothing more I can do for you tonight, I'd better get going."

"Thank you so much for the ride."

Katheryn paused. "Are you sure Lissa will be all right here tonight? I mean, if she needs to see a doctor, I could take you back to the emergency room."

Mellie tried to sound sure of herself, but inside... "I'll call her doctor in the morning." She wiped a tear from her daughter's cheek.

"Don't want to stay here," Lissa whispered, another tear following the first.

"There's nowhere else to go. All the hotels and places are full. Besides, we don't have any money for that." She ignored the money in Mr. Johnson's billfold. That was to be for emergencies only.

A woman with gray hair in a slipping bun stopped in front of them. "Will all of you be staying?"

"No." Katheryn shook her head. "I have a motel room." She patted Lissa on the back. "I'll see you in the morning."

"'Kay."

"Thank you again."

"I need you to sign this paper. Please print your names in the first box, then your address and signature." The woman whose badge read HI, I'M CAROL, held out the clipboard.

"I need to set you down."

Lissa shook her head and buried her face in her mother's neck.

"Here, I'll hold the clipboard. Is she injured?"

"No, just very ill."

"Flu?"

"No, leukemia." Mellie scribbled in the information while Carol tried to hold the clipboard steady.

"Poor lamb. Is there anything we can do to help?"

Find my husband? Turn back the clock? Mellie signed her name. "We just need a place to stay. My neighbor, who brought us down, had a heart attack and is in the hospital, or we'd have gone on home again. I'm sorry to be a bother."

"Now, never you mind. We're all in the same boat here. Dinner will be ready in fifteen minutes, so if you want to wash up, the bathrooms are over there." She pointed to the rest room signs down the hall to the right.

"Thank you."

"And you can set your things on two of the cots, wherever you want."

"Carol, do you know where…?" someone called from across the room.

Carol waved at the questioner. "I'd better go see what they need. As if I know any more than the others." She tsked her way back across the room, leaving smiles and comfort in her wake.

Minutes later Mellie held Lissa in her lap during the meal, encouraging her to eat tiny bits, the food tasting like dust to her.

"Come on, you like spaghetti. Take another bite."

Lissa, watching the two giggling children across the table, opened her mouth and took the food.

"You two behave yourselves now." Their mother tapped the older on the shoulder. "And don't you spill nothin'."

The boy slurped a string of spaghetti into his mouth.

Lissa half giggled.

The boy dug out another long strand, this one flicking him on the nose in a last-ditch effort for freedom.

Lissa laughed, a sound that brought a smile to her mother's mouth. Lissa used to laugh and dance and run like all the other kids they knew. Mellie kissed the part in Lissa's hair and smiled. Which encouraged the boy to more antics, which caught his mother's attention, which earned him a thump on the head.

"I warned you..."

"But, Mom," the round-faced daughter put in. "He made the little sick girl laugh."

The woman handed her son a napkin. "What's your little girl's name? Ol' spaghetti face there is Andrew and"—she patted her daughter's head—"this is Bitsy, 'cause she was so little."

"Tell them your name," Mellie whispered in Lissa's ear.

"Lissa Marie Sedor."

"That's a pretty name."

"Better'n Bitsy." Andrew poked his sister.

"Andrew Scott Bellamy, if you are finished eating, you may take all of our trays up to the window."

"Ah..."

"Now."

He untangled his legs from the bench seating and picked up his tray, and then his mother's.

"What about Sissy's?"

"Mo-ommm." The groan on his face made Lissa smile again.

"You want to come down to the TV room with us? We got a video of *Cinderella*."

Lissa shook her head.

"She's pretty tired." Mellie hugged her daughter closer.

When the two ran off, Donna, as she introduced herself, leaned across the table. "There's going to be a story read later, around bedtime, if you want to come listen."

"Thanks." Mellie set Lissa on the bench so she could get up, then scooped her up again. After a bathroom run, they sat back down on one cot.

"You're going to have to sleep in your T-shirt. I didn't bring your jammies."

"I didn't brush my teeth." Lissa clutched her bunny with both arms.

"I know. You ready to say your prayers?"

Lissa dug in the bag and pulled out a book. "Read this first?"

Mellie complied, having memorized *Goodnight, Moon* by now. The simple little story was one of Lissa's favorites.

"You should have read it to me."

"I can't read."

"But you know all the words."

"I know. I like...*Moon.*" She lay still, then turned her head to see her mother's face. "You think Daddy can see the moon?"

Mellie fought the instant burning behind her eyes. "I hope so, baby. I sure hope so. Let's say your prayers, and then I'll give you your medicine." *Please, God, let Harv see the moon tonight.*

"Now I lay me down to sleep..." After she'd finished the old verse, Lissa continued, "And make my daddy come home again and make Mr. Johnson all better and God please make me all better too. Amen." She opened her eyes, then clamped them shut again. "And if Jesus isn't right beside You, please tell Him I love Him lots. Amen."

"Amen." What more needed to be said? Now, if only they would turn out the lights and make everyone go to sleep.

She'd finally crooned Lissa to sleep when the baby began to fuss again. Lissa whimpered and shifted, a sure sign the pain was back. The medication should be taking effect by now. Mellie, who'd moved their cots close to the wall so she could prop herself against it, stroked her daughter's hair and murmured love into her skin. *How can I continue without Harv?* Fear snuck up her legs and squeezed her insides, up around her heart and her lungs so she could hardly breathe. Run. Where could she run?

Lissa settled back down. The frown smoothed away between her eyes, and her breathing evened. The crying even hurt her skin, making her want to scream. *God, please get someone to care for that baby. Poor little thing.*

Katheryn couldn't get Lissa out of her mind as she drove south on I-5 and exited at Klammath. How could she help them? When she parked in the lot by the motel, she wished she'd been able to find something better, but the thought of driving clear to Vancouver every day was about as appealing as a dunk in the mud-clogged river. Driving this far was bad enough.

She opened her door with the key, sniffing and wondering about the vile odor. But once inside, it faded away.

"Hi, Kevin, no messages here, so I'm leaving one for you there. I'm back in my room after a totally frustrating and fruitless day. Everyone keeps telling me to be patient. Carol, the woman at the center, asked me to be a greeter of sorts this afternoon, and that helped the time pass. If I could concentrate on the writing..." She rubbed her forehead. "Hopefully, I'll be able to sleep better tonight. Tell Susan I'll call her in the morning. I love you."

She hung up, thought about a shower, washed her face instead, and took two sleeping tablets. *David, Brian where are you? If you are suffering, God hold you and carry you. If you are in His arms, I am glad for you. I am.* She wiped her tears with the bed sheet. *But I didn't want you to go now. I don't want to—can't—be alone. I want you here. Oh, God, I want my son and husband back.* She muffled her sobs in the pillow, when she really wanted to scream her agony.

Sometime later someone banging on her door woke her. "Coming." She stepped out of bed and at the same time realized what a terrible stench filled the room. The backed-up sewer water came to her ankles. She gagged, nearly adding more liquid to the effluent.

Within a few minutes she was packed and out of there, after washing her feet in an upstairs rest room. The management closed the hotel.

Groggy from the medications, she drove carefully back up the freeway and into the parking lot of the shelter.

"You have room for one more?" she asked the man at the door. "In fact, there might be others. Our hotel in Klammath flooded with sewer water."

Even he shuddered. "There're empty cots over on that side of the room. If you want to take a shower first, I wouldn't blame you."

"No, I washed, thanks." After changing in the rest room, she set her overnight case under the bed, having left everything else in the car, and crawled under the covers. What a night.

Someone a couple rows over snored loud enough to…to wake the baby.

David Sommers, I cannot believe all this. I know you had no idea what could happen, but right now I could strangle you myself. Along with the mother of that child.

37

Mellie and Katheryn

May 20, 1980

When did you come back?" Mellie stared at Katheryn.

"Middle of the night. The sewer backed up into my hotel room." She shuddered, making a face. "Walking through sewer water is..." She didn't bother to finish her sentence.

"Oh, ick." Mellie shuddered along with her. "So you came here?"

"It was here or drive another forty miles or so to Vancouver." She leaned forward and dropped her voice. "But if that man snores like that again—and that poor baby..."

"Lissa was up and down a couple of times, but she slept pretty well, considering."

"Poor tyke is probably so worn out she'd sleep anywhere. Have you heard anything about Mr. Johnson?"

Mellie shook her head. "And they haven't found any unidentified bodies that might be Harv. I keep hoping and praying he is still alive, but..." Her sigh carried all the lost hopes and dreams. "I've got to call the doctor today and tell him about Lissa's fever and fatigue. Guess we'll have to take the bus home." Home, how could that house ever be home again without Harv there?

"Well, let's get breakfast and then figure some of this stuff out. You want me to bring you some?" Katheryn nodded to Lissa, who slept on.

"If you don't mind. I don't want her to wake up and be frightened."

"No problem."

Mellie watched Katheryn cross the room. Even her walk spoke self-confidence. She greeted other people around her and laughed at the antics of the two children who'd sat across the table from them at dinner. And yet, she hadn't heard about her husband and son either. *How could she be so cool about it all? If it weren't for Lissa, I'd…I'd…* Mellie swallowed her tears and wished away her fears. Neither worked very well.

"I hope you slept better than I did." Mrs. Bellamy stopped beside Lissa's cot.

Mellie wished she could think of something to say and could remember the woman's name. Had she slept at all? She must have. The night passed and she didn't recall all of it. Even the nightmare that wakened her was only a shadow rather than the specters that so often lurked at her shoulder unless Harv banished them for her.

"She doing any better today?"

"Not really. I'm letting her sleep as long as possible." She'd almost shaken Lissa to make sure she was just sleeping and not unconscious. "Um, I forgot your name."

"Donna Bellamy. Can I get you anything?"

Mellie masked her surprise. Why were people being so nice to her? "Uh, Katheryn is bringing me some breakfast. Thank you, though."

"Maybe later Lissa will feel like playing with the kids or watching a video. There's a box of books over there in the corner along with some toys someone donated. Sure wonder if we got anything to go home to."

"Where did you—do you—live?"

"Up on the North Fork. It was hit the worst. What about you?"

"We came down from Tacoma to see if I could find my husband. He was driving truck for a logging company."

"No word?"

"No."

"I'm so sorry, honey. Leastwise we got all our family, even the cat—Andrew snatched her up as we run out the door."

"You're lucky." As if luck had anything to do with it. Harv always said you make your own luck, but he also believed that almighty God was in control.

"I'll be praying for you to find your husband. What's his name?"

"Harv. Harvey Sedor." Mellie choked on the words.

"M-mommy?" Weak as it was, at least Lissa was able to talk. "I'm wet."

"Don't you worry none, sweetheart. We'll get you some clean sheets." Mrs. Bellamy turned back to Mellie. "You got any extra clothes?"

"Just what's in the bag." Mellie cuddled Lissa. "We'll go change you and wash in the bathroom, okay?"

"Sorry."

"I know. Sometimes it can't be helped."

When they came back, Katheryn had set a tray on the cot and was folding up blankets and sheets. "You go ahead and see if you can get some food in her while I check to see if anyone has learned anything new."

No matter how she coaxed, Lissa kept turning her face into her mother's shoulder. Mellie ate some toast and scrambled eggs, wishing the two charmers from the night before would come over and make Lissa laugh again—and eat. Feeling the heat in her daughter's thin body, Mellie knew she'd better call the doctor. Last time Lissa had been like this, he'd ordered a transfusion. But he was in Tacoma, and they were here, and while the distance wasn't hundreds of miles, anything over a couple blocks was too long if she had to walk it carrying Lissa. Her back ached already, a leftover pain from yesterday.

"Here, at least drink some milk." She held the cup for Lissa, who took a couple of swallows before turning away.

Katheryn sat down on the cot, facing Mellie. "I called the center up in Toledo, but the man who answered the phone said there wasn't any news for either of us. I thought perhaps I could take you by to check on Mr. Johnson. I can stay with Lissa while you go up and see him."

"I could call our doctor from there."

"Easier than here. The line formed right after I called. Guess they all figured the offices were open finally." Katheryn stroked Lissa's leg. "You need some clothes for her? We could stop at Kmart or something."

Why are you being so good to us? Mellie wished she dare ask out loud, but just having someone talk to her like a friend helped keep the horror at bay. Were clothes for Lissa an emergency? Should she ask Mr. Johnson?

The door opened, and a tall woman with a camera around her neck and wearing a backpack stopped and glanced around the gym. She took a spiral notebook from the pocket of her vest, flipped it open, wrote a few notes, and closed it again. Once the notebook was back in her pocket, she removed the lens cap, which also went in a pocket before moving toward the three children playing with toys in the corner. Watching her walk, the sunbeam catching another in her hair, was like watching a river flowing easy, sparkling in the sun.

"Orange juice."

Mellie leaped to fill her daughter's request. Only a few sips, but Lissa held the plastic glass instead of giving it back—and drank some more.

"Mellie?"

She turned her attention back to Katheryn, who hadn't seen the woman with the camera. The woman who walked like she was somebody. "Yes?"

Lissa pulled at her mother's sleeve. "Mommy, who's that lady?"

"I don't know."

Katheryn turned to look over her shoulder. "The one with the camera?"

"Uh-huh."

"Probably works for a newspaper or something. Reporters keep looking for the stories. That's their job."

"She's pretty."

No, she's grace in motion. Mellie set Lissa back on the cot and packed their meager things back in the bag. "Get your coat on. We don't want to keep Mrs. Sommers waiting."

Katheryn held the jacket open for Lissa to stick her arms in.

"Are you a grandma?" Lissa asked.

"Nope, not yet. But my daughter is going to have a baby. Maybe I can practice being a grandma with you."

"Okay. I don't gots a grandma."

Mellie stood and picked up her daughter to perch on her hip, then reached for the bag. Katheryn took it instead.

"My car is out in the parking lot. I'll bet Mr. Johnson will be glad to see you this morning."

"He's probably been worrying about us all night."

"I hope not. That would be bad for his heart."

"I'll wait out here with Lissa while you go in." Katheryn reached for the little girl. "You can sit on my lap, can't you? I need to learn how…"

"To be a grandma?" Lissa let herself be taken.

"Thank you, I won't be long." Mellie glanced over her shoulder to see Lissa and Katheryn sit down on the sofa. *Thank you, God, for this wonderful woman. Did you send us an angel or something?* She pushed the button for the CCU and waited.

"I'm Mellie Sedor to see Mr. Johnson."

"One moment."

Mellie studied the instruction paper taped to the wall above the Call button.

"I'm sorry, Mr. Johnson is no longer here."

Mellie's heart stalled.

"He's on the second floor, room 210. We transferred him this morning."

Relief. She could breathe again. "Thank you." Returning to the waiting room, she smiled at the two, who looked up from the pad of paper they were playing with.

"I'm showing Mrs. Sommers how to fold a butterfly." Lissa smiled at her mother.

"She's very good."

"My daddy teached me."

"Mr. Johnson is down in a regular room now. You can see him too."

"We can show him the butterfly. Colored paper would be better."

"Maybe we can find some crayons and you can color it."

The women gathered their things, Mellie picked up her daughter, and they headed for the elevator.

When they found his room, Mr. Johnson was sitting up in bed and a young man was giving him a shave.

"Hi, Mr. J." Lissa waved to him.

"We can come back later."

"No, no, we're nearly done here. Don't go."

When the young man left with a smile, they entered the room.

"We brung you a butterfly, see."

"How are you feeling?" Mellie stopped at the side of the bed, holding Lissa as she leaned over to kiss his cheek.

"Much better. They even had me walk down the hall a door or two. You were at a shelter?"

Mellie nodded. "Oh, I'm sorry, this is Katheryn Sommers, our angel in disguise."

"No angel, but delighted to meet you."

They visited a few minutes before Lissa announced, "We're going shopping, and I get a new pink shirt. And pants."

He looked to Mellie. "You use some of that money for whatever you need."

"But—"

"No buts. What did the doctor say?"

"I'm going to call him now. We'll be back later, after our shopping trip."

"You heard me, right?"

"Right." Relief felt light, like the paper butterfly that he held in his gentle hands. Only relief also wore pink and purple and blue with even a touch of yellow.

"Bye, Mr. J." Lissa laid her head on her mother's shoulder and waved a blue veined hand.

Down in the main waiting room Katheryn sat down with Lissa while Mellie went to find a public phone.

Mellie dialed the sequence she had learned the day before. "Sorry, Dr. Thomas is not available now. I will give him a message and we will call you back."

Mellie groaned inwardly. "Please tell him that Lissa is much weaker, and in the past they have given her a transfusion to help her along. Can we do that now?"

"I see. I'll ask the doctor and call you back. What is your number there?"

Mellie searched the face of the public phone. "There is none. I'll have to call you again."

"I see. Give me at least half an hour."

Mellie agreed and hung up the phone. Why did everything have to be so difficult?

She passed on the news and picked up Lissa. How easy it was to tell her brief spurt of energy had already been used up. Her eyelids drooped, and she let her head fall on her mother's shoulder.

They drove to the Kmart, and Katheryn parked the car as near to the front door as possible. "If you want, Lissa and I can wait in the car."

"I want to go."

"All right, let's do this quickly."

In the store Lissa pointed to the things she liked, and with two new outfits, undies, toothpaste and other sundries, and a package of panties for

Mellie, they left the store. Stopping by the shelter gave them no news, so they returned to the hospital.

Mr. Johnson was sleeping, so the threesome returned to the waiting room, and Mellie placed the phone call to the doctor.

Her hands shook as she listened to the nurse pass on the doctor's orders. "I'm in a hospital right now. Can't it be done here?" Her head dropped forward and she closed her eyes. "I'll have to get back to you. Can I call you?"

Would pounding the wall help? "There's no number on this phone. I'll have to call you back again." Despair not only smelled bad but tasted terrible.

"But I can't come up there. I have no transportation. I don't drive." *God, why didn't I learn to drive?* She felt like wailing instead of just crying. *And why can't I at least talk to the same nurse?*

38

MELLIE, KATHERYN, AND JENN

MAY 21, 1980

"Mommy, she's here."

"Who?" Mellie looked to where Lissa was pointing. The photographer they'd seen at the shelter now stood just inside the hospital door, where they had come to find word about Mr. Johnson. The tall, elegant woman glanced around the room as she had before, smiling when she noticed the three who'd taken chairs together, and came toward them.

"Hi. I saw you at the shelter. My name is Jenn Stockton."

The others introduced themselves, with Lissa peeking out from her mother's shoulder.

"Are you working for one of the local papers?" Katheryn asked.

"No, freelancing. I've not done photojournalism before." Jenn smiled at Lissa. "I love photographing the mountain. I came back to do that, and all this happened. There are a lot of stories here."

"Came back?"

"From New York." She squatted down to Lissa's level. "Hi, sweetie. Do you like your picture taken?"

Lissa glanced up at her mother, then back to Jenn. "Sometimes Mommy takes my picture—with my daddy."

"Ah, I see." Her slate blue eyes darkened with compassion as she laid a hand on Mellie's knee. "I hope you hear good news soon."

Mellie nodded, tears blocking her throat again.

"You look familiar. Do I know you?" Katheryn, head cocked slightly to the side, studied Jenn.

"No." A slight head shake. "I've been gone from here for fifteen years. Where are you from?"

"Seattle."

"Nope, never been there." Jenn stood, turning just enough that Katheryn got part of her back. "If you'd let me take your picture, I'd make sure you got a copy."

"But I look so terrible."

Lissa looked up at her mother. "No. Not terrible. Nice." She leaned back against her mother's shoulder.

"I'd like you to be part of my story."

Mellie shrugged, but nodded at the same time. Making someone happy would be good for a change. With everything so overwhelming and people helping her, she needed to be a help for someone.

Katheryn pulled out her small portable typewriter and set up to write. At least she could take notes on everything that had happened.

"What you doing?" Lissa leaned slightly forward.

"Writing."

"Writing what?"

"I write books—for children."

"I like to draw."

"You do?"

"Have you made lots of books?"

"Some."

Mellie listened to the exchange, aware that Jenn was moving around, snapping pictures from different angles, changing lenses. Something niggled at the back of her mind. Katheryn Sommers. The name sounded familiar.

"What are your books about?" Mellie joined in the conversation.

"Oh, animals and plants and some with kids in them. I wrote about a little girl with a pony, and right now another one of my characters, Brandy, is in a new school."

"Did you write *Zoe and the Dancing Pony?*"

Katheryn nodded.

"That's my bestest book." Lissa smiled up at her mother. "Huh, Mommy?"

"Sure is. How wonderful to meet you. Harv's read *Zoe* so much, we all have it memorized." *And to think you've been helping me. What if Harv would never be there to read to Lissa again?* The black thought nearly took her breath away. No! She wanted to cover her ears and not hear those voices any longer. Surely Harv was coming back to them. Any minute now, they would learn that he'd made it out.

Katheryn smiled back. "That's good to hear. I'll have to send you an autographed copy."

"Really? Ours is about worn out." There, she could talk without crying.

"What is aut'graphed?"

"She will sign her name in your book."

"Why?"

"Because she wrote it."

"Oh." Lissa cuddled her rabbit in one arm and leaned back against her mother.

"Out of the mouths of babes…" Katheryn shook her head. "Lest we become prideful."

"I'm sorry."

"No, I'm grateful she likes the book well enough to request it."

"All the time. Third only to *Goodnight, Moon* and *The Cat in the Hat.* When her father reads, he acts out the parts, with his voice, you know." Mellie glanced up to see a man in uniform remove his hat as he stepped through the automatic door. He crossed to the desk, spoke softly with the receptionist, and turned to see whom she pointed at.

Mellie felt the point pierce her heart. *Good news, could it be good news?* She watched his face, hoping that his stoic officer's look would at least crack with a bit of a smile.

"Mrs. Sedor?"

"Y-yes." She clenched Lissa's blanket between her hands.

"I'm Cowlitz County Sheriff Frank McKenzie." He nodded at Jenn.

He glanced to Katheryn. "Are you a friend?"

"Yes."

"Could you all come this way, please?" He motioned down the hall, then shepherded them in front of him. "This room to the left."

Mellie clutched Lissa to her as if a drowning victim on a life preserver. *Move, feet, keep moving. Lord, what are we going to do?*

"Are you a friend too?" he asked Jenn as she followed them.

Mellie turned and caught Jenn's gaze. "Yes, she is." Surprised at her own answer, she followed Katheryn into the room, empty but for several folding chairs and a desk.

"I'm sorry to have to ask this of you, but a body that might meet your husband's description was brought in this morning. I need you to come down to the morgue and see if you can identify him."

Mellie closed her eyes. *Might be. Please, Lord. Oh, please, not Harv.*

Katheryn put an arm around Mellie's shoulder. "Isn't there any other way to identify him?"

"Yes, but getting dental records would take time. His fingerprints didn't match anything we have on record."

"I… I'll come."

"I'll go with you."

"Thank you." Mellie shifted a small part of trust to Katheryn, her slight weight seeking harbor in the woman's warmth. A friend, yes, a friend; she had so few. At least someone she knew would be with her.

"Lissa, you and I could read a book while they go with the sheriff." Jenn offered. "Or we could play with my camera."

"That's a very good idea." Frank nodded as he spoke.

"Lissa, baby, here's your blanket so you can cuddle up right here with Jenn."

"Can I take a picture?"

"You sure may. How about we set up your bunny and you take a picture of him."

"He's Harvey the magic rabbit."

"I see."

Frank took Mellie's arm and the three of them tiptoed out of the room. He led them back to the elevator and pushed the Down button.

"I don't know if I can do this." Mellie, eyes closed, collapsed against the wall behind her.

"We'll get through it." Katheryn took her hand.

"I have to tell you that the body is in really poor condition."

"Where did they find it?" Katheryn asked.

"Not far from here. Most likely been in the water and mud since Sunday morning."

Oh, Harv.

They walked down a narrow hall and stopped in front of a door marked MORGUE. Frank held the door open and ushered them into a small room with a large window showing into a stainless-steel room, the walls, tables, and all the apparatuses gleaming in the bright fluorescent lights.

Mellie ran into a blinding wall of orange scent overlaying a sharp smell of decay. It reminded her of the stench in her kitchen when she'd once burned a chicken to a crisp. Her eyes watered and her throat clenched against the gagging.

"Breathe through your mouth," Katheryn whispered, digging in her purse for a tissue.

"You stand here at the window, and I'll bring the body out."

"I...I can't do this."

Katheryn's arm around her shoulders held her tight.

The sheriff and a man garbed from head to foot in green scrubs pushed a sheet-draped gurney up to the window.

Mellie gasped and sucked in a breath through her nose. "Uh, uh..."

"Easy, you'll make it." Breathing through her mouth garbled Katheryn's words.

"Mrs. Sedor, did your husband have any scars or identifying marks, like a tattoo?"

Mellie stared at the white sheet that covered what looked like a jumble of puffy packages. "Ah, he had a scar with a jag in it about three inches or so on his upper right arm. Close to the shoulder." She indicated on her own arm where it would be. The man in green screened the area with his body, moved something around, and stepped back to point at what must at one time have been an arm.

Mellie nodded. "I think so."

"But you are not positive?"

Mellie fought the dizziness that threatened her vision. "He...he wore a ring, wedding ring that has three sort of Xs on it. They match this." She held out her hand to show the decorations on her own rings.

The sheriff and the man in green fussed over the gurney again, and Frank turned to the window.

"Yes, ma'am, they match. I'm so sorry."

Mellie sagged against Katheryn, a whimper, like that of a lost and frightened puppy, escaping her clenched lips.

Together they turned from the window, but Mellie spun back, spreading her white fingers on the window glass. "Harrrrvvvvvey!" Her cry echoed around the viewing room, ricocheting from wall to wall and burying itself in their souls.

"Come, dear." Katheryn took her by the shoulders, tears streaming down her cheeks.

Frank came back through the door to the viewing room, and another wave of the morbid stench hit them.

Mellie gagged and wretched before either of them could help her. Her eyes rolled back, and Frank caught her before she collapsed on the floor.

"You get the door. We'll take her out of here. George, bring us a basin and a wet cloth."

Gently, Frank lowered her into a chair, and Katheryn took the offered basin and cloth to tenderly wipe Mellie's face and hands. She rinsed the cloth and dabbed at the wet spots on her T-shirt.

"Mrs. Sedor, can you hear me?"

Mellie's lashes fluttered and her eyes opened. "Harv?"

"No, he's gone." Katheryn bit her lip.

Mellie gave a small nod and closed her eyes again, at the same time struggling to stand. "Lissa, poor Lissa."

39

The Mountain

As the rumblings dissipated, she wondered, *What have I done to deserve this decree that continues from everlasting to everlasting? Why has the Creator forsaken me?* Her glory, her rocky summit once her crown and the mantle of white, her royal robe, had been reduced to muddy relics of carnage and fire-streaked, ashen hills. Gray clouds shifted, and a hint of sun pierced down upon her like a needle. Survival, yes, for she had before, but inside she felt hollow and wondered if she would ever be beautiful and majestic again.

40

Mellie, Katheryn, and Jenn

May 20, 1980

S*urely that wasn't Harv. Of course it was. You know his scars and the ring. But…* The thought of that gurney of sheet-draped body bags made her gag, but she had nothing left to vomit. That had all erupted before she made it out of the room. That cold, terrible room. Death indeed lived in that room in spite of the white lights and stainless-steel everything.

She hadn't even been able to touch him. Not through the glass—not that the police officer would have let her.

He's in heaven now. Harv's in heaven, I know that. He reassured me so many times that he—we—would go straight to heaven because we believe in Jesus.

Lissa believes in Jesus. I can't say for sure about me. I used to believe that, but why, God, why did you let Harv die when we need him so bad? Why?

Are you there? Are you real?

Lissa stirred in her arms.

"Do you want me to take her for a while?" Katheryn, who'd been sitting by Mellie ever since they reached the hospital waiting room, offered again.

"No…thanks, we're fine." *We're fine. What a stupid thing to say. I'll never be fine again. I can't live without Harv.*

I can't get a job. I can't do anything. All I know is to take care of Harv and Lissa.

"I need to tell Mr. Johnson."

"Is there anyone else we should contact—parents, relatives, friends?" Jenn returned from somewhere. What people said seemed to float right on over Mellie's head. She took the chair on the other side of Mellie and picked up Lissa's rabbit that she had dropped in her sleep.

"Have you heard any more of when they'll be ready to do the transfusion?"

"I have to call the doctor back." The thought became words, as if it passed through a dense filter.

"Let me do that for you." Katheryn leaned closer. "Where do you have the number?"

"Number?"

"For the doctor for Lissa—the transfusion."

"My purse." Mellie fumbled with her purse, her hands like thick mittens.

Katheryn returned after a few minutes. "Dr. Thomas is setting things up here for you."

"When?" Jenn asked.

"Soon."

Soon, what a joke, nothing was soon when you waited for doctors. It wasn't like they were regular patients here. Mellie watched as Katheryn rose and crossed to the desk. She spoke softly so Mellie couldn't hear. *What could she be saying? More than I would. I'd just nod and...* Mellie felt like she was standing off in a corner, watching all this go on.

Sometime later a nurse in a blue-and-pink top motioned them from the door. "Mrs. Sedor and Lissa."

Mellie stood, her back aching as she tried to shift a sleeping Lissa into an easier carrying position.

"Let me take her." Katheryn took Lissa from her mother's arms and nudged her toward the door.

"We have a room ready now." The nurse led the way down the hall and into a room with a high child's crib, the sides lowered nearly to the floor.

"You can lay her there, and I'll be right back to undress her."

Mellie shook her head. "I..." She paused, the words not coming as they should.

Katheryn smiled over her shoulder as she laid Lissa on the white sheets. "Do you have a gown for her?"

When the nurse left, Jenn peeked in the door. "All right if I join you?"

"Okay by me—there's plenty of room." Katheryn motioned to the empty spaces. "Probably the only room in town."

Lissa whimpered, and Mellie leaned on the bed to speak into her daughter's ear. "Mommy's here." She smoothed her daughter's hair. Together she and Katheryn undressed the thin little body with skin so blue as to seem transparent.

"Has she had transfusions before?"

Mellie nodded. "Several."

"Is there anything else to do?"

"She's had chemo. We were supposed to see a specialist in Seattle on Monday, but we came down here instead. I had to find Harv."

The nurse handed them a child's gown with pink teddy bears on it. "We'll be ready in just a few minutes."

Lissa roused as soon as they tied the rubber strip around her upper arm. "No, Mommy, no." Her shriek could be heard down the hall.

"You'll have to hold her steady." The nurse waited, butterfly needle in hand.

"I'm trying." Mellie leaned closer to Lissa. "Easy, baby. Let's get this over with, and then it won't hurt anymore." She kept her murmuring, at the same time rubbing Lissa's arm.

Lissa writhed on the bed. Weeping now, a heart-wrenching cry that rose to a scream again as soon as the nurse touched her arm.

"We're going to have to restrain her."

But even with leg and arm restraints, Lissa bucked and fought.

"How can one little girl who has been too weak to walk be this strong?" Katheryn stood on the other side of the bed, stroking Lissa's leg.

Two tries and the nurse couldn't get a vein, even when they were able to hold Lissa still.

"Okay, let's try again."

"No." Katheryn took charge. "This is ridiculous. You bring in someone else, or we sedate her or something."

Mellie stared at Katheryn, blinking in disbelief. How did she dare speak like that to a nurse?

"Well!" The nurse left the room without a backward glance.

"Good for you." Jenn joined them at the bedside. "Hey there, little trouper, how about I go get you an ice cream."

Lissa opened her eyes—and nodded.

When Jenn left, Katheryn asked, "Is it always this bad?"

Mellie shook her head. "Been getting worse. Harv has always been there, and he can make Lissa laugh and get through it better." Her eyes widened and she clamped her jaw. Harv would never again make his daughter giggle, tease her into enduring the endless pokes and needles, read to her in the voice of the cat in *The Cat in the Hat.* Fire flickered.

"I hear we're having a spot of trouble in here." A young doctor with brushy hair stopped at the side of the bed.

Lissa's eyes widened. "You got a red nose."

"Really." He put a hand to his face and felt the foam rubber ball. "Well, how did that happen?" He leaned closer. "Did you give me a red nose?"

"No." Her giggle made two of the three hovering women smile.

"I wonder where it came from?" While he was talking, he opened a butterfly pack. "Now, I heard that a little girl in here was in need of some good red stuff to make her feel better. I think she needs a red nose, just like mine." He shook his head and made a funny *brr* noise, all the while snapping a blue stretchy tourniquet in place on her upper arm. "Don't you want a nose like mine?"

"Does it squish?"

He leaned closer. "Squeeze it and see."

Lisa reached out and squeezed the ball.

The doctor jumped back. "Ouch, did you have to squeeze so hard?" He pretended to cry big tears.

Lissa giggled again.

"You think you can hold real still for me so I can give you a big red nose?"

She nodded. "Is it gonna hurt?"

"I'll be as fast as I can. Here"—he handed her a red ball—"you put this on with your other hand and..." All the while he talked, he tapped her skin and slid the tiny needle into a vein while she giggled at her mother for trying to put the nose in place.

"Ta-da." He finished taping the IV hookup. "Now, I suppose you want a red sucker to go with your red nose?" He whipped two red suckers out of his pocket. "One for you and one for me." Unwrapping them, he handed her one and popped the other in his mouth. He hummed while he set up the IV pole and hung the bag of life-giving blood. "Now, isn't that a pretty color? And you, my little red-nosed kitten, will feel a whole lot better real soon." He leaned over and touched his red nose to hers. "Bye."

"Thank you, Doctor." Mellie forced the words through her tears. "You were wonderful."

"You have a mighty special little daughter there. I'm sorry for your loss. Can I get you anything? Sleeping pills tonight might help."

"I need to be here with Lissa."

"I'll stay too." Jenn stepped forward. "Lissa and I have some more books to read, and I think we might have to dress some paper dolls. Huh, kiddo?"

Lissa smiled up at her new friend. "I guess. Can I have my rabbit now?"

Jenn tucked the lanky bunny under the little girl's arm. "You get a nap, and I'll go find us some paper dolls. Okay?"

" 'Kay."

"Can I get you something?" The doctor looked directly into Mellie's eyes. "You've had an awful lot on your plate. This could help."

Mellie shook her head. She'd had pills before. Never again. Especially now, when everything depended on her.

"I'll check back in a bit later. I'm here if you need anything."

The filter had dropped back between Mellie and the rest. She tried to answer with some kind of assurance, but from the look on his face, she'd most likely failed. Like she did everything. How would she ever make it in this world without Harv? Her eyes burned, but her throat was dry as tumbleweeds that rolled in the winter. Big weeds ripped out by the wind and sent bouncing across a barren landscape.

Sleep, would sleep help? Perhaps, she should call him back and be assured of blessed hours of forgetfulness.

"Mellie, is there anyone else we need to notify?"

"Notify?"

"What about Mr. Johnson? Do you have a pastor?"

"Yes." Mellie sank down in the chair that faced the bed, seeing Jenn making Lissa laugh, but not even sure who she was.

Katheryn knelt in front of her. She spoke slowly or Mellie heard slowly; she wasn't sure which. "I am going to visit Mr. Johnson and tell him what has happened."

Mellie nodded.

A nurse stepped into the room. "There are some reporters out here who would like to talk with Mrs. Sedor."

Jenn stood. "I don't think so, not tonight."

"But they…"

"I said, not tonight. If you want, I'll handle them."

"Good." She checked the blood flow, the IV site, and asked Lissa, "You want some Jell-O, sweetie? Bet someone here could feed it to you."

"Ice cream?"

"You betcha."

Katheryn followed the nurse out. "I'll be back in a bit. Jenn, how about waiting to leave until I return?"

"Sure. I'll just take care of those news hounds first."

"Mommy?" Lissa raised up, searching the room.

Mellie heard her call and forced herself to sit straight. "Mommy's here."

"Daddy coming home?"

Daddy's already gone home, but how do I tell you? I can't. Not tonight.

Jenn shut the door behind herself. "Rather persistent they are." She picked up a book. "Okay, how about I read this one now?" She'd just settled down when the nurse came in with the ice cream.

Mellie watched as Lissa and Jenn grinned at each other ever each bite. When had Lissa ever taken to someone like that? Of course, she used to, before the disease ate her up.

Mellie leaned back against the chair. Her mind blank, as though she'd walked away and slammed the door shut on her memories. Especially that room, the horrible stench of that room.

"Can I get you two something to eat?" Jenn asked when Katheryn returned.

Mellie shook her head. Even the thought of food made her stomach coil in a knot.

"I'll get something on my way back to the shelter." Katheryn crossed to the side of the bed. "How you doing, sweetie?"

"Tired."

"I'll bet you are."

"I want to go home and see my daddy."

"Right." Katheryn glanced at Jenn, who shook her head just enough for her to see.

"I'm going to stay the night with them, but I'll go find paper dolls first. Can you stay until I get back?"

Katheryn nodded. "You going to take that pack outside the door with you?"

"I wish. I tried to appeal to their compassion for a sick little girl who lost her daddy, but you can guess how far that got me."

"So what did you do?"

"Promised them a story tomorrow. Perhaps we can scuttle out the back way in the morning."

"I take it you've handled reporters in the past."

"Once or twice."

Katheryn studied the woman beside her. "You look so familiar. What did you say your last name was?"

Jenn heaved a sigh. "Stockton." Her voice took on a chill, and she pulled slightly away.

"Jenn Stockton?"

"Yes."

"The model Jennifer Stockton?"

"Not for some time. I'm a photographer now."

"I wondered what happened to you. My daughter thought you were the most perfect woman on earth."

"Little did she know."

"You came from around here, right?"

"Yeah, innocent young girl from podunk county makes good in the Big Apple." Jenn shifted so she could see Lissa. "But no more."

"Someday if you'd like to tell me the full story, I'm known as a good listener."

"Thanks." Jenn headed for the door. "I'll be back in a few."

Katheryn glanced from sleeping girl to her mother, who was either sleeping or suffering in silence. When she saw the tear slip down Mellie's cheek, she knew it was the latter.

"Mellie, how about I turn that chair into a bed for you?"

Mellie shrugged, an insignificant motion that barely raised her shoulders.

"You'll have to move to the other chair, then." Katheryn brought a regular straight-backed chair closer to the crib where Lissa slept, bunny under her arm, one long leg flopped across her waist.

"I'm going to get some linens from the nurse."

A minute nod.

In a few minutes, Katheryn returned with sheet, blanket, and pillow in her arms. She took Mellie's hand to help her move, released the chair so it lay flat, and made up a bed, turning the cover back at an angle. "Here you go." She knelt down and removed Mellie's shoes, tucking them under the chair bed so they were out of the way.

"I need to watch Lissa."

"No, Jenn and I will do that. You sleep." Once Mellie lay tucked in bed, Katheryn crossed to look out the window. To think, working here with Jennifer Stockton. Life sure could be strange at times.

When Jenn returned they changed places, and Katheryn headed out the door.

"Mommy?"

Jenn leaned over the half-raised rail. "She's sleeping. I'm here, sweetie."

"I'm thirsty."

"You want water or 7 UP?"

"Juice."

"I'll be right back. Don't you go moving around now, hear?"

"I won't."

Jenn returned in less than a minute. "They'll bring some." But Lissa had slipped back into sleep.

A couple hours later, Mellie sat straight up. "Harvey?"

Jenn came to sit beside her. "Mellie, you need to wake up."

"Who are you? Oh…oh…Jenn. Harvey, he's gone." Tears coursed down her cheeks, and Jenn wrapped her strong arms around the sobbing woman.

"Go ahead and cry. It'll help in the long run." *So often I wished for someone to hold me when I cried. Thank God, at least I can do this for someone else.*

"I can't do this all alone."

Hardly able to understand the words, Jenn answered. "You don't have to. I'm here."

41

KATHERYN

MAY 20, 1980

"That poor baby. Maybe I should have stayed with Mellie." Katheryn stared at the lights in the school parking lot. "I could go back." *Here I am, talking to myself, in a parking lot of a school, planning to spend another night in this uncomfortable shelter, when I could head on home to my own comfortable bed.*

She rested her forehead against the steering wheel. "My bed, David's bed, our bed. God, where are You? Did You take them? I need to at least have some idea if they are alive or not. How can hope continue?"

He is my hope and my salvation, my very present help in time of trouble. Where had that verse come from? She didn't even remember memorizing it.

I don't want to be a widow! She felt like she was screaming the words, when she'd not even spoken them aloud. *And my son, my dearest son. I want to hear him laugh again, to see his face. Lord God, I want my family back.* Pressure, like that of a giant vise being turned by some fiend, clamped her chest, her throat, her head. She tried taking a deep breath, thinking, *Hope, hope in Christ,* but nothing helped.

"Focus on something else," she ordered herself, not even recognizing her fractured voice. "Think of Lissa. Mellie. They are far worse off than you are."

"You are the God of miracles. All I want is a miracle." She dug in her pocket for a tissue, but even that was denied her. "I've gone to church all my life, and now when I really need You…"

She shook her head. "What's the use." Taking her briefcase from the backseat, she exited the car, locked the doors, and lifted her suitcase from the trunk. A hot shower would indeed be welcome. Maybe she could drown her sorrows.

She dropped her things and clutched her middle. *Drown.* Her mind leaped back to the morgue and the ghastly sight she'd seen there. *Oh, God, not drowning. What a horrible way to die. Please not drowning.*

She sucked in a deep breath, squared her shoulders, and entered the gymnasium. From across the room, a salty voice announced her arrival, peppering it with several profanities.

"Why, I never—" Katheryn wheeled around, ready to lambaste such rudeness. And swearing like that—there were children here.

"Gimme a kiss, baby."

She glanced around to see half the people at the tables looking her way, most of them chuckling or at least grinning.

She plunked her suitcase by the door, setting her briefcase atop it.

"Don't be such a sourpuss. C'mon and gimme a kiss."

"Adolf, stop that." An elderly woman stood up, and at that moment Katheryn saw the bird cage. A cage not half big enough for the brilliant red Macaw parrot that was shifting from one foot to another.

"A bird, it's a bird." She clapped one hand to her chest and shook her head. "I thought…" *No wonder everyone's laughing.*

"Sorry, when he's upset, he reverts back to what his previous owners taught him. If I'd known he had such a foul vocabulary, I'd not have taken him in." The woman threw a sheet over the cage. "And this is just too small for him. Perhaps tomorrow I can locate a larger cage."

Katheryn joined her at the cage. "Is he mean, too?"

"No, just sounds like it. He loves to cuddle and have someone stroke under his wings. If you like, I'll bring him out later."

"I'd love that. I've always wanted an African Gray parrot. Ever since I read an article in *Reader's Digest* called 'I love you, Mrs. Pat.' "

"I read that too. People think birds are just dumb animals, but these guys can really think. He never asks for a kiss except when he sees a woman."

"He's sure beautiful."

"There's a place over by me. Get your tray and come sit down."

Katheryn had just seated herself when the two children from the night before came over.

"Did Lissa go home?" the boy asked.

"No, she's in the hospital."

"Is she dying?" His little sister's eyes saucered.

"No. They gave her a transfusion." At their questioning eyes, she added, "Some new blood. She has a disease called leukemia."

"Poor little thing." The parrot lady laid her hands in her lap. "I had a cousin died of leukemia. Hear they've learned lots of ways to help folks get well again since then."

"Yes, we're hoping and praying that happens for Lissa."

"Bye." The two ran off.

"Cute kids. But I'll let you eat in peace."

"No, I need…ah…I'm Katheryn Sommers."

"Attie Hartwell. I used to live up in Toutle, but I saw my house go floating down the river on the television, so who knows where I live now. Got me and Adolf out, the rescuers did. I'll thank God for them the rest of my life. Came right in the second-story window and took me and Adolf right out. Good thing his wings were clipped, or he'd a been lost for good. He clamped his claws into my shoulder all right, made 'em bleed, but I lost my husband two years ago in a logging accident, and Adolf is the only family around here I got left."

"No children?"

"One on the East Coast, one in Atlanta. They want me to come live with them, but this area's been my home all my life. Why would I want to go traipsing off across the country? The land will still be there. I can always build a new house."

Katheryn propped her elbows on the table and her cup in both hands. "You are very brave."

"No, not brave, about the biggest coward you ever did see, but God has taken care of me all my life. Why would He stop now?"

"You think losing all you owned and your husband dying was God taking care of you?"

"Ah, honey, those kinds of things happen to all of us at one time or another. People die when it's their time, and my Bill, I know he's lots happier where he is now. Why, if he still walked this earth, he'd be fussin' and stewin' 'cause his tractor was gone. He worked on restoring that tractor ten years or more. His baby…" She shrugged, her faded eyes lit with something Katheryn could not identify. "And he's so busy up there, that tractor don't mean nothin' to him now."

"What makes you think that?"

"Why would anyone worry about an old tractor when he's living in the light of heaven? He's probably took Jesus fishin' by now." Attie patted

Katheryn's arm. "Sorry, here I go on about me, and you've not told me nothin' about yourself, except for your name."

"I live in Seattle, I have—had—have two sons and a daughter. Susan is pregnant with our first grandchild. My husband, David, is a professor at the University of Washington."

"And who did you come down here to wait for?"

"David and our younger son, Brian. They went camping."

"Near the mountain?"

"Yes." On the mountain, near the mountain, what difference did it make? "So far, no one has seen them."

"They are still finding survivors."

"I know."

"Not knowing has to be the hardest part."

All the noises of families and children and babies, old men, old women and those in between, most displaced from their homes, with staggering losses, facing the unknown, just like her, receded as she stared into Attie's sweet face.

"You are not alone." Her voice came gently across the void.

"Feels that way, though my mind knows differently. I cannot bear the thought of..." She sucked on her bottom lip, teeth worrying the tender flesh.

"You needn't bear it."

"I know, think of something else, others who are worse off than I..."

"I only know one way, and that is Jesus. His name is the most powerful word in our world. I say His name, over and over, whenever things get so heavy and deep I cannot bear them. I say that name above all names until I can sing it. Only one word, easy to remember."

"You make it sound so simple."

"Simple but never easy." She took Katheryn's hands in her own, hands knobbed by arthritis and softened by love. "I'll be praying for you."

And Katheryn, looking deep into the faded eyes, knew she would. "Thank you. I hope He hears you better than He hears me."

"Oh, He hears you, all right." Attie's fingers caressed Katheryn's cheek, feather light and burning deep. "You listen and look. He's here."

"Mrs. Hartwell, could you take Adolf out of the cage, please. He's lonesome," one of the children pleaded.

"Why, yes, I'll do that." Attie stood and laid a hand on Katheryn's shoulder. "You want to come meet my friend?"

"I'd love to, but I need to go call my son and daughter. Another time, perhaps."

The older woman traipsed across the room to show off the bird to the children. Katheryn didn't have to wait to use the phone. It seemed like the shelter wasn't nearly as full as it had been the day before. *Perhaps some of these people have found their loved ones,* she thought. *Oh God, let me be one of them.*

"Hi, Mom. What have you heard?"

"Nothing. Not a thing."

"How about if I come down there so you can come home?"

Home, her yard, her office, an empty house. "Thanks, but I'll stay. I've met a young mother and her little girl. At least I can help someone here. They need me. And besides, I might hear something anytime."

"We need you too, you know."

She could hear the gruff fight against tears in his voice.

"Lucky knows something is wrong; she's under my feet every minute."

"Poor girl. Give her an extra treat."

"She misses you. Grandma's called half a million times. Can't you call her?"

"I will, tomorrow. It's too late now." *She's the last person I want to talk to. Besides, what can I tell her—nothing. And right now, I don't want to hear about Bernie. I just cannot handle one more thing.*

"I'll talk to you tomorrow. 'Night. I love you, son."

"I love you too, Mom. Come home soon."

He sounded more like six than twenty-four. Katheryn turned from the phone and went back to retrieve her things. The noise echoing off the walls made her head ache.

That does it. I'm going for earplugs.

When she returned from a drugstore near the hospital, she put the soft foam forms in her ears and, taking out pad and pen, tried to write.

Brandy would not play. The dialogue was stilted, no action and humor, what a joke. She'd do better to write a murder scene. Not for a children's book, that was for sure.

As soon as they dimmed the lights, she left off adding up her checkbook and slid under the covers. *Be grateful you have a bed,* she reminded herself. Would someone please take care of that baby? *David, where are you? God, where are You?*

42

Jenn and Frank

May 20, 1980

"You look like death warmed over."

"Glad I can't say the same for you." Frank stared at her through eyes glazed by only two hours sleep, and that on the cot in his office. Never had he seen such confusion as in the three days since the mountain blew. Three counties involved, with all their services, National Guard, state government, private companies, and people taking things into their own hands to search for survivors, pets, livestock, family keepsakes. Besides all the activity of a mountain that could blow again at any moment and a debris dam at Spirit Lake that threatened more death and destruction.

"Been bad, huh?"

"You can't begin to know the half of it. I hear you're helping Mrs. Sedor."

Jenn nodded. "How about that cup of coffee I promised you?"

"Now?"

"I'd say we both could use one."

"We'd better take my car. Sig doesn't like pickups. We'd crowd him."

"You aren't on duty?"

"I'm supposed to be going home to sleep."

"I'll take a rain check, then. Get some rest."

"No. You can leave your truck there in the public parking lot."

This time Sig greeted her with a slight wag of his tail and no lip lifting.

"He likes you. Backseat, Sig."

"I like him. One of these days he may even let me pet him." She slung her backpack in first and climbed in the Blazer. The odor of alcohol made her wrinkle her nose. "You keep it with you, eh?"

Frank started the engine and slammed the truck into reverse, rear wheels spitting gravel. "Anybody ever tell you to mind your own business?"

She stared at him as he checked both ways for traffic. Bloodshot eyes, new creases on top of old, slightly gray around the gills, and in the close confines, she could smell the booze on him too. The old adage, rode hard and put away wet, would be a compliment to the condition he was in.

"How about I drive you home?"

His jaw tightened. "Coffee or nothing."

Jenn nodded. "Pigheaded as ever."

"Jenn, I'm too tired to argue or play games. Now, can I have the coffee without a sermon or not?"

"Guess if you want to crucify or kill yourself, that's up to you. Huh, Sig?"

She turned enough to look over her shoulder at the dog, who looked back, tongue lolling and the tip of his tail brushing the seat. "You know, you are one handsome fella."

Both ears pricked, he stared at her.

"I swear he understands every word I say."

"Not only what you say, but he reads your body language, your scent, and most likely knows what you had for breakfast too."

"His sense of smell is that good? Even if I haven't had breakfast?"

"Yes." He flicked on his turn signal.

"How long you had him?"

"Five years. He was a year when I got him." He parked his truck and opened the door. "You coming?"

When she reached for her backpack, he added, "You don't need that in the restaurant."

"You never know." She slung it over her shoulder. "See ya, Sig."

Frank slid into a booth and waved away a menu. "The usual."

"Thank you." Jenn accepted hers and took the seat opposite. "What's the usual?"

"Two eggs over easy, burn the bacon and hash browns, wheat toast." The waitress's badge read ROSIE. "Oh, and an entire carafe of coffee. The blacker the better."

Frank set his broad-brimmed hat on the seat beside him and slicked his hair back with both hands.

"You look God-awful, Frank." Rosie plunked the carafe on the table.

"And a happy day to you, too."

"Not too many having happy days around here. Some guys came in, can't get their ships out, real unhappy campers." Rosie shook her head. "Ships, loggers, sportsmen, you oughta hear them complaining. You'd think The Lady did this just to spite them."

"Going to be months before they can dredge the Columbia, let alone the Cowlitz. Those rivers still so hot the fish've jumped up on the banks to cool off."

Jenn looked up at him in surprise. Was Frank McKenzie always this friendly with this waitress? Of course, she did know him by name, so he must come in here a lot. *Now, why can he be pleasant with her and such a bear with a sore paw at me?* Jenn schooled her face to keep any such thoughts inside where they belonged. Frank meant nothing more to her than an old friend, and sometimes she wondered if her memories hadn't happened to someone else. *Be fair,* she told herself. *He has taken you into some places you wouldn't have gotten otherwise. I know, and he's been through about the worst any human can endure but…*

A hand waved in front of her face. "You still in there, squirt?"

His voice had softened, and was that concern she saw in his eyes?

"Frank, how do you deal with all this, like yesterday?"

"At the morgue?"

She nodded and lifted the carafe to refill his cup.

"Thanks." He studied the coffee, as if seeking knowledge. "That was a bad one. We couldn't show her, but that corpse was so cooked from the heat of the river that we had parts of it in separate body bags. That we could find. Someone saw the head and shoulder, called us, and we dug it out." He scrubbed a hand over his eyes. "And you wonder why I hit the bottle sometimes. Lord, Jenn, I…" He took a slug of coffee. "That poor woman, little girl so sick, and now this. I don't know. After all this is over, I might just get another job."

Her hand ached to touch his. As if separated from her body and with a mind of its own, it inched across the table and stroked the base of his thumb, then curled around his wrist.

"Here you go, folks." Rosie set their plates in front of them. "Get you anything else?"

Jenn shook her head. "No, thanks." The heat of her hand surprised her. "Mom said if I saw you to let her know when you can come for dinner."

"I wish I knew." He basted his hash browns with ketchup and held the bottle up.

"No, thanks. I like my food naked."

His arched eyebrow brought heat to her neck. "Frank McKenzie, keep your mind on your meal. That's just a figure of speech."

"Not from around here. That the kind of thing you learned in New York." He put a slur on the name of the city.

"The city was good to me." *For a while,* she finished the sentence silently.

His snort more than conveyed his opinion.

She ate a few bites in silence, listening to the discussion going on in the booth behind her.

"Well, look who's here." A familiar voice brought her back to the moment. "The ice queen herself."

"Gee, Sergeant, how nice to see you."

Frank swallowed a chuckle. "Ross, how's it goin'? Got enough to keep you busy?"

"McKenzie, you heard the latest report on that sediment dam?"

"Seems to me they ought to see if they can siphon off some of the pressure."

"As if we could get up there without getting someone else killed, let alone any machinery in. You been up in any of the choppers?"

"No. I leave that for the rescue boys. I got enough to keep me at a dead gallop without tryin' to do someone else's job."

Mitch turned back to Jenn. "I haven't forgotten my promise to take you up again, soon as I can get in the air."

Jenn rolled her eyes at the black look on Frank's face. "Sure, thanks, Mitch."

"Good to see you." Mitch nodded to each of them and left.

"You really would go up with him?"

"Frank McKenzie, I'd go up with the devil himself if he would take me closer to the mountain."

Frank threw some bills on the table and stood at the same time, grabbing his hat. His mutter included some words he had castigated her for using back when she was a teenager.

Guess he thinks I'm adult enough to hear them now. Her thought made her roll her lips to hide the grin. She grabbed her backpack and followed him out the door that he didn't bother to hold for her. Somc things never changed.

43

KATHERYN

MAY 21, 1980

Coffee's hot!" The raucous cry of the parrot worked like reveille. "Coffee's hot!"

Katheryn lay in her cot, listening to the sounds of the shelter around her. At least the baby had cried only briefly during the night. Perhaps the young mother was coping better, or someone else had taken charge for the peace of those sleeping. Whichever, it was one small thing to be thankful for. Nevertheless, the nightmares that she'd ridden during the darkest hours still galloped in her mind. The ride started with watching David and Brian make camp under the whispering fir trees. They'd gone fishing and caught enough trout for dinner. Sunday morning they'd fished again as the sun was rising to cast a yellow glow through the majestic trees, catching glints thrown by the cascading creek. So many times she'd been getting the fire ready to fry the fish in cornmeal and bacon grease. Nothing tasted better in the world. But the world turned dark, the blast, the heat, the fires, hot gases that sucked out life, and floods, and…

She sniffed the welcome fragrance of coffee brewing. Adolf was right. She reached for her wrapper and, sitting, shoved her hands in the sleeves.

Another day, more waiting. How easy it would be, if she were at home, to crawl back under the covers and sleep.

Except for the horrible dreams.

Making her way to the rest room and shower, bag in hand, she returned the greetings of those around her, waved to Attie, and waited only a minute before a shower was available.

She'd just turned off the water and reached for her towel when a scream made the hairs on the back of her neck stand at attention.

The woman screamed again, more a shriek this time, and Katheryn could hear the sound of running feet. People shouting.

Hair streaming wet, she grabbed her wrapper and thrust her wet arms back in the sleeves. Did they need to evacuate the building? Had the mountain blown again? Her heart triple-hammered against the walls of her chest.

Along with several others in like stages of dishabille, she burst through the doors, only to see some folks standing on tables, others nearly collapsing in laughter as two boys, a little girl, and three men were scrambling about on the floor.

"What in the world?"

"Careful, don't hurt him."

"They're just frightened."

"Easy now, throw my hat over him."

"Got one. Use the hat again."

One boy stood up, something hidden in his closed hands to his chest.

Katheryn, one hand clutching her wrapper closed at the neck, asked, "What is going on?"

"My gerbils got loose, and we couldn't find them." The boy held out his cupped hands. "You want to see Snitch?"

"No, that's all right." While Katheryn had no fear of fuzzy critters, right now an introduction to the perpetrator of pure fright didn't appeal.

"Hope you catch the other one, too." She returned to brush her teeth and finish dressing, chuckling to herself. A shame Jenn hadn't been here to catch some pictures of life in the shelter. Surely Snitch and Adolf should be included in her collection.

Sometime later, after another futile call home again, she walked into the hospital to see how Mellie and Lissa had fared through the night.

All dressed, Lissa sat in her mother's lap, alternately eating a Popsicle and pointing out pictures in a book Mellie was holding for her. She waved her Popsicle at Katheryn, smiled, and stuck the purple end back in her mouth.

"See my new shirt?" She pointed to her chest. "Pink."

"Is this the same child we…ah…helped?" Subdued would have been a far more appropriate choice of words, Katheryn knew, but not as polite a term. Besides, hopefully, Lissa didn't remember the fight to hold her down for the transfusion.

"Amazing, isn't it? New blood is a miracle." Mellie kissed her daughter's cheek. "We'll be ready to leave as soon as the nurse returns with the paperwork."

"Have you seen Mr. Johnson yet?"

"No, but I talked to him on the phone. Since he's on the regular floor, he said they've had him up and walking, so he is far better."

"I'll stay with Lissa if you want to go see him."

Mellie looked like she'd had a decent night's rest too, some color back in her face.

"You look so much better."

"The doctor came back and gave me a sedative. I slept in that chair bed. Jenn stayed the night, but she left early this morning. Didn't realize how tired I was, I guess." Sadness darkened her eyes again. "So much I need to do, and I don't know where to begin."

"There's a man downstairs asking about you," the nurse said when she walked back in the room. "He's from a timber company. You want me to tell him to come on up?"

Talk about Bambi in the headlights. Katheryn gave Mellie a reassuring look. "Is that the company your husband worked for?"

Mellie nodded. "I don't—I mean—what would he…?"

"Lissa and I could go down to the playroom so you would have some privacy to talk here. Would you like that, sweetie?" The nurse smiled down at the little girl.

Lissa looked up to her mother for permission and, at her nod, slid to the floor.

The nurse took her hand. "I'll let him know where you are."

"Thank you."

"You want me to stay with you?" Katheryn asked.

"Yes, please." Moment by moment Mellie melted back into the chair, as if hiding. She laced her fingers till they whitened.

"My advice is, if he asks you to sign anything, tell him you cannot do that right now."

"Why? I mean…?" Her face screwed up like a little girl's.

"Just to be wise and give us time to read anything over carefully." Katheryn leaned against the metal bed. "My father taught me that we need to be gentle as doves and wise as serpents."

"I…I don't get it."

"I'll explain later. But don't sign, okay?"

"Okay." Mellie rubbed her forehead. "I…I can't do this. Harv…"

Katheryn was sure she could read her mind. Total fear and panic because she depended completely on her husband.

"Mrs. Sedor?" The man removed his hat, showing a silver fringe of hair framing a shiny dome. His face bore the weathered look of a man accustomed to the out-of-doors.

Mellie nodded but remained as far back in the chair as she could disappear.

"I'm Harold Buckmaster, supervisor for A-1 Logging." He held his hat close to his chest, as if wishing he could hide within or at least behind it. "The company your husband, Harvey Sedor, worked for?"

Another nod.

Come on, Mellie, don't act like you're terrified of him, after all he… But she is terrified. She's shaking like a leaf. Lord, how do I help her?

"I…I want to offer you my, our condolences. Your husband was a good worker, a good truck driver."

"He…he loved trucks." Mellie's whisper brought a lump to Katheryn's throat. Past tense. *Was. Loved.* Would that be the way she referred to David from now on?

"I want you to know that we will pay your husband's medical insurance for three months. There will be papers for you to sign and all, but I just wanted you to know that we will pay all the funeral expenses, too. I wish I, we could do more."

Mellie stared down at her numb fingers. A single tear tracked down her cheek. The silence in the room magnified the noises in the hall. He shuffled his feet.

"Thank you, Mr. Buckmaster." Katheryn stepped forward and took the card he held out.

"I have the home address and phone. We'll be in contact." He turned back to Mellie. "I hope your little girl gets better real quick." He fled the room.

"Thank you." Mellie leaned her head back. "I don't know how I can do all this. I just don't know."

"Well, all we have to do right now is get Lissa checked out of the hospital. I'm sure you want to go see Mr. Johnson."

"I want to go home, but I want Harv to be there."

Yeah, I want my husband to be there too.

"We had a good time, didn't we, honey?" The nurse and Lissa wandered back into the room.

"I put the bunny puzzle back together." Lissa leaned on the arm of her mother's chair. "Can we go home now?"

"Soon as the discharge papers are ready." The nurse patted Lissa's head. "I'll be back with those in just a minute."

They got Lissa checked out and took the elevator to the medical floor.

"Hey, look at that. You're walking on your own. How's my favorite girl?" From the chair in the corner, Mr. Johnson held out one arm, the other still connected to an IV.

"I got blood again." Lissa's voice had the air of one used to medical procedures. "A doctor with a funny red nose got it in." Standing in the circle of his arm, she looked up at her mother. "Where's my red nose?"

"In the bag." Mellie patted Mr. Johnson's shoulder. "You're looking a hundred percent better than when I saw you."

"Feel that much better too. They're saying I could go home if I had someone there, but since I don't, I'm going to have to go to a convalescent home for a few days."

"You could stay with us."

"Thank you, but you have too much to handle right now as it is. It'll only be for a few days."

"Where?"

"Down here, I guess."

"But if you come home, I can come and see you." Lissa tipped her head so she could look up at his face.

"You sweetie." He hugged her and smiled up at Mellie. "I'll have to take it easy for a while, is all. Bet the weeds have been growing in the garden."

"Mommy, who's taking care of Kitty?"

"Mrs. Robins."

"Oh." Lissa looked over to Katheryn. "Do you have a kitty?"

"No, I have a dog named Lucky."

Back to her mother. "Are we going home now? Daddy might be there."

Mellie exchanged a long look with Mr. Johnson. Tears filled both their eyes.

"Come on, Lissa, I have something really funny to show you at the shelter."

Lissa kissed Mr. Johnson's cheek when he bent to hug her goodbye. "You come home soon."

"I will."

She turned and waved one more time as they walked out the door.

"What kind of s'prise?"

"You have to wait and see."

How long do I stay? Wouldn't I hear just as fast at home? No, I need to be here. I don't want to go home. The empty house? Kevin will be there. My children need me too. I have to call Mother. Oh, Lord, this is beyond me. Mellie says she can't manage, and I give her platitudes. I hate platitudes. The thoughts raged like flotsam on the swollen rivers.

They were just about to the shelter when Katheryn said, "If you can wait until tomorrow, I can give you a ride home."

"Are you sure? I mean you haven't heard…"

"I know. But you need to be in Seattle on Friday, right?"

"Yes."

"We could swing by your place and get what you need, then you can spend the night at my house. I'm not really far from Fred Hutchinson."

"You are so kind." Mellie laid a hand on Katheryn's arm. "Thank you."

"Where's my s'prise?" Lissa asked when they walked through the door to the school.

"Over there." Katheryn pointed to a bird stand, where Adolf preened his wing feathers, running his beak from the base of each primary feather, clear to the tip, then to the next one.

Adolf stopped, shook himself, cocked his head. "Hey, gimme a kiss."

Lissa looked from the parrot to Katheryn. "It talks."

"You cute thing, gimme a kiss."

"Can I see him?"

"Sure." Together they walked over to the bird on the stand. "Hi, Attie. I'd like you to meet my friends. This is Lissa, and Mellie Sedor."

"You can call me Aunt Attie. You want to pet Adolf?"

Lissa's eyes rounded even larger. "Can I?"

"I'll hold him. He likes to be petted under his wing. I'll show you."

Katheryn glanced at Mellie. Fear rode her like an apparition. White of face, body stiff. What is she afraid of? Of course, she'd heard how parrots can bite. But Attie wouldn't invite them like this if Adolf were a biter.

"He's so pretty, so red." Lissa stroked the bird under the raised wing like Attie showed her.

Katheryn moved closer to Mellie and slipped an arm around her shoulders. "She's a brave little girl."

"I know, it's me, I..." Her voice came in spurts, as if breathing was a major accomplishment. "Harv always taught her to try anything, not be afraid like her mother."

Katheryn leaned closer to Mellie. "Last night he greeted me with a string of profanities, then yelled, 'Gimme a kiss,' and I had no idea where it was coming from. Let me tell you, that was a shocker."

Mellie smiled, a faint smile, but real nevertheless. Her breathing had calmed.

"You have panic attacks often?"

"Uh-huh. I can sometimes fight them off, but the last few days..."

"Anyone would suffer from a panic attack after all you've been through."

The door opened, and at the sound, Adolf straightened, saw the entering figure, and wolf whistled.

Lissa stopped petting him, froze for a second, then giggled. "Jenn is here."

"Ms. Stockton," Mellie corrected her.

"She said Jenn. She likes that better."

"Hey, sweetie, who's your new friend?"

"This is Adolf and Aunt Attie. He talks."

"Gimme a kiss," the parrot murmured.

"I'm pleased to meet you." Jenn smiled at the older woman, then squatted down beside Lissa. "Does he really give kisses, or is he all hot air?"

"Give me a kiss, Adolf." Attie leaned toward the bird and was rewarded by a nibble on her lip.

If Lissa's eyes had rounded before, they saucered now.

"Now, that's a picture you need," Katheryn said with a chuckle as Jenn took her camera out of the pack.

"Will he mind a flash?"

"Oh no, he's all ham."

Katheryn watched as Jenn went into photographer mode. Lissa and the bird could well have been the stars in a well-rehearsed act. Aunt Attie played the straight man.

When Jenn recapped her camera, Lissa leaned against Aunt Hattie's arm, one finger stroking down the bird's back. "I like Adolf."

"He likes you too."

Lissa turned. "Mommy, can we go home now?"

"How about we go sit on a cot and I'll read to you?" Jenn took her hand. "Oh, here." She dug in her backpack. "I found us some paper dolls."

Mellie and Katheryn watched the two walk off. "I'm going to go help back in the office for a while. Perhaps there is someone there who can answer some of your questions."

"Okay."

Hearing a spate of giggles behind them, they turned to see a hobo clown stroll through the door, a bundle of long skinny balloons under his arm. He drew children like a Pied Piper and began making animals and hats from his stash of blown balloons.

"People are so good." Mellie sighed. "I'm trying to be grateful like Harv always said, but…"

But right now, gratitude is in low supply. Katheryn murmured some kind of assent and approached the woman she'd helped before.

"Is there someone who can answer questions for my friend here?"

"A social worker arrived an hour or so ago. Let me introduce you." She performed the introduction, and Mellie followed the older woman into another office.

"How's her little girl?"

"Better, she had a transfusion last night. They found her husband's body yesterday morning."

"Ah, the poor thing. But better to know, I think. What about you?"

"Nothing. Or rather, they found our car. That blue bug roosting in a huge tree was ours. But no sign of"—she fought the closing of her throat and took in a much needed breath—"my husband and our son."

"I'm sorry."

"Thanks. I need to keep busy. I've decided to go home tomorrow if I don't hear anything today. Mellie needs a ride, and…"

"And taking care of someone else is easier than being alone."

"Right."

"I have some typing you can do."

"That will be fine."

Some time later Jenn ambled into the office. "I was looking for you. Wondered if I could take you and Mellie and Lissa out for early dinner tonight?"

"Fine with me. Where's Lissa?"

"Out with the other kids and the clown."

"She needs some laughter."

"True. Thanks for putting me on to the photo ops here. What a character, that Adolf. And Attie, too."

"There's a family here with two live-wire kids and their gerbils." She went on to describe the panic scene of the morning. "People seem to be helping each other."

"Yes, human beings can be real good in a crisis. Shame we need crisis to bring us together."

"Right." Katheryn rolled another form into her typewriter. "I should be writing, but there's nothing there. This helps."

"Speaking of help, Mellie said you were giving her a ride home tomorrow."

"Uh-huh. She could use a hand right about now."

"You know much about the bone marrow transplant she talks about?"

"No, but if it will help that little darling, I'm all for it."

"I'd better get going; see you tonight. I'll figure out a place and swing by here about four thirty. You tell Mellie, okay?"

That night after dinner at a local diner, where they began sharing their life stories, the three women returned to the shelter to keep on talking. They talked of childhoods, and, for the first time in her life, Mellie told someone other than Harv how bad things had been. Talk of dating and marriage, schooling and careers brought Jenn to admit to the debauchery to which she had succumbed. Katheryn confessed her frustrations at David's depression and the anger she kept within but recognized that it would need to be lanced someday. They put Lissa to bed and talked on, ignoring the people and goings-on around them.

"I think they're trying to tell us something." Jenn motioned toward the dimming lights.

Mellie looked from one of her new friends to the other. "I don't ever talk to anyone like this."

Katheryn put an arm around her. "Me either."

Jenn shook her head. "Me three. As my mother would say, God got us together for a reason."

"Thank you." Mellie reached out, took one hand of each of the others, and squeezed. "I can't believe…I mean, tonight, I…" She shook her head. "I don't know what to say."

"I'd say you are stuck with two new friends."

"But I…" Her voice dropped to a whisper. "I don't have friends, not like this."

"You do now."

"We adopted you." Katheryn squeezed Mellie's hand again. "That makes us family."

"I never had sisters." Jenn got to her feet. "Only a brother, and he died in Vietnam. Call me and let me know what's happening."

Mellie and Katheryn both nodded.

"After all, the kiddo and I have lots of paper dolls to cut out."

Mellie sniffed. "Thanks." Such a meager word for all they'd done. Now to get through the night.

God help me.

44

The Mountain

She once wooed them with her beauty, her glaciers so deep, the lakes of blue, teeming with fish, bordered by trees, green and tall, a playground for all. And now her friends came seeking their dead, trudging over ash and rock and burning pits beneath her surface. Like a victim of war, she lay spent and exhausted, trails of smoke rising like signals of despair. Was she to blame for the carnage even as she called out to the Creator, wondering why she was to endure this rupture, why she had to give birth to such blight?

45

Jenn and Frank

May 22, 1980

But, Frank, I have to do something to help."

"Taking pictures isn't enough?"

"No. Yes, but…"

"Okay, I'm taking some men out to check on their farms. Come on along."

Jenn slung her backpack up in the Blazer before Sig's hindquarters cleared the seat. She glanced back to see him wag the tip of his tail, tongue lolling without a hint of sneer. "Morning, Sig." She slammed her door shut and buckled the seat belt.

The farther they traveled into a gray no man's land, the more Jenn slumped in her seat. She used to ride her bike along this road, back before it had been widened. They had driven to Spirit Lake for picnics and for fishing in the spring.

The Blazer plowed through areas of gritty mud covering the road, then speeded up when the way was clear again. Jenn couldn't believe her eyes. The lush, green Toutle Valley was a solid sea of gray mud. Farms had disappeared; only hillside houses remained. The rest were buried. The few trees that hadn't been swept away looked like squatty bushes dotting the moonscape.

Several army trucks and local pickups nearly blocked the road as the Blazer topped the next hill.

"I thought we were to be the first out here." Frank braked the Blazer. He rolled down his window. "What's going on?"

A mud-covered man in drab green answered. "Animals caught in the mudflow. We're dragging them out."

Jenn jumped from the vehicle as Frank parked behind the others, her camera at the ready.

Ahead, three men worked over a bedraggled steer on the ground. Two cows stood spraddle-legged, heads hanging. Mud still dripped off their steaming bodies.

"Not sure about this one," one of them men said. "She was in pretty deep." He felt the cow's ribs and legs. "Can't feel anything broken on this side."

"Can we leave her alone for a while?" someone asked.

"No, better roll her up. She'll get pneumonia lying like that, if she hasn't already."

The men struggled with the cow. One pulled on her head while Frank and an old farmer tucked her legs under her. A teen boy knelt by her back, push-lifting and talking the cow into a response. Slowly, the cow rolled up to rest on her folded legs. She coughed, then dropped her chin to the ground.

"Better put her out of her misery."

The boy braced the cow with his knees against her back to keep her upright. "Give her some more time, please?" The cow coughed and shook her head.

"She's looking better." Jenn capped her lens.

"Let's get her up, now or never." One of the guardsmen slapped the cow on the rump.

The boy bounced his knees into her back. "Come on, do it." His voice broke on the words.

The cow shook her head resentfully and tried to lie back, but the boy's knees prevented her from rolling flat.

"Come on, you can make it." Jenn grabbed the halter rope someone had snapped in place.

The cow's chin balanced on the ground, her rump rising as her hind feet struggled for footing. The men braced her on both sides as she straightened her front legs and finally stood, head hanging, panting.

Crack! A rifle shot echoed across the valley. Jenn's heart leaped like a deer during hunting season. "What are they doing?"

"An animal was still alive but too far gone to pull out," one of the soldiers answered. "Can't leave 'em to suffer, so..."

Nausea churned in Jenn's throat. Shooting animals that had been through so much seemed cruel beyond measure, and yet she knew it was for the best.

Frank's warm hand clapped on her shoulder. "Can't be helped."

"I know."

One of the guardsmen pulled a bale of hay from the back of a truck and broke it open in front of the weary cows. Another set out a small water trough and filled it from the steel storage tank in the back of the truck. One of the cows drank immediately.

Jenn got a photo of that and followed Frank back to the truck. Mud reached halfway to her knees. "I'd not thought about the farmers losing their livestock like this."

"There's all kinds of loss no one thinks about until after."

Led by the Blazer, the caravan of rescue vehicles ground over the next hill. At the edge of the gray-mud wash, the blacktop disappeared. On the far side, the road picked up and meandered over the next hill. The mud looked like a dense fog had drifted back across the holler. Even in four-wheel drive, the wheels slithered and spun, unable to keep their traction.

Frank rocked the vehicle back and forth, reversed, and backed out onto the solid road. "We're going to have to backtrack to a logging road. Can't drive through that yet."

One by one the trucks turned in the narrow road and followed the Blazer about a quarter mile back to where a log barred the way on a turnoff. Two guardsmen jumped from their canvas-covered truck and rolled the log off to one side. Jenn waved their thanks as Frank shifted back into four-wheel drive and bumped up the hill.

Frank clicked on his CB. "Any news on that sediment dam at the lake?"

"Still holding, but the water's getting deeper with all this runoff. You'd better be ready to get out of there quick."

"Thanks, Maybelle. What would I do without you warning me?"

"Keep a zip on that lip, Sheriff." The last was said with her traditional emphasis. "Or I'll let the river have at you."

Frank snorted. "Over and out."

Back on the main road, the caravan topped another hill.

"Well, will you look at that?" Jenn grinned at Frank, who smiled back. White-faced cows and calves grazed calmly on the grass along the road. "Some kept ahead of it all."

"But look out farther."

Jenn saw the trapped cows but focused her camera on the barn roof that sat on the surface of the mud as if floating. The red door to the haymow was only a foot or two above the gray. She swiftly changed lenses, took her picture, then followed the men out to the cows.

A hungry calf trotted back and forth at the mud's edge, crying for his trapped mother. The cow mooed in a frenzy, frantic because she could move only her head.

Slowly, the rescuers slogged across the mud to the trapped cows. Using small army shovels, they dug carefully around the nearest animal. With mud up only to her belly, it didn't take long to dig a trench to free her legs. One of the men slipped a halter on the cow's head, and while he pulled, another pushed from behind. With a bellow, the cow lurched forward into freedom. She slipped and fell to her knees, but between the man on the halter and another behind, all of them slipping and nearly falling, they got her to the edge and to her hungry calf.

The last cow lay farther out, only her head and upper back visible. She barely flicked her ears when they approached her. The men dug down on both sides of her and tunneled behind her front legs, freeing a space to thread sling and ropes. They did the same in front of the rear legs, everyone by now resembling "abominable mudmen."

"She's a heavy one," one of the diggers muttered, wiping sweat and mud from his face. "It's going to take all of us."

"I'll get the halter on her," the boy said as he knelt in the mud to slip a rope around her neck and loop it over her nose for a makeshift halter.

"All together now." The men grabbed the ropes and heaved. Jenn clicked her camera; the cow moaned.

"We can't do this one."

"Please try again." Jenn couldn't keep the words back. What did she know about pulling cows from mud? In all her years in New York, she'd hardly seen any mud.

Frank shook his head. "All together." They strained, the sucking mud slowing releasing its captive. With a mighty heave the cow lay on her side, gasping as full breaths filled her tortured lungs.

"Oh, you poor girl." Jenn, her camera slung out of the way, knelt beside the cow. Rising, she glanced down in the hole to see a patch of red. "What's that?" She turned to Frank and pointed down in the hole that was fast filling with water.

One of the men dug a bit deeper to reveal a calf entombed in the mud.

"Oh, her baby." Jenn fought the tears that threatened, but when she saw the boy's tear-striped face, she turned away and let the tears wash away some of the mud. "I know it's life, but it sure isn't fair."

"No one ever promised fair." Frank turned back to the cow. "Let's drag her across the mud and give her some solid ground to stand on."

By the time they got the cow back on her feet and left hay and water, Jenn felt like she'd been doing as much digging as the men. The stench of mud and death coated her hands and heart. What else would they find in their search for survivors?

Two days later, her pictures of the men dragging the cow across the mud appeared on the cover of the *Portland Oregonian.* Jenn nearly cried again when she saw it.

"Good job," Frank said when he called.

"Thank you. I've sold others. I need to thank you for letting me come along on these rescue operations."

"None needed. At least you have enough sense to stay out of the way."

"Yeah, and I finally got the muck washed out of my hair too. I keep thinking about Harry. You think he had any warning?"

"Yeah, but when he felt the blast, if he wasn't in his tunnel already, there wasn't enough time to get there. And by now, he'd be out of air."

"Thanks, you're such a comfort."

"He'll be a folk hero now. Old man against the mountain."

"And he lost."

"All depends on your point of view."

Jenn found herself thinking of his comment more often than she'd have liked.

46

Mellie and Katheryn

May 22, 1980

Mellie wished she could disappear into the seat of the car.

"We're almost home, Mommy." Lissa turned to look up into her mother's face. "Bunny's happy too."

Mellie glanced over to Katheryn, who turned her head to share an encouraging glance. If she hadn't known better, she could have pretended that Harv had gotten home already and was waiting for them. He would swing Lissa up to sit on his hip and put his other arm around her, so he could squeeze his two girls at the same time. Something he'd done just that way since Lissa was big enough. Before then, he'd held the baby against his shoulder and his wife tucked under his arm.

The grass had grown half a foot since they were gone. She'd never started that lawn mower in her life. Old and cranky, it sputtered to life only through Harv's loving ministrations.

"How will I ever…?" She stopped, the enormity of it all rolling over her like those waves of mud that toppled houses and trees.

"Hurry, Mommy, I have to go potty."

Mellie dug in her bag for the house keys. "I'm coming."

The house smelled lost and unloved. And cold. She reset the thermostat. "Would you like a cup of tea?" Kitty wound around her legs, her plaintive cry an echo of the lonely house.

"Sounds lovely." Katheryn rubbed her hands together. "When did Mr. Johnson say he would be home?"

"Next week. He's always been so good to us."

"He told me it was you and Harv who had been good to him."

Mellie filled the teakettle and set it on the burner. "Just being neighborly. Harv met all the neighbors not long after we moved here. He was always so friendly to everyone." *Not like me. What am I going to do?*

"Your message light is blinking." Katheryn indicated the phone.

Mellie's heart leaped. *Harv. No, never again.* She rubbed her chest with the flat of her shaking hand. She crossed the room to press the Message button. The light blinked four.

The first from Mrs. Robins, a neighbor. The second a hang-up buzz, the third a bill collector—she cringed that Katheryn could hear such a thing—the fourth…

The doctor's office. "If you could be here at three on Thursday, we can work you in."

Mellie's gaze flew to the calendar. Today. And it was already one.

"That at Fred Hutchinson?"

"Yes."

"How quickly can you pack? You can spend the night at my house afterward."

"I'd better call them first and see if the slot is still open." Mellie played the number back and dialed.

She hung up, shaking her head at the same time. "That one was filled, but we already have an appointment scheduled for tomorrow at eleven."

"That's at the Fred Hutchinson Cancer Research Center up behind Swedish Hospital?"

"Yes."

"Let's see, that means I need to pick you up about nine thirty, unless of course you'd like to come home with me now."

"Mrs. Sommers, did you pet Kitty?" Lissa wore the cat draped over her arm like a shawl. Kitty's back feet hung clear down to her knees.

"No, but she sure is pretty." Katheryn stooped down to stroke the purring cat's head. "When you come to my house, you can play with Lucky. She's my dog." And she won't have anyone to play with her anymore. *Stop it. Remember, you promised you wouldn't give up yet. There is still hope.*

Her knees creaked as she stood again. "Mellie?"

"Uh-huh." She looked up from studying the note on the table. A simple note that read, "Nearly out of dried cat food. I cleaned the kitty litter box. If there is anything I can help you with, let me know. I'm going to miss Harv too. He was a fine man. Mrs. R."

"He was a fine man, best thing that ever happened to me."

Katheryn could barely hear her.

"Mommy, when is Daddy coming home?"

The women exchanged a glance, both of them blinking hard.

"How do I…?" Mellie gave Katheryn a pleading look.

I'm no help. How do you tell a child the daddy she adores is no longer coming home?

"I could go get the cat food for you."

Mellie looked as if she could keel right over. "Not now." She laid a hand on Katheryn's arm. "C-could you pray. I've got to tell her." One tear rolled down her cheek as she sniffed back others.

"Okay."

"Mommy?"

Mellie scooped kid and cat up in her arms and headed for the living room, where a dark wooden rocker with floral pads tied in the seat and on the back sat in front of the square picture window. Curtains that might once have been floral to match the pillows hung straight on either side.

Mellie settled them in the chair as she had done thousands of times. When Lissa leaned against her mother's chest, Mellie rested her chin on the top of her daughter's head.

Wishing she could be anywhere else but here, Katheryn perched on the edge of the blue plaid couch, resting her elbows on her knees, hands clasped in an attitude of prayer. Would God hear her prayer when she had to force her words heavenward? *Father, please make this possible for Mellie. Make it easy.* How could a task like the one before them ever be easy?

"Lissa, remember how Daddy said that when we die we go home to live with Jesus?

"Uh-huh. He said Jesus loves us."

"Daddy went to be with Jesus."

"Really?" A smile lighted her pale face. "When is he coming back?"

"He won't be coming back."

"But I want to see my daddy."

"I know. Me too."

"Can I go see him?"

"Someday, but not real soon."

"Oh. I think Jesus was glad to see my daddy."

"And he was glad to see Jesus."

"Yeah."

Katheryn slumped against the back of couch; sitting erect took more backbone than she had at the moment. She watched the two fair heads, hair so fine, the sun turned it to white gold, blue crescents under their now closed eyes.

The creak of the rocker and the purr of the cat, a child laughing on the sidewalk outside, all parts of peace for the moment. Was this His answer to her prayer?

Did Lissa understand?

Do I understand? Katheryn pushed herself to her feet. When Mellie's eyes fluttered open, Katheryn whispered, "I'm going for the cat food. Anything else you need?"

"Milk."

"I'll be right back. You decide if you want to come now or tomorrow."

"Tomorrow, but that's such a big bother."

"No, I'll be here." *Anything will be better than being at home.* The thought ran through her like an electric shock.

47

Jenn

May 22, 1980

Jenn, your agent called, said it was imperative that you call him back today."

Jenn stared at the black public wall phone. "Thanks, Mom."

"He sounded really upset."

I'm sure he did. Herman Edelmeir was most likely frothing at the mouth. She'd told him she'd be gone two weeks, and here it was already three. And she hadn't called him with her change of plans.

Not that she had any plans, just living day to day. But at least she was living, feeling, thinking. She was alive again.

"Jenn?"

"I'm here, Mom. I'll call him right now."

"Good, and Frank left a message too, said to call him at the office."

Jenn hung up the phone and glanced at her watch. Two. That made it five in New York, but good old Herman would still be in his office. Sometimes she was sure he lived there.

She dialed, wishing she were anywhere but with a receiver against her ear, waiting to get an earful. He could make a two-ton bomb appear insignificant when he really got going.

"Hi, Nancy, don't you ever go home either?"

"Hi, yourself. God's been trying to get ahold of you."

"I heard."

"Where in the world are you?"

I'm in the real world, that's where. "Out here in Washington State, where the mountain erupted." She knew that to New Yorkers, all areas west of the Hudson and particularly west of the Mississippi could as well have been frontier.

"Oh, that. You came from out there, didn't you?"

"Yes, I'm staying with my folks."

"Oh, well, I'll put you through. Be prepared."

"Thanks." *Not really, why don't I just hang up, call him back—in about a year?*

"Where in the...?"

His tirade blistered her ear. She rolled her eyes and held the receiver a few inches from her head.

"Are you finished now?"

"No, not by a long shot. I understood when you said you needed a bit of time off, and I made excuses for you, but a bit of time does not extend to three weeks. With no word in between."

"I'm sorry."

"Magazines have deadlines, you know, and you have missed one now and another by next week."

"I'm sorry."

He rode on without even acknowledging her apology. "If you don't get your skinny—"

"Herman! That's enough! My rear wouldn't be so skinny if you'd let up on the pressure. And if all you are going to do is yell at me, I'll hang up right now."

His silence soothed her ear. Good, let him be shocked. She'd never before yelled back at him, just gone along with the schedule he set, one that kept him in Courvoisier and Ferragamos, dinners at Four Seasons, and tickets to first-run box seats. And nearly killed her.

"You're not going to go *prima donna* on me, are you?"

No, I'm just trying to stay alive. And away from all that life that was killing me. She thought of the hangovers and uppers and downers, the nights and the rotten mornings, the guilt and the gore.

"So, when are you coming back?"

Like one of the lightning strikes that flamed trees up on the mountain, it hit her. *I'm not going back.*

"You have"—she could hear the rustling, knew he was flipping calendar pages—"a shoot for *Cosmo* next Tuesday, they've already rescheduled it once for you, the catalog for Neimans and the location for *Vogue* in St. Thomas. And that's the critical list. You want more?"

Jenn wished she'd just told him she quit when she asked for time off. Then they could have gotten another photographer. Now they'd be strapped. *Do I still care about my reputation or not?*

"Okay, here's what I propose. Ask *Cosmo* to start on Wednesday instead of Tuesday."

"What do you have that is so almighty important there that you—"

"Wednesday, Herman. And don't just pretend, push. You're good at that."

His muttering made her smile, though not a friendly action, more a triumphant one.

"That should give me two or three days to get to St. Thomas."

"That's taking the chance that all goes well. You're not leaving yourself any safety net here."

"So be it." She straightened her spine and squared her shoulders. "And anything else you have for me on your books, cancel them."

His roar could be heard clear across the street. Someone walking by turned and looked to see what was happening.

"Herman. Herman. Just do it. We'll talk later." She hung the receiver back in the cradle.

Thursday, and all she had left was five days, if she could get a red-eye out on Tuesday night. Five days. And she hadn't flown up to the mountain again. Was there any way possible? She climbed in her pickup and stared at the racing gray clouds above. Not since the day of the eruption had there been sufficiently clear weather to see the mountain anyway. Forest Service and rescue planes and choppers were all that were flying.

She ducked back out of her truck to the phone booth, address book with phone numbers in her hand. The man at Pearson Airpark barked a laugh when she told him she wanted a plane complete with pilot. "Lady, they might take the president himself up, but not you, nor me. Sorry."

Swallowing her pride, she dialed the number Mitch Ross had given her.

"Sorry, but he's out of the office. May I give him a message for you?"

"Tell him J.E. Stockton called regarding an upcoming flight."

"And your number?"

She gave her parents' number and hung up again. Three strikes and you're out.

She dialed the sheriff's number, and after a brief chat with Maybelle, Frank came on the line.

"Things have settled down enough, so I could come for dinner tonight."

She groaned. "Mom has a thing at church, and I've got an appointment."

"Hot date?"

"Get a life, Frank. If you call photographing the dinner hour at the Toledo shelter a hot date."

Should I tell him I'm leaving again? Why? What difference does it make to him? One less body for him to worry about.

"Tomorrow night?"

"I'll check and leave a message with Maybelle."

"Good."

The phone clicked in her ear. Frank never had been one for the niceties. How many years had it taken her to get over that schoolgirl crush she'd had on that older man? Six years back then made a lot of difference. And when he'd married, she'd put away girlish dreams, gone to the wedding with a smile on her face, and soaked her pillow that night. As soon as she graduated she headed for New York, sure that a modeling career awaited her. Frank had been the first to realize how the camera loved her. He'd been the first to tease the beanpole that she'd make a great model—and laughed at her gawkiness.

Well, the last laugh had been on him. The celebrated face of the '70s. Jennifer Stockton. She'd even made *Time* magazine due to her astute asset management that turned her into a household word and her investments into a portfolio, the envy of stockbrokers wherever she went.

But no amount of money would buy her a ticket to circle the mountain, to drop her off on one of the ridges so she could personally see the destruction through the eye of her best friend.

If the truck were her own, she'd put a CB or police radio in it.

What would life be like if she dumped her fashion photographer career? Closed out her apartment, left New York for ever? Could she make a living as a photojournalist? Freelance photographer? Did she need to worry about making a living? Instead, let her money make money. Would she be sorry, look back with regret if she lost her place, her edge in the world? After all, any number of photographers were ready and willing, nay, willing to kill to take her place.

She shifted into reverse and looked over her shoulder for traffic. As if this were really traffic. She never even drove in New York. Rented a car when she needed one.

God only knows, she quoted her mother. One of these days she might have to decide if God even cared. These last days made her wonder.

Thinking of God led her to Jesus, which led her to Lissa. *Wonder if her mother has told her yet.*

She dropped by the camera shop to pick up the rolls she'd taken in to have developed, and she bagged up six more.

"I've got those reprints ready for you too," the man behind the counter said.

"Good." She took the packet he offered, paid, and headed back out to the truck to drive up I-5 to Toledo.

After shooting another couple of rolls, laughing at the antics of a stand-up comedian who arrived to entertain those housed at the shelter, and listening as a woman storyteller enthralled her audience of all ages, she drove on home.

Time to call Mellie and Lissa.

"I don't know," Mellie said in response to her greeting. "I learned we won't get Harv's body back for days, perhaps weeks. I talked with our pastor about the funeral, and that's what he found out. I feel like I'm wandering in a fog, and when someone calls me, they disappear before I can find them."

"Your appointment is tomorrow?"

"Yes."

"Do you need a ride?"

"No, Katheryn is going to come get us."

"Good. You'll let me know what you find out?"

"Yes. If you want."

"I want. Is Lissa awake?"

"She's right here. You want to talk with her?"

"Yes." Jenn could hear the two of them chatting.

"Hi, Jenn."

"Hi there, Lissa."

"My daddy's in heaven with Jesus."

Jenn caught her breath. Talk about laying it right out there. "I know." *Do I know? Do I believe that?*

"Mommy said he won't come back."

That part I do know. "He loves you."

"I know." A small silence. "Jesus does too."

"Yes, He sure does."

"Do you love Jesus?'

Out of the mouths of babes. *I used to.* No, that wouldn't cut it. "I think so, yes."

" 'Cause He loves you and me and Mommy and Daddy and even Kitty."

The old tune tinkled in her head. *Jesus loves me this I know, for the Bible tells me so.* "Was your kitty glad to see you?" *Little ones to him belong.*

"Can you hear her purring?"

They are weak but He is strong. For when you are weak, then I am strong. "Yes. She has a good motor."

"I go to the doctor tomorrow, and then I get to see Lucky."

"Who is Lucky?" Never had she enjoyed a conversation more, in spite of the voices singing in her head.

"Mrs. Sommers's dog. Do you like dogs?"

"I sure do. Let me talk to your mommy again, okay?"

"Bye, Jenn. When we going to cut out more paper dolls?"

"When I come see you."

"When?"

"I don't know. Let me talk to your mommy now."

"Bye."

"Bye, Lissa." *Oh, God, if you can hear me, please keep her safe.*

"Call me, okay?"

"I will."

Jenn took a breath and exhaled a decision. "I have to go back to New York Tuesday night. Can I come up and see you before then?"

"Oh, please do."

"I'll let you know when tomorrow."

"Thanks for calling."

They hung up, and Jenn flopped back on the sofa. She'd bring the photo of Lissa and Adolf. That would make her laugh. Lissa had the most carefree laugh she'd ever heard. When she felt better. But what lay ahead? What could she do to help bring smiles to that precious little face?

48

KATHERYN

MAY 23, 1980

Snarled in traffic, Katheryn drummed the heel of her hand on the steering wheel. She should have left earlier—or later.

Seattle traffic was getting worse each year. Usually, she managed to avoid it by doing her errands earlier in the day, one of the joys of a stay-at-home writer. Not that the writer had gotten much done lately. Her deadline loomed closer by the day. She counted the weeks to D-day. Less than six.

David, you won't be here to read my draft. The thought smote her chest like one of those hot rocks tossed out by the mountain. He'd always read for her, making helpful comments, cheering her on and helping her improve. Three books published and a bunch of short stories and articles in children's magazines. Giving her the space to do something she'd always dreamed of—until this last book. He'd been too down to be much help. Would the quality of the book suffer because of that?

What if I can't write anymore? What will I do? Besides be a grandma, that is.

The baby will never have a grandpa. A spurt of tears blurred the rear end of the car in front of her.

"Stop this! Stop it right now. You are acting like there is no hope. You have to keep hoping." Talking aloud didn't help a lot when she had to sniff after every other word or so. She dug in her purse for a tissue and blew her nose, mopped her eyes.

Think of Mellie. She knows her husband isn't coming back. And with her darling little one so sick. How will she cope?

Lissa. *God, help that poor baby.*

Kevin and Susan, so strong and capable. But no Brian. The tears brought on sobs, sobs turned to howls, and she finally pulled over to keep from having an accident. She locked her hands around her shoulders and rocked in her grief. *Brian, my Brian, child of my heart, I am torn apart. Oh, God, Brian. This child late in life, such an unexpected gift. His smile, his sensitive heart, all the good pieces of both his father and me.*

Her howls abated, and she let her forehead rest on her clenched fists on the top of the steering wheel. Howls to sobs to sniffs and mopping up again. Momentarily drained of tears, she put the car back in gear, flicked on her turn signal, and watched for a chance to get back in the steady stream of traffic.

Nothing. No one backed off to allow her entrance. Shouting a stream of profanities at the faceless drivers, she finally gunned it and merged, causing the car behind her to brake and honk. She thought of flipping him or her the bird, but already remorse for the language she'd used made her want to duck her head.

Lucky's barking greeted her as she opened the door from the garage. Dancing feet, a whirling tail, happy yips and whimpers.

"There's a good girl, oh, you sweetheart." She leaned down to get doggy kisses and rub the liver-colored ears. When properly greeted, Lucky went past Katheryn and checked the garage for Brian, as she always did.

"He's not coming home, dog, sorry." Katheryn fought the tears again, but she had as little control over them as before. With rivers streaming down her face, she dug a dog biscuit out of the canister and gave it to the dog.

"Where is Kevin?" She retrieved a couple of tissues from the square box by the telephone and wiped eyes, nose, and cheeks again.

The house, wearing that forlorn smell of no one home, felt cold and empty.

After guzzling a glass of water, she checked for messages. On the bulletin board she found one from Kevin.

"Gone to work. Be back around six. Call your mother!" Your mother, not grandma. He must have fielded more than his quota of calls. Katheryn glanced at the clock, five thirty. Eight thirty in Florida, couldn't use time for an excuse. She shrugged off a deep breath and picked up the phone. Like a lifetime ago, last Sunday she'd been deciding what good things to make for a homecoming dinner. Rejoicing in the number of pages written, hoping The Lady had worked her miracles on David's heart. More than a lifetime ago.

With each number dialed she almost hung up the phone, but when her mother came on the line, it was all she could do to not burst out in tears.

"Have you heard anything?"

"No. There's no sign, but if they camped where we usually went, that was right in the blast zone."

"I'll never understand why he went up there like that."

"How are things with you?" Katheryn needed to change the subject. Why did she already feel like yelling at her mother?

"And to take Brian too."

Katheryn's thought exactly, but what good did it do to dwell on that?

"Did he ever take any medications for that depression?"

"Mother, can we talk about something else?"

"Well." Huffy came across the wires.

"When I know something, I will tell you. There have been no survivors since Tuesday." Just speaking the words made her sink down on the desk chair. No survivors.

The count was fourteen dead and ninety missing. So many others in the same position as she. Not knowing.

She half listened as her mother rattled on, making appropriate comments; at least she hoped they were appropriate.

Lucky leaned against her knee, brown eyes watching her every move.

When Katheryn could finally insert a reasonable goodbye, she did so and, with a sigh of relief, hung up the phone. She'd wait a few minutes to regain some semblance of sanity before calling her father-in-law. This was his son who was missing—and his favorite grandson. Brian and his grandfather had fished many a local river and taken the boat out in the Sound, Puget Sound, where they'd seen killer whales, harbor seals, sailboarders, Jet Skis, Wave Runners, and all manner of boats to seagoing ships and ferries that plied the routes between Bremerton, Bainbridge Island, Vashon Island, and Seattle, along with points north. Puget Sound with all its harbors, bays and fingerlings, islands and inflowing rivers. How would the old man handle the loss of two of his favorite people in the entire world?

How could she talk to him? What could she say?

The phone rang again before she picked up the receiver to dial. Hope leaped in her heart.

"Hello?"

"Any word?"

"No, Dad, I would have called you if I knew anything."

"They were right in the blast zone."

"I know."

"I introduced him to that area years ago. We loved it up there." His voice broke. "I looked at the maps."

"They might have gone somewhere else."

"No." The sadness pulsed over the wire. "I know my son. That was his thinking place, and he loved fishing that creek. We always caught fish there."

"Kevin told you that our bug was roosting in a huge tree?"

"Yep. Saw it in a newspaper."

Katheryn heard Kevin come to the front door. Lucky's toenails clicked on the hardwood floor as she went to greet him. Her joyful bark brought a sting to Katheryn's eyes again.

"How are you doing, dear?"

"Not too good. It's easier being down there than here."

"Is there anything I can do for you?"

"It should be me asking you that."

"Why? All I know is, God willing, we'll get through this. The valley of the shadow, I've walked it a couple of times now, but not for my son."

"I love you."

"Yeah, good thing we have each other. How are Susan and Kevin?"

"Kevin's right here. You want to talk with him?"

"Later. Call me when you can."

"I will. Bye."

Kevin's arms came around her waist as she stood to hang up the phone. She leaned against his strength and reached up with one hand to pat his cheek.

"Susan's on her way over."

"Okay." How could she comfort her children when she had no comfort herself?

"Pastor Steve called."

"I should call him."

"He asked what he could do."

How should I know? He needs to tell me what we do. "I don't know."

"What do we do?"

"Wait, I guess." Hope. For what? Bodies? Some piece that will say they are indeed gone? God, not like that awful time at the morgue. I don't want to do that again. Not ever.

"Have you eaten? Can I fix you a cup of tea?" She could hear herself in his voice. Do something, fix something, food and tea could make most anything right. Except for this. Nothing could make it right.

"Mom!" Susan burst through the front door.

"In the kitchen."

Kevin patted their backs as the two women cried together, locked in each other's arms. When the storm had passed, Susan confessed, "I am so mad at him I could…" She shook her head. "I mean, this, this was so unnecessary." She spit out the last word.

Katheryn shrugged, blowing her nose, now gone raw from all the wiping. "Don't. Please don't."

"I'm sorry." She hugged her mother again. "I'm so glad you are home."

Kevin set three mugs of tea on the table. "Sugar, honey? Milk?"

"Please."

The three added what they wanted and sat stirring the steaming liquid, the clink of spoons against pottery taking the place of words that no one could utter.

"So, what do we do?" Kevin broke the nonsilence.

"If you mean me, tomorrow I am going to pick up Mellie and her daughter in Tacoma and bring them up to Fred Hutchinson, then take them home again." That should use up a good part of the day.

"But what if someone calls?" Kevin asked.

"The machine will pick it up, and I'll call back when I can."

"You don't think there's much chance, do you?" Susan failed to disguise an accusation, if she'd tried. No matter what one's training, it all fled when one's own family was involved.

Katheryn understood. But right now she didn't need her own daughter making her feel worse.

"Susan." Kevin glared at her.

Katheryn tipped her head back, trying to ease the knots at the base of her skull. "I am trying my best to keep hope alive."

Lucky whined at her knee. "Kevin, would you please let her out?"

Susan clasped her hands around her tea mug. "I'm sorry." She tossed her hair back with a flick of her head. "It's just that...that you never think these things can happen to your own family."

"Ann Wholly called me and said Professor Williamson had turned down the appointment. Your dad would have been offered the deanship." Katheryn shook her head, ever so gently. "If he'd only known."

"You think it would have made a difference?"

"Perhaps. Who knows." She pushed the mug away. "If you two don't mind, I'm going to go take a shower, two sleeping pills, and go to bed."

Susan stood and kissed her mother's cheek. "I'm going home, then, and I'll talk with you tomorrow."

"You want me to stay?" Kevin asked.

"That's up to you." Katheryn dropped a kiss on the top of his head. "I'm too tired to make any kind of decisions tonight."

After her shower, she glanced at the bed she'd shared with David these thirty-two years. When tears blurred the room, she went down the hall and crawled into the guest bed.

Lissa's doctor appointment the next morning went about as expected. Katheryn waited for them in the waiting room until a nurse came to the door and called her.

"I think she needs some moral support," she said, leading her to another room. "As if this wasn't bad enough."

"Yes, is there anything I should know?"

"Dr. Thomas is the best in this new field. She's lucky to have him."

After the introductions, Katheryn took the chair indicated and located a small notebook in her purse. Long years earlier she'd learned the wisdom of taking notes in a doctor consultation.

"I've been explaining our procedures to Mrs. Sedor, and I have some brochures, too, for any questions that come up. While we have approved Lissa for the procedure, the sad news is that we have a waiting list for at least sixty days. I have taken the liberty of adding her into that slot, but if you decide to try something else, you need to let me know."

"What else is there?" Mellie looked from the child sleeping in her arms to the man behind the desk.

"I know. We'll do all we can to work with your local doctor in keeping her as healthy as possible. I just wish we had more units."

"So, is there anything else Mellie needs to do?"

"My nurse will give you the stack of forms to be filled out. You'll need to make copies of your insurance policies. Your doctor has already sent all of his files. You need to be prepared to come any time, since if there is an unexpected opening, we will call you. If you are not available, we will go to the next one on the list."

"I see." Mellie seemed to shrink further within herself at each word. Once they were out of the office, Katheryn reached for Lissa. "How about I carry you? Give your mommy a rest."

"'Kay. I don't like hospitals."

"This one is going to make you all better."

"Good." Lissa tucked her arms into her chest and snuggled against Katheryn's shoulder.

"How about some lunch?" Katheryn asked as they exited the parking lot.

"Please, could we just go home?" Mellie climbed into the car, and Katheryn placed Lissa on her lap.

"Sure. You have some soup or something I can fix there?"

"I think so." Mellie let her head fall against the seat back. Her sigh said more than words.

"Do you know where all your insurance papers are?"

"Harv keeps them in a brown accordion folder. I don't understand what half of it all means."

"I could help you with that if you like."

"Would you?" A silence lasted for several miles.

Katheryn thought both her passengers had fallen asleep until finally Mellie said, "I can't thank you enough."

"That's okay. Helping you takes my mind off things."

"Any word?"

"No."

"How's your story coming?"

Katheryn shook her head.

"But at dinner you said you have a deadline."

"I can't seem to concentrate." *Not that I've tried a whole lot.*

"Wish I could help you."

"You are."

Back at Mellie's house, Mellie showed Katheryn where the files were and went into the kitchen to make lunch. Katheryn pulled out the file and sat down on the chair in front of a card table that Mellie had called their desk. Feeling slightly like a Peeping Tom, she pulled the envelopes out of the slot marked INSURANCE and lined them up before her. One by one she removed the papers from the envelopes and, starting with the Teamsters papers, glanced over the paragraphs and columns of numbers.

Yes, the health insurance was in force with a maximum of a million dollars. With a sigh of relief, she set that one aside to take to a copy machine. She went through two that were out of date, then put them back in their envelopes and back in the file.

"How are you doing?" Mellie stood in the door with a plate and cup. "I can put this here for you. Only tomato soup and a grilled-cheese sandwich."

"Sounds good." Katheryn cleared a place for the plate. "You already eaten?"

"I fed Lissa. She was too tired to feed herself."

"And you?"

Mellie shrugged. "Not too hungry."

"Is she sleeping?"

"Um." And a nod. Mellie had her arms crossed over her middle, as if keeping herself either warm or together.

"I'm not too hungry either. Sit here and share my sandwich." Katheryn adopted her sterner mother tone, one she'd perfected through the years.

Mellie sat. And picked up half the sandwich.

"You have more soup?"

"No."

"Fine, get another spoon and share mine."

"I couldn't..." With a slight smile that softened her eyes, Mellie did as told.

Katheryn took a spoon of soup and stared down at the paper in front of her. Was she seeing right? She put down her spoon and held the papers in both hands. A life insurance policy for two hundred fifty thousand dollars, with double indemnity for accidental death. Another policy read the same. Both for Harvey Sedor with Mellie as his beneficiary.

When Mellie sat down, Katheryn pointed to the two policies. "Did you know Harv had this much life insurance?"

"He has a small policy with the Teamsters."

"I haven't read that one yet. What about these?"

"What are they?"

"They each total five hundred thousand dollars."

"No. We couldn't afford anything like that." She picked up the one on top.

"Look here." Katheryn showed her the lines to read.

"When?" Mellie read the dates of issue. "But..."

Katheryn watched confusion race across Mellie's face and then back again. Was there more going on here than she knew?

49

Frank

May 23, 1980

Memorial weekend. Isn't there some way we can cancel it for this year?"

"Don't I wish." Maybelle set another stack of papers on Frank's desk.

"You breed paper in that file cabinet of yours or something?"

"Hey, these you only have to sign. I typed them." She picked up the stack he'd put in her basket.

"Jenn called. Said to remind you that you're having dinner with her family tonight."

"I know. If there is an emergency, let Tanner handle it." He signed the first sheet and flipped it over to make an orderly stack.

"You seen any of her photos?"

"Just the one of the cow. You?"

Maybelle nodded, a slow smile and a lifting of eyebrows showing awe. "She has a gift. That's for certain sure."

"She always took good pictures."

"No, these aren't just good pictures. These tell stories and tug at your heart, and some even give you shivers."

"Come on, Maybelle, aren't you laying it on a bit thick?" He kept on signing, one stack melding into the other.

"Suit yourself. But have you ever accused me of exaggerating?"

Frank stopped his pen and stared at her. "She said anything about going back to New York?"

"Not in my hearin'. But that's where her job is."

"According to you, she could take pictures anywhere."

Maybelle picked up the stack and tapped the edges on the desk to line them up. "Why don't you ask her?"

"Maybe I will." He finished the signing, dropped his pen in the wide shallow drawer in the middle of his desk, and slammed it shut. "That's it for today."

"You mean to tell me you are leaving early?"

He glanced at his watch. "If fifteen minutes can be considered early, then yes. I'll be on my radio, but if anyone less than God himself calls, tell Bridget to notify Brownie."

"He hates that name."

"I know. But deputies got to learn to deal with anything their boss dishes out."

Maybelle snorted and shook her head. "Haven't seen you in this good a mood since—well, since I don't remember when."

Frank just shrugged, snagged his hat off the hall tree, and headed for the back door, where he'd parked so Sig could be in the shade and he could get away without being badgered by the media or stopped with requests for assistance from any of his staff. If he heard "Mac, do you know...?" one more time today, he might copy The Lady and blow his stack.

"Get over, dog." Sig sat full in the driver's seat and smiled at him, tail thumping the leather. His front feet danced, and he whined low in his throat.

"Yes, you big lug, I'm glad to see you too. You need a pit stop?" He motioned for Sig to leave the car and waited while the big dog watered one of the back tires, then leaped back in.

Frank followed the dog in and realized he was whistling "You Light Up My Life" as he slammed the door. *Well, I'll be.* He checked the rearview mirror. Same face. If Tanner really wanted that promotion, he needed more experience. Hmm. He'd even teased Maybelle for a change. No wonder she'd looked a bit shocked.

He ignored the static and chatter on the police band, passing the drive home with thoughts of Jenn's family. Her brother had been a year behind him in high school, and since the two played football on the Kelso team, they'd been good friends, the first friend he'd lost to the war, though not his first brush with death. Mr. and Mrs. Stockton, as he'd called them then, had been stricken with the death of their son. Jenn had come home for the funeral, but by then he was married and the father of toddler. That was the last time he'd seen her.

After a fast shower, he debated leaving Sig at home, then brought him along. From force of habit, most likely, that and the fact that the truck seemed empty without him. Besides, it was time Sig and Jenn got on a petting basis.

"You like her, don't you?" He slapped the dog on the shoulder. Sig leaned toward him, a mute suggestion that he do some earnest scratching rather than playful thumping. Frank complied, again amazed at the now tuneless whistle that covered part of the radio noise.

He stopped the car next to Jenn's pickup and motioned Sig to accompany him. He checked the lay of his collar before ringing the doorbell.

"Well, Frank McKenzie, you are one good sight for sore eyes." Clare reached out to hug him. "And you brought Sig along, how nice. Come in, come in."

Frank removed his hat and held it in one hand while he crossed to shake hands with the man in the recliner. "Good to see you, Norm. No, don't get up. You look too comfortable."

"Been too long, son. I remember when you half lived here at times." He waved Frank toward the leather sofa with an elkhide draped over the back. "Make yourself comfortable."

"Jenn will be down in a moment. Can I get you something to drink?"

"No beer here anymore since that dang fool doctor told me I had to lay off it. Sorry."

At the word *beer,* Frank's salivary glands kicked into running speed. "Coffee will be fine, if you have some."

"Unless you want a Coke or something?" Clare stopped in the doorway to the kitchen.

"Coffee will be fine."

"Hear you've been busier than a one-armed paperhanger." Norm had his dark green recliner part way back and his coffee mug propped on his slight paunch.

"No matter how ready we thought we were, the old girl went beyond predictions. Thought sure she'd go straight up, not lateral like she did. When you think of it, the loss of life has been pretty minimal."

"Darn fools that went up there when they knew better." Norm shook his head. "To think it happened on Sunday when so few loggers were working there."

"Grace of God, if you ask me. He tried to keep as many people away from that mountain as He could." Clare handed Frank a coffee mug that said "over the hill and picking up speed."

Frank smiled at the inscription, hoisted the mug in salute, and took a sip. "Think how much worse it could have been coming out the west side or the south."

"All that timber down. Wonder if any of it will be worth saving?"

"Oh, I imagine some, at least. Just getting to it will be a problem." Frank looked up at the sound of Jenn's steps coming down the hall. "Hi, Frank. Hey, you brought Sig along."

"He asked especially. Said he'd pout if he couldn't come."

"Right." Jenn knelt on the floor. "Hey, boy, remember me?"

Sig sat by Frank's right knee, black-rimmed ears full up, eyes never leaving hers. He glanced over his shoulder at Frank.

"Go on, you can talk to her."

Sig looked back at Jenn, his tail brushing the carpet. When she extended her hand, he leaned forward and sniffed.

"Hey, handsome." Her voice lowered to a purr. "You are one gorgeous dog, you know that?" She sat back on her heels and waited.

"He still good as a tracker?" Clare asked.

"Not as good as a bloodhound, but far smarter. Sometimes I think he figures out the mind of the one he's tracking. Don't care a bit for drug runners, nor users either. Hates drugs."

Slowly Jenn and Sig drew closer together. First she scratched his ears, then rubbed his head. He inched closer so she could reach his neck and shoulder. All the while she murmured sweet talk until he relaxed and leaned into her gentle fingers.

Frank ignored the pang that just might be jealousy if he thought about it.

"Hey, squirt, I hear you've been taking some good pictures."

"Who told you, Maybelle?"

"Uh-huh. You sure got a fan in her."

"Good. I just finished running some more black-and-whites in the darkroom."

"You're doing that again?"

"Why not? Had the entire setup."

He turned to Clare. "You kept it all?"

Clare shrugged. "Just never got around to converting it to a sewing room like I thought I would. Now I'm glad I didn't." She smiled at her daughter.

"You two look more like sisters than mother and daughter."

Jenn and her mother looked at each other.

"So, since you told me I looked close to death…"

"Then I must be looking a whole lot younger than my years."

"I wouldn't go there if I were you, son. You can't win," Norm said.

Frank raised an eyebrow at Jenn. Seems like he'd heard more words out of her father's mouth this evening than he did in all those years ago.

A buzzer went off in the kitchen.

"Dinner's ready."

Jenn rose to her feet from a cross-legged position, as gracefully as if she'd been sitting on a chair. "Is he allowed in the dining room?"

"Not if it bothers anyone. He can stay in here."

"No, that's fine. Old Baldy used to lie right at Jenn's feet, remember? That dog had the best manners." Clare went on into the kitchen.

"She forgets how I used to slip Baldy anything I didn't like."

"Well, don't go slipping Sig anything. He only eats dog food and steak bones."

When they sat down Norm bowed his head, said the grace that Frank remembered all these years later, and looked up to glance around the table. "I'm glad you're both here."

While the rest of them swapped "remember when" tales, Norm laughed in all the right places but never contributed another word, eating steadily, passing things when asked. Just like it had been all those years ago.

Frank felt like he'd taken a giant step back in time. Back to when life was good, when he was a hero on the playing fields or floors, and Jenn made sure she kept up to him and James as they traversed the mountain and the lakes and rivers dotted around her.

He and Jenn always had their cameras at the ready, and James clowned for their photos.

Wonder where mine all went? Had his mother thrown them away in that last move? Or were they in a box high in a closet in his house?

"Are you going to show me your pic—er—photos?" he asked when they'd finished off the huge slices of banana-cream pie Clare set before them.

"If you'd like."

"Put your slides up on the screen so we can all see them. Norm, you set it up while I clear off this table."

Frank stood and, taking Norm's plate, scraped it onto his own.

"You don't have to do that."

"I know. But this is the way we used to do it, only Jenn and James always fought about whose turn it was to load the dishwasher."

"We didn't fight."

Frank gave her a who-are-you-trying-to-fool look.

"We just argued."

"Huh." Norm's one sound comment made Frank grin.

"Come on, Sig. You can take a run while we do the chores." He picked up his stack of plates and headed for the kitchen, dog at his heels.

Later, with the slide projector and screen set up, they all brought their coffee cups into the living room, where Jenn had been organizing her slides into the Carousel.

For the next hour, she entertained them with times, places, and problems for the different shoots. At the end she included some from a couple of her fashion shoots.

"I like the first ones better. What do you think?" From her place on the floor beside the projector, she glanced back at Frank.

"I think they are all fantastic." Clare leaned back against the sofa pillows. "I like the local ones best, but since the others earn you good bread and butter, I'm glad you are able to make a living doing what you love to do."

"Maybelle was right. You are good."

"Thank you." Jenn clicked off the projector light. She looked to her dad, who nodded.

She smiled her thanks and turned to sit cross-legged in front of them. Sig came over and sat down beside her. "Seeing them in a series like that, it would be fun to put together a multimedia show, you know, with several projector and screens, music. Perhaps some graphics. If I just had time."

"What's your hurry?"

She turned her attention to Sig. "I have to get back to New York."

"Her agent's been calling, threatening to come get her even." Clare sighed. "I hate to see you go."

Jenn watched the door slam in Frank's eyes. This wasn't how she'd wanted to tell him, but sometimes things were easier in a group. Not that she needed things easier, but… She stroked down Sig's shoulder and rubbed his ears. If only she could reach Frank as easily. With an exhaled sigh, the dog lay down and put his head on her thigh.

Jenn looked from dog to master, feeling her delight clear to the tips of her fingers, which continued to stroke the dog.

"He likes me, Frank."

"Yeah, well, he's always been a sucker for a pretty face."

She tightened her jaw; her eyes narrowed.

Sig sat up, his gaze on Frank.

"Guess that's that, then." She rose. "I'll see you out."

"No need to rush off."

"I'd better be on the road." As he stood, Frank reached out to shake Norm's hand. "Everything stays calm, you should be back to work in a week or so. Good to see you."

Jenn donned her hostess smile, one that didn't reach her eyes.

"Thanks for the excellent dinner, Clare."

"Don't be a stranger, okay?" She patted his arm, then gave him a hug. "And be careful, what with all the mess you're involved in."

"Beats busting drug runners, searching out marijuana." He nodded to Jenn. "See you."

She nodded back. One nod, short, more like a jerk of her head. *I was going to tell you. You and your flamin' temper. Stubborn, stubborn, stubborn!*

50

Jenn

May 24, 1980

I've got to get up there before I leave. Jenn stood on the deck of her parents' home, staring at the cloud-covered mountain. Gray clouds scudded above her. For a change, she had no desire to go find places to take pictures, to seek the story. All she wanted was a view into that crater. The news said the mountain lost thirteen hundred feet in height, and she couldn't comprehend the amount of ash that had not only buried untold acres but scattered across Washington, Idaho, Montana, and parts east. The magnitude was being compared to fifty million tons of TNT, twenty-five hundred times the atomic bomb dropped on Hiroshima: 3.3 billion cubic feet of material. What did that mean in real life?

And all that was hidden by clouds. There was no way to get in on foot or horseback or motorized vehicle of any kind. Only a chopper would do.

There were Forest Service planes going up, and rescue choppers still plied the skies, staying high enough so they didn't blow up the ash. The ash was being blamed for more problems than anyone had ever dreamed. It clogged air filters and delicate instruments, and ground into any aperture available. Everyone in the zone wore gauze masks to protect lungs. The latest reports said the ash contained particles of silicone, which meant glass.

Jenn knew all this, studied every bit of information she could glean from print, radio, and television. She finished her cup of coffee in a gulp and went to make a phone call.

"Hi, Mitch, this is Jenn Stockton."

"Well, well, the ice queen herself."

She cringed, bit back a sharp retort, and forced a smile into her voice. "I've heard that there's a possibility the weather might clear this afternoon. And the dream is that you would be going up and willing to take along a passenger."

"There's a chance."

She straightened from her laconic lean against the wall. "Really?" Hope warmed her voice.

"Well, I'll be. Do I detect a crashing icicle?"

"From Pearson?" She ignored his comment but reminded herself to keep some warmth in her voice. The man managed to set her hackles straight up with only two or three words. Always the innuendo. Whatever happened to normal conversation between the sexes?

"Word has it late afternoon. I'll be flying if you want to come."

"Want to? Flyboy, you've got a passenger."

"I'm not promising the mountain."

"Hey, I know you're not God."

"But we'll give it our best shot." So many words that had double meanings. *God, I'm so tired of that life, those lines. How do I handle this?*

Interesting that she found herself not using God as an expletive but as a petitioner. *I want what I had at one time and have so carelessly thrown away.*

She sighed. "I really appreciate this, Mitch. I just have to see the damage myself before I leave."

"You headin' on home?"

"Let's say back to work. New York is not my home." Not any longer, not that it ever was.

"Okay, I'll see you at Pearson for preflight about two, two thirty."

There, he'd done it again. It was all in the tone of voice, had nothing to do with the words he used, well, not that he didn't do that masterfully too.

She hung up the phone and danced into the kitchen. "I'm going up, I'm going up."

Clare smiled around apprehension. "I'm glad for you and scared to death at the same time. What if she blows again while you're in the air?"

"Others outflew the big blast, and the odds of that happening again right now are fairly slim."

"By whose estimate? Has anyone figured anything out? Not that I've seen." She crossed the kitchen and put both arms around her daughter. "I'm just doing my job as a mother, you know."

Jenn smiled and kissed her mother's cheek. "Never give up, do you?"

"Nope, I pray for you every day, usually more than once, every time God brings you to my mind. I know there is no way I can help you, but I know He can and does."

"What do you pray?"

"Oh, for protection mostly. That you will find true happiness, that you will return to Him."

"What makes you think I left?"

"Ah, my dear daughter, your actions speak a language far too clearly."

If you only knew. No, thank God you don't know it all. I think I would die of embarrassment. "Thanks, Mom. Maybe that's what brought me home."

"Why did you come back now?"

"I was so sick of all that around me that all I could think was to get back to the mountain and see her again, especially if she was going to blow."

"You've always had a special thing for The Lady."

"I know. I think you and Dad started it. But I feel..." Jenn paused, trying to put her thoughts and feelings into words. "I feel like I'm connected to her somehow."

"Perhaps you feel closer to God there."

Jenn nodded, tonguing the right side of her lower lip. When that wasn't sufficient, she nibbled it. "I feel more alive, excited about little things that don't even show up otherwise."

"Little things like...?"

"Physical, like a perfect leaf, the sun through a branch, a smell, my senses are revved up, I look forward to the next discovery. I feel like I can run up hills. Superwoman, able to leap tall buildings, or mountains, in a single bound..." Jenn found herself laughing with her mother, something they had not done a lot of when she was growing up. Those were the grief years for her mother, the time after James died.

"Wish you would come with me." Jenn was as surprised by the statement as she could tell was her mother.

Clare hugged her daughter again, all the while saying, "You know me and any planes, let alone small ones. You want to see your mother puking out a window?"

"Well, that wouldn't happen on a large plane. They give you a baggie, but you might find the view so exciting, you could skip being sick."

"I'll have dinner ready when you get back." She gave her daughter another hug. "But you have no idea how much your offer pleases me."

Jenn arrived at the Airpark early, and that after she'd made herself drive clear out to Camas and back. Other than additions to the Crown Zellerbach Paper Plant, she'd not noticed a lot of change, at least from the highway. Surely there were plenty of new houses built up in the hills.

She parked her truck where she could watch planes coming and going and took a couple of deep breaths to help her relax. Cloudy still, not even a spot of blue. Would it break enough for a sneak peek at the peak?

She half smiled at playing with words. Pictures were her forte, as they all knew, rarely words, at least written words. Perhaps that was why titling and captioning her photos came with such difficulty.

Each time she heard a vehicle arrive, she checked her rearview mirror. Two thirty, two forty-five. No Mitch. Had something happened on the mountain? Something that detained him? If they didn't get in the air soon, dusk would hide the mountain's secrets again.

While all the geologists studying the mountain could get to read the data, most of the general public, Jenn included, had to depend on reports carried on the radio, television, or newspapers. Some she'd gleaned from Frank, but she always wanted to know more. Lady, what's happening with you?

Three o'clock and Mitch drove in to park beside her.

"Sorry I'm late, more reports to file."

"Sounds like with all the reports between all the agencies, they'd better retrieve every tree that was downed."

"You can bet the timber companies are screaming for just that. I need to file my flight plan. We're flying that red 182 over there."

She waited for him by the gate, mentally checking through her gear as to what would be most effective with all the cloud cover, anything to keep her mind off Frank.

He hadn't lost his quick temper, that was for sure. Or was it her? Was he only this way when they were together? Maybe she should ask Maybelle. She'd tell her. Honest and forthright. That was Maybelle Hartman. And from something Frank said, Jenn was pretty sure Maybelle knew him better than anyone and wouldn't take any guff from him.

So how had he gotten under her skin again, she who could tell the smoothest operators to take their lines elsewhere, case in point the man walking toward her.

You never quit loving him. The voice inside sounded both sad and wise.

Of course I have. She followed Mitch to the plane, watching as he did a preflight walk around.

He might be a philanderer, but he was extremely cautious with a plane. She'd heard rumors of his skirt chasing, along with basing it on her own experience.

"Does your wife like to fly?"

His fingers stopped mid caress on a prop, and he shot her a look that said "beware" over his shoulder.

"I hear she's quite an artist."

Another pause, only this time he covered his reaction. "You been checking into my life, ice queen?"

She glanced toward the north. "Oh, Mitch, look." She pointed at the patch of blue that might well be north of the mountain.

"I'm done here. Get in."

She did as he ordered, her heart picking up the pace, her hands shaking as she buckled her seat belt. *The crater, I don't need a long look but even just a glimpse. Although, the more pictures the better.* They'd help her remember her time on the mountain, not that she needed any prompts. She stared out the windshield, mentally counting down as Mitch continued his preflight check. Had she been piloting, she would have been sorely tempted to rush the process.

He started first one engine and then the other, their roar drowning any need for conversation. He finished his cockpit preflight and turned on the radio. "November 4834 Echo, taxi for takeoff."

After receiving final clearance, he positioned them on the runway, shoved the throttle all the way forward, and lifted into the sky. Cloud cover hovered at about five thousand feet, as they flew through wisps of fog, still seeing the terrain below, though spotty.

"I'm going around on the east side," he shouted now that the engine roar was more subdued.

"Good. How high?"

"Going up to fifteen thousand. Ash and steam are minimal right now, according to flight service."

"How close?"

"Three, four miles. Depends on the clouds."

Jenn nodded, all the time wishing she'd been able to ride in a chopper. That was the only way to get really close.

How close is close enough? This time her voice wore a teasing tone. *To be honest, close enough to see the whole picture, then...*

"Will you look at that." Mitch dipped the left wing to give them a better view.

Jenn couldn't answer. Awe took over her throat and heart and soul. The horseshoe-shaped crater yawned below them, so deep it seemed she could see clear to the base of the mountain. "Can we come around again from the west?"

"I'll try. If our weather window stays open long enough." He called in to the tower requesting permission to alter his flight plan. After some back and forth from the ground, he set the plane into a steep bank to the left and came back over it.

Jenn kept snapping as they passed. Mitch sang at what might be the top of his lung power, "Oh, the things we do for love."

Jenn ignored him, all her attention focused on the hole in her friend, her fingers clicking the shutter, adjusting apertures and swapping lenses without conscious effort on her part. As they banked again, the mist crept back over, as if the crater really did not exist but was a figment of her imagination.

"What did you say?"

"Just chatting with the Forest Service. They're as excited at the viewing as you are."

Thank you, God. I asked for this and you gave me the gift. Why? Only you have control over the clouds. But you made it happen. This was indeed something she would have to think about.

"Thanks. More than I can say."

"I'd like prints of those."

"Of course." She leaned back and closed her eyes, the better to see the crater. *Awesome* was the only word she could come up with.

"Some of those should be easy to sell. Newspapers, magazines, get your name out there."

"I don't need my name out there."

Yes, you do. Big difference between shooting fashion layouts and shooting a mountain crater. How quickly could she get them processed?

"You have any contacts at the *Oregonian?*"

"No, but I do at the Vancouver paper, the *Columbian.* Why?"

"Perhaps they would develop the black-and-whites."

"I'll take you down there when we get back on the ground."

Another favor. How would she repay them all?

Fog was teasing the perimeters of the airport when they landed.

"Just in time." Mitch rolled to a stop. "You chock the wheels while I shut this baby down."

"Yes sir!" She put plenty of emphasis on the "sir," even so far as touching two fingers to her forehead. Pushing open the door, she scrambled out, then reached back in for her backpack. If those frames were anywhere near what she thought them to be… She set the chocks and kicked each one to make sure they were secure. Capricious winds could create havoc at a small airport like this one. They would pick up plenty of turbulence roaring through the Columbia Gorge.

She didn't need to check the windsock to know that right now the winds were blowing from the west, and moisture-laden from the ocean.

After chaining the wings of the plane to the earth, Mitch ushered her ahead of him into the office. He hung the plane keys on a board of hooks, slapped his logbook on the counter, and held up a hand.

"Give me a minute and I'll be right there." He headed down the hall.

"Where's the rest room?" she asked the man behind the counter.

"Follow that man. That's where he's headed."

Jenn waited outside the one bathroom door, restless, pacing. She might indeed have a scoop here, not that there hadn't been other crater photos, but none for three days. The mountain had been noticeably reticent about viewing.

"Couldn't stay away, eh?" Mitch touched the bill of his baseball hat.

Jenn rolled her eyes.

Back outside, she met him again at the pickup. "You want to ride, or follow?"

"Follow. Then I don't have to come back out here."

"Suit yourself." He waited for her to get her truck started, then turned right onto Mill Plain Boulevard, back to the declining downtown district of Vancouver. They parked in the parking lot and approached the building.

"You think anyone will be here?"

"Oh, my friend Jerry will. They've been working round the clock since the mountain started."

"Even if they don't put out a Saturday paper?"

"Got to get the Sunday edition ready."

"True."

He held the door for her, then motioned her toward the reception desk.

Within minutes they were back in the darkroom with Mitch's friend, Jerry.

"Will you look at that?" The photo showed the crater in all its glory, a small puff of ash rising in the center of the floor and a bit of cloud fuzzying the west rim.

"I'll buy it."

Jenn eased a couple more prints out of the tray and clipped them on the drying rack. As they'd thought from the negatives, the first one was the best.

"I'll develop some more of these when I get home and send you one."

"Home, as in...?"

"I have a darkroom at Mom and Dad's."

"You want to stop for a cup of coffee?"

There, it was back. That suggestive tone again. She'd almost begun to like him, and then this.

"You know, Mitch, you and I could be good friends if you'd leave off the leering."

"I didn't leer. I just asked if you wanted a cup of coffee. I have to get back to the office."

"It's your tone, your stance, you don't even know you do it." Jenn wanted to throw her hands in the air, but she had too much in them. *Why doesn't he get it?*

"A cup of coffee, that's all I'm asking."

Jenn sighed. "All right." But don't make me regret this. "Burgerville?"

"No, Denny's."

All the way to the restaurant, she argued back and forth. *Go, stay.* She needed to say thank you. *Call him; it's safer.* She wanted to...to what? Send him home to his wife, that's what. With that in mind, she followed him into the restaurant.

Once seated at a booth in the back, and full cups in front of them, she struggled to find the words. Words that he couldn't twist.

"How do I thank you?" She knew that was stupid when the words left her mouth.

"Oh, I'm sure you'll find a way."

"There, you did it again."

"No, I didn't."

"What did you mean then? 'I'm sure you'll find a way.'"

"Ah, Jenn, you're just too sensitive. Can't a guy even tease you?"

Follow through—back off. He's right. I am sensitive. I'm sick and tired of that life.

"Mitch, I'm telling you this as a friend. Teasing is one thing. Affairs are another. Mitchell Ross, go home to your wife before you lose her. And your kids." She kept her voice soft, but she enunciated each word, clearly, carefully. She leaned slightly forward. "Before it's too late."

She tossed two dollars on the table and left without a backward glance.

Now, if only she could have a chance to talk with Frank.

51 The Mountain

The Lady languished like a patient regaining consciousness, slow to wake, dazed, but coming to her senses. Again, again. But all around her, only ash and steam and stink. The new ash veil, ripped from her heart, blew toward the sea and the Sound. *Oh, foolish friends, why are you so hurried? Can you not see that there is more?*

52

Frank and Jenn

May 25, 1980

The phone ringing on a Sunday morning would make anyone swear, and Frank did. His eyes hurt, his head had become a thudding drum, his throat felt raw as though he'd swallowed glass.

"Not another hangover." Disappointment traveled well over the phone wires, and Maybelle's sigh made her message even clearer. "I thought you'd turned over a new leaf."

"If you want to preach, go get a pulpit."

"Are you getting ash there?"

"How in the…?" Frank heaved a heavy breath, cleaned up his vocabulary, and mumbled something into the phone while he fumbled the shade aside. "Some."

"Some is nothing like what's hitting I-5. Traffic's in a snarl like you won't believe. Give me the word and I'll call in support."

"State Patrol asked for assistance?" He sat on the edge of the bed and rubbed his eyes. No way could he take a chance on a drink now. No matter how bad he needed it. "I thought I told you not to call me."

"Now, Frank, you know and I know that if I hadn't, you'd have had my head."

"You've already called Tanner?"

"He's on days today."

"We talking feet or inches here?"

"Who knows? It's still coming down."

"I'll be there as soon as I can."

"Thought you'd see things my way." Her chuckle irritated him into another snarl.

As soon as he got in his truck, he turned up his police-band radio and listened to the chatter. No one was counting the accidents caused by low visibility and drivers who saw no need to slow down. Twenty-five miles an hour was the speed limit in an area usually traveled at sixty-five, seventy if no one was watching. He heard of three pileups in the stretch from Longview to Tacoma going on right then.

So far, it had been mostly fender benders, but a massive pileup could bring fatalities instantly.

"Stupid, idiotic people don't have the sense of a peahen."

Sig whined and glanced toward his master.

"Not your fault, fella. You'd have more sense."

By evening every tow truck, emergency vehicle, squad car, and maintenance crew was answering aid calls and patrolling the freeway and other major roads. Ash clouds billowed up, erasing the line between gray clouds overhead and earth itself.

In spite of the raining mud caused by rain and falling ash, Jenn, knowing she was leaving on Tuesday, decided to drive to Tacoma on Sunday to see Mellie and Lissa.

"This is absolute craziness," her mother confirmed, her father just shaking his head and rolling his eyes.

"She don't listen to you, Mother, so give it up."

Was it Jenn's imagination or had her father been talking more than he used to? Whatever, it was good. "I do listen, but time is so short before I leave, and the way things are going, it could get worse by tomorrow. Those two need every bit of encouragement anyone can give them."

"If your car starts to cough and act sluggish, get out and blow out the air filter. You do remember what one of them looks like?"

Jenn nodded. Her father had made sure his daughter could change oil, tires, air filter, and batteries. She didn't bother to tell him she'd not seen the innards of an automobile since she'd left for New York. Her closest contact was the backseat of a taxi.

"You take water along." Her mother went to the pantry for a picnic thermos and filled it. "They canceled church this morning so people would stay off the roads, you know."

Jenn ignored the hint, put all the supplies they insisted she take into the pickup, and headed down the road. Slowly, as her father had firmly suggested.

The drive took forever. Three times she almost ended up in the ditch; once to miss a sliding car, another because of a two-car accident still on the road, and the third because the road was slicker than the pond frozen in winter. Her shoulders felt like iron bands when she drove into the street marked on her map. At least here the falling ash was minimal and had been easing up ever since Olympia.

"You came." Lissa's smile made the horrendous drive worthwhile.

"I didn't think you would." Mellie ushered her into the living room.

"So, how's my favorite model been doing?" Jenn folded herself down on the floor, and Lissa scrambled into her crossed legs.

She leaned back against Jenn's circling arm. "I been missing you."

"I missed you too." Jenn touched the little girl's nose with the tip of her finger. *Been missing,* what a wonderful way of saying it. *Frank, I been missing you. How am I ever going to get time to see you again before I go?*

"You want to see Kitty?"

"Of course. Does Kitty like to have her picture taken?"

"Don't know. Didn't ask her."

Jenn's laugh belted out. "You, my dear little one, are a true realist."

"What's a 'list?"

"Someone who sees and hears things just the way they are. You'll make a good photographer someday."

"Like you?"

"Tell you what, when you get to feeling better, I'll bring you a camera, and we'll take pictures. How's that?"

"Would you please take a picture of Kitty?"

"I sure will. Let me get my camera."

By the time Jenn was ready, Lissa wandered back in the room, the cat draped over her arm.

Jenn clicked a couple of shots, suggested girl and cat cuddle on the sofa, and took some more.

"I know"—Lissa scrambled off the sofa—"Kitty likes the toy Mr. Johnson got us. Where is it, Mommy?"

"In your room, on your chest of drawers."

"How is Mr. Johnson?"

"Supposed to come home sometime this week. Said he's been flirting with the nurses, and they're about to chase him out."

"He's quite the gentleman."

"*Gentle* is a perfect word for him. He has been so good to us."

Jenn leaned back against the sofa, wrists resting on her bent knees. "When I called, you said you had a surprise."

"Oh, I forgot. Katheryn was helping find the papers for the hospital, and you wouldn't believe what she found."

"What?"

"Life insurance policies."

"So?"

"Harv took out two life insurance policies without telling me. Because of double indemnity in case of accidental death, they are worth a million dollars." Mellie's eyes filled with tears. "I wish Harv were here," she whispered into her hands, then brushed her hair back with both palms. "I can't dwell on that."

"That's a lot of money. How wonderful for you. I'll bet Harv is dancing a jig with joy that you'll be taken care of."

Mellie smiled around her tears. "And A-1 Logging is going to pay for the funeral. I don't know how long it will take the insurance companies to pay." Mellie wiped her eyes. "Harv would say God has provided for us, but I think he did."

Me too. It'd better not take long for them to pay up and without a hassle. "Has your pastor been by to see you?"

"Yes, but we can't have the funeral until the officials release the body." Her voice quivered on the last word.

"Here." Lissa came back into the room and dangled the fur-tipped string above Kitty. The cat lay on the couch, her white front paws curled over the edge of the sofa pillow. She reached up with one paw and batted at the bit of fur, rolled on her back, and used both front paws. Lissa giggled, Jenn clicked the shutter, and Mellie watched the antics, chuckling at them all.

Jenn put her camera away after taking one with Lissa in her mother's lap. "I'll send you some of these for your photo album."

"You are so good to us. Can I get you something to drink?"

"I thought perhaps I could take the two of you out to lunch." She turned to Lissa, who sat beside her with the dangle, still playing with Kitty. "Where would you like to go?"

"Hamburgers."

"Any place special?"

"Hamburger Haven is her favorite. They have place mats to color on there."

Lissa fell asleep in the car on the way back.

"Do you need anything from the grocery store?"

"Well, I could use bread and milk and a couple other things."

"How about you go in and I'll stay in the car with Lissa?"

"If you don't mind?" Mellie wore that scared rabbit look again.

"Mellie, listen to me. I wouldn't offer if I didn't want to. So you take as long as you need."

Sitting in the truck with Lissa leaning against her sound asleep, Jenn had time to think. About Frank. One moment she ached to just see him. The next she wanted to push him off a high place, with a safety net to catch him, but the fall might help him get the point. But which point? Why did she care? He'd made it patently clear that he didn't. Or as one drunk knows another, perhaps he cared too much. Men, how to ever understand them. She thought about returning to her other world. Even the thought made her wish for a drink or a pill, and if she, who'd been sober for over three weeks now, felt that, who was she to condemn Frank? She stretched her head from one shoulder, then to the other, pulling the knots out that had been gone for weeks.

What was her body telling her? Well, not to go back, that was simple. But she had to. To honor contracts she'd made. As her father both lived and taught her, you did your job to the best of your ability. And her job was fashion shoots—for the next three weeks or however long it took to wrap them up. Then she was out of there, no looking back. Flipping burgers at McDonald's was better than the New York scene. Well, maybe not really, but then she had enough money to live on quite comfortably for the rest of her life if she managed her assets right. But not in New York. Out here on the West Coast where she belonged.

She glanced down at the sleeping child, who seemed better, but Jenn knew the ticking bomb had been appeased, not disarmed. *What do you say to a child when she asks if you know Jesus?*

I used to. Can I go back?

"Thank you," Mellie said when she opened the truck door.

"You are most welcome. Set those bags on that skinny seat behind." Jenn scooted Lissa over so the seat could be leaned forward.

"Mommy?"

"I'm here, pumpkin." Mellie climbed in and eased Lissa around to lay her head in Mellie's lap.

Jenn's side felt a chill. Maybe she did have a maternal instinct or two somewhere inside her after all.

Shortly after dropping them off, Jenn headed back south, figuring the return trip would take as long as the first. She was right. Only it took longer, since there'd been another pileup, and it took more than an hour to clear. She quit counting the cars off to the side after five and kept her total focus on the pickup that threatened to slither into the median any time it had a chance.

"Thank God," her mother said when Jenn walked through the door.

She took her backpack to her room and stopped at the phone on the way back. She dialed a number and got an answering machine. "Frank McKenzie, I have some things I need to talk over with you before I leave. I know this ash is creating havoc, but you have to eat, so meet me at Barney's at six on Tuesday. I'm on the red-eye; that is, if the mountain behaves herself. If you can't do that, call me and we'll set another time. If you're chicken, I'll nail your sorry hide to a barn wall somewhere the next time I see you. Have a good day." She added the last, tongue firmly ensconced in her cheek.

Her mother raised one eyebrow as Jenn entered the kitchen.

"Don't bother. I know what you're thinking, but this is all your fault."

Clare handed her daughter the beaters from the chocolate-chip cookie dough. "Enjoy."

53

KATHERYN

MAY 26, 1980

"Katheryn, are you all right? I've called three times and left messages..."

Katheryn blinked and tried to sort through her foggy brain to come up with a response. "Mellie?"

"Yes."

Katheryn glanced at the clock, reached over for her glasses, put them on, and looked at the clock again. Six. Was that a.m. or p.m.?

"Are you all right?"

Of course not. I'll never be all right, ever again. Just like you.

Lucky whined, darted to the door, looked over her shoulder, and yipped this time.

"Can I call you back? Lucky needs to go out."

"Okay, but you sound sick."

"No, just woke up. Bye." She hung up and swung her legs over the edge of the bed. "I'm coming, girl, I'm coming." Feeling like she was looking at the world through the wrong end of a telescope, she padded down the stairs to let Lucky out in the backyard. How long had it been since she'd performed this simple service? First of all, it was evening, the sun hanging toward the horizon. But on what day? Sunday, of course. Kevin and Susan had both been there that morning. Then why did her mouth feel like it had been a month since she'd brushed her teeth?

Lucky woofed at the door, and on entrance headed for her dishes, both of which were empty.

Katheryn found a note on the table. "Hi, Mom. Came over this morning and fed Lucky. You were sleeping, so thought you must have had a hard night and could use the rest. I'll bring dinner by this evening about six or so."

Katheryn fed the dog, patted her, and, using the rail as a lifeline, made her way back upstairs. Monday, she'd lost an entire day. Actually more like a day and a half. She'd lain down shortly after noon.

David? Brian? Had there been any news? She rushed back downstairs, stumbling and nearly falling in her hurry. Sixteen messages.

She flipped through them, listening only to voices she didn't know, hoping one would be an official of some kind saying her family had been found. Condolence calls, Pastor Steve, Mellie, her mother, her mother, and her mother.

Let the kids answer them.

She wiped away the tears she hadn't realized were falling and pulled herself back up the stairs. Looking down she groaned. Sweats, she was wearing David's sweats. No wonder she felt like she'd been standing in front of the furnace. Or perhaps it was a grief-induced hot flash, if there was such a thing.

Lucky woofed downstairs, her welcome home bark.

"Mom?" Kevin called before closing the door.

"I'm up here. Be down in a minute." But when she saw herself in the bathroom mirror, she knew it would take more than a minute. She needed a shower, shampoo, and… Using a word she'd forbidden her children to say, she shucked her borrowed clothes, pulled jeans and one of her own long-sleeved T-shirts from the closet, and, after using the deodorant stick, Katheryn dressed. She brushed her teeth, pulled a brush through her hair and swept it back in a club, then slid her feet into clogs. There, she'd made it; dressed, that is. And now all she felt like doing was crawling back under that down comforter and dropping down into the void again. A place of no pain, no sorrow, no nothing.

Instead, she went back downstairs, the smell of pepperoni pizza nearly gagging her.

"You just get up?"

"No."

"You all right?"

"No." She poured a glass of water and drank half without pausing.

Kevin looked in the fridge. "You didn't eat the sandwich I brought you."

"Sorry. I wasn't hungry."

"When did you eat last?"

Katheryn struggled to remember. Finally, she shrugged. "You sound like my mother."

"Did you call her back? She even called me to make sure you were all right."

After he stayed with her the first night, she'd insisted she would be all right by herself and sent him home. At least she could remember that. The phone rang. Katheryn stared at it as if it were a snarling rat. Or a hissing cobra.

"You want me to get that?"

"Please." *What's the matter with you, woman, you haven't lost an arm or a leg? The phone can't bite you.*

Kevin covered the receiver. "It's Grandma."

"I...I can't talk with her, please."

"She's busy right now, Grandma. Can she call you back later? I know, I know, I'll tell her. Sure, I promise. Bye." He hung up and shook his head. "I'm to tell you that if you don't start returning your calls, she is going to get on the next plane and come out here."

Katheryn massaged her temples with the first two fingers on each hand.

"Now, if you don't want that, which, by the way, I think is a good idea—you need someone here with you—you'd better take five minutes and call her back." He pulled a breadstick from the flat box. "Here, eat this first so you have energy enough to deal with her."

"Thanks, Son. I owe you one."

"Aw, Mom, if only there was some way I could really help you." He put his arms around her and rocked her as she had him so many times.

The tears spurted. She wept on his shoulder, soaking his sweatshirt, and wrinkling the parts she clenched in her fists. When the rampage finally subsided, she could hear him murmuring comfort and feel him stroking her hair. He handed her a fistful of tissues and stepped back so she could mop up.

"Susan gave me strict instructions to make you cry."

Sniff. "Oh, she did, did she?" *Mop, sniff, blow.* Katheryn sank down on a chair, the strength leaving her legs as the tears had left her eyes.

"Yep, and I didn't even have to work at it, or make you mad or nothing. I know the trick. Threaten you with a visit from Grandma, and the dam bursts."

"Kevin." She found herself almost laughing. "You are a nut."

Lucky, her brown eyes worried and her tail barely moving, pushed her wet nose into Katheryn's hand.

"I'm sorry, girl. It's all right." Katheryn leaned down and hugged the dog, rubbing her soft ears, earning doggy kisses and small whimpers of sympathy. Lucky hated for anyone to be sad. She'd even tried to comfort her by climbing in bed with her sometime in the long hours of sleeplessness the first night. Last night she was so comatose, an elephant could have climbed in bed with her and she'd been none the wiser.

"Are you going to call Grandma?" Kevin turned from listening to her messages. "I saved the ones I think you'd better listen to."

"Thank you."

"Coffee?"

"That might help. You got any industrial strength backbone? Either IV or pill form?"

Kevin gave her a one-arm hug and dropped a kiss on the side of her forehead. "We'll get through this, Mom. We really will."

How strange it felt to be comforted by this tall, lean son of hers. Like the first time she went to Susan's apartment for dinner and didn't have to do the cooking, acted like a real visitor. *Sure your kids grew up, that's what they are supposed to do…* At that thought another came screaming from some corner of her mind. *Brian will never grow up. He will always be eleven, a boy who loves to fish and climb mountains and read and ask questions.* She rolled her lips together, fighting the onslaught. But one sniff and she was a goner. How could she have any tears left after that last deluge?

"What happened?" Kevin stared at her in total confusion.

"I...I thought of Brian and how he will never grow up, and it's just not fair." She slammed the heels of her fists against the wall. "God, I cannot do this!"

Kevin grabbed her pounding fists. "Mom, Mom, take it easy. You're going to hurt yourself. Here, pound on me."

She slumped against him, held up by his strong arms, when all she wanted was to curl into a puddle and melt away.

"Have you been like this all day?"

She shook her head. "No, I slept since you and Susan left yesterday afternoon." *Or at least I think I was sleeping. Perhaps unconscious. But anything is better than this. I'm bleeding to death from this gaping crater in my heart, and no one can see it but me.*

Kevin pushed her gently down on a chair. "You are going to drink a cup of coffee and eat a piece of pizza."

She shook her head. "I can't eat pizza. How about a glass of milk and a piece of toast? No, wait. Tea. That's what I want: tea and toast. That might stay down."

"You've had the heaves?"

Again she shook her head. "No, just feels like it." Besides, if you've not eaten, you have nothing to throw up.

Kevin put the teakettle on, popped a slice of bread in the toaster, and lifted a piece of pizza from the box. "Do you mind if I eat?"

"Not at all." Katheryn dutifully ate her toast and sipped her tea, the fluid making the tasteless bread slide down more easily. She felt like she would choke if she tried it dry.

The phone rang, and again he went to answer it.

Please, not Mother, please.

"Can I tell her who is calling?" He clamped the phone to his shoulder and turned. "Someone named Mellie. Will you take it?"

Katheryn nodded and held out her hand. The long cord she'd so carefully measured to make sure she could do anything in the kitchen while still on the phone stood her in good stead right now. She wasn't sure yet if her legs would hold her up.

"Hi, Mellie. Sorry I didn't get right back to you. Kevin came and is taking care of me."

"You sound more like yourself. I'm glad. Have you…you heard anything?"

"No." Short, sharp and to the point.

"I'm sorry."

"Me too."

"Jenn came to visit us. She said she has to go back to New York for a couple of shoots she'd contracted for."

"Yeah, life goes on. How's the little sweetie?"

"Still responding to that transfusion. It helps for a time."

"And Mr. Johnson?"

"Says he will be home later this week. That's pretty soon, isn't it?"

"He didn't have a bad one."

"You know, those insurance papers?"

Do I ever. "Yes."

"I called the agent listed, and he said they are all in order. But I need a death certificate to st-start the claim."

Katheryn fought the tears she could feel at the sound of Mellie's sniffing. *At least you know.* As if that were any help.

"Thanks for helping me."

"You are most welcome. I'll call you soon, and if you hear anything from the cancer center, you call me immediately. I can be in the car to come get you within minutes."

"I...I was afraid you didn't really mean that."

"Mellie, I never say anything I don't mean. Give Lissa a hug for me, and I'll see you soon."

Kevin took the receiver from her hand and hung it up. "You did good, Mom. That poor little kid, so sick and no daddy." He choked on the *d* word.

"Dad would say you're the man of the family now." Katheryn could barely get the words out, then swallowed and took another drink of her now lukewarm tea. Iced tea was good, hot tea was good, but this—blah.

Kevin finished off another slice of pizza. "You think you're strong enough for Grandma now?"

"I guess so." She tipped her head back. *Lord God, giver of small favors, grant me this one, an easy conversation with my mother.* She took the receiver and propped it on her shoulder, lifting her mug for another cup of tea.

That night Lucky shared her bed, still in the guest room.

54

Frank and Jenn

May 27, 1980

"I hate to have you leave again." Clare hugged her daughter one final time.

"I'll be back before you miss me."

"Half an hour?"

Jenn turned to her father. "You be careful up in those woods."

"Lot safer than where you are going."

"I know, Dad. And I agree. When I get back we'll have to go looking for a truck for me, okay?"

"I'll keep an eye out."

Jenn smiled to herself. Little did he know that when she came back, they were both getting new trucks. And there wouldn't be any monthly payments either. She'd be willing to bet a year's livelihood that her father had never had a brand-new-off-the-lot-zero-mileage truck in his entire life.

As she drove along the winding roads, she kept the speed down to keep from stirring up the ash. Sunday, at least, the rain had kept it on the ground in the form of slick mud.

The closer she got to Longview, the greater the butterfly acrobatics in her belly. What if he never showed up? Well, that would certainly tell her a message. What if he showed up with the same chip on his shoulder from the other night? She'd dealt with hardheaded men in her life, starting out with him. She was an adult now. They should be able to talk this out. *Should.* Right.

She'd been practicing what she needed to tell him. Mainly, that she was coming back and she hoped—ah, the hope of every woman in love with an alcoholic—that he'd give up the booze for her. Voluntarily. After all, perhaps he wasn't an alcoholic—yet. Just a man who drank too much too often. *Ah, Jenn, don't kid yourself.* You're fighting and losing the battle here, and the only one who can change it is Frank with the help of God. And no matter what the songs said, the love of a good woman wouldn't cut it.

She pulled into the parking lot ten minutes early and drove past the cars lined up like pigs at a trough. Barney's served the best barbequed ribs in Southwest Washington. Or maybe further afield. And booze.

She parked and leaned her forehead against the steering wheel. Why hadn't she chosen someplace without a bar? As if any of the good restaurants in the area didn't have a bar.

You can't make the choices for him. Remember that, you dimwit. Her self was growing impatient with herself.

She stepped from the truck, straightened black silk slacks, adjusted the black leather belt that nipped in the waist of a black silk turtleneck. Should she take the black suede jacket with her or not? She glanced at the sky, overcast like all the nights lately, as if Mount St. Helens needed to hide behind clouds. She slipped the long, fine leather strap of a Gucci minibag over her shoulder and folded the jacket over her arm. It might be cool when she came out. She needed to be at the airport by ten. Most likely she'd get there early.

She knew she looked good. The appreciative glances of two men coming out assured her of that. Would Frank notice?

She told the maître d' her name; she'd called ahead for reservations. "Frank McKenzie will be meeting me." *I sure to heaven hope so.*

"He's already seated." One worry off her mind.

"Thank you."

Jennifer Elizabeth Stockton, you are not thirteen any longer, so cut the dry mouth and put your best word forward. "Hi, Frank. I didn't think I was late." She slid into the booth, folding her jacket on the seat.

"You remind me of a puma, black and sleek, all pure grace and..."

He's been drinking.

"Thanks for the compliment." *You look like you haven't slept in three days.* "And for coming." *Get it out quick.*

"My lady commanded and I obeyed."

"My lady? Come now, you were ready to strangle me two days ago."

"Yes, well, it's not nice to drop bombs on your friends."

"I was planning on telling you."

"Would you care for something to drink?" the waiter stopped at their table, tablet in hand.

"I'd like iced tea, extra lemon, please."

"Sheriff?"

"Coke, please. I need my wits about me to spar with the lady here."

Besides, you've already had a snootful. Unable to look at Frank, Jenn watched the waiter walk away. But she didn't smell booze on him. Perhaps she was wrong. Perhaps... *Do not get your hopes up, girl.*

"So, how was your day, things settle down any on I-5?"

"Did you hear what happened this morning?"

"No. What?"

"Have you been watching the news?"

"Anything to do with the mountain and not a lot else."

"Well, you know how bad the ash is?"

She nodded, deciding not to tell him she'd driven to Tacoma on Sunday. Oil on troubled waters and all that.

"We've given out tickets, posted with flashing signs, everything, but those stupid drivers just get in a hurry. Can't seem to slow down to a safe speed. So the truckers took over."

"The truckers?" She caught the glint of laughter in his bloodshot eyes.

"Using their CBs to communicate, they set out three across and drove the slow speed, so no one could get around them. They spaced themselves out about seven miles, which gave the ash time to settle in between. Whoever came up with that idea deserves a medal. No one would 'fess up, but it sure took care of the ash and traffic problem."

Jenn shook her head. "Ingenious. You ought to put them on the payroll. Hmm."

The waiter set down their drinks. "Are you ready to order?"

"Sorry, I haven't even looked at the menu." Jenn picked hers up. "You know what you're having?"

"Ribs."

"Good, me too. Baked potato, salad with blue cheese on the side. And extra sauce, extra hot."

"Make that two."

"Thank you." The waiter collected their menus and left.

Jenn resisted the urge to study her fingernails, but she knew they were cut short, as always, with a coat of clear polish. Once she'd resigned from the front side of the camera, she'd worn her fingernails the way she liked them. In fact, she'd worn her life the way she liked it, until the last few years. She could feel Frank staring at her, so she raised her gaze to lock with his. Another urge, to reach out and stroke a tender finger down the side of his face, ease away the lines and… *Stop it right now, Jenn. He reads body language like you read a book.*

He leaned forward, and now she could smell it. She'd been right. He'd had at least one. For courage? Or for need?

"I was planning on telling you."

"Telling me what?"

His eyes slitted just enough to let her know he was deliberately keeping a cap on his anger. She wasn't bad at reading body language herself, especially when it came to him.

"To tell you I have to go back to New York, but…"

"Here you go, folks." The waiter set their salads in front of them, whipped a tall pepper mill tucked in the waistband of his apron behind his back, and held it poised above her salad. "Pepper?"

She nodded, as did Frank. "Thank you."

"Look, can we postpone this discussion until after we eat? I haven't had a decent meal since dinner at your mother's, and I'm really hungry."

Jenn nodded. "Of course." Her salad looked much more appetizing now.

"Remember when…" Frank started the ball rolling, and she passed it back like any decent soccer player. Memories carried them through the salads and the main course, all the while, Jenn was wishing they could talk about now. But a cheerful dinner companion was worth the wait, and she had always enjoyed Frank's stories. One time they'd even talked about putting a book together. He'd do the stories and she'd take the pictures, a historical about the land they loved.

Jenn shoved her plate slightly forward and used the warm wet cloth provided to make sure she wasn't wearing any of the sauce. "You remember that idea we had about collecting the old stories around the mountain?"

"Sure, haven't thought about that in ages."

"I've been thinking about it, for when I come back."

"Come back?"

"You didn't give me a chance to tell you the other night. I have to go back to New York because I have three contracts to fill. Should take about three weeks, and I have to close up my apartment."

"You're coming back here."

"Yes."

"I hear a 'but' in your voice."

She tongued her teeth on the left side, wishing she were anywhere but right here, right now. This man knew her too well.

She gave a small nod. "I gave up drugs and booze."

"Congratulations." His eyes did that narrowing trick again. "So?"

"So, in order to stay clean and sober, I know that I cannot be around others who drink, at least for a time—until I get stronger, you know?"

"And you're saying..." He leaned back, his shoulders rigid, one finger tapping the shiny table.

"I'm saying that for my own salvation I..."

"No, you're saying that my drinking is causing..."

Jenn grabbed her courage by the neck and hauled it up in front of her. "I'm saying that your drinking is wrecking your life, and no matter how much I love you, I can have no part of it." She heard herself use the *l* word but hoped it slid right by him.

"Is that love as in friendship, or…?"

She met his gaze. "I don't know, Frank, and right now I'm afraid to find out." She tried to keep her gaze steady and not look away first. But could she control the size of her pupils? Most likely not, since she could feel her heart kicking up a notch.

"So, you're saying if I keep drinking, you won't come back?"

"No. I'm coming back, but I can't stand by and see you destroy your life." She closed her eyes for a moment, and when she opened them, she slowly shook her head. "I just can't."

"But it's my life."

"Yes."

"And what I drink is my choice. I'm not hurting anyone but me, and I don't see that I'm hurting myself. I know I tie one on once in a while, but, lady"—he leaned forward, menace making her swallow—"no one tells me what to do."

"I wasn't telling you, Frank. I was pleading. And trying to explain myself."

"Funny, it didn't sound that way to me."

"I'm sorry." Jenn picked up her coat and, standing, slung her purse over her shoulder. "Goodbye, Frank."

Walking out of that room was the hardest thing she ever did. Especially when she heard him call, "Waiter." She knew what he was doing. Ordering another drink.

"God, save him. I sure can't."

She replayed the scene in her mind fifty times between Portland and New York. And never could make it come out right.

When the flight attendant offered her a drink, she almost accepted. After all, what did it matter? She could always go home and drink along with Frank. And when she couldn't sleep, she had sleeping pills in her carry-on. But again, the fear of one more kept her not only awake but more sober than she'd ever been in her life.

Watching dreams die had that effect on one.

55

Mellie

May 27, 1980

"Mrs. Sedor, have you chosen a funeral home yet?" Telemarketers sounded more personal than the voice on the phone.

"No, I…" Panic attacked like a starving lioness with cubs, ripping her throat, clamping her heart, and shredding the edges of her vision.

"Mrs. Sedor. Mrs. Sedor, is there someone there with you?"

"No, I…" Her breath came in gasps.

"Are you all right?" The calm voice upped a degree in insistence.

Take a deep breath. Easy, you can do this. The voice comforted, held, and encouraged her. The voice, a voice, deep, melodious, and constant like the song of the sea. *There now, very good, another breath, hang on to me, I will hold you up, see with my strong right hand I will hold you.*

She took another breath, this one actually going down into her lungs. The lioness backed off, and Mellie could hear.

"I am all right now." She spoke each word cautiously, as if carelessness would bring back the attacker. "Please, continue."

"Whew, you scared me there for a minute."

"Me too. I'm sorry for—"

"No, don't be sorry. You have had a great shock, and today I compound it. Forgive me for being abrupt."

The gentleness was nearly Mellie's undoing. Tears slipped down her cheeks. "Please tell me what to do. I…I mean, my husband…Harv took care of everything." She sniffed and reached for a tissue. "But now I must, and I know my Father—my heavenly Father—will get me through. He promised."

There was a pause on the line, then a sniff and the sound of a nose being blown. "Thank you for the reminder."

"You are welcome. Now, what is the next step?"

"You need to call a funeral home. You might ask your pastor whom he suggests. Then you tell us, and we will ship your husband's remains to where you decide. All of this will be taken care of thanks to A-1 Logging."

Mellie thought back to the man who had called on her at the hospital. They were indeed doing what he had said they would.

"Then you need to discuss with them or with your pastor how you want the rest of the arrangements handled."

"I see."

They finished the conversation with the woman giving Mellie a phone number to call and then she hung up.

Lissa was asleep, so Mellie called their pastor and explained where they were.

"Ah, Mellie, I know this is terribly hard for you. Would you like me to call them for you?"

Yes, please, take it all away. She closed her eyes. *My right hand will uphold you.* "Thank you, but no. I need to do these things. Harv always said God would be here for us, for me, and He is. Just tell me what the procedures are."

Pastor Dahlquist laid out the usual plan. "But, Mellie, I don't believe you should go down there alone. I will go with you. Can you go this afternoon?"

"Yes. But I cannot take Lissa to a funeral home like that."

"I know. I'll bring someone to watch her. Now, you need to call the mortuary and then call the number back from Longview." He paused. "And, Mellie, we need to talk about a memorial service for Harv."

"Do we have to do that?"

"No, but I believe it will be good in the long run. He touched far more lives than I think you realize."

"I'll think about it."

"Good."

Strong right hand. She dialed the numbers, answered the questions, and, when she hung up the phone, she sat still, held close in a circle of comfort.

Jenn, Katheryn, Mr. Johnson, who came home from the nursing home that day, and Pastor Dahlquist surrounded Mellie and Lissa as they lowered the casket into the ground on Friday afternoon.

"Dust to dust, ashes to ashes, we commit this body to earth from which we come, knowing Harv's soul is already home, rejoicing with our heavenly Father. In the name of the Father and the Son and the Holy Spirit. Let us pray."

As he led them in prayer, Mellie made no effort to stem her tears, as if she had any control. Katheryn put her left arm around her waist and

Jenn her right. Lissa laid her head on her mother's chest, and Mr. Johnson put his hands on her shoulders.

Pastor Dahlquist drizzled dirt in the shape of the cross on the simple coffin, stepped back, and raised his hands in blessing. "Now may the God of all peace and love, comfort and strengthen you in the days ahead. Go in peace."

They stood there a few moments while a house finch sang his song in the tree above them. The fragrance of newly cut grass and newly turned earth floated around them as they returned to the waiting cars.

"Thank you for coming." Mellie rocked Lissa, who remained in her arms, legs locked around her mother's waist. "I never dreamed"—she looked to Jenn—"that you would come so far."

"Thank God for red-eye flights. I think there is a reason they are called that."

"The church ladies have brought food and beverages to your house, so if you would all like to go to Mellie's, we can visit there." Pastor Dahlquist held open the door of his car, and Mellie settled into the front seat, Mr. Johnson in the back.

"We'll see you there." Katheryn and Jenn both nodded.

They had all just walked in the door when the phone rang. Mellie set Lissa down and went to answer it. Who would be calling? All her friends were right here, and what amazing friends she had.

"Mrs. Sedor, this is Anika from the Fred Hutchinson Cancer Research Center. We have had a sudden opening, and if you can be here with Lissa first thing tomorrow morning, we will start the procedure."

"T-tomorrow? But that's Saturday."

"I know. Is there a reason you can't be here?"

"No." She smothered the rising panic with a firm breath. "We will be there."

She hung up and, sucking in a lung full, turned to the waiting group. "We start treatment at the center tomorrow morning."

"We'll be there with you." Jenn and Katheryn exchanged nods as they looked back at Mellie.

"Praise God." Mr. Johnson shook his head. "God is healing our little girl. And I'm right here to take care of Kitty for you."

Lissa looked from her mother to Mr. Johnson. "Did God make you all better?"

"Yes. And pretty quick too."

"He made my daddy all better?"

Mellie blinked but nodded. "Yes."

"He's all better." Pastor Dahlquist blinked a couple of times. "Better than he's ever been and happier than he's ever been."

"You promise?" Standing in the circle of adults, Lissa stared up at him.

"I promise."

She nodded. "I'm hungry."

"Good for you, Lissa. Let's go see what all they brought." He took her hand, and they walked toward the kitchen.

"Do you feel like we're caught up in a whirlwind?" Jenn asked.

"I mean, things like this just don't happen."

"I know. Harv is talking to the higher-ups and convincing them to get cracking on taking care of his little girl, since he can't be here right now." Jenn did a little tap and shuffle dance step. "Yes, Harv."

"Not sure how scriptural that is, but the Bible says the Holy Spirit pleads for us when we don't know what to say."

"It also says we have a heavenly host of those who've gone before cheering us on." Katheryn scrunched her eyes. "I don't remember where, but I do remember a pastor preaching on it one time."

Mellie smiled at her friend. She knew that Katheryn had spent a good part of the week in bed, with no will to get up. But here she was, looking much more like herself than Mellie expected, although thinner and with well-concealed dark circles under her eyes. And Jenn flew clear across the country to be here.

Mr. Johnson smiled at her, his face once more with healthy color, not that gray she'd seen in the CCU. "I don't know where you found these two, but they are keepers." He motioned to each of her friends.

"I know. You too."

"Wish I could drive you up there, but the doctor said I can't drive for a couple of weeks yet."

Mellie sucked in a deep breath to calm her heart that leaped at the thought she was about to share. "I have a favor to ask."

"Sure, whatever you need, you know that."

"When the insurance money comes, and we have time to go buy me a car, I want you to teach me how to drive."

The three of them stared at her. She could feel them drilling into her heart.

"Well, I'll be..." Jenn was the first to recover, her smile broadening by the second.

"You want to learn to drive?" Katheryn shook her head, little movements from side to side, as if this was beyond possible.

"Mellie, dear, I would be most honored."

They all hugged her at once.

"I don't want to go to the hospital."

"I know."

"In the next couple of days, a real big surprise is going to come visit you."

Lissa turned from her mother to Jenn.

"What s'prise?"

"I'll never tell." The four of them stood under the portico of the Fred Hutchinson Cancer Research Center.

"Will I like it?"

"You'd better. And you have to call and tell me what you think."

"I don't have a telephone."

"Oh, I'm sure we'll find you one."

Katheryn checked the bag she carried. "Yup, books and color crayons. Oh, and a funny long bunny."

"Harvey, like my daddy." Lissa reached for the bunny and hugged it with both arms.

"Okay, we've got everything. Here we go." Jenn held open the door and, with a sweep of her arm, ushered them in.

Mellie wanted to take Lissa and run the other way, but with her friends on either side, and Lissa laughing at something Jenn said, she had no choice. *Not that I'm ungrateful, Lord, just overwhelmed. Things are moving so fast.*

Just hang on, darlin', hang on tight.

Did everyone who'd lost someone seem to hear their voice? Or was she going crazy along with everything else? She wanted to ask Katheryn but somehow couldn't dredge up the courage.

Hang on.

56

JENN

JUNE 2, 1980

Gold sandy beaches, white-frosted waves on an ocean so blue it didn't look real, a breeze that teased the models hair just so. Perfection.

Unless, of course, one's mind is in a hospital room with a deathly pale little girl in Seattle.

Jenn forced herself to concentrate on the shoot. She wanted to go out with a bang, not a whimper. She hadn't told the advertising director for Neiman Marcus that this was her last shoot for them. That was Herman's job, after all.

She slathered on some more sunscreen, resettled her khaki squish hat so it shaded her eyes, and reset her camera.

"Okay, ladies, let's make this a good one. The sooner we get it right, the sooner you can go play."

While they shifted, she shot, glancing eastward at the thunderheads gathering on the horizon. Knowing that a storm could cost them not only hours but days, she pushed hard, leaving no one with breaktime.

"Have a heart," one of the models complained.

"I don't. Let's set up the next one."

They had no need of a wind machine to blow skirts and tresses by the time she set her camera down. The sky had turned an ominous silver gray shot with purple and flashes of lightning in the distance.

"It's coming our way, so let's get out of here." They all clambered into the waiting vehicles; rain dotted the windshields as they wound their way up the steep dirt track back to what could barely be called a road. Whoever had found that location had been an intrepid searcher.

It would be called a gullywasher back home, Jenn thought, staring out her hotel window some hours later. They'd driven through a couple of streams that caused her to hold her breath, but they made it back.

The only bad thing, no planes would be flying in this. But the shoot was done. A full day ahead of schedule. Or rather, ahead of the revised schedule, since they'd put it back for her. A day less of shooting would save the ad department a chunk of change. Which would make them even happier. She'd known the shots were good. Everything came together for a change, something unheard of in this *prima donna* world.

As soon as she entered her room, she called Katheryn, grateful when she heard the connection go through. Storms could disrupt the phones, too.

"What have you heard?"

"Your present got here. Takes a lot to make her smile right now, but that did. Where did you find such a huge gray cat?"

"FAO Schwartz. That size is usually more for display than sale, but I wanted something she could look at from a distance and still see."

"She can see it. They are disinfecting the little one so she can have that in her bed. What a good idea to send both."

"It's so little."

"I know. When I'm there I feel so helpless."

"So how are they holding up?"

Katheryn sighed. "She's doing well enough that the surgery is scheduled for the day after tomorrow."

"I'll be there."

"I'll tell them."

"How are you doing, Katheryn?" Jenn knew if there had been word, someone would have let her know. Not Frank, of course. She might have fallen off the face of the earth for all he cared. Or knew.

"Time for truth?"

"Would you tell me anything else?"

"I'd sugarcoat sometimes."

"But now?"

"I'm impatient when I'm awake, and while I'm not taking anything, when I do sleep, I fall into this soundproof pit where I sleep twelve, fifteen hours. No one needs that much sleep, or that kind of sleep."

"They say that grieving takes a lot of energy."

"Sometimes I…"

Jenn could hear a sniff. Was Katheryn crying? Should she ask? What would it take to break Katheryn's barriers down?

"You don't have to be Ms. Super Capable with me, Katheryn. I will love you no matter what."

"Who in the—" A choke covered by a cough. "Sorry, excuse me." She turned aside to cough again.

"Who in the heaven or the other place, gave me permission to talk to you like that?"

"Something like that."

"Katheryn, I don't know why, but I feel God put the three of us together for a reason."

"You believe God does things like that?" Her voice still wore a tinge of sarcasm.

"I tried not to believe, I tried to run, drown that voice, quiet it with whatever it took, but it's still there. Songs from my childhood in Sunday school come into my mind, now that I have a clear mind again. Wisps of Bible verses. I see what is going on with Mellie. Why, when she asked Mr. Johnson if he would teach her how to drive, I almost shouted, 'Miracle! We have a bonafide miracle right here!'"

"Yeah, me too." Another silence fell. "Why can I talk so much easier with you on the phone than with my Susan and Kevin? I have friends, friends I've had for years, and I want to run, hide when they call or come by."

"I don't know. Strange creatures we are."

"How are things with Frank?"

Ah, she needs to change the subject. "Frank who?"

"That bad, huh?"

Yeah, now who needed to be honest? "I haven't heard a peep from him since I left. And yes, he has my phone number. Or if not, he could get it from my mother." Hope flared like a tiny birthday candle. And blew out just as easily. He wouldn't call. He had too much pride. Unless he got real drunk and was feeling maudlin, then he might call. If he had her number.

"You love him a lot, don't you?" Katheryn's comment was more statement than question.

"Yeah, for most of my life. You'd think I'd outgrow it, wouldn't you?" Jenn glanced at the clock. "Please tell them I called. And thanks."

"Me too."

The storm passed on overnight, leaving behind downed palm fronds and coconuts, high seas and a foot of water on the tarmac. As soon as that was swept away, their plane readied for takeoff.

Jenn leaned her seat back and closed her eyes, wishing only to be left alone. *God, I know You are there, and if I believe all I've learned through the years, I know that You love me. I just don't feel very loved, not by You, by my parents as much as they are able, since they have no understanding of my life, and I thank You that they don't. And if You've noticed, I don't have a lot of real friends. I thought Frank was one, and You know I wanted more than friendship, but I guess he and I have different definitions of friendship, let alone love. I do have these two women whom I would never have chosen as friends, and yet—they have shown more concern for me and desire for my companionship than anyone. And Lissa, what a kid. God, You've got to heal her, You just have to. I know I have nothing to bargain with, not that you are of a bargaining persuasion, but if there is anything I can do to help make this easier for them, please let me know. I have so much, and they have so little. Give me wisdom and an open heart. I've already told You how sorry I am for these dissolute years, and if I understand Your plan, I'm forgiven.* A great rush of gratitude welled up and, like an incoming wave, nearly swamped her in its magnificence. Tears rushed up and out, and all she could hear, even above the roar of the plane engines, was *I love you, I love you, I love you.* Repeated over and over until she drifted off to sleep on a swell of peace.

She booked a flight for Seattle for the next morning.

One more shoot to go.

Frank, what's happening with you?

57

The Mountain

She stood bereft and spurned by those who once claimed to love her. Dust-coated and blackened with ash, she wished that she might sink and implode into the crater-wound on her flank. *Am I cast off and with no worth in your sight, my Creator? My friends prod and study me but do not rejoice over my survival.* She groaned in despair. Would life ever return to the wasteland she'd become?

58

Frank

June 5, 1980

He could feel eyes drilling into his back. Did he look so bad that Maybelle was glaring at him? He sucked in a deep breath and nearly coughed on the fumes. The peppermint gum had not helped. Nor the mouthwash. He should have tried the cloves. Someone told him they helped. But to chew a real clove, he shuddered at the thought. He'd accidentally cracked one in a pickle and that woke him right up at the time.

Lay off, lady. This is my life, and I don't need any more sermons. The last one I heard was enough to... He slammed the door to his office, setting the vertical blinds to clacking.

Right now he wished he'd kept a stash in his desk, but he'd been neither that far gone nor that stupid.

"I am not an alcoholic." He spoke the words distinctly. After all, he was not drunk. He had a hangover. Big difference. He did not drink on the job. He did not need a drink to get through the day. He was able to stop drinking when he wanted to. He had never missed a day's work because he was drunk or hungover. He only drank for one reason—to forget.

If only the headache would cease and desist. He opened a desk drawer, pulled out a bottle of Tylenol, and popped two, washing them down with the pitcher of water he kept full on his desk. They said to stay healthy one must drink eight glasses of water daily, and he came pretty close to that.

A knock at the door brought forth a gruff, "Enter."

He knew who it was by the pattern of knocks.

"You got a minute?" Maybelle stood in the doorway.

"Not if you are going to lecture me."

"Why ever would I do that?" The sarcasm in her tone nearly gagged him.

"You don't do saccharine well, so out with it."

"I'm only saying this for your own good."

He rolled his eyes. "You've got two."

Maybelle crossed the room, keeping her gaze on his. "You look like you feel."

"I know that. What next?"

"There is scuttlebutt that the powers that be are about to go after you."

"For what?"

"The drinking."

"It's not slowed me down. I do a better job than three men."

"That's because you work untold hours so you don't have to go home. Sleeping here does not constitute as work." She shook her head. "I'm sorry, Frank, I just want to help."

"How'd you hear this?"

"I can't tell you."

"Maybelle, you can be fired so fast you couldn't get your desk cleaned out quick enough."

"So what, fire me and I'll have you up on unjustified termination along with sexual harassment so fast your head will swim. Besides, I can retire any time I want, and if you badger me too much, I might want tomorrow."

"Are you finished?"

"No."

He propped his head in his hands. "Maybelle..."

"No, you need to know this. I heard someone say rehab or the road. Frank, they are coming after you."

"What grounds do they have? I've never shirked my job. I've never..."

"You have been stopped for weaving..."

"No ticket."

"Of course not. You're the sheriff. Who would lay their job on the line by arresting or even ticketing you?" She stepped back. "Frank, you gotta get some help."

He half rose as if he were coming across the desk at her. "I can stop drinking any time I want."

"Prove it." Nose to nose now, she lowered her voice. "You lost your family in the worst way, and now you lost a fine woman who's loved you all her life. What more do you need to lose before you listen up?" She spun on her heel and marched out the door, leaving him slack-jawed and sucker-punched.

If he ever needed help sobering up again, he knew who to go to.

Fury helped. After calling her every name he could think of, he roared through the stack of forms to be signed, met with his officers, gave out assignments, and caught up with what had gone on with the mountain in the last two days. He dug out the résumés of the three people he'd narrowed out of a field of twenty for the open position of deputy and had Maybelle call them to set up appointments.

By the end of the day everyone was tiptoeing to stay out of his way.

Frank McKenzie was on a roll, and no one wanted to be rolled over.

"So much for being Mr. Good Guy," he muttered as he studied the revised roster. He'd used up most of the rest of his year's budget on the mountain, and he had six months left to go. What would they do for funds? Another form to fill out.

"I hate all this paperwork." He slammed his pen down so hard it bounced and rolled off the front of his desk. "And I hate being a desk jockey."

He left at five. "Fools think they can tell me what to do. I want a drink, I'll have a drink. But tonight I choose not to have one."

He didn't stop at the restaurant for dinner, and he didn't stop at the bar for a drink either. He headed on home all aglow in his "I can do it myself" pride.

Until he entered the dark house where no one really lived, where he just existed. Dirty dishes in the sink, but not many, for he rarely ate at home, mouse droppings on the counter, dog food trailing across the floor. In his bedroom the shards of untold broken bottles glinted from their pile against the wall.

"What a sorry mess I've made of things, Sig." He slumped on the edge of the bed that missed more washings than he wanted to count and, propping his elbows on his knees, scrubbed at his hair with his fingers.

"First Barbara and now Jenn. I don't have too good a record with women. They up and leave me."

Sig sat beside him, leaning into his knee, as if offering what comfort he could by his presence.

"This place is a pigsty." He heaved himself to his feet, went for a broom, dustpan, and garbage can. Took him half an hour, but all the glass was cleaned up. He vacuumed the entire room just in case some got away. *Sig could have cut his feet. I could have cut my feet. Where has my head been?* He stripped the bed and threw the sheets in the washing machine. *They aren't going to tell me what to do. I can beat this by myself. Just watch me.*

He started on the kitchen, found a bottle half full of bourbon, and set it aside so he could wipe off the counter. *Who do they think they are? Whoever they were. Leave it to Maybelle not to tell me who. Ha, I can figure it out. Bust my rear all these years and this is the thanks I get. Rehab or the road.*

He took one swig just to prove he could, finished the dishes, and looked in the fridge for something to eat. Nothing. The freezer? Several frozen dinners. Nothing looked appetizing.

But the bottle. "Just like an elephant in the middle of the room. Don't think about the elephant. What the…? One more drink isn't going to make me or break me. No one will be any the wiser."

He took his cleaning spree into the living room, folded up all the papers, stacked the magazines, and hauled his dirty clothes out to the washing machine, while there tossing the washed sheets into the dryer. Sig followed him from room to room.

When he sat down with a peanut-butter sandwich to watch the news, he took another swig. By ten he was sound asleep in the chair, bottle on the floor almost empty.

Sometime later Sig barked and barked again until finally Frank heard and realized the doorbell was ringing and someone yelled his name.

"Come on in."

"Door's locked."

"Oh, for…!" He staggered slightly but shook himself alert. He unlocked the door and pulled it open. "Tanner, what are you doing here?"

"There's a possible domestic violence situation going on, and they're calling for you."

"Oh, all right." Frank turned and ricocheted off the wall.

"No, Frank, not tonight."

"Just a minute, get my gear."

"You're drunk, man. You can't go out there."

Frank came out the door like he was going to pound the young deputy into the ground.

Tanner sidestepped, and Frank kept on going. He crashed into the side of his Blazer and slumped to the ground.

"Thank God I didn't have to hit you." Tanner climbed back in his vehicle and headed out.

Sometime later Frank woke with his cheek in a patch of water. Sig lay beside him. "What in the…?" He shook his head, rubbed his eyes. "Wasn't I sleeping in my chair? How'd I get out here?" His words mumbled together as he heaved himself to his feet and stumbled back into the house. This time he made it to his clean bed, shucked off his clothes, and fell back into the nightmares that always rode him.

No one would look at him when he entered the office, only half an hour late. After six cups of coffee, he'd been able to shave without cutting himself, shower, and make sure no one had any indication that he had been drinking the night before.

"Hey, Maybelle, what's for today?" The look she gave him stopped him in his tracks. "All right, now what?"

"You didn't listen to your radio?"

"When?"

"Last night?"

"No, I finally slept. There a law against the sheriff getting a decent night's sleep?"

"You don't remember Tanner coming out to get you?"

"Ah, no."

"He's in the hospital. A domestic violence case where they were calling for you. He said you were sick and went on ahead. He got shot."

The way she said *sick* let him know she knew what he'd had. "Is he going to be okay?"

"Still in surgery."

"I swear to God, Maybelle, I—"

"No, Frank. Don't do any more swearing. Just get your life cleaned up before it's too late."

Tanner took a bullet for me. If I'd been there I might have talked them down. He's too inexperienced, and then he lied for me too. Dear God, what have I done?

59

Jenn

June 5, 1980

Hey, Miss Kitty, I brought you something."

"I not Kitty." Lissa halfway opened her eyes.

"Oh, guess I got these two mixed up." Jenn held up a poster-size picture of Lissa with Kitty draped over her arm. "I'll put this on the wall where you can see it."

"You look funny."

"You don't like my new outfit? And here I thought I'd go buy you one just like it." Jenn put on a wounded face.

Lissa smiled, a slight crack in a face so pale it disappeared against the pillow in dim light.

Wearing her full sterile garb, with every inch of her covered by scrubs, booties, gloves, hat, and mask, she pushed pins into the wall to hold up the poster that had been through the decontamination process too. Nothing could come into the room without being sterilized first. She glanced over her shoulder to the bed shrouded in clear plastic, a system called LAF, for Laminar Air Flow, which created a room within a room, to protect Lissa, who had no resistance to any kind of illness. With all the radiation and chemotherapy, Lissa had no white cells to combat anything. *Please, God, make this treatment that's killed all the cancer cells work so now the new, clean bone marrow can take over and rebuild her body.*

Smiling was not the easiest thing right now, when one look at the little girl made one want to burst out in tears.

Lissa lay sleeping again.

Jenn took out the book she'd sent through the disinfecting and went back to reading. The three of them were taking turns, sitting by the bedside, being there for Lissa when she woke up, praying for her when she slept.

Each of her rest shifts, Jenn drew a couple of cartoons, and then Katheryn told stories using the cartoon of Miss Kitty and her adventures.

"We might have to see about publishing these one day," Katheryn had said. "At least I'm getting some writing done."

Jenn leaned back in the chair and thought about Katheryn. She was stuffing so much and either didn't realize it or refused to acknowledge how much she hurt. Once the initial grief eased, she went about her business as if nothing were wrong. *God, Father God, please help her. The not knowing is beyond comprehension. I know she feels they are gone, but hope flares, flickers, and dies. Please, God, do something.*

She watched the nurse check the machines and Lissa's vitals.

"She's hanging in there. Doesn't look strong enough to lift a glass, but she's a fighter."

"I know." *Because watching her fight has changed my life, that's for sure. All the time and energy I've wasted. Running away from my God who loves me.* All the hours of watching a little girl battle for her life had given Jenn plenty of time to reevaluate her own and come to the right conclusion. Life without faith at the center was no life at all.

"How do you do this, working with such terribly ill children?"

"Some live, more now than before. So there is hope. Can I get you anything?"

"No thanks."

"Mommy?"

"Mommy's sleeping right now. You have to put up with me."

"I love Kitty." Lissa gazed across the span to the poster. "I'm going to throw up."

Reaching through the portals, Jenn held the emesis pan, wiped Lissa's mouth with a wet cloth, and patted her as she curled in a ball under the blankets.

"My turn." Katheryn entered the room. "Mellie is sleeping, so I left her with a note and came instead."

"No change. More vomiting. Nurse said she's a fighter."

"Doesn't look like it from here, does it?"

Jenn got out of the chair and motioned for Katheryn to sit down.

"How're you doing?"

Katheryn shrugged. "Susan came over for a while. She's having a hard time talking about her father. Still pretty angry."

And you're not? Jenn hoped the thought didn't show on her face.

"Hey, that's some poster."

"Thanks. I was hoping it would get through quarantine before I had to leave."

"When do you go?"

"Tomorrow. I'll wrap things up, get a mover, and be back in a week or so." *I hope. I'm certainly more needed here than there.*

"We'll miss you."

"Thanks. I think when I come back I'll find an apartment."

"There's always room at my house."

"Thank you, Katheryn, but I'm realizing I'd better be thinking about the rest of my life. What I'm going to do."

"Why, you're going to be a famous photojournalist with a specialty in Mount St. Helens, and you can live anywhere you want."

"You dreamer." *The only place I really want to live is with Frank, and that's not a possibility.*

"Some of us have to have dreams come true so the rest of us can keep living." Katheryn stared down at the sleeping child.

"You have to let go, my friend."

Katheryn stared at her out of eyes so bleak that Jenn raised her hands to reach for her, but let them fall again when Katheryn took an invisible step back. Her withdrawal was so obvious that Jenn wanted to weep for her.

"Of what? What more can I lose?"

Your sanity? But this was not the time to preach. Jenn had learned that the hard way. "I'll keep praying for you."

"You do that. Maybe God will listen to you. He seems to have a deaf ear where I'm concerned." Katheryn sat down in the chair and turned to face the bed.

Jenn understood a dismissal when she saw one. "I'll bring Mellie back when she wakes up."

"Thanks."

Katheryn had invited them both to stay with her, since she was only a ten-minute drive from the Pill Hill, as the conclave of hospitals and medical offices located on Boren Street was called. Right across the street from Swedish Hospital and bounded on the south by Odea High School, the Fred Hutchinson Cancer Research Center was leading the investigation into bone marrow transplants to fight cancer, especially leukemia of many forms.

Jenn read everything she could about the place and the people pioneering there. Indeed, Lissa being there was another one of God's miracles. She glanced up at the concrete portico as she left the building. *And I who such a short time ago was no longer sure I even believed in God, I am now recognizing miracles in action. Surely that makes me one too. Lord, get me in and out of New York quickly.*

That night as she sank into a first-class seat on the red-eye to New York, her mind did another of its one-eighties, and she could see a younger Frank, clear as if he stood right in front of her. His grin made her heart smile. Another miracle needed, *Please Father, for Jesus's sake, turn Frank's life around.*

60

Frank

June 6, 1980

"Oh, dear God, let him live." Frank knew he'd not been a praying man for too many years, but if anyone deserved to be prayed for, Deputy Lucas Tanner did. He lay hooked up to every machine known to medical science, and he still looked like he could die at any second. He had yet to regain consciousness.

Lord, he stood in my place. Because I was too drunk to do anyone any good, he went. And look what happened. The knowledge that his own skills in dealing with violent and half-crazed people might have prevented an officer down and a man in the morgue ate at him like a hyena on a kill.

"Tanner, son, you shouldn't have gone." This bright young man who dreamed of a career in local law enforcement and was doing everything right had been a special protégé of Frank's. Frank rubbed his jaw. He had a feeling the bruise on it came from a certain young man's fist.

And then you lied to save my hide. And unless you or I tell them differently, I still have my badge and what reputation I have left.

He took Tanner's hand. "You get better, you hear. No malingering. You can beat this." He squeezed the flaccid hand, all the while ignoring the tears dripping off his chin. Not a flicker of an eye or a hint of a smile.

But—the barest squeeze of a hand. Tanner could hear.

"Lucas, thanks to you I'm on my way to check into rehab. You saved that woman's life, and you saved mine. See you when you get out of here and I get out of there. Then you can tell me what really went on last night."

Another faint squeeze.

Frank squeezed back, long and hard. "God bless." After sucking in and releasing a deep breath, he saluted the man in the bed and left the room, blowing his nose as he went.

That night, lying in a strange bed in a place he'd dreaded to the depths of his fear, he couldn't get Tanner out of his mind. *He stood in my place. By his deliberate choice. And he might die. Christ stood in my place by His deliberate choice. And He died. For me. For me. Oh, God, He died for me.* He clenched his teeth and jaw against the scream that threatened to choke him.

The scream escaped as a whimper. *Is everything too late? My job? My life? Jenn?* He tried to rise but fell back on his bed, arms flung wide. *Is it too late?*

Frank McKenzie aspired to the principle that one should keep one's dirty laundry within the borders of one's own family, and since he was the only remaining family member, that didn't leave many knowing the family secrets.

The rehab counselor had other ideas.

"And then?"

Frank crossed his arms over his chest, to keep from exploding or from hitting the man, he wasn't sure which. "I filed my report." *What do you think I did? I'm a cop. I filed my report and I…*

When the silence drew too long and made his feet twitch, Frank narrowed his eyes. "And I tried to nail him to the wall, but the court let him off, sent him to a psychiatric hospital where he can watch television and play games and perhaps do a little watercolor. To calm his demons, you know."

"I see. Let's go back to the night you found your wife and son."

"Dead?"

"Yes."

"Murdered by that psycho that drew Sig and me up on the mountain to search for a lost child."

"Yes. Did you find the child?"

"No, it was a false alarm." Frank left the chair as if on fire and stared out the window, his body rigid, locked so tight breath could hardly enter.

"Tell me what you saw when you entered the room."

"They were dead."

"In bed?"

"No."

"How did they die?"

"They were just dead."

"How did he kill them?"

"I don't remember." Fist clenched, he slammed it on the arm of the chair.

"What did you see when you first walked in?"

"A hand." He paused. "My son's hand—on the table." He fought the memory, writhing and flexing.

"Nooo!" His scream ripped the air and flayed the walls. "He dismembered them. They were lying in pieces all around the living room. My son's hand lay on the table with a note stuffed in it. Blood, blood everywhere." He sank to the floor and curled in the corner. "Oh my God, blood and body pieces everywhere." His sobs pooled around him, reflecting the pain that poured from his body.

Sometime later, when he could move, he raised his head. "And so I began drinking."

"To forget."

"What else could I do? They wouldn't let me kill him."

61

The Mountain

The mountain sighed in the knowledge that her travail had ended. *Come see, come see, there is green sprouting through the ashes. My friends come seeking, nibbling at my seeds and sprouts that are washed clean by heaven's water. I will live by the bounty of the Creator's hands.* Days passed and the sun shone through the haze of ash clouds fading thinner and thinner like worn cloth. Her grieving would continue, but seeds of hope pressed through the surface.

62

Mellie, Katheryn, and Jenn

June 30, 1980

"How is she?" Jenn asked as Katheryn and Mellie came through the kitchen door.

"I think stronger." Mellie hugged her Bible to her chest, her favorite reading matter ever since she started at Genesis and was reading all the way through for the first time in her life.

"Dr. Thomas said we might be through the worst. If only we can keep her from contracting any illness." Katheryn set her purse on the counter and sighed. "My stomach aches in sympathy pains for all her throwing up."

Mellie leaned against the counter. "I heard one of the nurses say seventy days of vomiting is not unusual."

"Mr. Johnson called, just to check up on her. Wondered if she'd gotten his cards. I told him they had to be decontaminated first." Jenn set her mug in the sink. "I'll be on my way, then. Oh, Katheryn, I bought groceries. Stuff's in the fridge and..."

Mellie looked from one to another, sensing the change in the air. She followed Katheryn's glance. The cup left in the sink. Katheryn moved to put it in the dishwasher, but Jenn beat her to it. Katheryn had a thing against anything left in the sink.

Or anywhere else, for that matter.

Sharing a house with two women was indeed a different lifestyle for her. She bent down and petted Lucky. "You are such a good dog." Perhaps when they got to go home again, she should get a dog for Lissa. If Kitty would let one in the door. Harv had always wanted a dog.

" 'Night, you two. At least I think it's night. Thank you both for all you do."

" 'Night. I'm outta here." Jenn picked up her canvas tote. "Call me if you need anything."

Mellie stopped long enough to watch her head out the door. Jenn, always smiling. Katheryn, now, that was a different story. Little things seemed to bother her more and more. Of course, it wasn't easy having permanent houseguests. She'd be moving into that apartment by the cancer center in another week. Along with Lissa. They had to stay there for a hundred days for Lissa to be closely monitored. Would they all have to wear the gowns and stuff? She'd not thought to ask that yet.

She looked at the message Jenn had left on her dresser. "Call the insurance company. Ms. Fairchild at extension 301." She included the phone number. It was too late to call now, one more thing to do at the hospital. She and the phone booth in the lobby were getting to be close friends.

Perhaps in the morning she could ask Katheryn if she could help with the weeding, or perhaps she should just go out and do some. If she could wake up early enough.

Sometimes, while Lissa slept, she did too, in the chair by the bed.

Just before she fell asleep, she heard a man's voice downstairs. Kevin must have come by again. Good, that meant that Katheryn might be in a better mood in the morning.

"Lord, if there is any way I can help her, will You please let me know? She is doing so much for me, and I don't want to be a burden."

One good thing about being in Katheryn's house rather than at home, there were no memories of Harv here. She couldn't go sniff his clothes in the closet or his aftershave, she didn't see his tools in the garage, nor could she reach across the bed to where he always slept.

Sometimes she dreamed that this had all been a dream. But when she woke, she was alone.

The next afternoon she walked into the hospital gift shop for a candy bar and saw friendship mugs on the display. One said, "Friends forever," another, "Friends are the chocolate chips in the cookies of life," and, "A best friend is a sister you choose." She picked out two of the sisters kind.

"Could you gift-wrap these for me?" Never had she done such a thing. To walk in to a store, see something she liked for someone else, and just buy it. Without it being a birthday or Christmas gift.

She had the gaily wrapped boxes in a bag on her arm and was out the door when guilt leaped out from behind the post and grabbed her by the throat. She couldn't breathe.

No! I am not afraid. I can buy something if I want. It is not wrong. She felt her breathing calm, her heart settle back down.

Next stop, the friendly telephone. When she hung up again, she stared at the wall. The insurance company would be sending her a check for five hundred thousand dollars, to arrive tomorrow. She'd given them

Katheryn's address. She would have to be there to sign for it. Five hundred thousand dollars. She'd never heard of having so much money at one time. *Now I can pay Mr. Johnson back.* The thought buoyed her steps as she ate the candy bar on the way up to the floor.

"Hi, Mommy."

"Hi, baby." She sat down in the chair and put her hands up against the plastic. Lissa did the same so they were palm to palm.

"Need to snuggle."

"Me too. Just think, next week we'll be together again."

"At home with Kitty."

"No, right near here." That was another thing she needed to do, find out what kinds of things she could bring there, which of Lissa's toys, her blanket, clothes. Did everything have to be sterilized first?

"I'm hungry."

"That's good to hear. I'll call for something."

"Ice cream?"

"How about a Popsicle?

" 'Kay." Lissa sat cross-legged in the middle of her bed. For a change a bit of pink tinged her cheekbones. Her bald little head made bathing her easy, since they didn't have to wash hair. The chemo took care of that. Mellie looked closely.

"Hey, guess what? Your hair is growing back. You've got peach fuzz, no, longer than that."

Lissa scraped her hand over her head. "I don't feel anything."

"Go like this." Mellie held her hand about a quarter of an inch above her skin and moved back and forth.

Lissa did so, and both she and her mother giggled.

Never had Mellie heard a more delightful sound.

When she saw Jenn and Katheryn, she burst out her news. "Lissa was laughing today, and her hair is growing back." She paused. "And…!"

"And what?" Katheryn and Jenn spoke at the same time.

"And that call from the insurance company—the check for five hundred thousand dollars will come here tomorrow. I have to be here to sign for it."

First Katheryn, then Jenn hugged her, and then the three of them hugged together.

"Group hug, group hug." Jenn squeezed tighter. "I haven't had a group hug since…since I don't know when."

"Ah, Mellie, she is doing great." Katheryn stepped back. "What a miracle. All this good news on one day."

"Oh, I have something for each of you." Mellie dug the boxes out of her bag and handed them to her friends. She watched with delight as they each opened their box and pulled the tissue paper back to read the saying.

"I never had sisters, but if I did, I'd want them to be like you two. Lissa and I, we can never say thank-you enough."

"You don't have to. Our friendship is something special." Jenn held up her mug and touched it to Katheryn's. "Cheers to friendship, long and true."

"Thank you, Mellie." Katheryn kissed Mellie on the cheek.

"Yes, thank you. I gotta be off. Our girl awaits."

Our girl. Mellie hugged the words close. *Harv used to say "my girls." Harv, if you are watching, thank you. I'll do my best.*

63

FRANK

JULY 1, 1980

"What can I get you to drink, sir?"

"Coke, please." Frank smiled up at the flight attendant. Attractive, nice eyes.

She handed him a packet of peanuts, along with a cocktail napkin, then set the plastic glass on the napkin.

He stared at the glass. First time he'd had a soda onboard in many a year. He opened the nuts and munched them one at time.

You should have called, told her you were coming. I want to surprise her. Oh, you will. Are you sure this is the best course?

Second-guessing, a bad habit and one he usually overcame. Now he had too much time on his hands. A five-hour flight to JFK and then a long ride into New York City. All he had was an address.

What if she is out? I'll wait. He handed the plastic back to the attendant and flipped his tray back up. He had work to do, right there in his briefcase at his feet. Work that would take his mind off the meeting ahead. Instead, he tipped his seat back and let his mind roam back through the years.

He'd taken her for granted. Any fool could see that. But she'd been only a kid. He'd never thought of her as more than a friend.

Until she showed up at the mountain. Talk about a punch right to the solar plexus. Seeing her turned the sunshine on, sun that he hadn't seen for a long time.

He fast-forwarded past the scene at Barney's. That one he'd replayed far too often. So, what was keeping her in New York? He'd have sworn she planned to stay in Washington, right near home, in fact. Never once had she mentioned her life in New York, at least not with any longing. If she considered the Big Apple her home, she'd done an Oscar-quality acting job.

She'd said she loved him. Like a brother? He shook his head. Not with the sparks that flew between them. Nearly burned him a couple of times.

What to say when he got there? *Jenn, I'm sorry. I've gone through rehab and turned my life around. You don't have to worry about me getting drunk ever again.* Could he say never taking a drink again? *Yes. I can.*

He landed at JFK and lifted his carry-on out of the bin. Two pieces of luggage but a lot of baggage, much of which he'd been dealing with in the last weeks.

He caught a cab into the city and gave her address. Sometime later, they drew up in front of a glass-and-brass building with a canopy clear to the street.

"Thanks." He added a tip and stepped out onto the sidewalk. If this was the place, she'd been doing right well for a skinny little girl from Longview, Washington.

A man in a navy coat that reached mid thigh and gold-trimmed epaulets on his shoulders greeted him.

"May I help you, sir?"

"I'm here to see Ms. Stockton."

"I'm sorry, sir, she's not here."

"I'll wait."

"No, I mean she has moved."

"Do you have a forwarding address?"

"No sir."

And if you did, you'd not tell me either. That's the kind of protection you are paid to give. "No phone number, no nothing?"

"Correct, sir. The moving van took her things three days ago."

"I see." Frank thought a long moment. There was nothing else in New York he wanted to see. "Can you call me a cab, please?"

"Certainly, sir, and I'm sorry. Are you an old friend?"

"Yes. Since childhood." *And tonight I'm feeling very old.*

The man blew a whistle and a Yellow Cab pulled up to the curb.

"To the airport," Frank ordered as he settled in the backseat. How soon would it be before he could be back on a plane, flying the only direction that counted. West. Toward home.

Several hours later the flight attendant stopped beside him. "What can I get you to drink, sir?"

"Bourbon and water."

Another bag of peanuts, another napkin, but this time a glass of ice and water and a small bottle of Jim Beam. The label gleamed in the spotlight over his seat. He broke the seal with a twist of the wrist and poured the amber liquid into the glass. It swirled and spread as he shook out the last drop.

Ignoring the voice clamoring and screaming in his head, he lifted the glass and inhaled. Ahh. Setting it down again, he moved it in circles on his tray table. The liquids had melded now, the ice cubes knocked against each other, companionably, inviting him to toss one back.

He stared at the drink. She wasn't there. Surely one drink would not matter. He'd find her. She was worth the wait.

"Here, miss." He handed her the untouched drink and let his seat back. *Thanks* seemed too small a word, but he sent it heavenward anyway.

"She went to Seattle? Whatever for?"

"Lissa, the daughter of the woman she met here, is in a cancer treatment program up there. Jenn went up to help."

"When is she coming home?"

Clare shrugged. "Not sure she is."

"Well, I'll be. Here I fly clear to New York, and she's not a hundred miles away. You got an address for her?"

"You sure she wants to see you?"

"I got to take that chance, don't I?"

Clare touched his arm. "Good luck, Frank McKenzie. I'll be looking for some good news when you come home."

"You'd better say a prayer or two. She was mighty upset last time I saw her."

"Frank, I spent most of my life praying for her and you, too, more than you know. Congratulations on your new direction. God bless you, boy, God bless you."

"Yeah." He waved the paper with the address. "Thanks. In Seattle, well, I'll be."

64

FINALE

Is it too much to ask you to put your dishes in the dishwasher?" Both fists glued to her hips, Katheryn glared at Jenn.

"Sorry, I'll take care of it."

"Never mind, I will." Katheryn's nostrils flared. She took the mug, David's favorite, one she'd not used since— She stared at the mug in her hands. The stupid cup, he'd never put it in the dishwasher in all the years since Susan gave it to him. WORLD'S GREATEST DAD and a fishing pole. A fishing pole. They'd gone fishing, for crying out loud. Traded their lives for a few stupid fish and the vain hope of healing. Katheryn choked on the fury burning her insides.

"Why couldn't he have taken the Valium?" Like the mountain herself, Katheryn could no longer hold the flow within. Grief mushroomed, dragging out the rocks of despair, melting the walls of ice she'd built to protect her heart.

"Who?" Jenn stood beside her.

"David, dragging Brian up there, going to see The Lady." She rounded on Jenn, as if to attack. "The Lady who killed my husband and my son. Why couldn't he have gone to Mount Rainier? Stayed home? I tried to get him to stay home, but he wouldn't listen. And now they are gone, and I'm all alone."

Mellie took the cup from Katheryn's shaking fingers and set it carefully in the dishwasher.

"I want them to come back. Please, God, if You love me, let them come home." Katheryn slid down the cupboard door and huddled against the cold wood. "There could be a mistake, let them come home." She covered her face with her hands, but Jenn knelt beside her, taking Katheryn's hands, warming them with her own.

Joining them on the floor, Mellie put an arm around Katheryn, and like a child seeking its mother, Katheryn burrowed into Mellie's shoulder.

With the three of them locked in one another's arms, Jenn and Mellie rocked the woman between them as she wept deep, tearing sobs that shook them all.

Nothing could be said, only arms that comforted, hands that soothed, and hearts that cared. Tears poured down their faces. Jenn rose and fetched a box of tissue, handing Katheryn a handful.

Much later when the storm passed, Katheryn asked, "How am I going to live with never knowing for sure?"

"You will. And perhaps they will find something to tell you." Jenn handed Mellie the box of tissue.

"And if they don't?" Katheryn sat up, still propped against the cabinet. With bent knees and feet flat on the floor, she stared down at the kitchen tiles.

"In the military they call it MIA, missing in action." Jenn assumed the same position as Katheryn. "I should know—it was three years before they found my brother's grave."

"Vietnam War?"

"Uh-huh. Thought it might kill my dad, too."

"Thanks, you two. Sorry I was being such a snip."

"Oh, is that what you call it?" Jenn tipped her head back. "I had a better word."

"Rhymes with witch?"

"Something like that."

Mellie sat cross-legged in front of them, elbows propped on her jean-clad knees. "I'm glad you let us be with you. I mean, you have helped me..." She shook her head. "I can't begin to count all you've done for me."

"That's different. I like helping people."

"Right, but when the shoe is on the other foot...?"

"I know. Katheryn the capable. My mother's favorite saying, 'Don't ever let them see you cry.' "

"Things any better with her?"

"Give me a break. My mother wrote the book on difficult." Katheryn pushed herself to her feet. "Anyone for a cup of tea, and then I have to get Mellie back to the center."

"After all, tomorrow is the day."

"The big day. Lissa goes to the apartment."

"Thank You, heavenly Father."

Still masked and gowned, the nurses were wheeling a masked and gowned Lissa down the hall.

"You're going to a new apartment, sweetie. We have it all ready for you."

"Will Kitty be there?"

"Sorry, no, but the big Kitty will be waiting for you."

"And my poster?"

"Yup." Jenn carried Harvey the bunny and her canvas tote full of cards.

"Look, balloons." Lissa pointed to the door.

"And they are all for you." The nurse leaned down to give Lissa a quick squeeze.

Jenn laughed along with the others until her gaze caught the sight of a broad-shouldered man with hair shot through with gray. "Frank."

"Where?" Katheryn looked around. "Oh, my word, what have we here?"

Jenn's heart did a triple-time dance and threw in a kick step for good measure.

"You are one hard woman to track down." He stopped in front of her, ignoring all that was going on around them.

"You're looking good."

"Better than last time?"

"Yes."

"I went clear to New York, but you weren't there."

"I left New York."

"I know. Your doorman told me."

Frank stared into Jenn's eyes. "I… I've made some changes since we last saw each other."

Oh God, help me. Jenn couldn't have torn her gaze away if she tried—or wanted to. "I see." *Oh, no you don't. Give him a chance.* "What changes?" The words fought to stick in her throat.

"I've been through rehab, and by the grace of God, I'll not drink again."

"Good for you." Staring into his eyes was like toppling over into a sun-warmed pool. He took her hand and tried to draw her off to the side, but she refused. "You can say what you want in front of my friends."

Frank shrugged, but kept hold of her hand, as if afraid she might run again. "You said you loved me. What kind of love are we talking about? Is that the man-woman kind of love or friendship kind of love?"

"If I have to explain, then I think you're missing something. I think you know how I love you."

"Good thing, then, 'cause I don't want to have to do any more growing up before you'll marry me."

"Marry you? Frank, are you sure?" Jenn tipped her chin slightly, never taking her eyes from his.

"Surer than I've been about anything in a long time. I love you, Jennifer Elizabeth Stockton. So, will you be my wife?"

Jenn turned at the sound of clapping and cheering. They were surrounded by hospital personnel, Lissa in her wheelchair, visitors, Katheryn, and Mellie.

"Tell him yes," someone called.

"Quick, before he gets away," added another.

Frank put his hands on her waist. "Please."

The love she saw shining in his clear eyes did it. "Yes."

More clapping and cheering erupted as Frank locked his arms together with her in their circle and kissed her. The kiss was all she'd dreamed of. When he pulled slightly back, she leaned forward and kissed him again. "Come on, Officer, we're blocking traffic. And that little girl needs to get to her new temporary home."

Frank took her hand, and the two of them joined the others walking through the earth-bound balloons.

"Here, honey, one for you to keep." One of the attendants handed Lissa a red balloon.

Out from under the portico, Lissa looked up at the balloon bobbing above her head and let go of the ribbon. "That's for my daddy. He lives in heaven with Jesus."

They all watched the balloon ascend, a gentle floating rather than an eruption.

EPILOGUE

Some days were indeed for remembering.

The visitor rose, stretching legs gone numb from sitting. The hoopla had died away, the press packed up cameras and recorders, the sightseers gone off to recount their memories or overheard stories.

Remembering. Can life go forward without looking back? Can one face the past but not live there, let go but learn? For life is in the now, not yesterday and not tomorrow, but the now. But today was for remembering. And now is for looking forward, looking within and shutting the door on the might-have-beens. So much loss, like timber downriver, passing along on its way to some unknown destiny. Who would have thought so much life could come out of the ashes?

The visitor saluted The Lady with a slight bow. "May you rest in peace and beauty." And walked back down the trail that had denied access all those years ago.

About the Author

Lauraine Snelling is a member of the more-than-two-million-books-in-print club. With her dream to write "horse books for kids," an actuality, researching her Norwegian heritage inspired her to craft *An Untamed Land,* volume one of the Red River of the North family saga, which quickly became a bestselling trilogy chronicling the Bjorklund family.

Writing about real issues within a compelling story is a hallmark of Lauraine's style, shown in her contemporary romances and women's fiction, which has probed the issues of forgiveness, loss, domestic violence, and cancer. For example, *The Healing Quilt* explores the relationship of four diverse women who come together to supply their community with a much needed mammogram machine.

All told, she has had over fifty books published and her works have been translated into Norwegian, Danish, and German, as well as produced as books on tape. Awards have followed Lauraine's dedication to telling a good story: the Silver Angel Award for *An Untamed Land* and a Romance Writers of America Golden Heart for *Song of Laughter.*

Lauraine frequently teaches at writer's conferences across the country and at her home in the California Tehachapi Mountains. She mentors others through book doctoring and with her humor-laced Writing Great Fiction tape set. Lauraine also produces material on query letters and other aspects of the writing process.

When she's not trying to keep up with reader demands for her books, Lauraine enjoys gardening amidst the flowers, fountains, and hummingbirds of her backyard as well as playing Rummikub. She and husband, Wayne, have two grown sons and a daughter in heaven.